MARATHON

MARATHON

A JONATHAN STRIDE NOVEL

BY

BRIAN FREEMAN

Quercus

New York • London

Quercus

New York • London

© 2017 by Brian Freeman
First published in the United States by Quercus in 2017

ISBN 978-1-68144-241-9

Library of Congress Cataloging-in-Publication Data

Names: Freeman, Brian, 1963- author.
Title: Marathon / Brian Freeman.
Description: First edition. | New York : Quercus, 2017. | Series: A Jonathan Stride novel
Identifiers: LCCN 2017000663 (print) | LCCN 2017005927 (ebook) | ISBN
    9781681442419 (hardcover) | ISBN 9781681442402 (softcover) | ISBN
    9781681442396 (ebook) | ISBN 9781681442389 (ebook library edition)
Subjects: LCSH: Stride, Jonathan (Fictitious character)—Fiction. | Murder—
    Investigation—Fiction. | Police—Minnesota—Fiction. | Duluth (Minn.)—Fiction.
    | BISAC: FICTION / Mystery & Detective / Police Procedural. | GSAFD: Suspense
    fiction. | Mystery fiction.
Classification: LCC PS3606.R4454 M37 2017 (print) | LCC PS3606.R4454 (ebook) |
    DDC 813/.6—dc23
LC record available at https://lccn.loc.gov/2017000663

Distributed in the United States and Canada by
Hachette Book Group
1290 Avenue of the Americas
New York, NY 10104

Manufactured in the United States

10 9 8 7 6 5 4 3 2 1

www.quercus.com

For Marcia

Times of heroism are generally times of terror.

—RALPH WALDO EMERSON

The backpack is proudly made in the USA.

It is constructed of tough navy-blue canvas to stand up to the Minnesota ice and snow. It's the kind of bag you can take with you wherever you go: to college, the office, or into the wilderness. In an outdoors-loving city like Duluth, hundreds of people carry the same backpack.

From the outside, this backpack looks like all the others.

From the outside, you cannot see the fifty pounds of metal, shrapnel, black powder, and wires contained within.

From the outside, you cannot see hatred, but that is what the backpack actually holds.

At 12:32 p.m. on the third Saturday in June—marathon day—the contents of the navy-blue backpack will receive their awakening signal. The signal will come via radio waves and be transmitted to a cell phone taped to the handle of the eight-quart pressure cooker within.

Everything that happens next will take no more than a millisecond. Once started, the process cannot be stopped. It is basic physics.

The cell phone sends an electrical impulse to a blasting cap.

The blasting cap, wired through the lid of the pressure cooker to the supply of black powder, triggers an explosive reaction.

The gases of the explosion expand under pressure until their outward force exceeds the structural integrity of the pressure cooker.

The pressure cooker shatters.

Thousands of ball bearings and nails launch with the speed and force of bullets shot from a gun. They will maim or kill anyone in their path. In that millisecond, lives will change.

You cannot stop physics.

You can only stop hatred.

SATURDAY

1

Jonathan Stride watched dozens of runners emerge from the Lake Avenue overpass and make the last turn on the way to the finish line in Canal Park. Sweet victory was in sight.

The rain, which had dogged the course all morning, didn't stop the athletes. The rigors of traveling twenty-six miles by foot in just a few hours didn't stop them. They came, one after another, dressed in neon colors, crossing under balloon rainbows that decorated the last two-tenths of a mile. Stride knew that the final, short stretch of pavement could feel as long as all the miles that had come before. Some runners smiled. Some cried. Some had beet-red faces twisted in pain. Some looked lost, their eyes wide, as if they could barely contemplate what this physical accomplishment meant to them. Regardless of their condition, completing the marathon was a moment they would remember all their lives.

More than two hours had passed since the leaders—a cadre of amazing Kenyan athletes—sprinted across the finish line as if the race were no more than a hundred-yard dash. Because of the weather, no one had set a record today, but Stride admired anyone who took on the entire distance from the small town of Two Harbors to the city of Duluth, with the shore of Lake Superior in view along the way.

Next to him, Cat Mateo consulted her phone. "According to the tracking app, Serena should be here any minute now. This is so cool! She did it!"

Cat put two fingers into her mouth and produced a shrill whistle. She raised a red cowbell over her head and clanged it for the runners. So did a hundred other spectators crowded beside them, huddled under slickers and umbrellas. Rain didn't stop the cheering section, either. On every marathon day, regardless of the weather, the people of Duluth poured into the streets to show their love for the runners. It didn't matter if someone finished first or five thousandth or limped across the line six hours after starting. They all were treated like winners.

Stride was pleased to see joy in Cat's face as she watched the race. The seventeen-year-old had battled melancholy as long as he'd known her. Fifteen months earlier, he and Serena had rescued Cat, who was pregnant and undernourished at the time, from a life on the streets, and she'd lived with them ever since. It had been a rocky road for all of them. Today, though, none of that mattered. Today, she was happy. Stride put an arm around the girl, and she leaned her head into his shoulder.

Near them, two teenage boys eyed the beautiful girl and murmured, "Wow," and Stride had to resist an impulse to knock their heads together. He felt like a father to Cat, which was a responsibility that he'd never expected as he turned fifty years old.

While the crowd watched the runners, Stride watched the faces in the crowd. The spectators pushed ten deep against metal barriers that blocked off the street. Drizzle spat on their hoodies and hats from a charcoal sky. It was a chilly morning if you weren't running, but these were Duluthians, and most wore shorts despite the cold. They were young and old, laughing, cheering, sipping hot coffee, and dancing to Eagles and Steely Dan songs blasting out of loudspeakers.

This was always one of Duluth's best days. Since the first race decades earlier, the Duluth Marathon had grown from a local event for a handful of die-hard runners to a Minnesota institution drawing tens of thousands of athletes and visitors from more than forty countries.

The North Shore route, steps from the Great Lake and cutting through miles of wilderness, was probably the most beautiful marathon course in the country.

Every year, Stride relished the excitement of the event, but he was also a lieutenant in the Duluth Police, and he felt the tiniest unease seeing so many people crowded together in such a small area. Crowds were vulnerable, and after the Boston Marathon attack, they'd learned that the threat of violence lurked wherever people gathered. That was why they had a black tactical van parked at the entrance to Canal Park, along with bomb-sniffing dogs and armed officers patrolling the street. That was why he and his team watched individual faces, looking for something in a person's eyes that shouldn't be there.

Hatred. Calculation. Evil.

He was taking no chances today. Duluth had been an uneasy place this spring. An activist named Dawn Basch had taken up residence in the city in preparation for a so-called free-speech convention. Basch called it a defense of First Amendment rights; her opponents called it a thinly veiled assault on Muslims. The resulting protests had divided the Northland, and social media was lit up with bitterness and finger-pointing. Everyone was angry, and anger had a way of spiraling out of control. He didn't like having the marathon take place in the midst of the city's worst unrest in years.

Stride brushed rainwater out of his wavy black-and-gray hair, which he kept shorter than he had in his younger days. He was a tall man, nearly six-foot-two, with a weathered face and intense dark eyes. He'd crossed the half-century mark a few months earlier. His friend and doctor, Steve Garske, had told him he'd quickly a notice a difference between his fifties and forties, and Steve was right. Whenever Stride rolled out of bed in the morning, his body felt knotted together, and it took a hot shower and a pot of coffee before he was loose and ready to face the day.

He wasn't young anymore, but as far as he was concerned, youth was overrated. He'd known loss and recovered from it. He'd made mistakes and learned to live with them. Imperfection had made him who he was. It had taken most of his fifty years to learn that lesson, and for the first time in a long time, he wouldn't trade the present for the past.

Ten feet away, in the crowd, Stride spotted a twenty-something male with his arms tightly folded across a camouflage jacket. The man's mouth was a thin, angry slash, and he wore a baseball cap with **#noexceptions** embroidered in large white stitching across the crown. The slogan on the hat was a red flag for Stride. The recent troubles in Duluth had a name, and the name was **#noexceptions**. That was the hashtag Dawn Basch used whenever she posted on Twitter. According to Basch, free speech was free speech. No ifs, ands, or buts. No exceptions.

The young man didn't look like a threat, but Stride adjusted his leather jacket so that his badge was visible on his belt. Most of the people who sported the slogan were harmless, but some were spoiling for a fight, and he wasn't going to let anyone disrupt the marathon. The mayor had spread the word in a press conference the previous day: No protests that could endanger the runners or the crowd would be tolerated.

His radio earpiece crackled to life.

"Hey, boss, I'm at the Guppo station," his partner, Maggie Bei, announced. "It's a party over here."

Stride grinned and tapped his microphone. "What's on the menu this year?"

"Fried mac-and-cheese balls. The things are amazing."

"Are the runners actually getting any?" he asked.

"Yeah, Gina's making sure that Max doesn't eat them all."

Stride laughed out loud. Over the years, the "Guppo station" had become legendary among marathon runners. Max Guppo was one of his detectives, built like a snowman, with a pumpkin-shaped torso and perfectly round head. Normally, marathon day meant all-hands-on-deck for the police, but Guppo had been excused for the past two decades to run an elaborate "nutrition stop" for the runners. It had started small, with Guppo, his wife, and their oldest daughter, Gina, handing out lemonade and crackers. Today, the Guppo station featured Max, his wife, all five of their daughters, a dozen volunteers, live music, and an endless supply of homemade, carb-heavy treats. They staked out a location near the race's twenty-two-mile mark, just after the shallow slope called Lemon Drop Hill that nonetheless loomed like Kilimanjaro in front of the tired runners. At the Guppo station, they could get a jolt of encouragement and energy for the final miles leading into the heart of the city.

"Did Max see Serena?" Stride asked.

"Yeah, he says she's looking good," Maggie replied. "Did she get to you yet?"

"No, but she'll be here soon, according to Cat."

"Well, good for her. She's crazy, but good for her."

"Hey, she asked you to run with her, Mags," Stride said, smiling.

"Yeah, no thanks. If I'm going to travel twenty-six miles, it'll be in my truck."

"With you driving, it's safer to run."

"Ha-ha," Maggie replied sourly.

"I spotted one protester here in Canal Park," Stride said. "Any issues up where you are?"

"No, we're good for now. Guppo saw a couple people in **#noexceptions** T-shirts, but there haven't been any serious altercations with the Muslim runners. A few slurs from one jerk, but people in the crowd shouted him down."

"Okay. Keep me posted."

Maggie supervised the police security detail for the marathon. She sped up and down the race route in her yellow Chevy Avalanche all day, checking every detail from first aid stations and medical emergencies to parking and traffic.

This year, everyone was on high alert.

"Any sign of Dawn Basch?" Maggie asked Stride.

"Not so far."

"Do you think she'll stay away?"

"It's not like her to be out of the spotlight, but let's hope so," he said. Stride signed off the call and switched off his microphone.

Dawn Basch lived for controversy, regardless of the consequences. She dared Islamist extremists: "If you want to shut me up, you'll have to kill me." At her last convention, in Portland, she'd nearly gotten her wish. A Muslim radical had stormed the hotel with an assault rifle and been shot dead by police in the lobby. The incident had sparked national headlines and made Basch even more famous. Or infamous. Hatred accompanied her wherever she went.

Now it was marathon day, and Basch was in their city. Stride was on edge.

"Hey, there's Serena—there she is!" Cat shouted, grabbing the sleeve of Stride's jacket.

Stride spotted Serena immediately among the runners making the turn toward Canal Park. She ran gracefully on her long legs, with no obvious sign of the fatigue she had to be feeling. She'd been training for an entire year, and her lean body showed the results. She wore black Lycra running shorts, fluorescent green sneakers, and a vibrant green-and-yellow tank top. Her black hair, tied in a ponytail, bounced behind her. Her expression was intense. Her skin was damp with sweat and rain. Beyond her, the city's lift bridge loomed over the ship canal just behind the finish line. She was within steps of her goal.

Cat screamed with an ear-splitting volume that only a teenage girl could manage. "HEY! SERENA STRIDE!"

Her voice was so loud that other spectators giggled. Serena couldn't help but hear her. Her face turned, and her lips creased into a smile. She winked at Cat and at Stride, and then she was gone, swept by onto Canal Park Drive, immersed in the pack of runners pounding out the last steps of their 26.2 miles.

Serena Stride, formerly Serena Dial.

His wife.

It was still strange for him to think of her that way. After several years of living together, they'd gotten engaged the previous summer and married in January at a tiny church on Park Point five blocks from the cottage where they lived. It had been an intimate ceremony, and they could count on two hands the people they'd invited to share the moment with them. Taking that step hadn't come easily for them. He'd been unsure for years if he could truly say good-bye to his first wife, Cindy, and put his heart at risk again after her death. For her part, Serena had been unsure whether she could close the door on the child-hood abuse that had made her reluctant to trust anyone who claimed to love her. They'd struggled in their relationship and even separated for a while, but they'd finally discovered that they weren't afraid of the future. They didn't *need* to be together, but they wanted to be together.

The day after he'd asked her to marry him—the day after she'd said yes—she'd told him of her plans to run the marathon the following year. He thought that it was her way of binding herself to the life she'd made there in Duluth. Marathons defined every kind of human commitment. Physical. Emotional. Spiritual. That same day, she'd started training.

"Can I head down there and wait for her to come out near the finish line?" Cat asked.

"Sure, go ahead."

Stride watched Cat disappear into the crowd at a run, and that was when he heard Maggie in his headset again. Her voice had turned dark.

"Hey, boss? We may have a problem."

"What's up, Mags?"

"We've got a report of an unattended backpack," Maggie replied.

It was 12:09 p.m.

2

The brace on Michael Malville's foot made it uncomfortable for him to stand for long periods of time. He and his son, Evan, had staked out their place on Superior Street three hours earlier, and he now found himself favoring his good leg. He was ready to go home, but Evan was entranced by the marathon. They'd been here to see the wheelers speed by in low-slung wheelchairs as sleek and aerodynamic as a Corvette. They'd seen the lead runners keeping an unimaginable pace at mile twenty-four. Now the heart of the pack jogged past them dozens at a time.

"Those girls are wearing *bikinis*!" Evan shouted with the amazement of a twelve-year-old boy who couldn't decide if the sight of women in sports bras and short-shorts was interesting or gross.

"They're not really bikinis," Michael told his son. "But you do see runners wearing some strange things."

That was true. They'd seen tutus, leopard skins, superhero costumes. Even a wedding dress. If you were willing to run twenty-six miles in the rain, you could wear whatever you wanted.

Michael and Evan watched the marathon from the sidewalk outside the Electric Fetus music store. He was annoyed to be on the sidelines of the race, not running it. After years as a swimmer, he'd decided on his fortieth birthday to train for the Duluth Marathon, and whenever Michael Malville set his mind to something, he did it with one-hundred-percent intensity. His plan had been to break four hours, and he'd been on track to meet his goal. He'd run a half marathon in Milwaukee in April in one hour, forty-eight minutes, and he was confident that he could meet or exceed that pace in Duluth.

Then, a week earlier, his wife, Alison, had asked him to take a laundry basket down to the basement of their Cloquet home. He'd set one foot wrong on the last step and fractured two metatarsal bones. His marathon dreams were done for the year and, depending on how the bones healed, possibly for good. He'd been angry about it ever since.

Michael was a big man. He was six-foot-one with a broad build. He'd had curly blond hair for most of his life, but when his hair started to thin in his mid-thirties, he'd shaved his head and kept it that way ever since. He wore narrow, rectangular Prada glasses. He was dressed well, in chinos, a burgundy golf shirt, and one tan loafer on his uninjured foot, with a long, open, seersucker trench coat to stave off the rain. Anyone who looked at him could tell he had money, but his life had never been about wealth. He was an adrenaline junkie, and right now, being a marathon spectator rather than a runner was making him restless.

His cell phone rang. It was Alison. "How's it going up there?" his wife asked.

"Evan loves it," Michael told her. "One of the runners was dressed like some kind of zombie. That was his favorite."

"Dad, he was a character from *The Walking Dead*," Evan explained to him impatiently. The boy pointed at his own T-shirt, which showed an actor with a crossbow and the words KILLIN' IT in red letters. Michael had no idea what the slogan meant, but the shirt apparently had something to do with the television show Evan was obsessed with.

"Are you coming home for lunch?" Alison asked.

"No, we already grabbed hot dogs at Coney Island."

"How's the foot?"

"It sucks," Michael said.

"Well, don't kill yourself, okay?"

"We'll only stay a little longer."

He hung up the phone. Runners flooded past them on the street, and the spectators kept up a loud chorus of cheers, regardless of how much time or how many people had already passed. A woman sitting in a canvas chair shouted over and over, "You've got this! Less than two miles to go!" Michael knew her heart was in the right place, but he wanted to tell her that runners hated being reminded of how far they had to go. They all knew, and most of the time they didn't want to think about it.

"Hey!" a runner shouted from the street. He was big, like Michael, but at least fifteen years younger, with long, wet brown hair and a bushy beard. "Hey, no exceptions, man! No exceptions!"

It took Michael a moment to realize the runner was talking to him. The younger man wore a **#noexceptions** bandana tied around his head, and he'd spotted the large red button on Michael's trench coat that said the same thing.

"No exceptions!" Michael called out, giving the man a thumbs-up. He was always pleased to find other conservatives here, because he didn't meet too many kindred spirits in the "People's Republic of Duluth."

"What does that mean, Dad?" Evan asked, looking up at him. "No exceptions?"

Michael squatted to stare the boy in the eyes. "It means we live in America, and nobody can tell us what to say or what to think. It says so in the Bill of Rights, in the First Amendment to the Constitution."

"Oh."

"That's something to be proud of," Michael added. "Always remember that."

"Okay."

Michael straightened up with difficulty, because his foot was bothering him, and that was the exact moment when a pedestrian pushing quickly along the sidewalk collided hard with his shoulder. Michael lost his balance. Pain, like a lightning bolt, jolted through his leg. He staggered into Evan, and his son stumbled into the street, where a pack of runners had to dodge around him. Michael grabbed Evan's wrist and yanked the boy back to the safety of the sidewalk.

Furious, he spotted the man who'd struck his shoulder, walking away as if nothing had happened between them. "What the hell!" Michael shouted after him. "Watch where you're going!"

The man didn't break his fast stride, but he glanced back and caught Michael's eye. It lasted a split second, no more. Michael had an impression of someone younger than himself but similarly tall and solid. In that instant, Michael saw one thick eyebrow and one cold, hostile eye in a bronze-skinned face. A waft of musky cologne lingered in Michael's nose, and he knew it came from the man on the sidewalk. The man wore black jeans and a loose, untucked, button-down shirt.

A navy-blue backpack hung from one of the man's shoulders. It sank low on his back, as if weighed down by something heavy.

Michael felt the animosity across the distance. He was sure the collision had been deliberate. The angry moment was there, and then it was gone. The crowd swallowed the man with the backpack as he marched toward the Lake Avenue overpass leading to Canal Park. Michael tried to fix the details of the man's face in his mind, but the image was already growing blurry, like a photograph you weren't fast enough to snap. The man was just another immigrant on a busy city street.

Michael made sure Evan was okay.

It was 12:17 p.m.

* * *

Crowds made Khan nervous. He didn't like them.

This was a happy crowd, but it didn't matter. As he came out of the doorway of the Duluth Outdoor Company shop, his senses rebelled at the loud music, the laughter, the clapping, the clanging of bells, and the cheering. He felt an urge to cover his ears to drown out the noise. The squirming closeness of so many bodies made it hard for him to breathe, and they all smelled of rain, sweat, perfume, and tobacco. It overwhelmed him, as if he were fourteen years old again in the streets of Lahore. He trembled in agitation, wanting to run away, wanting to go back to the empty alley behind the shop, but he had work to do.

Behind the silver frames of his glasses, his eyes darted from face to face. It was hard to find one particular man among the hundreds squeezed along the cobblestoned sidewalk. This was where everyone wanted to be. The finish line. It was such an American place: confident, pushy, full of dreams, full of ambition. All the shops were open, hungry for business. Posters lined the street for banks, car dealers, gas stations, and cell phone companies. Runners with flushed faces mingled with their friends, their finisher medals proudly hung around their necks. The beating heart of the marathon was in this place.

Khan thought: *If Malik is here, this is where he will be.*

His phone rang in the pocket of his black jeans. He dug it out from under his flowered batik shirt and saw that it was Ahdia calling. Even the sight of her name made him smile. His wife, his beautiful wife, who had given him their beautiful son. Khan lived for the two of them.

"Have you found Malik?" Ahdia asked.

"No."

"So maybe he's not there."

"I hope that's true, but I can't reach him, and he won't answer his phone."

"Are others searching, too?"

"Yes, but no one has seen him."

"How are you?" she asked.

"You know how I feel about crowds."

"I do. Come home, Khan. There is nothing more you can do. Pak misses you. So do I."

He lowered his voice to avoid drawing attention to himself. He was as skinny as a street sign, but he was also tall and handsome, with a mane of jet-black hair and a neat beard. His dark, Arabic features were enough to attract suspicion on the street, especially today. He didn't really blame people for that. Evolution had programmed the human heart to fear what was different. When he saw a muscled, tattooed man eyeing him, he turned around to hide his face.

"If Malik is here, I have to find him," Khan whispered.

"Then be careful."

"I will."

He didn't want to tell Ahdia that if he found Malik, it was possible that neither one of them would come home alive.

Malik was one of his closest friends, but he'd crossed to the wrong side. The side of violence. Online recruiters and angry radicals in the Cedar-Riverside coffee shops of Minneapolis had poisoned him with talk of *jihad*. All of it was so foolish, so pointless. A deadly game played by stupid boys. It made Khan want to tear out his hair, because if he lost Malik, it would be like losing his own brother all over again. Another brother dying in a crowd for nothing.

He wanted to shout: *Where are you?*

Because he was sure that Malik was close by. Somewhere. Khan needed to find him before the police did. Find him and stop him before he threw away his life, along with the lives of others.

Khan left the spectators packed in front of the Duluth Outdoor Company shop and walked quickly toward the other end of Canal Park.

It was 12:26 p.m.

* * *

"I am *so* sorry," Max Guppo told Stride and Maggie. His round white face was even paler than usual, and his mustache drooped. Next to him, his youngest daughter, Gloria—eight years old—clutched her Barbie backpack to her chest. Her wide eyes and white bubble coat made her look like a snowy owl.

"Well, I think we can call off the SWAT team," Stride said, struggling not to laugh. He knew Guppo and his daughter both felt bad. At least a dozen officers had surrounded the bag before the girl wandered between them and casually grabbed her backpack from the ground.

"Honestly, boss, I had no idea Gloria left it behind," Guppo went on. "And then when the call came in . . . I didn't realize—"

"It's all right, Max." Stride bent down to Gloria's level and smiled. "You okay there, Glo?"

The girl nodded without saying a word.

"Good. Now you keep your backpack with you from now on, okay? You don't want somebody walking off with it, do you?"

She shook her head silently.

"Okay." Stride tweaked her pudgy cheeks and straightened up. He patted Max on the back. "Go on, Max, get back to your mac-and-cheese balls. You've still got a lot of hungry runners coming through here."

"Thanks, boss."

Guppo took Gloria by the hand and led the little girl away. Stride and Maggie watched them go. When father and daughter were out of earshot, smiles broke across both of their faces, and the laughter they'd been holding back bubbled out of them. The other cops around them laughed, too. Stride shook his head.

"A Barbie backpack," he said. "That's one for the record books."

"Needless to say, the woman who called 911 didn't mention that," Maggie told him.

"Well, we tell people, if you see something, say something. And she did."

Maggie zipped up her red jacket against the rain. Her bowl-cut black hair was soaked. She pointed at her yellow Avalanche, which was pebbled with dents in the doors and fenders. She was a terrible driver. "You want a ride back down to Canal Park, boss?"

"I'm not that brave, Mags."

"Hey, I got the airbags replaced," she pointed out.

"Still no."

"Okay, suit yourself." She chuckled again, her hands in her pockets. "I guess we've had our excitement for this year's marathon."

"I guess so," Stride said.

It was 12:29 p.m.

* * *

Wade Ralston checked the rubber fitness tracker on his wrist. Despite the rain and the perspiration on his skin, it was working fine. Even so, he was upset with himself, because he was way behind the schedule he'd mapped out. He'd pulled his right hamstring at mile sixteen and had to walk off and on since then to shake off the pain. What should have been a three-and-a-half-hour pace—bringing him to the finish line at 11:15 a.m., his record time—was now a frustrating four-hour-and-forty-five-minute jog. He'd never fallen so far behind in a marathon, and he'd run twelve races in ten years.

Other runners passed him, because he was limping. The finish line wasn't even a hundred yards away, but the distance loomed like ten more miles. The race clock on a banner stretched across Canal Park Drive ticked off the seconds, reminding him of his failure.

Someone shouted at him, "You're bleeding!"

Wade looked down at his white tank top, which had been specially printed to advertise his business: RALSTON EXTERMINATION: THE BUG ZAPPERS. Where cartoon ants and cockroaches marched across his chest toward two men carrying foggers, his nipples had begun to bleed from the friction with his shirt. The bugs appeared to be walking into two crimson pools for a swim.

A volunteer medic on the street offered help, but Wade waved him off. A little blood didn't matter. He'd developed a blister while running the Chicago marathon four years earlier, and by the time he reached the finish line, his left sneaker had turned cherry red.

He jogged another step and then another step. That was what it was all about. One foot in front of the other, one step at a time, adding up to 26.2 miles.

Thanks to his running regimen, Wade didn't have an ounce of fat on his body. He was a compact package, no more than five-foot-five and a rock-hard 120 pounds. In school, as a child, his small size had worked against him. Girls had teased him and bigger kids bullied him mercilessly, but as an adult, he had always been determined to outrun everyone else, outwork them, outsmart them, and out-earn them. He'd had the last laugh. If you were willing to do things that no one else had the guts to do, you could always get what you wanted. Not many people wanted to deal with bugs and rodents.

He found himself getting dizzy, but he had to keep moving. Nothing else mattered. Just keep moving forward.

The finish line was fifty yards away.

He looked for his cheering section. They'd promised him they would be here, but he was so late that he wondered if they'd given up on him and gone for a beer. It wouldn't mean a thing if he couldn't see their faces. He peered through the crowd lining the street—and there they were, all three of them, in front of the Duluth Outdoor Company shop, exactly as they'd promised, so they could watch him take the last steps across the finish line.

Travis Baker was there, in front of a tree and built like a tree. They'd worked in the bug business together for five years, ever since Travis's sister, Shelly, had introduced them. Wade and Travis went down into the places no one else would go, taking out cockroaches from building basements by the shovelful. Travis spotted him first and cheered wildly, as if Wade were a football player scoring the winning touchdown.

"Wade! Wade! Wade!"

Shelly stood next to Travis. She took up the cheer, too.

And so did Joni. Wade's wife. Ex-cheerleader. Joni had always been the ultimate proof of what life could bring a short, scrawny, C-average kid who knew how to work his butt off. She waved at him and whistled, and her blond hair bounced, and so did everything else. He couldn't take his eyes off her.

"Wade! Wade! Wade!"

"Cross the line! Cross the line!"

That was all he had to do, but Wade wasn't moving. He'd stopped. His limbs became rubber. He bent over, his hands on his thighs. Mouth open, panting, he stared at the finish line. He stared at Joni, Travis, and Shelly, wildly waving him on. Dozens of others in the crowd took up the cheer.

"Cross the line! Cross the line!"

But he couldn't move. His heart beat crazily. His chest heaved as he tried to suck in a breath, but tightness grabbed his ribs in a choke hold. He swayed and crumpled to one knee. He grabbed his wrist. The world spun.

The finish line teased him, with the race clock ticking off second after second after second. He was so close.

"You can't stop now!" someone said, and he realized it was his own voice. He'd come too far to quit now. He staggered to his feet and took another step toward the end of the race.

He was almost there.

Almost there.

It was 12:32 p.m.

@runnerbae81 tweeted:
Oh, shit.

@edbrown_cpa tweeted:
Saw it on the finish line feed. OMG.

@mrrdevlin tweeted:
Something happened at the Duluth Marathon a few seconds ago.
Anybody got details?

@talkischeap_mn tweeted:
Got this screenshot before the feed went down. Bad.
126 people retweeted @talkischeap_mn

@sallybrl tweeted:
Bomb.

@luvicecaves tweeted:
My sister lives up there. She says bomb.

@duluthnative55 tweeted:
Sirens going crazy. #marathon

@shirleyctate tweeted:
Still nothing on the news? WTF?
#marathon

@mndude_msp retweeted The Associated Press:
Explosive device detonated near finish line of the Duluth
Marathon. Multiple injuries reported. Details to follow.

@kimberlyandjohn_fl tweeted:
Prayers.
#marathon

@asweetsole tweeted:
Anyone killed? Prayers.
#marathon

@duluthcity tweeted:
All residents/visitors asked to remain indoors and away from
Canal Park to allow access for emergency responders.

@zenithcityguy tweeted:
Runner friend was picking up her sweat bag when it went off. She
thinks several dead. #marathon

@marythechurchlady tweeted:
Lord, when will this madness stop?
#marathon
#prayers

@peteclay_noex tweeted:

Now we get to hear "Don't leap to conclusions" for a week.
Yeah, right.
#marathon
#islamismurder
84 people favorited @peteclay_noex

@dawnbasch tweeted:

Tragedy is no time for political correctness. We all know what this is and who did this.

#marathon

#terrorism

#islamismurder

#noexceptions

1604 people retweeted @dawnbasch

3

Stride sprinted down Lake Avenue against a wave of hundreds of people pushing back in the opposite direction. As he headed toward the clock tower at the threshold of Canal Park, smoke grew like a giant spider against the dark sky. The stench of sulfur hung in the air. Emergency chatter exploded over the radio. He heard shouts for triage and trauma units at the finish line.

Multiple victims down.

"Everybody out! Everybody out! Clear the area!"

Parents carried children on their backs. Runners pushed seniors in wheelchairs. Some of the crowd headed east toward the lakeshore, some toward the convention center to the west, some toward the streets downtown. A few gawkers lingered, taking photos and video. Stride jerked a hand toward the nearest officers to herd those stragglers away. Where there was one bomb, there could be two. Or more.

Glass crunched under his shoes as he ran the last block, the way thousands of runners had already done today. The entire street was a field of glass. Ahead of him, people tore at the metal barricades lining the street and heaved them into a pile to clear space for the victims. Fallen balloon arches draped across the pavement like multicolored snakes. All the joy of the day had popped like the balloons and morphed into fear.

Stride stopped where it had happened. The blast site. He was outside the Duluth Outdoor Company shop, yards from the finish line. He looked down. The mottled cobblestones were soaked with blood that the light rain couldn't wash away. Bricks had been torn up and scattered. He saw severed body parts and torn flesh. Dozens of victims lay on the street and sidewalk, some with clean white bones protruding from their limbs. He counted five people who appeared to be fatalities. Others, the lucky ones, sat against the walls of the shops, their faces cut, their clothes shredded, their legs bleeding.

He didn't have time for emotion, but he couldn't completely swallow down his anger and sadness. The marathon was a day of oneness for everyone in Duluth, and to have it violated like this made him furious to his core.

Overlapping sirens wailed, drawing closer from the downtown hospitals. Everyone had trained for the worst-case scenario, and with the worst case in front of them, the emergency responders went about their business with dead-serious determination. Police. Marathon workers and volunteers. Firefighters. EMTs who'd been on hand to treat exhausted runners but now were pressed into service as battlefield medics.

Stride grabbed one of his men by the shoulder. The man's face was dotted like a constellation with pinpoint shrapnel wounds.

"Are you all right? Get yourself bandaged up."

"I'm fine, sir. Others are worse."

"Where were you when it went off?" Stride asked.

"Across the street on the hotel side. The force knocked me to the ground."

"Suicide bomber?"

"I don't know, sir. With the rain, so many people had bulky coats and slickers. Somebody could have been hiding something, but we didn't get any warning from the dogs."

"Okay. Have someone tend to your face."

"I will."

Stride added, "Have you seen Serena? My wife?"

"I'm sorry, sir, I haven't."

Stride's eyes swept the street. The shop windows for half a block were shattered, and the dark interior of the Duluth Outdoor Company revealed a smoking ruin. Across the street, all the windows in the nearest hotel had been blown out, and he grabbed an EMT to make sure emergency personnel were going door to door inside to check for guests in need of medical attention. He was sure people had been standing at those windows when the bomb went off.

The trees on the street had been sheared of leaves and stripped of bark. They looked naked. Most of the nearby cars in the hotel parking lot had been damaged by the impact of the blast. Car alarms blared through the still air, like wailing puppies who'd been left alone. Six feet away from him, Stride saw an EMT crouched over a tattooed blonde in the street. The woman wasn't moving; her blue eyes were fixed. The EMT looked up at Stride, and the man shook his head.

Dead.

Not far away, another woman awakened from the blast and screamed as the pain caught up to her brain. Her legs were a mess of blood, bone, and tissue. Stride felt a wave of anger again, hard and deep.

He heard Maggie on the radio over his headset.

"We're evacuating the entire route," she told him, "but nearly everyone bolted as word spread through the crowd. Buses are en route to pick up the runners. I've got people driving the course to make sure we don't have any other devices left behind."

"Make sure the schools and the mall are cleared before we take runners inside," Stride told her. "I don't want anyone walking into a trap."

"On it. How bad is the situation there?"

"We've got dead and injured on the ground. Trauma teams are on the way."

"You need me down there?"

"Not yet. Secure the rest of the route."

"Okay. Have you found Serena and Cat? Are they safe?"

"I'm still looking."

He grabbed his phone and dialed Serena's number, but the call failed. He tried again with Cat's number and got the same result. Bad news traveled instantly on social media; cellular bandwidth was already overloaded in the wake of the explosion. Across the country, thousands of people were dialing friends and family in Minnesota. Across Duluth, nearly everyone was calling everyone else.

Stride pocketed his phone. He stepped out among the dead and dying, most of whom were in a semicircle outside the Duluth Outdoor Company shop. Nails and ball bearings littered the street, along with popcorn fragments of glass. The silver thermal blankets that typically kept runners warm after the marathon now covered the victims. He checked each face, afraid that he would recognize one of them, but he didn't see his wife or the girl he loved like a daughter among the injured.

Then he saw a man lying on his back on the street, away from the immediate blast zone. A female marathon runner bent over to tend to him. The man's eyes opened; his limbs moved; he was alive. As Stride watched, the runner who was helping the man stood up and flagged an emergency medical worker for assistance.

When the runner turned toward him, Stride saw her face.

It was Serena.

* * *

Wade Ralston opened his eyes. He stared up at a gray sky, and individual raindrops streaked toward his face. The world was absolutely silent. No voices. No wind. No waves on the lake. He opened his dry mouth to speak—"Where am I?"—but he didn't know if he'd said anything at all. He didn't hear anything except a hollow rushing sound, as if he were holding a seashell up to his ear.

He blinked and shook his head.

Then, with a roar, noise rushed back. His hearing returned, overwhelming him with its shattering volume. Men and women shouted. Sirens screamed. Footsteps ran. He squirmed, trying to get up, but his brain spun, and he sank back in confusion. Everything was a blank; nothing made sense. He had no memory. He remembered only the coolness of a lake breeze and the deep green of the trees and the sound of his breathing, and then—

Nothing.

"What happened?" he asked aloud.

Wade heard his voice, but it sounded far away.

"Don't try to move," someone said.

A woman knelt over him. He tried to get up again, but her hands pressed his shoulders back onto a hard, uncomfortable surface. He stared at her, not understanding. She was a stranger, but she could have been an angel. Her black hair was tied behind her head, emphasizing the angles of her face. She wasn't young, but she looked ageless. Her warm eyes were as green as emeralds, and her lips were pale. She was statuesque, with tanned, muscular arms and legs. A medal dangled from her neck.

A runner's medal.

He remembered now: the marathon.

He remembered everything. The miles from Two Harbors. The pain and exhaustion. The finish line, so close. Joni, Travis, Shelly, all cheering for him. Then time stopped.

"Where am I?" he murmured.

The angel spoke. "We're in Canal Park. Don't worry, you'll be okay. We'll get you to a hospital very soon. Just lie still."

She stood up. From the ground, Wade saw that she was tall. Her legs were sleek, but on her calves, which were near his face, he saw scars. He watched her gesture to someone, and moments later, a medic knelt at his side. He was dressed in an orange T-shirt, with an orange baseball cap, and he draped a thermal blanket over Wade's body. The medic studied his eyes.

"Are you in pain, sir?"

"I don't know," Wade said. "I'm not feeling anything."

"How many fingers am I holding up?"

Wade saw two fingers, and he said so.

"That's good. Try not to move. There's blood behind your head. You may have banged it when the blast knocked you over. You have shrapnel wounds, too."

"Blast?"

"Somebody set off a bomb," the man told him.

Wade said the first thing that came into his brain, along with the image of his wife. "Where's Joni? Is she okay?"

* * *

Stride and Serena crossed the distance between them and embraced on the street. He held her tightly, and relief poured from both of them. He'd already dealt with the death of his first wife, Cindy, nine years earlier, but when the bomb went off, he'd felt a wave of certainty that Serena was dead, too. He'd felt darkness stalking him like a serial killer.

But the darkness hadn't come for him. Not this time.

"Are you okay?" he asked.

"I'm fine." Serena knew how to read his mind, and she could guess what he'd been thinking. "Really, Jonny, I wasn't even there. I was in the runner recovery area when it went off."

"I was afraid that you—"

"I know. I was worried about you, too."

He held her again, but they didn't have time to say anything else. The clock was already ticking on the investigation. Once the victims were transported to St. Mary's and St. Luke's, he and his team needed to secure the crime scene for the FBI. Rain was now washing away evidence. As cops liked to say, blood got cold fast.

He knew this would be a federal investigation. Any hint of terrorism moved the case up the food chain and out of the hands of the locals. In another hour, maybe two, Stride and his team would be playing supporting roles. The FBI would be in charge.

"Where's Cat?" Serena asked. "Did you send her over to Maggie's place to wait for us?"

Stride stared at Serena. The chill of fear returned to his body. So did the anticipation of loss.

"I thought she was with you. Weren't the two of you together?"

"No, I never saw her. I told you, I was still in the recovery area after the race. They don't let anybody but runners in there."

"Cat came down here to find you," Stride said. His voice was hollow.

Serena grabbed his arm like a vise. "Oh, my God, Jonny, where is she?"

4

"What are you doing, Dad?" Evan asked.

Michael Malville opened his eyes. "I'm trying to remember somebody's face," he said.

He and Evan stood in front of Sammy's Pizza, a block from the marathon route. The street was deserted, as if they'd taken refuge in a ghost town. They'd heard the bomb blast from the corner of Lake and Superior and seen the smoke rising out of Canal Park. People had begun to run. He'd dragged Evan away from the danger zone and made an immediate call to Alison to let her know they were safe, but he wasn't ready to go home yet.

He used his phone to scroll through his Twitter time line. The top trending hashtag was #marathon. Below it, the next hashtag on the list was #noexceptions. He read through the speculation about who was behind the bombing, and he wanted to put out a tweet to say: *I saw him.*

"Whose face are you trying to remember?" Evan asked.

"That man who bumped into me on the sidewalk," Michael told his son. "Did you see him?"

"No. Why do you want to remember him?" Then Evan whispered, as if they were part of a conspiracy, "You think he was the bomber, don't you? You think it was him!"

"I don't know, Evan. I have no idea who the man was. I just want to be clear in my own mind about what I saw, in case anyone asks me."

"Why do you think he did it?" Evan asked, as if Michael had already put the man in a police lineup.

Why?

Because of the look on his face. Because of the backpack he was carrying. Because he was heading for Canal Park.

Because—Michael had no trouble admitting to himself—the man reeked of Islam.

"I told you, I don't know whether he did it," Michael said. "He was probably just watching the marathon like us."

"Okay," Evan replied. "Can we bring home pizza?"

Michael glanced at the restaurant behind them. "Sorry, bud, it's closed."

All the shops were closed. The city was shut down. A handful of parked cars lingered on the street, and the police had stopped to check each one. Everyone was nervous about more bombs.

Two separate police officers had already checked his identification and suggested he take his son and go home. He'd seen another cop pass by ten minutes earlier, and this time, he saw the man grab a radio as he eyed Michael from inside the squad car. Michael could imagine the report: *That man on the corner of First, the one with the kid, is still there.* On any other day, no one would have cared, but this wasn't any other day.

Five more minutes passed.

A yellow Avalanche swung wide around the corner and stopped in front of Sammy's, halfway over the curb. When a tiny Chinese woman hopped down from the dented truck, Michael realized that he knew her. Her black hair fell in bangs across her forehead, and her eyes were hidden behind honey-colored sunglasses. She wore a red leather jacket, tapered black pants, and burgundy boots with block heels. She was a Duluth police detective, and their paths had crossed before.

He could see that she recognized him, too.

"You're Michael Malville, aren't you?" she said. "I'm Maggie Bei with the Duluth Police. We met two years ago during the Spitting Devil investigation."

"Yes, I remember," Michael replied coolly.

He strained to be polite. He didn't have fond memories of Maggie Bei or her boss, Jonathan Stride. Two years earlier, a serial killer had terrorized Duluth, targeting victims who all bore an uncanny resemblance to his wife, Alison. When a cloud of suspicion fell over Michael, the investigation had nearly cost him his marriage, and Alison barely escaped with her life. Michael blamed the police.

"You're Evan, aren't you?" the detective continued, eyeing Michael's son. "You were quite the hero back then."

Evan beamed at being remembered. "I got a badge from the police chief!"

"I know you did. You earned it. So you're a Walking Dead fan, huh?" She pointed at the boy's T-shirt.

"You bet!"

"Me, too," the detective told him. Then she said to Michael, "What are you doing out here, Mr. Malville? My colleagues tell me you've been hanging out on this corner for quite a while. We're encouraging residents to go home and stay home. Just until we're sure the city is safe."

He shrugged. "I've been watching all the police activity. It's interesting."

"Were the two of you in the marathon crowd when the bomb went off?"

"Yeah, and my Dad saw the guy who did it!" Evan shouted.

Michael winced. "Evan, don't exaggerate. I told you, that's not true."

The detective cocked her head. "What exactly did you see, Mr. Malville?"

"I saw a guy with a backpack. He bumped into me."

"Where was this?"

"Lake and Superior. I saw him heading toward Canal Park. This was like fifteen minutes before the bomb went off. So the timing made me suspicious, that's all."

"What did the man look like?" Bei asked.

"I've been trying to remember, but it all happened fast. Dark hair. Black jeans, I think, and some kind of colored shirt. I'm pretty sure he had a beard."

"Pretty sure?"

"I only saw him for a second," Michael said.

"Would you recognize him if you saw him again?"

"I think so, but look, I'm not saying he did it. Believe me, I know what it's like to have the police suspect you of something you didn't do."

"Yes, I'm aware," the detective replied, "and I'm sorry about what happened to you back then."

"All I'm saying is, I saw him, he had a backpack, and he was heading toward Canal Park."

"That's all?"

"Well, he—he looked Muslim, too."

"Muslim," Bei said. "Do you mean Middle Eastern?"

"Yes, that's right." Michael folded his arms across his chest. "Don't pretend that doesn't mean anything to you."

Bei said nothing. She eyed the empty street. "Okay, I appreciate your sharing this with me, Mr. Malville. If you remember anything more, please call me. In the meantime, I'd suggest that you and Evan head home now."

Michael felt a cool brush-off in her tone. He knew that he'd committed a politically incorrect sin. He'd dared to say the word *Muslim* out loud, even though that was what everyone was thinking.

"Whatever you say," Michael replied.

Bei headed back to her Avalanche, but he could read the tilt of her head, and he watched her checking out the red button prominently displayed on his trench coat. The button that Dawn Basch had handed him personally.

#noexceptions

* * *

Serena had already run more than twenty-six miles, but adrenaline, which had kept her going through the marathon, kept her going again. This time it was driven by fear.

An hour had passed. She couldn't find Cat.

She'd gone up and down Canal Park Drive, checking everyone who had taken refuge in the doorways. She'd described Cat to every cop and every emergency worker she encountered. No one had seen her. She called the girl's phone again and again, but there was no answer. She had visions of Cat's phone destroyed by the blast. She pictured Cat, bleeding, injured, hidden in some corner of a building near the lake, unable to summon help.

This was how it was at mass crime scenes. She'd been on the other side of it, as a cop, but she'd never been personally affected. Something terrible happened, and all you could think about was finding the people you loved and making sure they were safe. And always, always, every empty minute without news made you fear the worst.

She watched ambulances come and go, carrying victims to the hospitals. The street was largely empty of civilians now. Only the police stayed behind, taping off the scene and protecting what they could from the weather. The drizzle through which she'd run had turned to a downpour, filling the curbs with rivers that were tinged red. Shrapnel washed downstream. What should have been a day that was electric and alive had become a gray funeral.

And still no Cat.

Serena shared a bond with Cat that was different from what Jonny felt. He saw her as a daughter. Serena saw her as a much younger sister. They'd lived similar lives, both growing up with abuse, both unwanted and alone. Serena had escaped her drug-addicted mother and remade herself as a cop in Las Vegas. She was convinced that Cat could remake herself, too, but nothing came easily for the girl.

When they'd met Cat, she was pregnant. She'd been desperate to keep her child, but in the end, she'd let a Duluth family adopt him and give him a good home. Making the right choice didn't mean it was the easy choice. Her baby's new parents had invited Cat to be a part of the child's life, but so far, she hadn't even had the courage to visit. Just seeing her son, she said, would tear out her heart.

Helping Cat was the hardest work Serena and Jonny had ever done, but Serena was also convinced that it had brought the two of them together as never before and let them put aside their own pasts and doubts and get married. She felt a debt of gratitude toward the girl that would be impossible to repay.

Sheer, wicked tiredness began to take its toll, but she couldn't stop searching.

Serena thought about Cat, on her own the previous year, and she remembered the girl taking refuge inside the city's infamous Graffiti Graveyard. A killer had been chasing her, and she'd hidden from him among the graffiti-covered concrete pillars of I-35. It wasn't the first time she'd sought protection there, she'd told Serena. The homeless hung out under the freeway, like a city within the city.

Suddenly, Serena knew that Cat had hidden there again. When she was scared, when she was alone, when she was hurt, she would go back to her roots. It was a sister's intuition. Cat was back at the Graffiti Graveyard.

Serena didn't know where she found the strength to run, but she ran. She was on the boardwalk near the lake, and she reversed course, sprinting between two hotels. She headed for the old ore ship, the *Charles Frederick*, which was docked in the harbor, and then she ran along Railroad Street bordering the freeway. When she reached the short slope that led to a flooded ravine beneath I-35, she skidded downhill and splashed through the shallow water to an iron ladder propped against the opposite wall. She climbed it and dropped down into a narrow tunnel between the freeway ramps. Normally, traffic buzzed by in both directions overhead, but not today.

Immediately, she shouted Cat's name. The long stretch of grass and mud was deserted, and her voice echoed back to her, but no one answered. Concrete slabs propped up the freeway, and wild graffiti turned every square inch into a rainbow of guerilla art.

"Cat?" she called again. "Cat, are you here?"

Serena heard something from behind one of the pillars. Someone was crying.

"Cat? It's Serena."

The noise of the sobbing guided her. Thirty feet away, she spotted the girl sitting on the wet ground, her hands wrapped around her knees. Serena hurried to her and knelt at her side.

"Cat, are you okay? Are you hurt?"

The girl couldn't talk. Her black hair was plastered to her face in ropes. Tears streamed down her pretty skin, mixed with dirt and blood.

"Let me get you to the hospital," Serena said.

"I don't need to go there."

"You're bleeding," Serena told her.

Cat shook her head. Her eyes were haunted. "It's not my blood."

Serena understood, and there was nothing to say. She reached out and gathered up the girl tightly in her arms. She held on, letting Cat cry herself out in a muffled wail that echoed from everywhere in the tunnel. Above. Below. From the shadows of the ravine.

Eventually, the girl grew quiet, but Serena didn't let go.

"Can you tell me what happened?" she asked.

Cat separated herself from Serena and grabbed something from the ground beside her. It was a dark-colored beret, which the girl twisted between her fingers. She held it out for Serena to see.

"What's that?" Serena asked.

Cat sniffled. "I stole this."

"What?"

"I was coming to find you at the finish line, and I saw this in the window of one of the shops. I went inside, and I took it."

Serena shook her head. "Why? You have money."

"I don't know why. I just did it."

It was always that way with Cat. Two steps forward, one step back. The girl had made progress, but she kept doing things—making mistakes—that gave her a reason to justify the self-hatred she felt. *You gave up your baby, so you must be a bad person.*

"Why are you telling me this?" Serena asked.

Cat's voice rose. "Don't you get it? If I hadn't stolen this hat, I'd be dead. I went inside, took it, and as I walked back out, the bomb went off. If I'd kept going past the store, I'd be dead. I'd have been right there where the explosion was. What does that mean, Serena? Why would God do something like that?"

"Oh, Cat," Serena murmured.

"I should have been punished, and instead He saved me. That doesn't make any sense."

"Nobody deserves that kind of punishment. Nobody. This had nothing to do with God. This was someone cruel and evil who did this. Period."

"You can't imagine what it was like. There was this huge explosion, and smoke, and I felt like I'd been hit in the chest. A woman ten feet away got struck by something, and the blood sprayed from her face onto mine. I saw people on the ground. I saw somebody's *hand*, Serena. A hand, just lying there. Everybody was screaming. And there I was, with this beret I'd stolen, and all I could think was: I'm supposed to be dead."

"No, you're not," Serena said.

"Who could do something like this?" Cat asked. "I mean, everybody looks forward to the marathon. It's something good for the whole city. Who could rip it apart like this?"

Serena wanted to say something, but she had no explanations.

"You know what I feel?" Cat asked.

"Tell me."

"Helpless," Cat said, sounding older than her seventeen years.

"I understand."

"This is just how it was when I was living on the streets. I mean, yeah, I was scared all the time, but you get used to being scared. You deal with it. The worst part of it was feeling helpless. Like there's nothing you can do to change it. Like things are going to be bad forever, and you might as well give up."

Serena realized she was crying, too. She wasn't a sister to this girl. She was a parent, and she wanted to make it better for her, and she couldn't. She knew exactly how Cat felt, because she felt the same way. It was how the entire city of Duluth felt at that moment.

"That's what these people want," Serena told her. "That's why they do this. To make us give up. But you know what? We can't."

5

Special Agent Gayle Durkin of the Minneapolis office of the FBI kept one photograph on her desk. Otherwise, her cubicle was impersonal, perfectly organized, and all work, which was a good description of Gayle herself.

The photograph showed her twenty-six-year-old brother, Ron. His face was at arm's length to the camera on his phone; he was taking a selfie, with a sly grin on his face. He had shoulder-length brown hair and a rainbow-colored headband, and Gayle could see his Che Guevara T-shirt, which he'd probably worn just to annoy her. Brother and sister couldn't have been more different. Ron was the hippie; Gayle was ultraconservative. She could see the Paris street and outdoor café tables behind her brother, and on the horizon, the upper half of the Eiffel Tower. He'd taken the selfie and texted it to her in Minnesota, with the caption: You're at work. I'm here. Who's got life figured out?

Ninety seconds later, the bomb went off. Six people died in the Paris bistro, including Ron and the ISIS radical who'd worn the suicide vest.

That was two years ago.

And now another bomb. Close to home.

Gayle watched the television footage streaming on her computer monitor. One of the local stations already had a helicopter hovering over Lake Superior, with a camera angle on the destruction in Canal Park. She recognized everything. Duluth was her hometown. She'd grown up there, and her parents still lived in the same house on Martin Road near Amity Park they'd owned since they got married. She and Ron had watched the finishers at the marathon a dozen times from the exact site of the blast, and she'd run the half marathon once herself.

The camera panned, and she could see the rest of the city. Away from the lake, Duluth climbed sharply, with streets as steep as those in San Francisco. She saw the towers of the antenna farm atop the hillside, framed like metal soldiers against black clouds. The cluster of downtown buildings terraced on the skyline—the Greysolon, the circular Radisson Hotel, the sprawling St. Mary's hospital complex, and the stone clock tower of the old high school—made Duluth look like a big city, when it was really just a small town dressed up to look more sophisticated, like a girl wearing her mother's clothes.

For an old city, Duluth was young. Thousands of college students filled the breweries and coffee shops and kayaked on the lakeshore, and they'd made the city strangely hip. A town that had been carved out of the winter wilderness by the raw, hard labor of mining and shipping was now the artsy, outdoorsy hub of Minnesota.

Gayle had only been back to Duluth once since Ron died. His ghost was everywhere, which made the city oppressive to her. Her parents had learned that if they wanted to see their daughter, they had to drive two and a half hours to Minneapolis, but even those visits were rare and awkward. She worked twelve-hour days six days a week, and she didn't like taking time off—her job was her life. Her sterile apartment in Brooklyn Center, not even a mile from the FBI headquarters building, wasn't made for overnight guests, so her parents stayed at the Super 8 when they came to town.

After spending eighteen years in Duluth, she'd joked to Ron that she wanted to go somewhere warmer for college—so she went to the University of Minnesota in the Twin Cities. She double-majored in psychology and sociology and then stayed for a psych master's degree.

She got a job with Hennepin County conducting applicant interviews for sensitive positions dealing with the public. Her specialty was reading faces and body language, and she was so good at sniffing out people who were misrepresenting their backgrounds that her colleagues began calling her the Lie Detector.

She'd worked at the county for three years and then passed the test and training to join the FBI. At that point, she was twenty-seven years old. Now she was thirty-three.

To survive in the FBI boys club, she had to be twice as tough as the men, physically and mentally. Her life was simple. She worked long days; she exercised at the gym during the evening. She slept six hours each night. She'd never had a serious romantic attachment, and she didn't want or need one. She was confident that she was generally the smartest person in the room, and it was usually true.

Gayle was five-foot-nine and full-figured, but her extra weight was muscle, not fat. She kept her brown hair in a short, practical cut with slightly messy spikes across her forehead. She had brown eyes, a rounded nose, and a V-shaped chin. She wore women's suits from Penney's. Nothing expensive. Nothing fancy. Whenever she was outside, she hid her eyes behind sunglasses, so she could watch the world unseen.

Nobody at the Bureau really liked her, but they respected her. She was frustrated, though, because she'd been trapped in the penalty box—behind a desk—for more than a year. It was her own fault. Ten months after Ron died in Paris, she'd interviewed a teenage Somali immigrant in St. Cloud about his online contacts with Islamist radicals. The kid had lied to her. It was all over his face. Her job was simply to pass her notes up the food chain, but Gayle kept seeing Ron's face with every lie. She imagined this kid walking into a crowded space, somewhere like the Mall of America at Christmastime, and blowing up everyone around him. She lost it. She threw the kid into a wall and fractured his shoulder. The case against him fell apart, and the Bureau settled a lawsuit brought by his family.

Gayle kept her job, but since then, she'd been a paper pusher, analyzing videos of interviews conducted by other agents and writing reports. She hated it, but the only way to get back into the field was to take your punishment without complaint. Despite what she'd done, nobody blamed her. If anything, she'd won some fans among agents who felt the way she did, even if they couldn't say so out loud.

Her phone rang in her cubicle. Gayle tensed.

She'd been waiting for the phone to ring since the first report of the marathon bombing had come in. Patrick Maloney was calling. He was the Special Agent in Charge of the Minneapolis office, and he'd only be calling her for one reason. He was going to bring her in from the cold. It was a disaster, it was Duluth, and they needed her.

"Agent Durkin, I'd like to see you," he said.

"I'll be right there, sir," she told him.

Gayle practically ran to the elevator. The small wait to get to the top floor made her impatient. She smoothed the lines of her suit as she made her way to the corner office, and she used a pocket mirror to make sure she had no remnants of her lunch salad stuck in her teeth. When she reached Maloney's office, the door was open, and she could hear him inside, on the phone. The secretary told her to wait, and she sat in a cushioned armchair with her knees squeezed together.

She heard snippets of the conversation and realized that Maloney was talking to the president. That was when the import of what was going on really dawned on her.

Fifteen minutes later, Maloney appeared in the doorway and motioned her inside.

She liked him. Everyone in the office did. He was from the old school. Despite being the top man in a cocky organization, he projected an aura of calm, organized efficiency, with no ego at stake. He was sixty years old, extremely tall and thin, but there was nothing fragile about him. Gayle suspected that Maloney could have easily outpaced her in a marathon. His gray hair never varied in length, because he had it trimmed every week. She'd never seen a single hair of his mustache or eyebrows longer than any other. His suits were dark and perfectly pressed.

Maloney was a workaholic like her, but unlike her, he'd managed to maintain a family life. He'd been married for thirty-five years. He had four children and six grandchildren. He was soft-spoken and not given to shows of enthusiasm or emotion, because emotion didn't solve crimes. He simply got the job done, and he declined to play political games.

That tendency hadn't served him well in the agency's bureaucracy. Maloney had begun his career in Baltimore and then D.C., and for years, he'd been on the fast track. Agency watchers had buzzed about him as a future director. However, he'd made the mistake of not toe-ing the administration line on a domestic terrorism case in the 1990s. Maloney chose facts over politics, and not long after that, he'd been transferred out of Washington to lead the Minneapolis office. It was a promotion in name but not in fact. They were exiling him to the wilderness.

Maloney had accepted the new reality with grace, and he'd built one of the top field offices in the country out of his heartland beat. He had no chance of heading back to D.C., but he never expressed disappointment at the direction his career had taken.

Gayle sat down in front of Maloney's desk. His eyes were direct. She was accustomed to reading people's faces, but in this case, her boss was taking the measure of hers.

"You know what's going on," Maloney said with almost no inflec-tion. If he'd read bedtime stories to his kids in that tone, they'd have fallen asleep in no time.

"Of course, sir."

"We'll be taking over the investigation," he went on.

"Yes, sir."

"There's considerable interest in this case at the highest levels in Washington."

Maloney's voice never betrayed how he felt, but Gayle knew that "considerable interest" was probably an understatement. The betting in the field office was that the president would be weighing in on Twitter about the bombing before midnight, and he wasn't likely to be nuanced in assigning blame.

"I'm sure that's true," Gayle said.

The field director assessed his agent for a moment in silence.

"You grew up in Duluth—is that right, Durkin?" Maloney asked, even though she was sure he could have recited her entire biography from memory.

"I did, sir. My parents still live there."

"This is a painful day for your hometown."

"Yes, it is."

"I'd like you to serve as our liaison with the Duluth Police during the investigation. We'll be in charge, but they know the terrain."

"Thank you, sir. Yes, absolutely."

"Normally, I'd use our resident agency in Duluth, but we lost our supervisory agent there after Special Agent Harrison passed away last month."

"I understand," Gayle told him.

"The lieutenant in charge of major crimes in the Duluth Police is a man named Jonathan Stride. He's good. He has a strong team."

"I look forward to working with them," Gayle said.

"Be ready to leave in thirty minutes."

"Yes, sir."

Gayle stood up, but before she could leave, Maloney stopped her with the smallest motion of his hand. "One more thing, Agent Durkin. The eyes of the country are on us. Whatever we do will be scrutinized and second-guessed. It's very possible that politicians may get ahead of the facts in this case, but the only thing I care about are the facts. Understood?"

"Yes, sir."

"No matter what we uncover about the people who did this, or their motives, I will not tolerate the slightest unprofessional behavior from anyone on my team."

"Of course. I appreciate the opportunity."

"You know why I'm telling you this, don't you? I want assurances that you'll be able to separate any personal feelings you may have from this investigation. Because if you have any doubts about that, say so now, and I'll find someone else to do this."

Gayle knew he would have to bring this up, and she knew what he expected her to say. She had no doubts. She had no emotions. Or if she did, she would set them all aside to solve the case. That was how the FBI worked.

"You don't have to worry about me, sir," Gayle told him.

"Good."

Gayle left the office, exhilarated to be back in the field. It was what she'd wanted for a year. In truth, she did have doubts about whether she could handle the case with professional detachment. She did have emotions. When she first heard about the bomb in Duluth, she'd thought about Ron, and she knew exactly what she felt about the terrorists who'd launched the attack.

She wanted to kill them.

6

Khan turned his taxi into the driveway of his small home on Vassar Street at three o'clock in the afternoon. They had no garage, so on winter mornings, he had to shovel his cab out from the snow before he drove off to pick up his first fare of the day. He parked on the gravel and sat in the car with his hands still on the wheel. Tall trees soared over his head, full of summer greenness. The rain had stopped, but the ground was wet and shiny with puddles.

The front door of his house flew open.

His wife, Ahdia, burst onto the wooden deck that was lined with geraniums in clay pots. She saw him and clapped both hands over her mouth in relief. She bolted down the three steps and ran to the car. He opened the taxi door, and when he climbed out, she threw her arms around him.

"Khan!" she breathed into his ear. "I thought you were dead. I was so scared. I called, and you didn't answer! Why didn't you answer?"

They stood at arm's length with their hands still entwined. He stared at the face he knew so well. The dark, teasing eyebrows and brown eyes, so vivid against her ivory skin. The mouth that was always laughing at whatever he said. The blooms of her cheeks, pink, puffy, and round. Her bright *hijab* making a circle around her face. She was small, and to him, she was perfect. A treasure.

"I'm sorry. I went back to help after the explosion, and I lost my phone in the chaos."

"I can't tell you all the thoughts that were in my head."

"I know. There were people stranded everywhere. I wanted them to get home, so I made several trips in the cab. I'm sorry you were worried."

Ahdia dragged him toward the house, but her eyes never left him. She wore a cherry-red sweater and long black skirt. "Come inside. I'll make you tea."

She led him up the old porch steps, which shifted unsteadily under their feet. Their house was small, nothing more than a tiny box with a pointed roof, but it felt like a castle to him. The lawn grew fast and always felt overgrown. They lived in a quiet neighborhood, on a street that dead-ended in deep woods. They'd bought the house a year ago. Some of their new neighbors ignored them; some had welcomed them with strange Minnesota dishes like green bean casserole. Others, the fearful ones, whispered or stared when Khan drove by in his cab, but he smiled at them anyway. He was a happy man.

But not today.

Inside, sandalwood incense relaxed him. He dropped into the worn armchair near the front window. A yellow embroidered tapestry took up most of the wall beside him. Whenever he saw it, he thought of his mother, who had made it over a stretch of months. She was long gone. So was his father. And his brother, who'd died in the riot in Lahore. None of them had made it out of Pakistan.

Ahdia brought him tea in a blue ceramic mug, which he cupped between his palms. His wife curled up on the wooden floor at his feet and lay her head against his knee.

"How is Pak?" he asked.

"He's sleeping."

Khan smiled. "Impossible."

His four-year-old son, with his mop of black hair, had limitless energy. He could already run like the wind, and he had astonishing grace on the soccer field. Khan was sure that Pak would be a star player.

"Tell me what happened," Ahdia said. "People outside were talking. They said there was a bomb."

Khan nodded. "Just a minute earlier, I'd been standing right there."

"Were you hurt?"

"No. I'm fine."

"Did anyone die?"

"I think so. That's what I heard."

Ahdia took his hand. "Awful. So awful."

Khan stared down at his wife. Yes, it was awful, but he knew the troubles in their community were just beginning. "These are going to be dark days for us, you know."

"I know." She added after a pause, "Did you find Malik? Was he there?"

"I never saw him," Khan replied. He sipped his tea, but he had no thirst for it now. He took off his silver glasses and wiped away the smudges with the tail of his shirt.

"So maybe he wasn't involved."

"I hope that's true."

Ahdia stood up and folded her arms across her chest. "You should rest, Khan. You look exhausted."

"I wouldn't be able to sleep. I'm going to take a walk to put this all out of my head."

She bent down and kissed him. "All right, but don't be long. Pak will be up soon. He'll want to kick the ball with you."

Khan got up and went outside into the damp afternoon. He passed his yellow cab, where he spent twelve hours every day. Later, he would wash it. The rain had left it dirty, and he was fanatical about keeping a clean cab. He wandered into the empty street, which was quiet except for the songs of birds and a hushed wind. Where the road ended, he made his way onto a dirt trail leading into the woods. The silence of this place was a blessing. Growing up in Lahore, he'd never known what silence was. There was tumult everywhere, people shouting, animals baying, cars and bicycles honking horns or ringing bells as they clamored for space in the street. He missed very little about his homeland, where his memories were mostly of hunger and loss. He didn't always understand America, but he was proud to be American.

As a fourteen-year-old orphan, he'd been brought to Chicago by his uncle. Khan was grateful to have been rescued, but his uncle's children had resented him and wanted nothing to do with him. Instead, his friends became his family, most of them young immigrants like him. He didn't have money for college, so at eighteen, he drove a cab instead. His life followed a strict but sterile routine. Drive all day, pray, go to the mosque, share an apartment with four other ex-Pakistanis with similar lives. Looking back on those days, he understood how young men could go wrong. He wasn't starving, but he'd had no clear purpose, and the purposeless life yearned for any kind of meaning.

Everything had changed when he was twenty-three. His uncle introduced him to Ahdia.

She was a Pakistani, like him, but her parents were both technology professionals, and she had a degree from the University of Chicago in computer science and a job with a local medical device manufacturer. She was traditional but strong-minded, and she was beautiful. He learned about life from her in a way he'd never appreciated before. She made him a better person. It was Ahdia who convinced him to become a citizen, and Ahdia who suggested they leave Chicago and move somewhere quieter and smaller, where they could build a family.

They married. Ahdia got a job offer from the high-tech aircraft manufacturer Cirrus, and they made the move to Duluth. Khan continued to drive a cab. Pak was born a year later, and they bought their little house a year after that. The Muslim community was much smaller here than in Chicago, but they had built a small circle of friends at the mosque, some from Pakistan but others from places like Somalia and Iraq. Right now, today, Khan had everything he wanted in life, and the only thing he needed from the rest of the world was to leave him in peace.

As he walked through the quiet woods, though, he realized that the world always catches up with you. He hiked a trail he'd hiked a hundred times before, and he saw someone waiting on a bench near the bank of Amity Creek. It was Malik.

His friend stood up when he saw him. They didn't embrace.

"*Salaam Alaikum*," they both murmured.

Ironically, Malik looked more American than Khan did. He wore American clothes and kept expensive sunglasses tucked into the V-neck of his white shirt. His black hair was buzzed and came to a sharp point on the peak of his forehead. He had a chin curtain beard that followed the line of his square jaw. Malik, at twenty-two years old, was more than a decade younger than Khan. He was a senior at UMD, studying engineering, and his parents in Detroit were both doctors, but his privileges masked something hollow.

Like Khan years before, Malik had no purpose, and the purposeless life always looked for meaning.

Khan wasted no time getting to the point. "Did you do this?"

"Nice to see you, too, Khan," Malik replied.

"No games! I want the truth. Was it you?"

"Does it matter? They will blame us. They always do."

"And what if it *was* us? People died, Malik. People were blown to bits. Men, women, probably children, too."

His young friend sat back down on the bench. Behind him, water gurgled over the rocks, gathering strength. Barely two miles away, the creek crashed downward in waterfalls on its way to Lake Superior.

"They bring it on themselves," Malik replied.

"How can you say that? This was a vile act. If a Muslim did this to innocent people, he is no Muslim to me."

"Nobody in this country is innocent," Malik told him.

Khan sat down next to him. "I was there. It could have been me, too. One minute this way or that, and I'd be dead."

For the first time, Malik looked concerned. "Why were you there?"

"Looking for *you*," Khan told him.

Malik said nothing.

"I wasn't the only one," Khan said. "Many of us have been worried about you. The things you've said lately? All the anger? The threats you've made against this awful woman Dawn Basch?"

"Are you saying she doesn't deserve them?" Malik asked.

"I'm saying she is baiting us! She wants to incite violence. She only needs one fool to give her what she wants. These are not children's games, Malik. Our community is trying to protect itself."

"If you think I'm guilty, turn me in."

"I think you're hiding something," Khan said.

"My plans don't concern you."

"If they put you at risk, they do concern me. You know how I feel about you."

Malik's angry eyes softened. "Yes, I know that, and I love you like a brother, too. That's why I don't want you involved. You have a family. A life to protect."

"So do you."

Malik stood up. "I have dedicated my life to something else now."

His friend walked away toward a bridge that crossed the creek. Khan called after him. "Malik! How can I reach you? Where are you staying? You haven't been at the dorm in days."

"It's better that you not know where I am," Malik replied.

"Then turn on your phone."

Malik retraced his steps. "I destroyed my old phone. I have a new one now. Memorize the number, but don't use it except in emergency."

Malik rattled off a number, and he made Khan repeat it several times to be sure he had it right.

"Tell me what's going on with you," Khan urged Malik, but his friend simply walked away. In a short time, he'd become someone different. He was older and harder, with a cold line to his jaw. He looked like a man who'd found his purpose, and that was what worried Khan. It was too easy to find purpose in evil.

"Go home to your wife and boy," Malik called to him without looking back. "Keep your head low, Khan. Bad things are coming our way."

@AP tweeted:
Press conference under way in Duluth. Minnesota governor asks for calm, advises people to remain indoors.
#marathon

@AP tweeted:
Governor introduces Patrick Maloney, Special Agent in Charge of the Minneapolis office, FBI, to lead investigation.
#marathon

@AP tweeted:
FBI's Maloney cites "multiple casualties" from one explosive device. No other devices found.
#marathon

@AP tweeted:
FBI's Maloney says no suspects or motive, no claims of responsibility, investigation "wide open."
#marathon

@myopeneyes tweeted:
No motive, Pat? How about allah akbar. Wake up.
#marathon
#copsareblind
17 people favorited @myopeneyes

@a_private_i tweeted:
Marathon photos showing up on diggitt.com. Got photos? Post
them. Let's solve this thing.
#marathon

@fredsissel tweeted:
Thousands of photos at diggitt already. Come on, people, we can
find this asshole.
#marathon
182 people retweeted @fredsissel

@dawnbasch tweeted:
Motive? This was terrorism.
This was an attempt to silence me.
I will not be silenced.
#marathon
#islamismurder
#noexceptions

7

Stride stood with Special Agent Gayle Durkin in Canal Park. The lift bridge, which separated the city from the strip of land known as the Point, loomed like a gray steel monster two hundred yards away. He could see the deep blue of Lake Superior from the street. The entire area around them had been taped off as a crime scene. FBI personnel swarmed the half block surrounding the Duluth Outdoor Company retail store, laying down numbers to mark evidence to be collected.

Shrapnel. Metal. Fabric. Human tissue.

The FBI Special Agent in Charge, Patrick Maloney, had cornered Stride after the press conference to introduce him to Durkin. Stride, in turn, had introduced Durkin to his cops at the bomb site. It helped that she was from Duluth. That gave her credibility as a police liaison, because she knew the local area, but no one—including Stride—was naïve about her role. Liaison was just a fancy word for the fact that Durkin would be telling his team what to do.

"Was there any chatter around town before the marathon?" she asked him.

"You mean threats? No, nothing specific. We were on high alert because of Dawn Basch and the unrest she's caused. There's been a lot of angry rhetoric back and forth. Campus protests. Things like that."

"Yes, Basch already called us about the death threats she's received. She's sending over copies of the hate mail. We need to review any intelligence you gathered on the protesters, too. E-mails. Videos. News reports. Social media posts. I want names and faces."

Stride took a long time to reply. "This isn't the NSA, Durkin. We're not spies up here."

"Yes, and Duluth's not New York City," Durkin fired back. "It's a small town. I know how it works here. Nobody's a stranger. Everyone is connected to everyone else. Chances are, somebody knows who did this. And a smart cop like you must have a pipeline to these people."

He thought: *these people*. He knew what she meant, but he wanted to hear her say it.

"So what exactly are you looking for? Are you asking if I have a mole inside the Muslim community in Duluth?"

"Do you?"

Stride turned away from the crime scene in Canal Park and focused on the young agent in front of him. Maloney said she was smart, but she was also ego driven and impulsive. He knew about her background. A brother killed by Islamist extremists. An emotional response with a terrorism suspect that almost got her fired.

"I know the FBI's job is to find whoever did this," Stride said. "But part of *my* job is to make sure this city doesn't tear itself apart. We're the locals. We still have to live here after you guys have packed up and gone home. That means building trust with different communities, and that's not easy when some of the people in Washington seem intent on setting us at one another's throats."

She took a deep breath. "I'm not trying to undermine relationships you've built, but let's not kid ourselves, Stride. We know where we need to start asking questions, and it's not at the Lutheran prayer breakfast."

"Aren't you skipping a few steps?" he asked.

"I'm not jumping to any conclusions. We'll go where the evidence takes us. But a bombing in a city that's had weeks of protests over a 'free-speech' conference that openly insults Islam? It would be naïve not to reach out to contacts in the Muslim community and find out if there's been any buzz. I'm assuming you have someone you can talk to."

"Yes, I do," Stride acknowledged.

"Good. Call him. Set up a meeting. I want to be there."

He shook his head. "I'll call him, but the meeting is just me."

"This is what I do, Stride. I read people. I know if they're lying."

"I'm sure you're good at it, but I've spent three years getting this man to trust me. Our politicians haven't exactly been helping me make my case. If I bring in a stranger, from the FBI, particularly someone with your personal history, that trust is gone. You won't get what you want from him."

"Then tape it. I'll use the inflections in his voice to analyze whether he's telling the truth."

"No. No surveillance."

Durkin exhaled, long and slow. She hid her anger, but Stride could feel it like a cold lake wind. "I could get the SAC to order you to do it."

"Go ahead and try, but Maloney will back me up," Stride told her.

He'd read her correctly. Durkin was bluffing.

"Okay, fine, do it your way, but I want to know every word your mole says and how he says it," Durkin told him.

"Of course."

Stride heard a voice calling to him. He spotted Maggie Bei approaching from between the lakeshore hotels. She always had the same cocky, clip-clop walk in her chunky-heeled boots. Her bangs bounced. She stopped in front of him and dangled a plastic evidence bag before her. The bag contained a mangled piece of steel, blackened by scorch marks, about eight inches by six inches in size.

He noticed that Maggie's pants were soaking wet from the thighs down. The plastic gloves on her hands were wet, too.

"You guys need to see this," Maggie said.

Durkin studied the tiny cop from behind sunglasses. "It's Sergeant Bei, right?"

"That's me. And you're the FBI liaison? Special Agent Gherkin?"

The agent's face was stone. "Durkin. Gayle Durkin."

"Right. Sorry."

Durkin reached for the evidence bag and examined the contents while holding the seal with two fingers. "What is this?"

"You guys are the experts, but it looks like part of a pressure cooker to me," Maggie replied.

"Where did you find this? And why did you move it? Next time don't touch a thing, Sergeant. If you see something, get someone over there from the Evidence Response Team. We can't afford to have anything contaminated."

Maggie, who was also wearing sunglasses, blew the bangs out of her eyes. She showed more patience than Stride expected. Maggie made no secret of her dislike for the arrogance of the FBI. Not that she was short on arrogance herself. "I found this in the lake. I was afraid it was going to wash away if I waited to call for one of your techs."

"In the lake?" Durkin asked.

Maggie pointed at the Inn on Lake Superior across the street. "Yeah, given the power of the blast, I figured some of the debris might have shot completely over the top of the hotel, so I've been climbing around on the rocks next to the boardwalk. I saw this chunk in the water near the shore, and I climbed in to retrieve it before the waves carried it away."

Durkin frowned but didn't say anything more. She didn't offer thanks. She marched away with the bag in her hand toward the head of the FBI's evidence team. Stride stood next to Maggie, and he waited until the FBI agent was out of earshot.

"Special Agent Gherkin?" he murmured.

A smirk played across Maggie's lips. "Innocent mistake," she said.

"Uh-huh. Play nice, Mags."

"Always," she replied.

"Look, nobody likes this, but we knew the FBI was going to take over. It's too high profile to leave it to the locals. And the fact is, they have resources and experts for a case like this that we don't."

"Yeah, but this is *our* town, boss," Maggie replied. "Some bastard killed our people and blew up our marathon. I don't like playing second fiddle to the feebs on this one, and I don't like the idea of this investigation becoming another political football."

Stride understood. For many people, Duluth was the marathon, and the marathon was Duluth. Everyone was emotional about what had happened.

"I hear you, but I know Patrick Maloney. He's solid. He doesn't blow with the political winds on either side."

"What about Durkin?"

"Maloney tells me that Durkin is bright, even if she can be a little headstrong. Let's give her the benefit of the doubt."

"In other words, you don't like her, either," Maggie said.

Stride smiled. "No, but I want you and Serena to work with her, okay? Share whatever you find. I don't need the chief accusing us of hoarding information."

"You know it'll be a one-way street, right? We tell them everything, they throw us crumbs?"

Stride knew that was true, but he couldn't change it. "It is what it is, Mags."

Maggie sighed. "Where's Serena?"

"I told her to go home. Cat wasn't in any shape to be alone, and Serena already ran a marathon today."

"You want me to call her with an update?"

"Thanks. I doubt I'll make it home tonight."

He was grateful that Maggie had volunteered to call Serena. He knew that the relationship between the two women was complicated. They'd started out as friends, and then, for a while, they'd become enemies. At one of the lowest points in Stride's life, he and Maggie had had a short-lived affair that temporarily derailed his relationship with Serena. After he and Serena put their lives back together again, the two women had spent a year of cold separation, until some of the bitterness finally wore off. Now that he and Serena were married, the two women were trying to coexist peacefully as cops and friends.

"Good find on the pressure cooker," Stride told her.

"Thanks. I want to show you something else, too."

Maggie led the way to the other side of the street. The two of them picked their way among the FBI evidence team toward the Duluth Outdoor Company shop. The store was a ruin inside and out, its windows gone, the cobblestones in front of the store torn up, its brick walls seared. Nothing had escaped the devastation.

"The bomb went off here," Maggie said. "Ground zero."

"Yes."

"Okay, but check this out." She took him inside. The floor of the shop was scattered with remnants of the store's merchandise. Burnt and torn clothes. Shredded satchels. Stride saw colorful shards of plastic water bottles that had been imbedded like knives in the rear wall by the sheer force of the bomb.

"What am I supposed to see?" Stride asked.

"It's what you don't see. Glass."

He looked down and realized what Maggie was showing him. Amid the debris, there was very little glass on the floor of the shop. Outside, glass fragments littered the entire street—but not here. He realized immediately what Maggie was suggesting.

"You think the bomb was *inside* the store," he said. "The windows shattered outward."

"Right. Leave a backpack with a bomb inside a store that sells hundreds of backpacks. Who's going to notice? Somebody brought it inside and left it behind. Either they used a timer or a radio trigger to set it off."

"What about the people who were inside the store?" Stride asked.

"Two dead, one critical, a couple others with serious injuries. They won't be talking to us for a while."

"Does the FBI know about this?"

"Yeah, they have it figured out, too. I heard them talking. I wasn't sure when we'd get the news."

Stride wandered back outside the store. The street was filled with police and FBI, not the people who should have been there on marathon day. Runners. Tourists. Locals and visitors who would have crowded Canal Park in the aftermath of the race. That night, there was supposed to be an awards ceremony and live entertainment, but it had all been cancelled.

Cancelled because of a madman with a bomb. Or madwoman—terrorism was becoming an equal-opportunity profession.

Stride didn't know who the bomber was, but he could see a shadowy image of that person in his mind's eye, walking into the Duluth Outdoor Company shop with a heavy backpack casually slung over one shoulder. And then leaving without it. How far away was the bomber when the explosion went off? Fifty yards? One hundred? Far enough to be safe but close enough to witness the trauma caused by the attack.

"The FBI is gathering up cameras and video footage from Canal Park," Stride told Maggie. "Somewhere in all those photos, we'll find the person who did this. They can't hide for long. Whoever it is has a face."

8

Michael Malville loved the long summer evenings in the Northland. Daylight lingered into the late hours like an old friend. The scent of flowers blew in the air, and hawks circled overhead. This should have been a perfect Saturday night, but a strange emptiness ruled in the aftermath of the bombing. Even in the town of Cloquet, which was twenty miles outside Duluth, people stayed inside. The grassy land across from Michael's front porch typically bustled with children playing baseball until it was nearly dark, but not tonight.

He lived in a historic district, with roots going back to the town's lumber milling days a century earlier. The homes were expensive; his neighbors were wealthy. A few years ago, he and Alison had built a mansion in a rural area much closer to Duluth, but they'd sold it after Alison's violent encounter with the serial killer there. Alison had never wanted to go back to that place. In a small town like Cloquet, they now had neighbors who looked out for one another.

Their home was two and a half stories, built on a slope above a cul-de-sac, with white clapboard siding and columns lining the porch. The lawns were lush. Evergreens ringed the neighborhood. Sometimes it felt as if they'd gone back to a simpler time. Alison loved it here, and so did Michael, but he was restless.

He'd spent most of his life building a successful technology business, but he'd sold it two years ago, along with their Duluth house. For a year, he and Alison had focused on putting their marriage back together and putting the Spitting Devil nightmare behind them. She still had the occasional panic attack, but she was better, and they were sleeping together again, which had taken months of therapy to achieve. Evan, caught up with his cartoon monsters and TV zombies, seemed unaffected by his close encounter with a real-life monster.

They had plenty of money. The sale of his company had given him enough assets to retire comfortably, but Michael wasn't the kind of man who could play golf every day. Alison had thrown herself into projects at Evan's school and into the Cloquet arts community, but Michael was adrift. He'd made a few angel investments, but making money on top of money didn't appeal to him. He felt as if he had no purpose in life, and every man needed a purpose. Without it, he didn't know why he was here.

He stared at the lengthening shadows in the cul de sac. Lights had come on in the other houses around them. On the porch, citronella candles burned to keep away the mosquitoes. He sipped a gin and tonic. He'd hoped, by loosening his mind with alcohol, that the image of the man on the street would come back, clear and sharp, but it didn't work that way. Every time Michael dug into his memory, the recollection came out muddier than before. The man's face changed. His clothes changed. He wasn't sure of any of the details now.

The man had collided with him; he'd looked back; they'd shared a glance. Face. Eyes. Hair. Expression. Skin tone. Clothes. Michael had seen it all, but the moment had tiptoed in and out of his brain without leaving clear footprints. Every day contained more than eighty-six thousand seconds, and if you didn't know that one of them was going to be important, you didn't really pay attention.

"Are you okay?"

Alison stood in the doorway. His wife cupped a glass of Riesling.

"I'm still thinking about it," he said. Then he added, "It makes me mad."

She came and sat in an Adirondack chair beside him. Once upon a time, she'd had long, natural red hair, but now she colored it blond and kept it in a bob. Her long legs were bare below her shorts, and she wore a tan blouse with the sleeves rolled above her elbows. She was slim, and she preferred to go without makeup. To him, her natural face was even more attractive, with its laugh lines and freckles.

They were both forty-one years old. He didn't know where the time had gone. Just yesterday, he'd been thirty.

"I really don't understand how any human being could do this," Alison murmured. "It makes no sense to me. Some person had to plan this. Someone had to make it happen, knowing what it would do."

"I know. It's insane."

"I don't want Evan playing alone outside until they catch whoever did this," Alison said.

"We're safe here in Cloquet," Michael told her, but he didn't want to argue with her. After what they'd gone through two years earlier, it didn't take much for Alison to feel threatened. "But yeah, okay, we'll stay home with him."

He grabbed his phone from his belt. He used his thumb to swipe through the Twitter time line. Everyone was talking about the bombing. He wasn't used to Duluth being the center of the universe, but the world now had its eyes trained on Canal Park. He watched a video clip from the FBI press conference. Next to the agent in charge, he recognized the Duluth police lieutenant, Jonathan Stride, who'd called Michael a murderer two years before.

"I want to caution everyone not to jump to conclusions," the FBI agent, Patrick Maloney, warned the public.

Don't jump to conclusions.

Jonathan Stride should have thought about that before he nearly destroyed Michael's life in a single night. Later, when the real killer was dead, the lieutenant had apologized. The sergeant, Maggie Bei, had apologized, too, but it didn't matter. The damage to his life and his marriage was already done.

A serial killer targeting redheaded women who looked like Alison? Michael must be guilty.

A pressure-cooker bomb at a marathon? Don't jump to conclusions.

Michael had heard the same song before, over and over, around the world. San Bernardino. Paris. Brussels. Fort Hood. London. Sydney. Don't jump to conclusions. And in the end, it was always the same. Islamic names. Islamic faces. People got tired of being told to believe everything except their own eyes.

He thought again: *I was there. I saw him.*

"Twitter?" Alison asked.

Michael looked up from his phone. "What?"

"I always know when you're looking at Twitter. Your face gets so angry."

"Come on, Alison."

"You should look at yourself in a mirror sometime. See what I mean. That's why I prefer Facebook. On Facebook, it's mostly about the cat videos, you know? But you and Twitter—I don't like it, Michael. I really don't."

"Okay, yes, I'm angry. This guy killed people. I was there. You expect me to be smiling about it?"

"That's not what I mean," Alison said.

"Then what do you mean?"

His wife reached for his hand. "When I heard about the bombing, the only thing I wanted to do was hold on to you and Evan. We are *blessed* to be alive at all. Didn't what happened two years ago prove that to you? I needed you with me today, Michael, and you didn't come home. Where were you?"

"I'm sorry. I just couldn't leave."

"Why not? Everyone else did."

"I know that, but you weren't there. I saw—"

His wife interrupted him. "I know. You told me. You saw someone with a backpack. It's fuzzy, and you can't really remember the person's face. Hundreds of other people who were at the marathon are probably saying exactly the same thing right now. It's okay, Michael. You told that police officer about it. You did the right thing. Now you have to let it go."

"How can I let it go? His face is in my head somewhere. Maybe they could hypnotize me or something, and I could remember. It drives me crazy to have them stand up and say they don't know what this is, when I know what I saw. A Muslim guy with a backpack heading toward Canal Park. And fifteen minutes later—boom."

"The fact that he was there doesn't mean he did it," Alison pointed out.

"Okay, sure, maybe not, but what if he did? He *bumped* into me on the street, Alison. The bomb could have gone off right there. I'd be dead. Evan would be dead, too."

Her eyes welled with tears. "Don't talk like that. Don't even say that."

"I'm sorry, but I just want you to understand why this is so hard for me. You haven't been to the rallies when Dawn was speaking and seen the faces of the protesters. The hatred in their eyes? It's unbelievable. That's what I saw in the guy who passed me. That's what I remember. Hatred. He heard me talking about No Exceptions, and he deliberately slammed into me. I know that's what happened."

His wife sighed and closed her eyes. "I just wish—"

"What?"

Alison shook her head. "Nothing."

"Tell me," he insisted.

"I just wish you hadn't gotten so caught up in Dawn Basch and this whole No Exceptions crowd. They make me uncomfortable."

He sat up in his chair. "What are you saying? This is *her* fault?"

"No, of course not."

"Dawn is defending free speech and the Constitution. Nobody else is standing up for the First Amendment. They're all too politically correct to say anything. For God's sake, these people riot and murder over *cartoons*, Alison."

Alison sat up, too, and put a hand on his knee. "All I'm saying is that the whole city got a lot angrier after Dawn Basch came to town. *You* got a lot angrier. I don't think that's a good thing."

"Some things are worth getting angry about," Michael snapped.

He got up and walked away, leaving Alison on the porch. She called after him, but he slammed the door. A feeling of uselessness washed over him. Throughout his life, he'd needed a cause, but his business was gone, and he'd found nothing to fill the void.

Michael climbed the stairs to the master bedroom, but he wasn't ready to sleep. He took the twisting iron staircase up to the half floor at the top of the house, where he kept his man cave. The small space was paneled in dark wood under a low, angled roof. Wet bar. Framed Vikings posters. High school and college swimming trophies. A television the size of Wyoming. His desk and computer.

He booted up his Mac, and he scrolled through his Twitter feed again. Yes, the people out there were angry, but they spoke his language. They didn't need the police and the government to tell them what had happened at the marathon. They already knew.

He could see the reflection of his face in the monitor. Alison was right; his expression looked chiseled in stone.

Michael tapped on his keyboard and tweeted under his handle @malvileo:

I was there. Think I saw the guy. What's the site where everyone is posting marathon photos?

Ten seconds later, a user named @danmink59 replied.

diggitt.com. *Go get him, man. #noexceptions*

Michael found the website, where a link to the cache of uploaded photos was in a banner on the home page. A counter kept track of the users accessing the site. Thousands of online detectives were already examining photos, all of them showing places he knew intimately, taken along every mile of the marathon route.

He went to the wet bar and made coffee. He needed caffeine for the long night ahead of him. He clicked on the first photo and zoomed in on the faces, and he studied them one by one.

He was looking for a man with a backpack.

A terrorist.

Where are you?

9

Stride waited in the parkland by the olive-colored waters of Chester Creek, near the bridge at Skyline Parkway. At dusk, the area was empty and silent, except for whispers in the dense trees. The cool wind rustled his wavy hair. By instinct, he reached for a pack of cigarettes in his pocket, but he'd quit long ago. The craving came back at moments like this, when he was alone after a long, difficult day. His middle and index fingers rubbed together, as if a Lucky Strike were still between them.

He checked the time on his phone. Haq was late.

They usually met here, down the hill from the dormitories of UMD, where Haq Al-Masri was a professor of religion and the faculty advisor to the Muslim Student Center. Haq didn't like to be seen with Stride; he couldn't afford to be perceived as a spy in his community. It had taken Stride three years to win the man's confidence, but trust was a fragile thing, particularly in the current climate. They both knew they served different masters. Haq was a Muslim first, and Stride was a cop first.

As he waited, he texted Serena. *Is Cat okay?*

His wife texted back almost immediately. *She's struggling.*

Stride frowned. Serena had told him about Cat and the stolen beret, a stupid act of rebellion that had saved the girl's life. It took his breath away, to know how close she'd been to the bomb, to know how easily it could have gone another way.

Does she remember anything?

Cat had been there when the bomb went off. On the way into Canal Park, she probably passed the bomber, escaping in the opposite direction as the timer ticked toward zero. It took Serena a long time to write back. He wondered if she was irritated with him for pushing the question so quickly. Then finally she replied: *No, Cat didn't see anyone suspicious.*

He texted: *I had to ask.*

She wrote back: *I know that.* And then she added: *Maggie called me. So the device was inside the Duluth Outdoor Company shop?*

Looks that way.

Her next message was delayed again, but finally, she wrote back: *Something happened at that store a few days ago. Do you remember? A homeless man caused a disturbance. Cops had to be called.*

He remembered the incident. *So?*

She wrote back: *It's an odd coincidence.*

That was true, and Stride normally didn't trust coincidences, but for the moment, he didn't see a plausible connection between the two events. He heard footsteps on the grass and looked over his shoulder and saw Haq jogging into the park. Without looking at Stride, the man slowed to a walk and checked the pulse in his neck. Haq took a squirt of water from a plastic bottle on his belt.

Stride texted: *I have to go.*

Haq approached the bench. Sweat and cologne clouded the air. When Haq wasn't running, he was cycling; when he wasn't cycling, he was lifting weights. He was a dark, handsome man, in his mid-thirties, the kind of teacher who caught the eye of college undergrads but who never looked back. He had a shock of jet-black hair and a prominent, aquiline nose. His skin was like gold, except for the neat line of his beard. He wore a black UMD long-sleeved T-shirt and nylon running pants.

Stride didn't think he'd ever seen Haq smile or laugh; the man was relentlessly serious. He was smart, too, with an encyclopedic knowledge from his academic studies. Over the years, they'd discussed religion, philosophy, politics, and the Constitution. They brought opposite values to nearly every debate, but they'd found a way to be civil with each other and to respect their disagreements. The only thing he disliked about Haq was that the man could never quite shake the elitism of his upbringing, as if he still looked down on everyone else around him. He'd grown up in Egypt and now held dual citizenship. His father had a senior post in the Egyptian embassy in Washington, D.C.

Haq sat down on the other side of the bench. "I knew you'd be calling," he said.

He had a high-pitched, slightly singsong voice, and although his English was perfect, he retained a Middle Eastern accent.

Stride heard the veiled accusation and felt bitterness coiled in the man's body. Impatience. Exasperation at knowing that Stride would knock on his door. It wasn't entirely misplaced.

"When Americans see a house on fire, they assume it must be dragons," Haq went on. "Muslim dragons."

Stride let the silence linger, but then he said, "This is your house, too."

"Yes, I'm aware."

"Did you see the FBI press conference?" Stride asked. "The Special Agent in Charge was clear that the investigation is wide open. We don't know if this was terrorism. If it was, we don't know who's behind it."

"Tell that to the president."

"I'm not a politician, Haq," Stride said.

"And yet here you are, Jonathan."

"I'm just covering all the bases."

"Please. You're looking for dragons. It doesn't matter what the FBI says or doesn't say, or what the president says or doesn't say. A bomb explodes, and Muslims are guilty until proven innocent. We are *all* guilty, every one of us. You accuse us of not sharing American values, but at the first sign of trouble, you jettison those values yourself."

"People were murdered, Haq. People had their limbs blown off. This was a heinous crime."

"I know that. It's an awful, awful thing. I'm not minimizing the horror or pain of those affected. However, for us, for my community, I know what comes next. While you're looking for evidence, I'm looking for pitchforks in the village square. They'll be coming for us. Haven't recent events made that clear?"

"I understand your concerns," Stride said. "You know I appreciate your honesty and directness. One thing we've never done is play games with each other."

"That's true."

"So now I'm going to be honest and direct with you," Stride went on.

Haq looked back over his shoulder for the first time, and their eyes met in the semidarkness. "Go ahead."

"Your community has more than its share of dragons," Stride told him.

Haq didn't protest or get angry. Instead, he dug into the zippered pocket of his sweats and removed a flat object wrapped in cloth. He unfolded the cloth and held up a runner's medal by its ribbon.

"See this? I ran the marathon last year. And the year before. I would have run it again this year, but I spent months leading an effort to educate the Muslim community about the marathon and to get more Muslim runners involved. I recruited more than forty runners from the five-state region and arranged housing and transport this weekend. I coordinated with everyone at the race. I saw this as a way to bring us *together*, Jonathan. To focus on what we share instead of what divides us. And then this happens, and where do we end up? Even farther apart."

Stride hated what came next. He didn't like it, but he had no choice.

"These people you brought in—" he began.

This time, Haq exploded. His fist slammed down on the bench. He leaped to his feet, and his voice was loud in the peacefulness of the park. "What, you want their names? Their addresses?"

"Yes, I do."

"So you can interrogate them! For what? What's their crime? Running while Muslim? These people did *nothing*. They came here to run twenty-six-point-two miles from Two Harbors to Duluth. For most people, that would be an amazing thing. For us, apparently, it's nothing but probable cause."

Stride stood up, too. "I'd like to say we live in a perfect world, but we don't. There hasn't been much peace around here lately, and a lot of the unrest has to do with religious differences. I can't ignore that."

"You mean since Dawn Basch came to town?" Haq asked. "And whose fault is that?"

"No one in city government welcomed or encouraged her, but we also can't stop her from holding a private conference. You know that. She can say whatever she wants. That's her right. It doesn't mean you have to listen."

"So we should ignore her? We should just laugh when she insults and degrades us? Well, I'm sorry, but to us, it isn't funny. Think about it, Jonathan. You're married to a lovely woman. I've met Serena. Now imagine someone came to town and got in your face and screamed at you that your wife was a pig. A whore. I think you'd be angry about that."

"You're right. I would."

"Would you strike back? Would you punch whoever said that?"

"I don't know. Maybe. But that's my point, Haq. People lose control. There's a lot of anger in Duluth because of Dawn Basch. More than anger. *Rage.* The question is whether someone decided to act on that rage. I know you. You have your ears to the ground. Everyone talks to you. Is there anyone that the community was worried about?"

Haq held the race medal in his palm. He balanced it on his hand as if measuring its weight.

"When this Dawn Basch tweets, she also uses the hashtag #islamismurder," he said in measured tones. "People talk about #noexceptions as if she's defending free speech, but that's not what she means. When she says #islamismurder and #noexceptions together, she is saying that every Muslim is a killer."

"You're probably right," Stride replied.

"You think no one else feels anger? That we're the only ones with extremists in our midst? We're not. Now, because of the bombing, the rage of Basch's bigots will get turned against us even more. Mark my words. It always does."

"And I'll do everything in my power to stop that. You know me."

"One man can't stop a tidal wave," Haq said.

"Then the best thing right now is to find out who did this," Stride told him. "Maybe this happened because of Dawn Basch, and maybe it had nothing to do with her. I don't know. Until we get the truth, we'll be fighting rumors and speculation, and that's dangerous for all of us."

Haq sat down. Silence lingered between them. Crickets chirped in the weeds. "I hate this," Haq said finally.

"I understand, but I need your help."

"I could ruin an innocent man's life."

"If he's innocent, I won't let that happen," Stride told him.

"Don't make promises you can't keep."

"Then I'll do my best."

Stride wondered if that was enough. Haq hesitated, and he looked around to make sure they were alone. He lowered his voice.

"All right, fine. You're right, everyone is angry about Basch, but one young man—well, he's been saying things that frightened some of us. We were all conscious of the fact that marathon day was coming. It's hard not to think about Boston."

"You should have talked to me," Stride said. "Warned me."

"I'm sorry. We decided to deal with it ourselves. We wanted to counsel him, not have him arrested."

"That was foolish."

"Perhaps, but we've seen what happens when the police get involved. Naïve, reckless talk becomes the basis for federal charges, and just like that, you put someone away for years."

"Who's the young man?" Stride asked. "And where is he?"

"I don't know where he is. He disappeared a few days ago. That's what worried us. We've been trying to find him."

"And his name?"

"His name is Malik," Haq replied.

10

The parasail floated high above the turquoise waters off Key West, making the people on the beach seem no larger than the bugs that Wade Ralston hunted in the subbasements of Duluth. He heard nothing but wind, but even at this height, the Florida air was warm. A single, slim tether connected him to the boat, which was churning ripples and white water in its wake. Being up here made Wade feel on top of the world, like the king of an infinite domain. Like a god.

However, good things always came to an end.

He felt the winch dragging him downward to the boat. Back to reality. The Gulf got bigger and closer, full of reefs and sand and shadows. His three friends waited for him.

Travis, meaty and tall, with long brown hair and tattoos covering both arms.

Travis's sister, Shelly, looking pudgy in her one-piece bathing suit as she sucked a fruity drink through a straw.

And Wade's wife, Joni, hoisted on Travis's shoulders, swaying as she tried to keep her camera steady.

Joni was ridiculously hot in her string bikini. Joni, with the breast implants he considered one of the best investments he'd made in his whole life. Joni, blond, twenty-eight years old, who made every male head snap around as she walked by. Short, skinny Wade Ralston—Wade the bug zapper with the comb-over—had the hottest wife in the Keys. He'd dreamed of saying that every day since he was a teenager in high school.

The three of them waved with their arms over their heads. Grinned. Laughed. Pointed. He drifted closer to the boat, and he could hear their voices shouting at him.

"Wade! Wade! Wade!"

"Cross the line! Cross the line!"

Huh? That didn't make sense.

And then—*snap*.

The tether broke like a guitar string. He was free. The parachute ballooned behind him, dragging him back to the sky. He shouted for help, but it was as if no one in the boat cared that he wasn't coming down, that he was unmoored, that he had no way to land. They laughed, watching him as he disappeared, turning and twisting lazily on the ripples of air. The island grew small; the water became a sea, far below him. He sailed up and up toward the clouds.

"Wade?"

Up and up, spinning and rising, growing dizzy . . .

"Wade?"

He awoke with a violent start. He blinked, and the Key West sky vanished from his brain. He was warm, because the hospital room was warm. The tether was a tube that tied him to a plastic bag hung on a metal pole, from which IV fluids dripped into his vein. It was dark in Duluth outside the St. Luke's window, and the lights in the room were low. He could see his bruised, swollen feet.

Someone said again, "Wade?"

Travis Baker stood at the end of his hospital bed, but Wade wasn't sure what was real and what wasn't.

"Travis?" he murmured. "What the hell, man?"

"Hey."

Travis was really there. It wasn't another dream. His friend's voice was subdued, which wasn't like Travis at all. Travis was loud. He was loud when he was sober and when he was drunk. He was loud when he got into fights and when he squeezed into utility tunnels to check the bait in a rat trap. But not now. Now Wade could hardly hear him.

"Jesus, you're alive," Wade said. "We're both alive."

"Yeah."

Most people would be happy to be alive, but Travis didn't look happy. His face was wet with tears, and Travis Baker never cried. Extermination wasn't for the sentimental. Poisoning creatures for a living didn't get you a TV movie on the Hallmark Channel.

"They say they dug shrapnel out of my stomach. I was in surgery?"

"Yeah," Travis replied again, no louder than a whisper.

"Where's Joni? Is she with you?"

"Joni? No, man. I—I just got here."

"She must be in the cafeteria or something. I've been asleep pretty much all day. Whenever I wake up, the nurse tells me to rest. TV's unplugged. Somebody put on ocean noises to help me relax. I dreamed about our vacation in Key West. Man, that's the place to be. If you've got the money."

Travis gave him a cracked smile. "You bet."

Wade lifted up the collar of his hospital gown and winced as the incisions in his skin tugged with the shifting of his muscles. He could see bandages taped to his abdomen, and red stains seeped through the gauze.

"I'm a mess," he said. He studied his hands and his bare wrists. "Hey, where's my Fitbit? And my phone? Shit, I hope I didn't lose them. What's the point of running a marathon if you can't see all the steps, right? Can you check the closet or something?"

Travis pointed to a plastic bag on the window ledge. "It's all in there. Phone, clothes, Fitbit, shoes."

"Good." He added, "Did I make it across the finish line? I can't even remember."

"I don't think so, man. Sorry."

"Sucks. Nobody cares if you run twenty-six-point-*one* miles, huh?"

"No."

Wade was confused. He was missing something. He didn't know what it was.

"I figured you'd be dead," he told Travis. "How come you're not dead?"

"It was a tree," Travis told him.

"Huh?"

"I was in front of a tree when the thing blew up behind me. Blast hit the tree trunk and missed me. I barely got a scratch."

"Wow. Lucky."

"Yeah. I guess."

"How's Shelly?" Wade asked. "She okay?"

Travis didn't answer. He wandered over to the window and leaned his elbows on the ledge and chewed on the cuticle of one thumb. He was young. A year younger than Joni, seven years younger than Wade. He had big arms, big legs, and a baseball cap planted backward on his head. He had a Fu Manchu mustache and a silver stud through his lower lip. He wore a Bug Zappers T-shirt and paint-smudged sweatpants.

In high school, Travis had been the kind of guy Wade hated. A bully. Cocky and full of himself. Always a stash of pills and weed. That worked in school but not in the real world. Travis went straight from high school to a job on a garbage truck, the kind of job where you had to shower before you went home because you always smelled like four-month-old cheese. Travis dumped trash bins during the days and drank beer and screamed at the UFC fights on the bar's TV in the evenings. He went nowhere in life, until his sister Shelly, who was Wade's accountant, suggested that Wade hire Travis to grow the business. More clients, more dead bugs, meant more money. That was four years ago.

On the job, they got along okay. Wade had a vintage Mustang he'd restored in an old storage locker. A speedboat. And Joni. All of it impressed Travis, who was usually a month away from having his truck repossessed and crashed on Shelly's couch most nights.

"Travis?" Wade said again. "How's Shelly?"

"She's in surgery. Been there for hours. They won't tell me anything."

"Shit. No wonder you're upset."

"Her legs were a mess. I saw it. A real mess. Bones sticking out. One foot, man, it was like hanging by a thread."

Wade closed his eyes. He tried to swallow, but acid burned in his throat. "That sucks."

Travis breathed through his mouth, like a fish. "Yeah."

"What about Joni? Can you ask the nurse where she is? I mean, is she in the cafeteria, or did she go home to get some sleep?"

Travis turned away from the window. His eyes looked as if they'd sunk back into his skull. "I—I don't know, man."

"Well, can you find out? Come on, Travis."

"Sure. I'll ask somebody. You get some sleep or something."

"I don't want to sleep," Wade said. "I've been sleeping all day. I want to see my wife."

"I guess she must be around here," Travis said.

There it was again. Something in his voice. Something in his face. "Travis?"

"Yeah, man."

"Joni's okay, right?"

"What did they tell you?" Travis asked. "Did they tell you anything?"

"I don't know. Everyone said, don't worry, just sleep. The thing is, Joni was standing right next to Shelly, wasn't she? I mean, right next to her, Travis. I saw her. If Shelly's so bad off, how could Joni be okay? She wasn't in front of a tree like you, Travis."

Travis came and stood over the bed. Tears poured down his face. "No, no tree."

"She was right next to Shelly," Wade said.

"Yeah."

"Tell me the truth, man."

"Hey, you've been through a lot, Wade. Just close your eyes, buddy. We can talk tomorrow."

"*Tell me the truth, man.*"

Travis sank down by the bed and gathered up Wade's hand in his bear paw. The kid didn't know his own strength. "I'm sorry, man. I'm so sorry. Joni's gone. She died out there on the street. The bastards killed her."

Wade closed his eyes and said nothing at all.

He'd known all along.

SUNDAY

11

"I'm here to express my solidarity with the people of Duluth," Dawn Basch told the crowd in the ballroom of the downtown Radisson Hotel. No one would mistake her accent for a "ja sure, you betcha" Minnesotan's. Her voice made her sound like one of the *Real Housewives of New Jersey*.

"Yesterday, terrorists tried to silence the voices of freedom-loving people in this city, just as they've done in so many other places around the world. Well, I have a message for them. You won't succeed."

Stride watched from the back of the room. Basch stood at a podium with two beefy private security guards on either side of her. He had his own police officers just outside the room, at the elevators, in the lobby of the hotel, and on Superior Street. He wasn't taking any chances with more violence, but what bothered him was that violence was exactly what Basch wanted.

Violence brought publicity. Attention. Credibility.

Violence sold tickets to her conferences.

Violence rang up sales of bumper stickers, T-shirts, and hats.

Worse, the media played right along with her. The ballroom overflowed with television reporters who'd arrived to cover the marathon bombing. Basch gave them the raw meat that drove up ratings, and ratings trumped journalism every time. She was live on CNN, CBS, NBC, and Fox.

"Special Agent Maloney says that he can't draw any conclusions yet about yesterday's bombing, but I believe the American people have made it clear that they are sick of political correctness in the face of terrorism. So let me just say what we all know. This horrible event was almost certainly committed by the Islamic extremists who have been protesting this free-speech conference since I arrived in Duluth. I've received dozens of death threats, and we've made those e-mails available to the FBI. Somewhere among those radical Islamists, I'm sure they will find whoever perpetrated these outrageous, senseless murders. In the meantime, I hope that the entire city of Duluth will act as a kind of Neighborhood Watch to help the authorities locate these murderers before they do more harm. These people must be stopped, and all of you can play your part."

Stride swore under his breath. A city of vigilantes was the last thing they needed, but Basch was the kind of person who played with matches at a gas station.

She was fifty years old, trying and failing to look forty. She had long, dark hair that fell into a tornado of messy curls at her shoulders. She was tall and bird-thin. Her smile was slightly misshapen, and she used overly bright lipstick. Her skin had a lumpy, masklike quality, as if it had been shaped in Play-Doh and then painted with crayons. Her long eyelashes and dark mascara made her eyes look like two vampire bats, flapping their wings as she blinked. She wore a red jacket and a tapered black skirt.

"Naturally, I'm seeing my usual attackers in the liberal press," Basch went on. "*The New York Times* calls me a reckless provocateur, and you know what? I am. I'm proud of it. When it comes to free speech, I say No Exceptions. I don't care who I offend. If somebody wants to make a movie about Muhammad cutting the heads off Barbie dolls, I say, go right ahead. In this country, we have an absolute right to make fun of anything we want, and if you don't like it, you can go somewhere else. Of course, it's rather ironic, because the media 'experts' who say we can't jump to conclusions are also blaming me for creating a culture of

violence by offending Muslims. Obviously, they know I'm right about
who's behind this crime. And as for causing offense, I don't negotiate
my First Amendment rights at the barrel of a gun. We can talk about
civility as soon as the other side stops blowing people up."

Basch was smooth. No doubt about it. She had the gift of every
demagogue to wrap up her prejudice in a pretty package, so you
couldn't see the ugliness within. Stride didn't even believe that her
basic message was wrong. Between protecting free speech and avoiding
offense, free speech always won. Even so, he had no respect for people
who threw insults simply because the Constitution said they could.
He hated painting a diverse community of faith with a single brush,
because his own experience of Duluth's Muslims was that they were
honorable people who worked hard, loved their families, and wanted
to live in peace.

He also knew, as he'd told Haq Al-Masri, that the Muslim community had more than its share of dragons. And a single dragon could
burn down a whole town.

As Basch began to take questions, Stride ducked out of the ballroom. He exited the hotel on Superior Street, across from the downtown library. The Sunday streets were deserted. Businesses were closed.
Only the police and media patrolled the city. He waved away a handful
of reporters and walked alone down Fifth Avenue past the Depot.

This was his home. He'd grown up here. Gone to school here. Lost
his parents here. Lost his first wife, Cindy, here. There was something
about loss that bound you to a place forever. Most outsiders saw
Duluth only through the lens of its brutal winters, but to Stride, it
was also ore boats and icebreakers. It was folk bands at Amazing Grace.
It was Bent Paddle ales. It was the Curling Club. It was the famous
Christmas lights display at the home of his neighbor Marcia Hales.
It was the marathon. He'd seen highs and lows in this city in his fifty
years, from recessions to floods, but nothing drove Duluthians away.
They were a tough breed.

He made his way to the Duluth Entertainment Convention Center,
which the FBI had taken over as a staging ground for evidence collected from Canal Park. The sheer scope of the operation impressed

him. If there was one thing the FBI did well, it was to organize and sift through massive amounts of data. He knew he was seeing only the tip of the iceberg here at the convention center. Across the county, hundreds of agents were analyzing photographs, video footage, e-mails, phone records, bank records, call-in tips, website search histories, and social media posts, looking for any kind of connection to the marathon bombing.

Someone had researched how to make a bomb.

Someone had bought the components for a bomb.

Someone had assembled a bomb.

Someone had brought the bomb to the Duluth Outdoor Company and detonated it.

Every one of those steps left electronic footprints, if you knew where to look and how to recognize what you were seeing.

Stride found Special Agent Maloney in an office borrowed from the DECC director, surrounded by laptops and whiteboards. The agent hadn't slept in twenty-four hours, but he looked none the worse for wear. His suit showed no wrinkles. His tie was perfectly knotted and snug against his neck. Stride was tall, but Maloney was an inch taller, and he was thin to the point of being gaunt.

Maloney wasn't a friend, but their paths had crossed regularly on investigations over the past twenty years, since Stride had been a young Duluth detective.

"I was just over at the Dawn Basch press conference," he told Maloney.

"Yes, I saw it on CNN. Don't worry, I've already got Agent Durkin putting to bed this Neighborhood Watch concept."

"Good," Stride replied.

"We're asking people to stay out of the downtown area today. The mayor and governor are talking about whether to ask businesses to close again tomorrow, depending on how the investigation unfolds."

"Do we have any more details on the device?" Stride asked.

"Some. Sifting through the remains of hundreds of shredded backpacks hasn't made the process easier, but the team thinks the source backpack was navy blue. We also know that the triggering mechanism was a cell phone. So the detonation could have been done by radio signal at close range, or the bomber could have called it in and watched the thing blow up on TV."

"In other words, we can't be sure he was even in Canal Park?" Stride asked.

"Yes, except someone had to be there to place the backpack itself," Maloney replied. "Durkin asked one of your officers to talk to the owner of the store to see if we can find out more about how and when the placement could have been made."

"Yes, Serena and I know Drew Olson, who runs the camping store. He'll help if he can." Stride added, "About Agent Durkin . . ."

One of Maloney's trimmed gray eyebrows twitched, which was his only hint of surprise. "Is there a problem?"

"I already have one bull in my china shop, thanks to Dawn Basch," Stride said. "I don't need two."

"I know that Durkin speaks her mind. She can be difficult. If it makes you feel better, she was complaining about you, too. She wasn't happy about being excluded from the meeting with your source."

"It's a delicate relationship."

"Understood. You made the right call. Durkin is many things, but delicate isn't one of them. However, she knows Duluth, and she's one of my brightest agents, especially when it comes to reading people."

"She seems to have something to prove on this case," Stride said.

"Yes, she does. You know what happened to her, and you know I had her out in the cold for a year. This investigation is her way back in, but if she screws it up, she'll be behind a desk for the rest of her career. She knows the stakes. Candidly, I hope she learns something from you and your team."

"Just so we're on the same page," Stride said.

"We are."

"What about the name I gave her?" Stride asked. "Malik Noon."

Maloney smoothed his mustache and plucked a single sheet of paper from the encyclopedia-size pile of materials stacked on the surface of the desk. He knew exactly where everything was. "Noon is twenty-two years old. Engineering student at UMD. Born in Pakistan, parents live in Detroit. Mom is a radiologist; Dad is a thoracic surgeon. Smart kid, and no shortage of money. Has he shown up on your radar screen before now?"

"No."

"Well, he's not a fan of Dawn Basch," Maloney went on. He grabbed another file and laid out three photographs one after another. They'd been taken at No Exceptions rallies in Bayfront Park. "Our boys found him *here* and *here* and *here*," he said, jabbing a finger at faces in the photos.

Stride studied the smiling picture of Malik Noon in his university student ID, then shifted his attention to the photos of Noon taken at the Dawn Basch speeches. He saw no smile, no hint of the easygoing, Americanized student attending the University of Minnesota at Duluth. The man at the rallies had an expression twisted darkly into hatred. His mouth was open as he shouted. He carried the same sign in each of the photos.

It read: BREAKING DAWN.

The image on the sign showed a digitally altered photograph of Dawn Basch with blood pouring out of knife and gunshot wounds in her head and body.

"Have you been able to find him?" Stride asked.

"No. In fact, I'd like you to talk to anyone who knew Malik Noon at UMD, and do it fast."

"Understood."

"And Stride?" Maloney went on. "This time, take Durkin with you."

12

Serena watched Drew Olson push his eight-month-old son in a swing tied to a huge oak tree in his backyard. She knew a lot about the baby. His name was Michael, taken from the name of the baby's grandmother, which was Michaela. He had thick black hair and a big, easy smile that never went away. He had a birthmark on his thigh in the shape of Florida. He'd been born at 4:07 a.m. on October 14 at St. Mary's, with Jonny and her in the hospital room.

He was Cat's baby. Drew and Krista Olson had adopted him.

Serena had met Drew almost a year earlier, when she'd gone into the Duluth Outdoor Company store in Canal Park to find out what she needed to begin training for the marathon. She'd liked him immediately. He was thirty years old and the kind of man who found twenty-five hours in every twenty-four-hour day. He and Krista ran. Kayaked. Skied. Volunteered at food shelves. Grew their own rhubarb and tomatoes. And all of that on top of two demanding full-time jobs.

They were busy people who'd wanted to add a child to their busy lives, but none of their efforts to get pregnant had been successful. When they found out about Cat, they'd made a tear-filled pitch to be the ones to adopt her baby. It was Cat's first decision as a mother, and it had turned out to be a good one.

"This little guy is about the only thing that's kept me going since yesterday," Drew told Serena. "When something like this happens, you realize what you need to hold on to."

"I understand."

"Krista pulled an all-nighter in the ER. She's sleeping now. She said the injuries she saw were horrific. Like something out of a war."

"Thank God for nurses like her."

"Yeah." A little smile of pride played across Drew's face. Then the smile washed away. "I lost two people at the store. Seth was just nineteen. Candice was twenty-one. Both of them the nicest, sweetest kids you could meet."

"I remember Seth. He helped me last year when I was in training."

"Another girl from the store is critical. They don't know if she'll make it. Two others suffered concussions and burns."

"I'm so sorry, Drew."

"When you find the guy who did this, you'd better not let me near him," he told her.

Serena nodded. She'd already heard that sentiment over and over again. Among the police. Among the runners. Among the Duluth people who'd had their marathon stolen from them in the worst way possible.

In the swing, Michael fussed, and Drew slid him out of the harness. The rocking of his father's arms quickly settled the boy. Drew was a small man, but he had an athlete's strength. He wore runner's shorts, a yellow soccer jersey, and sneakers without socks. His kinky, straw-colored hair was tied in a rubber band behind his head.

"Do you want to hold him?" he asked.

"I was ready to grab him as soon as I got here," Serena replied, smiling.

She lifted Michael under his chubby shoulders and held him against her chest. He was warm and smelled clean and fresh, and he was already more boy than baby. She put out two fingers, and he grabbed them in a pincer grip. His eyes never left her face. She could see a strong reflection of Cat in his eyes.

She'd never thought of herself as maternal. There was little from her own childhood she wanted to remember. She'd run away from her mother after years of abuse. A teenage abortion had left her unable to have kids of her own, and she'd had to make peace with that part of her life. It wasn't that she had regrets. She was forty, Stride was fifty; they'd already decided that they were beyond the age where they wanted to adopt. Even so, holding Michael in the hospital eight months ago had changed her. After that moment, she'd understood for the first time what it really meant to be willing to give up everything for another human being.

"He's getting heavy," she said.

"Twenty-one pounds. He's crawling, too."

"Really?"

"Oh, yeah. Nothing is safe." Then Drew added, "How's Cat doing?"

"Nothing is ever easy with her," Serena said. "Has she been by to see you?"

"Not yet. She knows she's welcome, doesn't she? We'd like her to feel close to Michael and to play a role in his life. It's not just talk. Krista and I both want her involved."

"Stride and I keep encouraging her to visit," Serena told him.

"Do you know why she's reluctant? Does she regret giving him up?"

"It's not that. She wanted to keep him, but she knew she wasn't in a position to give him the life he deserved. She loves the idea that he has such a great family with you and Krista. I think she's genuinely happy about that."

"Then what?"

Serena shook her head. "I don't think she believes she has anything to offer him right now."

"That's silly," Drew said.

"I know. I've told her you and Krista don't expect anything from her except love. It's just something she has to come to in her own time."

"Fair enough. I understand."

"Cat was in Canal Park yesterday, too," Serena said.

"Oh, my God. Is she okay?"

"Physically, fine, but she was very close to where the bomb went off. She feels guilty. She wonders why she was spared."

Drew pushed the tree swing back and forth with one hand, even though it was empty. "I know how she feels. Krista and I both ran the marathon. I should have gone over to the store when I was done, but instead, we just hung out and drank beer in the finisher's tent with our friends. If I'd gone back, I'd be dead. Instead, my employees paid the price for me."

"Do I have to give you the speech I gave Cat?" Serena asked. "About none of this being your fault?"

"No, I get it. It's just that the world feels pretty fragile today."

"Yes, it does."

"The FBI told me the bomb was *in* my store. Is that really true?"

"It is."

"Unbelievable. Somehow that makes it even worse, you know? They let me inside this morning to assess the damage. It's a total loss. All the inventory was destroyed. The space is unusable. I feel bad thinking about that, given what happened to my people, but it's going to be hard to rebuild, even with insurance. Retail is always tough. We've been struggling to stay afloat despite a decent economy. But after this, I don't know what happens to tourism around here."

Serena thought: Every crime has ripple effects that people don't see.

"Listen, Drew, I have to ask you a couple of questions," she told him.

"Of course."

"Did you have security cameras in the store?"

"We did, but the video archive was on a DVR near the register. I don't think there was much left of it after the blast."

"Did you talk to any of your people in the store after you finished the race?"

"Yes, Candice was in charge. I called her from the finisher's tent. She said everything was fine. She was the one who told me to relax and not bother coming over to the store."

"What time was that?" Serena asked.

"About eleven-thirty."

"Did she mention anything out of the ordinary?"

"No, nothing."

"How hard would it be to sneak a backpack into the store without being noticed?"

"In a camping store? Not hard at all. We're more concerned with backpacks sneaking *out* of the store. Assuming the pack looked new, I doubt anyone would pay attention to it. Anybody could slide it off their shoulder and walk away."

"Okay, that's what I figured."

"Sorry I can't be more help."

"I do have one other question. Last Tuesday evening, you called 911 because of a problem in the store. Something about a homeless man causing a disturbance. Can you tell me about it?"

"Oh, sure," Drew said. "I felt bad, because I really didn't want to get the guy into any trouble. I was more concerned that he should be in a hospital. Why are you asking about him?"

"I like to check out everything. What happened?"

"Well, this guy came into the store. It was pretty obvious he wasn't a tourist. Let's just say he smelled like he hadn't seen a shower in a while. The staff and I were keeping an eye on him, because frankly, we thought he might be looking to do a little grab-and-go. He climbed up to the loft level, and the next thing I know, he's screaming and rolling around on the ground, banging into fixtures, throwing merchandise. We ran up to calm him down, and I called 911, but before the cops arrived, the guy bolted."

"Did he steal anything?" Serena asked.

"No."

"Have you seen him in the store since then?"

"No."

"What did he look like?"

"Medium-height. Forties. Beard, long brown hair, stocky build."

Serena stood up and delivered Michael back into Drew's arms. "Okay. Thanks for taking the time to talk to me. Tell Krista I said hi."

"I will. Congratulations, by the way."

"On what?"

"On finishing the marathon."

"Oh." Serena shrugged. "Thanks. The weird thing is, I almost forgot about it. Getting through the race doesn't feel so important today."

Drew shook his head. "Not true. Don't let this asshole take it away from you. Finishing a marathon is a big deal."

"You're right. I appreciate the reminder."

"Please tell Cat we're serious. Krista and I would love it if she came to see Michael."

"I will."

Serena walked away toward the street.

She was thinking about the homeless man who'd caused an incident inside the store. It was probably nothing. The percentage of mental illness and addiction among the homeless was extremely high, and the out-of-control behavior Drew had described happened in public parks and detox centers every night. It wasn't unusual.

Even so, it had happened inside the Duluth Outdoor Company shop, and so did the marathon bombing. Just four days later.

Two unusual events in the same place always got her attention.

She needed to find that man.

* * *

Fifty yards away, Cat sat by herself on the asphalt of an outdoor basketball court in an elementary school playground. She could see Serena and Drew Olson. In Drew's arms, she could see Michael. Her baby. Her son.

Serena had told her she was going to see Drew, and she'd suggested that Cat come along. Cat had said no, she wasn't ready. Then, after Serena left, she'd taken her own car and followed. It wasn't the first time she'd hung out near the Olson house. Ever since the weather had gotten nice, she'd come over here a couple of times a week. Drew and Krista had a cute little matchbox home at the corner of Central and Elinor. The house was old, but they kept it well. It was next to the elementary school, which would work out nicely when Michael got older.

Sometimes Cat got lucky, and she'd see them playing with Michael in the yard or pushing him past the school grounds in a stroller.

Sometimes she crept close enough to the house to hear their voices as they talked to him.

They loved him.

She'd done the right thing, letting them take her child.

She wished she could walk over there right now and hold him. Talk to him.

"Hi there. I'm your mom. I'm the reason you're here, and you're the one thing I did right in this whole world."

But that wasn't fair. Michael didn't need a mother, because he already had one. He didn't need a single thing that Cat could give him. Not one thing. He was better off never knowing where he came from.

Cat waited until Serena was gone, and then she walked down the alley behind the houses to her car. She didn't look back.

13

Khan opened the door to Malik's attic studio in the student house near UMD. The room smelled of the honey-scented candles that Malik liked to burn. One white plate sat on his desk, a puddle of ochre wax congealed in the center. An engineering book lay open next to a mug of cold tea and a square of sweet *burfi*. Behind his desk, next to the single window looking out on the alley, was a poster of championship Pakistani wrestlers. Malik, despite his scrawny physique, had never lost a wrestling match in high school. He knew how to turn an opponent's greater size and strength to his own advantage.

Clothes lay on the wooden floor. His bedsheets were twisted. It was as if Malik had left in a hurry and would climb back up the steep stairs any minute now, but Khan knew he wouldn't. He'd taken his prayer mat for *salat*. His Qur'an was missing from the table by his bed. Malik was gone.

Khan had only been there once before. Most of the time, when he and his friend met, it was at Khan's house, or at the mosque on Friday, or in the parkland around Duluth where they could walk and talk privately. For the first time, he wondered if Malik had been protecting him from suspicion.

They'd met when Khan and Ahdia moved to Duluth. That was three years ago, when Malik was a student from Detroit who was also new in town. He was different then. Funny. Happy. For Khan, it was like seeing what his brother should have grown up to be. They'd become friends, and Khan could see a bright future for Malik. He was smart, an excellent student; he would be a professional, a builder of bridges and buildings.

Then, a year ago, things had changed.

Malik grew darker, as if he were living under a shadow. Where the two of them used to talk, they now argued. Malik became prone to hostile outbursts at the mosque. He began to disappear on weekends to Minneapolis and refused to talk about the people he met there. He spent hours on his laptop into the dead of night, making connections with Muslims around the world. The wrong kind of Muslims. Extremists.

They all talked about it in hushed voices. Everyone was afraid.

When Dawn Basch came to town, Malik went further than the others in his protests. He began to brag about the violent things he could do to her. It was the kind of talk that no one wanted to hear, because if word got out, it would bring down the hard hand of the FBI on the entire community.

And then, a week ago, Malik disappeared.

A day ago, a bomb tore open the city.

Khan studied the room for answers. He yanked open each drawer in his friend's desk, which overflowed with cables and circuit boards and engineering newsletters. He overturned Malik's wastebasket onto the floor and sifted through the garbage. He found food wrappers and an empty can of sweetened milk. A pencil, worn down to a nub. Clippings from Malik's beard.

And a brochure.

A brochure for the marathon. Map. Race times. Locations.

Khan dropped the brochure as if it were a hot coal. He told himself that half the homes in Duluth had that same brochure. It was in perfect condition. The brochure had no markings or folds to make him think that Malik had studied it in detail. It meant nothing.

Unless it meant everything.

He thought about seeing Malik in the forest near his house. *I've dedicated my life to something else now.*

Khan faced a choice. Talk to the police and tell them his suspicions. Or walk away and stay uninvolved. Ahdia had told him he shouldn't be there at all. He was leaving fingerprints behind; he was putting himself at risk. Once the whirlwind started, it sucked up everyone in a torrent of dust and debris, innocent or not. And yet here he was.

Malik was a friend, but murder was murder. If Malik was guilty, Khan couldn't stay silent.

But was Malik guilty?

Khan spotted a pair of jeans on the floor. He grabbed them by the cuffs and turned them upside down and shook them. Coins sprinkled out of the pockets. A crumpled dollar bill. A receipt for ice cream. He picked up the receipt and saw that it was from the Cold Stone Creamery shop in Canal Park.

Three doors down from the Duluth Outdoor Company. Oh, Malik, Malik, Malik.

He told himself: It was ice cream. Malik had a sweet tooth. It meant nothing.

Or it meant everything.

Khan saw that something else had spilled from Malik's pockets. Something shiny, no more than an inch long, like a bright, tiny thread. He got down on all fours and delicately retrieved it between his thumb and middle finger. What he saw made him want to cry. Sweat bloomed on his neck and face and made his glasses slip.

It was a piece of copper wire.

As Khan held the wire in his fingers, he heard something below him, and his eyes shot to the doorway of Malik's apartment in horror.

Someone was coming up the stairs.

* * *

"I met your brother once," Stride told Agent Durkin as they crossed College Street from the UMD campus.

Durkin swept her sunglasses off her face. "You met Ron? When?"

"A year before he was killed. He was part of a volunteer team trying to live-trap an injured bobcat. He stumbled onto the body of a missing hiker in the woods."

"I remember that. Ron was freaked out. He was sensitive about things like that."

"It was big news around here when he was killed in Paris," Stride told her. "When I saw his picture in the *News-Tribune*, I remembered talking to him during the investigation. I liked him. He was a nice kid."

Durkin's face, which was normally as hard and expressionless as marble, softened. "Yeah, that was Ron."

"Anyway, I just wanted to tell you I was sorry. Losing family is never easy."

"No, it's not." She put her sunglasses back on, and just like that, her mask was back. "I guess you know about my screwup with that Somali kid. Don't worry about me, though, Stride. I've got things under control now."

"I'm sure you do." But he wasn't sure at all.

"Do you think I'm biased against Muslims?" Durkin asked.

"I don't know. Are you?"

"Look, what's in my heart is my business. As long as my feelings don't get in the way of the job, then there's no problem. I'm good at what I do. That's all that matters."

They walked through a neighborhood of square green lawns and modest houses dating back to the 1920s. Old trees overhung the street. Stride shoved his hands into his pockets.

"How old are you, Durkin?" he asked.

"Thirty-three. Why? Do you think I'm too young?"

"Not at all. Thirty-three is a good age for a lot of things. When I was thirty-three, I knew everything. I knew a hell of a lot more than my bosses, that's for sure. It pissed me off that they didn't realize it."

"Funny," Durkin replied sourly. "I get it."

"What makes you think I'm joking?" Stride asked. "I was pretty damn smart back then."

Durkin finally laughed. "Yeah, okay. I know a lack of confidence isn't exactly my problem. Sorry. If you show weakness around the FBI boys, they eat you alive."

"Don't apologize for it. Maggie is the same way. There's nothing wrong with being cocky if you can back it up. And believe me, I wasn't kidding. Getting older hasn't made me smarter. It's more like the reverse. Now I have a lot more respect for everything I don't know."

"Yeah? Like what?"

"Like how to separate my heart from my job," Stride told her. "I can't be a cop without being a human being, too. My feelings get in the way all the time. But if you've figured out how to do it, Durkin, then good for you."

Durkin said nothing at all. He hadn't expected to reach her, and he didn't.

They got to the end of the block, and the FBI agent checked her phone and said in a stony voice, "This is the alley. Malik Noon lives down here. Let's go."

The alley was cracked and patched over with shovelfuls of asphalt. Greenery made a wall on their left, growing up to the height of the telephone wires. On their right, they passed detached garages and postage-stamp backyards. Halfway down the alley, Durkin pointed at a two-story house with peeling pink paint. Four cars squeezed onto the narrow lot next to a collapsing fence. A plastic lawn chair and rusted charcoal grill sat forlornly in the long grass. In the driveway, Stride noticed a yellow cab that was several years old but as clean as if it had just come off the manufacturing line.

"This is it," Durkin said.

As they approached the back door, a Somali student emerged, pushing a bicycle. He wore a *kufi on his head*, a paisley shirt, and blue jeans. Stride didn't need to show a badge. The kid knew the look of cops.

"Does Malik Noon live here?" Stride asked.

"Top of the stairs," the young man replied, "but he's not here."

"When did you last see him?"

"A week ago. Why are you looking for Malik?"

"We just have some questions for him," Stride said.

The Somali student shrugged and climbed onto his bicycle. He didn't look at them as he headed down the alley, with his back straight and his arms outstretched to the handlebars. He pedaled fast.

"He knows what questions we want to ask," Durkin said.

They went inside. A dusty corridor led deeper into the house. On their left, worn stairs climbed at a steep angle toward the attic. The house smelled of dirty laundry. Stride went first, with Durkin behind him. Halfway up the stairs, he froze. Leaning back, he whispered, "Door's open."

Stride swept back the flap of his jacket, giving his hand ready access to his gun. "Malik Noon?" he called. "I'm Lieutenant Stride. Duluth Police. I want to talk with you."

Five seconds of silence passed.

Then someone above them called, "Malik is not here."

A man appeared in the open doorway at the top of the stairs. He wasn't a college student; he was older, in his thirties. The man was good-looking, with swept-back black hair, a long face, and a beard that neatly followed the line of his chin. His dark eyes, behind bright silver glasses, were nervous.

"Who are you?" Stride asked.

"My name is Khan Rashid."

"Do you know Malik Noon?"

The man hesitated. "He's a friend of mine."

"Is that your cab outside? Do you drive a taxi?"

"Yes."

From behind him, Durkin called, "What you are doing here, Mr. Rashid?"

"I was looking for Malik, but he's gone."

"Do you know where he went?" she asked.

A trace of belligerence crossed Rashid's face. "Obviously not, or I would be there."

"Why are you looking for Malik?" Stride asked.

"I told you. He's my friend."

"If you're his friend, do you know why we're here?"

"I have no idea," Rashid replied.

"People in the local Muslim community have been worried about Malik. They say he's been radicalized. Do you know anything about that?"

"No."

"And yet you're his friend?"

Stride watched Rashid hesitate. His eyes flicked to the ceiling, and there was emotion in his face. Stride took another step closer. "Mr. Rashid, if you were worried about Malik, you should talk to us."

"I don't know anything."

Behind him, Durkin murmured, "He's lying. He knows something."

"If Malik is in trouble, the best thing would be to tell us where he is," Stride went on.

"I don't know. Really, I don't. I have to go."

"Do you believe Malik had anything to do with the marathon bombing?" Stride asked.

Rashid hesitated again. He looked to be having a fierce argument with his conscience.

"I'm not a police officer. I don't know about such things. Please, may I go? I have to get back to my family."

Stride nodded. "Of course."

Carefully, step by step, Rashid walked downward, getting closer and closer. Stride watched him with a careful eye. He thought the man was innocent, but he wasn't prepared to risk his life on it. Rashid watched him, too, with the same fear, as if Stride might suddenly pull a gun and fire.

They were inches away and so very, very far apart.

Rashid squeezed past Stride and then Durkin, but the FBI agent stopped him with a firm hand on his shoulder. Stride watched her. She was under control. Rashid, on the other hand, looked like a rabbit ready to run.

"Mr. Rashid, were *you* at the marathon yesterday?" Durkin asked.

His eyes widened. He opened his mouth and closed it again. His agitation and the closeness of the stairway made him sweat.

Then he said, in a voice no louder than a whisper, "No. No, I wasn't."

He hurried down the rest of the stairs and disappeared. Stride heard the taxi engine as the cab roared away.

"What do you think?" he asked Durkin.

She didn't hesitate.

"He was there," she said.

14

Maggie sized up the two men in the hospital room. Wade Ralston, who was in bed, was wiry and small, with blond hair stretched across a mostly bald skull. He was in his early thirties. Travis Baker, who sat in a chair next to his boss, was younger and built like a gorilla. The two of them watched the television, which was tuned to CNN, but every few seconds, Ralston got impatient and switched channels.

"Mr. Ralston?" she said. "My name is Maggie Bei. I'm a sergeant with the Duluth Police."

He fixed her with suspicious blue eyes. He wasn't an attractive man, and his skin had a post-surgery paleness. "Yeah? About time you showed up."

She couldn't blame him for being angry. "I heard about your wife, sir. I'm very sorry for your loss."

"Don't tell me how sorry you are," Ralston snapped. "Tell me you got the guy who did this."

"There are literally hundreds of law enforcement personnel around the country working twenty-four hours a day to identify and capture whoever was responsible," she told him, but she knew it didn't offer any comfort. She'd said the same thing to dozens of witnesses and victims today.

"So in other words, you got nothing," he concluded.

The television was loud, and Ralston switched it off with the remote control.

"How are you feeling?" Maggie asked him.

"Let's see, somebody ripped up my stomach with glass and nails, and the docs had to go in and fish it out. They're feeding me through a tube. So the answer is, I'm feeling like shit, Sergeant."

"Yes, I understand. Have the doctors told you when you'll be released?"

"Maybe tomorrow. Maybe the next day. They need me back on solid food first. In the meantime, I'm losing money."

"You own a local extermination business?" she asked.

"Right. It's mostly commercial rather than residential. I've got contracts with dozens of downtown buildings."

"Was this your first time running the marathon?"

"No, marathons are my thing. I've done Chicago twice, Twin Cities twice, and Milwaukee twice, too."

"That's impressive," Maggie said. "Did you notice anything out of the ordinary while you were running the marathon route this year? Any odd behavior from spectators, or something that looked unusual?"

Ralston thought for a moment, then shook his head. "No, nothing."

"How about on the last block through Canal Park?"

"I was focused on the finish line, not the crowd. I saw Joni, Shelly, and Travis cheering me on—that's it. The next thing I knew, I was on the ground."

Maggie switched her attention to Travis Baker, who dwarfed the chair in which he was sitting. He wore a T-shirt that showed off his physique, which was molded like stone. For women who liked their men big and dumb, Travis was a prime specimen. Maggie had a bit of a weakness for muscle-bound weightlifters. Her boyfriend, Troy, was built the same way.

"Mr. Baker, where were you standing when the bomb went off?" she asked him.

"Right in front of the Duluth Outdoor Company, with Wade's wife, Joni, and my sister, Shelly."

"You're lucky to be alive," Maggie told him.

"Yeah, I know it. A tree saved me. It took the brunt of the blast." Travis looked down at his friend on the hospital bed. "If I'd known what was going to happen, I would have pulled Joni in front of me. I'm so sorry, man. If I could trade places with her, I would. You know that."

Ralston didn't say a word.

"How is your sister, Shelly?" Maggie asked.

Travis's fists grabbed on to the hard plastic shell of the chair, as if he could lift himself off the ground. "I haven't been able to talk to her yet. She's still unconscious. Docs say she'll pull through, but they had to—shit, they had to take both of her legs below the knees. Can you believe that? My sis ain't never gonna walk again because of those shithead terrorists."

"I'm terribly sorry," Maggie said. "Did the three of you go to Canal Park together?"

Travis wiped his nose, which had begun to run. "No, I picked up Joni at Wade's place. Shelly lives in a Central Hillside apartment, so she walked and met us there. That sucks, huh? She walked. And her apartment is on the fourth floor. No elevator. What's she going to do when she gets out?"

Maggie could have talked about the magic of prosthetics, but that was for the doctors to do. And it wouldn't change the long, tough road his sister faced. "Did you spend the entire time in that same spot near the Duluth Outdoor Company?" she asked Travis.

"No, we met Shelly at Starbucks. Joni is—was—a big Frappuccino fan. We hung out at the coffee shop until maybe half an hour before Wade was supposed to be finishing, and then we made our way down the block. Joni knew Wade would be looking for us, so we stayed there until the bomb went off."

"And you were completely uninjured?"

"I got some cuts on my arms and shoulders," Travis told her, "and I couldn't hear too good for a couple hours. I still got this ringing in my ears. Otherwise, I'm fine."

Maggie felt her phone vibrating in her pocket. She excused herself and went into the hospital corridor to take the call. Through the outside windows, she could see that the evening sun was waning.

"Serena," she said. "How's the body today?"

"Feels like someone has been hitting me with a hammer," Serena replied.

"Well, next time, skip the marathon, and I'll bring the hammer," Maggie told her.

She was on thin ice making a joke like that, but Serena laughed, anyway. They'd gone a long way in repairing their relationship over the past year. Maggie looked back on the brief months when Stride and Serena had been apart—and the even briefer months when she'd slept with him herself—as a kind of dark winter among the three of them. She didn't blame Serena for freezing her out after she got back together with Stride. The truth was, Maggie blamed herself for crossing a line with Stride that she'd known would be a mistake. He was better off with Serena and happy being married to her. She liked seeing him happy again.

For as long as Maggie could remember—from her earliest days as a cop—she'd had a crush on Stride. His first wife, Cindy, had known about it. Serena had, too. It had served mainly to give Maggie an excuse not to pursue a real relationship, and every time she did try to get serious with someone, the results were disastrous. If the affair with Stride had done one good thing, it had broken Maggie's fever. She wasn't in love with him anymore. She'd found a new boyfriend, and she'd broken her personal record by spending nearly a year with him without the relationship imploding. She and Troy made an odd pair. Troy Grange was a single father who looked a little like Mr. Clean and acted that way, too. She was an overly horny comedian with a bad haircut. They didn't see each other often—and they'd avoided "the talk" about whether they were in a real relationship—but for the time being, it worked.

"So what's going on?" Maggie asked Serena.

"Last Tuesday, there was an incident at Duluth Outdoor Company. Do you remember it?"

"Sure, a homeless guy had a fit," Maggie said. Her memory was near-photographic. "What about it?"

"Did you ID the guy?"

"Yeah, Guppo confirmed it with one of the store clerks. His name's Gary Eagleton, but his street name is Eagle. That's what everyone calls him."

"Did anyone talk to him?" Serena asked.

"No, we never found him. Guppo figured he was laying low. Tracking him wasn't a high priority, because he hadn't done anything wrong. The most we could have done is make sure he was okay."

"All right."

"Why are you asking about this? Do you think there's a connection to the bombing? Eagle doesn't strike me as a terrorist."

"I just don't like the timing," Serena replied.

"Did you tell the Gherkin?"

Maggie heard Serena laughing on the other end of the phone. "I did. She wasn't too interested. Then again, neither was Jonny. It's probably a dead end, but I'd like to find Eagle myself and make sure that's true."

"Well, if I wanted info on a homeless guy, you know who I'd talk to first," Maggie said.

"Cat," Serena said with a sigh.

"Yeah. Good luck with that."

Maggie hung up the phone and went back into the hospital room. Wade Ralston and Travis Baker were deep in hushed conversation, but they stopped when Maggie returned.

"Sorry for the interruption," she told them. "Mr. Baker, I have just a couple more questions. You said you, your sister, and Mrs. Ralston were all outside the Duluth Outdoor Company shop for about half an hour prior to the explosion?"

Travis nodded. "That's right."

"Did you see anyone there who aroused your suspicion?"

"Yeah, there *was* one guy, actually. Wade and I were just talking about it. This guy was standing right near us, but he left a couple minutes before the bomb went off. Seemed like he was in a hurry."

"What did he look like?" Maggie asked.

"Tall, good-looking guy but built kind of scrawny. Black hair, beard. He was alone, nobody with him. I'll tell you something else, too. He looked foreign to me."

"Foreign?"

"Yeah. You know the look. Son of a bitch was Muslim. That figures, huh? If you ask me, you find him, you find your bomber."

15

"You *lied* to the police?" Ahdia said in astonishment. "Oh, Khan, what were you thinking?"

Khan mussed his black hair with both hands on top of his head. He'd finally confessed his mistake to his wife, and they were both frantic. "I wasn't thinking! They took me by surprise. I just wanted to get out of there. I didn't want to be in the middle of it."

"And now that's exactly where you are," his wife told him. "This is what I warned you about!"

Khan stared out the front window of their house. His yellow cab was in the driveway. Long shadows stretched like giants from the woods at the end of the road, and in the distance, he heard a rumble of thunder. Around him, the house still had a delicious smell from the chicken pilau that Ahdia had made for dinner.

"What was I supposed to do?" Khan asked. "I was in Malik's room! How could I explain that?"

Ahdia leaned her head into his shoulder. "With the truth. He's your friend. You were worried about him."

"The truth? The truth is, we're Muslim. That's all they see." Khan shook his head. "Maybe they won't find out that I was there during the race. They won't know I lied to them."

"Sooner or later, they will find out. You know they will."

He saw the first drops of rain on the window. He wondered if it would be a summer storm, over and done in minutes, or whether it would linger long enough to drown them. Next to him, Ahdia's face was dark with worry.

"What did you find in Malik's room?" she asked.

"He left things behind. A brochure about the marathon. A small piece of wire."

"Could it really be him? Could he have done this?"

"His soul has been poisoned this year. He's not the same person he was. We all saw it happening."

"And you were there. The police saw you in his room."

Khan nodded. "Yes."

"I wish you had never gone to the marathon," she said.

"Malik is my friend. Practically my brother. I was trying to stop him. To save him. To save innocent lives, too."

"If he did this, he is *nothing*," Ahdia hissed. "You owe him *nothing*."

"I know that."

"They will find out you were there, Khan. As soon as they do, you are a suspect. Do you realize that?"

"Yes, of course, I do."

Ahdia put her arms around him, and he could feel her fear. It was a fear that every innocent Muslim knew. The religion he found beautiful and held sacred, around which he'd built his entire life, could also be a brand: You must be violent, like the others. You are all guilty. You are all terrorists.

"So how do we make this go away?" Ahdia asked.

"I don't know. Maybe it's too late for that."

Ahdia smoothed her dress. She stared at the rain. "No. Here is what you must do, Khan. Tomorrow morning, you will go to the police. You will tell them everything. Your worries about Malik. The efforts that you and the others made to stop him from violence. You will say you lied today because you were scared, and you will give them whatever information they want to know. You will help them find Malik in any way you can."

Khan thought about the number that he'd memorized. The phone number where he could reach Malik in an emergency. If he gave it to the police, they would find him. They would arrest him, or, more likely than not, they would kill him.

"I'm not sure I can do that," he murmured.

"You must think of your family first," Ahdia told him. "You may love Malik as a brother, but he's not your family. If he killed these people, he is not even Muslim. He is no different from those butchers overseas, building their so-called caliphate."

Khan closed his eyes as tightly as he could. His world was chaos. He'd only known such turmoil in his life once before, when he'd found the trampled body of his brother in Lahore. Ever since that moment, he'd been running, trying to find peace and shelter. He'd thought that in Duluth, he had finally run far enough, but now he worried that happiness was about to slip through his fingers once again.

"Papa?"

He looked down when he felt a sharp tug on his pant leg. His son, Pak, gazed up at him with his wide, dark eyes. Ahdia had cut the boy's hair today, but it grew like a weed and wouldn't stay tidy for long.

"Papa, it is time for *Maghrib*."

"Is it?" Khan asked. He reached for his phone to check the Athan app, which tracked the daily times of prayer as the sun changed throughout the year. *Maghrib*, the fourth of the five prayers of *salat*, had a narrow window between sunset and the end of twilight. However, he had no phone; he'd lost it in Canal Park. He checked the grandfather clock in the corner of the living room and confirmed the time.

"You are right," he told his son. "Come, let us do our ablutions and pray."

They washed themselves carefully in the ritual known as *Wudu*, and then Khan took Pak's hand and led his wife and child up the stairs. Rain thumped on the peaked roof. Their small house had only a narrow attic, which the previous owners had used for storage of their Christmas lights. Mice, spiders, and wasps had made a home there, too. When Khan moved in, he'd cleaned up the attic and made it into a space for daily prayers. It was neat, lit by a single window, and lined in wood paneling, with a niche that he had built into the wall to mark *Qibla*, the direction they faced during prayer.

Nothing offered Khan more contentment than the time he spent in prayer, and nothing brought him more love than doing so with his son at his side and his wife behind him. At four years old, Pak was too young for obligatory prayers, but Khan wanted him to make it a habit early in life, and he and Ahdia were proud that their son already took *salat* as a serious responsibility.

He stood on the prayer mat with his head bowed, and he cleared his mind, pushing out all other thoughts. To him, prayer was a direct conversation with God, and he wanted nothing unclean between them. Sometimes passengers in his cab asked him if it was difficult to find the time to pray five times a day, but he told them that those moments of his day made more sense than anything else in his life.

When he was ready, he cupped both hands behind his earlobes and chanted the *Takbīr*.

"*Allāh u akbar.*"

Standing straight, he took hold of his wrists with his arms over his heart, and, in Arabic, recited the opening verses of the Qur'an:

In the name of God, Most Gracious, Most Merciful
Praise God, Lord of all that exists
Most Gracious, Most Merciful
Master of the Day of Judgment
You alone we worship, You alone we ask for help
Show us the straight way . . .

Ahdia followed smoothly behind him, and next to him, Pak did a sweet, clumsy imitation. Pak didn't know all the words of the prayer yet, but every time he heard Khan say, "Allāh u akbar," he repeated it earnestly, and he said "Aameen" loud and long at the end of the opening verses. When Khan bowed and put his hands on his knees, Pak did, too. When Khan prostrated himself and lay his forehead on the floor, Pak did, too.

Subhana Rabbiyal A'la.

Subhana Rabbiyal A'la.
Subhana Rabbiyal A'la.

Khan completed the ritual of the entire *rakat*, and then he performed it again, repeating the prayers aloud, and then one more time, silently, with only his lips moving as he recited the verses. Finally, he saluted the angels of his good deeds and misdeeds over each of his shoulders with the *salaam*.

They were done. Not even ten minutes had passed.

Pak scrambled to his feet, and as Khan stood up, too, his son wrapped his arms tightly around his father's legs.

"I love you, Papa."

"I love you, too."

Ahdia went downstairs first. Her face was grave; prayer hadn't soothed her anxiety. When she was gone, Khan hoisted Pak in his arms and carried him from the attic. He knew what he had to do. He let Pak scamper off to play, and he found Ahdia in the kitchen, where she was drying a dinner plate with a towel. Her tension was evident in how she held herself, stiffly, as if she was squeezing her emotions inside.

He stood beside her and said, "You're right. Tomorrow I will talk to the police."

She put the plate down. He could see her eyes fill with tears. She turned and threw her arms around his neck. "Thank you, Khan."

"We will get through this, won't we?" he asked.

"We will."

The darkness lifted from her face. She was his wife again, with pink roses on her cheeks and teasing eyes and a smile that never went away. "Now I have an even more important errand for you," she told him.

"Oh?"

"One of the women in my office is coming back from pregnancy leave tomorrow. I want to make *laddu* for her, and I have no coconut. Could you run out to the market and get me some?"

"Now?" he asked, eyeing the heavy rain that hammered the kitchen window.

"Please," Ahdia said.

He smiled, because he could never resist her or say no to her. "I'll get soaked, you know."

"You'll dry," she told him.

"Just coconut?" he asked.

"That's all."

He turned to leave, but Ahdia took his hand and leaned close to him and placed a soft kiss on his cheek. "You're a good man, Khan."

His heart felt full. He grabbed his jacket and went to the front door, but he stood at the threshold without opening it. Music played from Pak's room. He heard the clatter of dishes in the kitchen. He smelled the sweetness of ginger from dinner. They were little things, but he closed his eyes and concentrated, wanting to remember them forever. Then, not looking back, he ventured into the thick of the storm and left behind his perfect house, his perfect wife, and his perfect son.

16

That's him, Michael Malville thought.

He examined the photo that had been posted online by a Twin Cities tourist named Janet Waller. She'd been standing near the Hampton Inn, facing Canal Park Drive, using an old camera phone that took two-megapixel images. The time stamp on the photo was seven minutes before the bombing. In the crowd across the street, in profile, he saw the torso of a tall, bearded man with dark hair and what looked like a casual, untucked, button-down shirt. When Michael enlarged the photo, the resolution made the details of the man's face impossible to distinguish.

Even so, he repeated to himself: *That's him*.

Or was it?

He'd had similar breakthroughs throughout the day, but each time, he'd concluded that he was wrong. There was no way to be sure based on a single photograph, particularly a low-quality jpeg taken at a distance. After hours of frustration, Michael had developed a system. As he analyzed photos, he classified them in a spreadsheet by time and location, so that he could easily call up corresponding images of the same crowd scene at the same time from different angles.

Instead of the back of someone's head, he could see his face.

Instead of a partial image of a head or body, he could see the entire person.

The photo taken by Janet Waller showed a crowd of marathon spectators in front of Caribou Coffee. He searched his spreadsheet: *Caribou*. And then he narrowed down the photographs he'd reviewed near Caribou Coffee to those taken six to eight minutes before the bombing. Half a dozen photos met the search parameters, and he loaded them to his screen.

A minute later, he knew he was wrong.

He matched the man in Janet's photo to one of the other Caribou photos and realized that what had looked like a beard from a blurry distance was actually a shadow. This man was clean-shaven.

He wasn't the man who'd bumped into him on Superior Street.

Michael rocked back in his chair and exhaled in frustration. He grabbed his mug and drank cold coffee. He didn't realize that his wife, Alison, had joined him in the attic, until she called to him from the doorway.

"Are you ever coming downstairs?" she asked. "You've been up here in front of that computer all day."

"I know. Sorry."

She came up beside him. Rain pummeled the roof over their heads. "Are you having any luck?"

"Not so far," he admitted. "There are thousands of photographs posted, and I have to examine each face in each picture. When I see one that's a possibility, I cross-reference with other photos, but a lot of the pictures aren't time-stamped, which makes it harder."

Alison chuckled. They'd been married a long time, and she knew he had an OCD streak that came out in projects like this.

"Seems to me there are people who do this for a living," she told him gently. "People called the FBI."

"Yes, but they weren't there," Michael replied. "They didn't see this guy."

"Honestly, did you really see him yourself? It happened so fast. Will you ever be sure?"

"I don't know, but I have to try."

She bent over and kissed him. "Well, come down soon. Evan misses you. So do I. I'm not going to let you stay up all night again. I have other plans for you tonight."

"Another hour, and I'll stop for today," he promised her.

"Deal."

Alison left him alone. He got up and stretched, and he made fresh coffee. He put his 1980s music collection on shuffle, because he was afraid the rain would lull him to sleep. He sat down and opened up the next series of photographs.

He blinked, and an hour passed.

And then another hour.

The process had a strange, addictive quality to it, like a video game. He felt as if he were peering into the lives of strangers. Some of the people showed up again and again in different pictures, and he began to think of them as friends. He saw the faces of people who were laughing. Arguing. Kissing. Singing. He watched face after face after face, until it felt as if he'd seen every runner and every single person on the sidelines cheering them on. He'd seen the entire marathon over and over, every mile, every inch of Duluth and the North Shore, every tree, every house, every store, every street sign.

The evening quickly bled away. Alison didn't return to hassle him; she knew he'd come down when he was ready, or he wouldn't come at all. Another hour passed.

He yawned. He clicked. His mind wandered, and he had to pinch himself to stay awake.

And then he saw him.

The photo was part of a collection that had been uploaded only half an hour earlier. A man with the screen name Shoe Geek had watched the race in the heart of Canal Park in the hour leading up to the explosion, and he'd posted dozens of high-resolution photos. Michael opened up a picture that was time-stamped ninety seconds before the bomb went off. Shoe Geek had taken a picture of the sidewalk heading up Canal Park Drive toward the lift bridge. When Michael enlarged the image on his screen, the resolution was crisp and sharp. He could see every face, and he could even clearly see the sign for the Duluth

Outdoor Company shop suspended over the cobblestones. He was so focused on the crowd that he almost overlooked the empty, closed-off parking lot across from Grizzly's restaurant.

There, framed against the brick wall of an old paper mill, was the man he'd spent the entire night and day hunting. He zoomed in, and he could see exactly what the man looked like. Tall. Dark hair. Beard. Loose, untucked, flowered shirt. Black jeans. The photo captured him in mid-stride, alone, rushing, looking back over his shoulder.

As if he were waiting for something. Waiting for the noise. The blast. The fire. The screams.

And one more thing: His backpack was gone.

Michael lurched out of the chair and paced under the high roof. His breathing accelerated. So did his heartbeat, thumping in his chest. He pounded his fist rhythmically against his chin as he went from wall to wall. He tried to concentrate, but he knew he was exhausted and light-headed. He was overwhelmed with the sheer volume of information he'd pumped into his brain during the past twenty-four hours.

He asked himself: *Are you sure?*

He went back to the desk and enlarged the photograph until only the man's face filled the screen. Then even larger, until they were eye to eye. This man wore silver glasses. Had the man on the street worn glasses? Was that what had made his eyes seem so large and hostile?

Yes.

It was him.

This was the man on Superior Street. Thousands of people lined the marathon route, thousands with dark hair and beards—but *this was the man*. He was absolutely sure. This man had hammered into Michael and pushed Evan into the street. This man had looked back with nothing but cold hatred in his face. This man had continued on to Canal Park, shouldering a heavy navy-blue backpack.

There, in the parking lot near Grizzly's, ninety seconds before the explosion, this same man didn't have a backpack anymore. He'd left behind a killing machine in the Duluth Outdoor Company shop.

Michael had found him.

He'd found the bomber.

He was too tired and drunk with adrenaline to think about exactly what he was doing. His emotions carried him down a rushing river. He opened up his Twitter feed and dragged the photograph of Canal Park into a new post. He tapped out three simple sentences, and then he slid his mouse over the button labeled Tweet.

He hesitated for a moment.

A moment that was no longer than the entire time he'd spent staring into the man's eyes during the race.

Michael thought: *I'm about to change the world.* And his finger tapped the mouse.

* * *

@malvileo tweeted:
This man passed me with a backpack on way to Canal Park. Photo here is 90 seconds before blast. No backpack.

* * *

Dawn Basch stood at the window of her hotel room at the Radisson, where her tenth-floor view was of the lake and the silver lift bridge. It was almost dark, and the rain fell in a steady downpour. Her long fingers with their red-tipped nails held a glass of minibar Chardonnay. She was still dressed for business, but she'd kicked off her heels, and she stood in stocking feet. She kept the room ice-cold. A late room-service dinner—egg-white spinach omelet, fruit, whole-wheat roll—was on the way.

It had been a long day of interviews. TV. Radio. Bloggers. Newspapers. The phone never stopped ringing. She was exactly where she wanted to be—at the center of everything. It didn't matter that some people hated her. It didn't matter that some people wanted to kill her. Sooner or later, one of them might get lucky, but if the Islamists could be martyrs, so could she.

With her phone in her hand, she reviewed the tweets about herself. She was pleased to see that she was trending and that her followers were winning the fierce tweet war. Whenever a liberal called her a racist, an army of defenders rose up to slap that person down. She'd gained ten thousand new Twitter followers from around the world since the bombing. People were listening. They were finally paying attention.

Dawn had traveled a long road in twenty years. She'd been one of the early online-news pioneers, starting her own website in the days before HuffPost and hustling ads from her Jersey City office while she wrote most of the content herself. It was all about clicks, because more clicks meant more ad money. That was why every serious post about politics and trade policy usually also teased readers with photos of celebrity nipple slips. Everybody clicked on those.

She'd never set out to be a First Amendment activist. Islam found her, not the other way around. After her website expanded to Europe, she'd published a freelance profile of a bizarre Swedish artist who liked to decorate his penis and take photographs of his erections. One of his strange creations was a turban-clad, bearded version of his genitals that he photographed in mid-orgasm and titled Spewing Muhammad.

Seeing it, Dawn had never laughed so hard in her life.

After she posted the article, it went viral, blowing up like a bomb. Lots of clicks. *Millions* of clicks. It also led to days of riots in Stockholm in which six buildings were burned and two people were killed. The artist himself fled the city, but a radical Islamist found him in Gothenburg, and he was castrated and beheaded.

Live. On video.

From that moment forward, Dawn Basch was never the same.

What horrified her almost more than the violence was the reaction from the left-wing media in New York and D.C.—people she'd considered colleagues and friends. They blamed her. They blamed the artist. They called his satire a needless provocation of Muslims. When they talked about the First Amendment, it was always with an asterisk for critics of Islam: "Free speech, but"; "Free speech, although"; "Free speech, unless."

Their attitude made Dawn furious. In response, she sought out every portrayal of Muhammad she could find and posted it on the home page of her site. She began planning a First Amendment conference to send out the message that censoring anyone's speech to avoid violence was the first step in giving up your free-speech rights altogether. That day, she coined the phrase "no exceptions," which had become the slogan for her entire movement. It had made her enemies, but it had also made her rich.

Dawn didn't care if people called her a hater, an Islamophobe, or a racist. If Christians were blowing up people over cartoons, she'd attack Christians, but they weren't the threat to civilization. Only one religion was trying to stamp out freedom and kill nonbelievers, and that was Islam. People didn't understand that this was a battle between two completely incompatible visions of human values. There was American freedom, and there was Islamic tyranny, and the former would never bow to the latter. Not as long as Dawn Basch was alive.

As she searched through tweets in front of the hotel window, she spotted a retweet in which she'd been tagged by one of her many followers. The woman's message was:

Hey, Dawn, did you see this?

Dawn checked out the tweet from a user named @malvileo. He'd posted a note and a photograph just minutes earlier, and when Dawn examined the picture, she couldn't suppress the smile of triumph that crept onto her face. This was what she'd been waiting for, and she didn't hesitate.

She knew exactly what to do next.

Over to you, Special Agent Maloney.

* * *

@dawnbasch retweeted @malvileo:
Is this the marathon bomber? Duluth, have you seen this man?
#marathon
#islamismurder
#noexceptions
#surprisehesmuslim

17

When Stride opened the attached photograph in the retweet from Dawn Basch, he recognized the marathon scene in Canal Park, and he recognized the face of the man heading through the parking lot. They'd met a few hours earlier on a musty set of stairs in a student house near UMD.

"His name is Khan Rashid," Stride told Special Agent Maloney. "Agent Durkin and I ran into him at Malik Noon's apartment. Rashid and Noon are friends. We checked him out. Cab driver, married, one child, lives in the Woodland area. Born in Pakistan, naturalized citizen."

"Criminal record?" Maloney asked.

"Nothing. He's clean."

"What about radical connections?"

"He's never been on our radar, but Rashid lied to us today. Durkin asked him directly whether he was at the marathon, and he said no."

Maloney's forehead creased into a deep seam. He'd been angry at the tweet by Dawn Basch, but his anger had already turned to calm again, like the quick passage of a summer storm. The closer he got to a perpetrator, the more his decades of experience took over. He smoothed his gray mustache.

"Get some uniforms over to Rashid's house to keep it secure," Maloney said. "This thing is going viral, and we don't need any vigilantes popping up among the No Exceptions crowd. And let's make sure Rashid doesn't rabbit. Guilty or innocent, as soon as he knows his picture is all over the Web, he may try to bolt."

"I'm on it," Stride said.

"I'll get Durkin over there, too, while we wait for a search warrant. What about this @malvileo character who made the underlying tweet? Who is he?"

"I know him. He was part of a murder investigation a couple of years ago, but he was exonerated. His name's Michael Malville. He was a spectator at the marathon yesterday, and Maggie talked to him during the evacuation. His story matches what he tweeted. He told her he was with his son on Superior Street during the marathon, and a Muslim man with a backpack bumped into him."

"All right, this could be a serious break," Maloney said.

Stride reached for his phone to order teams into the Woodland area, but as he did, the phone started ringing. The caller was Haq Al-Masri, and Stride knew why Haq was calling. Word had already spread through the Muslim community about Khan Rashid.

"Haq," Stride said. "It's a bad time."

"You know what's happening on Twitter?"

"Yes."

"It's a mistake," Haq said. "Khan isn't involved."

"How do you know?"

"Because I know the man. I know his wife and son. There is no violence in him. None."

"He's a friend of Malik Noon. He was at Malik's apartment."

"Of course, he was! They're friends. Khan was the one who first warned me about Malik. He was concerned that Malik was becoming radicalized. He wanted us to do everything in our power to help him."

"Khan was in Canal Park during the marathon," Stride said.

"Yes, I know—looking for Malik. We were all trying to find him to make sure no violence occurred."

"Khan lied about being there. To me and the FBI."

He heard Haq exhale sharply in frustration. "Well, that was foolish of him, but really, what do you expect? If you were a Muslim fifty yards away from where a bomb went off, would you admit it to the police?"

"I'm sorry. I have to go."

"He's not your man, Jonathan," Haq added quickly. "Believe me."

"I hope you're right, but that doesn't change what we have to do. If you can reach Khan, tell him to come directly to the FBI headquarters at the DECC. We can talk to him, and we can keep him safe. If he's not involved, we can get the word out and clear his name."

Stride hung up.

He looked for Agent Maloney and saw that the FBI agent and a cluster of his men had gathered around a large-screen television in the conference room. Maloney kept switching channels, from CNN to Fox to ABC to NBC to CBS. On each channel, Stride saw the same thing. Every news show was already broadcasting the photo of Khan Rashid that Michael Malville had tweeted.

In half an hour, Rashid had become the most wanted man in the country.

* * *

Travis Baker held his sister's hand. Shelly's eyes were closed. Morphine had kept her mostly asleep since the operation. She wasn't going to die, but she had the grayness of death. Her plump face looked sunken, and she breathed with a raspy snore. He could see the outline of her body under the white sheet. Below where her knees were, the sheet sank down to the bed. He hadn't had the courage to look.

The doctors hadn't told her yet. They'd asked him if he wanted to do it, but he said no, he just wanted to be there when they broke the news. They'd told him that she might cry, she might scream, she might not believe it. Travis knew Shelly. She'd just close her eyes and say that life gives you a challenge and Jesus gets you through it. He wished he could believe that, but he didn't.

It was just the two of them in this world. Their parents had been gone since Travis was fifteen. Car accident. Shelly was eight years older, and she'd been as much a mother to him as a sister ever since then. He hated that he'd been such a disappointment to her. She never yelled at him for his mistakes; she just urged him to do the right thing or to stop doing the wrong thing. He tried, but he couldn't stay away from the flame. When the Devil came to Duluth, he always looked up his old buddy Travis.

Shelly kept saying that Jesus had a plan for him, but Travis didn't think that was true. Life wasn't about plans. Life was about whatever shit happened to you on any given day. Just ask Joni.

"Hey."

He looked at Shelly's face and saw that her eyes were open. Her fingers squeezed his hand.

"Hey, Shell."

"My legs hurt," she said. Her voice slurred the words.

"There's a button. You can get more morphine."

She shook her head back and forth. "Not yet. Want to stay awake."

"Okay."

"Nurse said it was a bomb."

"Yeah."

"You okay?" Shelly asked.

"Yeah. Good as new. Lucky Travis."

"Not luck. Nothing is luck."

"Aw, Shell, don't. Not now." He didn't want to hear about Jesus. Not when his sister was never going to walk again.

"People killed?" she asked.

"Yeah."

Her head turned. Her eyes bored into him. "Joni? What about Joni?"

He'd told himself that he would be strong when he told her, but he wasn't. His eyes filled with tears. His lower lip quaked like he was a scared dog. Hearing Joni's name, he could still see her face, so clearly that if he reached out, he was sure he could touch that bottle-blond hair. But she wasn't there. She'd whispered in his ear at the marathon, and those were the last words she ever spoke. Five seconds later, she was dead on the ground.

He couldn't even say the words or shake his head, but Shelly understood.

"I can't believe she's gone," she said. "I'm sorry, Travis."

"Yeah. It sucks. There's nothing else to say."

"What about Wade?"

"He needed surgery, but he'll be okay."

"And me?" she asked.

Travis pasted a smile on his face. "You? What about you?"

"What happened to me?"

"Hey, come on, nobody messes with my big sister."

"Travis," she murmured, because she could see right through him.

"What?"

"What's up with my legs?" she asked.

"What do you mean?"

"I can't move them," she said.

"Aw, well, what's the rush, huh? You got somewhere else to be?"

"Travis, be strong and tell me the truth."

He opened his mouth, but the words stuck in his throat. He shook his head over and over. "Don't make me, Shell. Don't make me. I can't do it."

She stared at him silently for a long time. It was as if, without saying anything, he'd said everything. Her face softened. She looked at the ceiling, and she smiled, which made no sense to him at all. Shelly always said when she smiled like that, she was seeing angels.

"Push the button for me, Travis," Shelly told him. "It hurts. I want to sleep."

"Okay."

He did, and he watched his sister close her eyes. Her body relaxed as the drugs worked their magic. In no time, she drifted away. He stayed to make sure she didn't wake up again, and then he got up and went into the hallway and closed the door behind him. He was right across from the hospital lounge.

The television was on. A crowd of people watched it.

Travis went inside, and he saw a picture of a man frozen on the television screen. He knew exactly who that man was. That was the man who had stood right next to him in Canal Park during the marathon.

That was the squirrely son of a bitch who ran away right before the bomb went off.

Before Joni died. Before Shelly lost her legs.

"That's the one, huh?" he said to a nurse. "That's the guy who did it?"

"Looks that way," she said.

Travis walked out of the lounge, because if he'd stayed there, he would have pulled the television off the wall and thrown it through the third-floor window. He was filled with rage in a way he'd never felt in his entire life. If that man had been there, he would have put his fingers around the man's neck and squeezed until the bastard's eyes bulged and his skin turned blue and his lungs screamed and his heart gave up and quit beating.

Travis knew what you had to do to people like that. Every single murdering terrorist.

You had to exterminate them like bugs.

18

Khan parked his yellow cab in front of the Woodland Market, which was half a mile from his home. This was a quiet, small-town neighborhood in the northeast corner of the city. Pak's favorite pizza restaurant was across the street. There were other small shops nearby, too. A barbershop. A hardware store. A bakery. A gas station. Tall trees ringed the intersection of Woodland and Calvary behind the buildings. In Duluth, no matter where you were, you were never far from the woods.

Rain assaulted his windshield, making the late evening even darker. He waited to see if the storm would dissipate, but it kept on in torrents, blown by a heavy wind. Finally, he shoved open the cab door and ran for the market. By the time he made it inside, he was soaked, and he stopped to shake off water from his hair and clothes and dry his glasses. The floor was slick where rain had swept inside. The store was cold.

He saw people in the checkout lines. A nurse in purple scrubs chatted with one of the clerks; a father wrangled two young kids; an overweight, twenty-something man in a wet leather jacket checked his phone; a teenager and his girlfriend bought a six-pack of Pepsi and a large bag of potato chips. Pop music played from overhead speakers.

Khan wasn't familiar with the layout of the store. Ahdia typically did the grocery shopping. He spotted a store employee wearing a tie, and he approached him to ask a question.

"Excuse me."

"Yes, sir, how can I help you?" Minnesotans were invariably friendly.

"I'm looking for shredded coconut. Can you tell me where to find it?"

"Of course. Aisle four, with the baking supplies."

Khan nodded. "Thank you."

As he headed past the checkout lines, he noticed the overweight man in the leather jacket staring right at him. Catching his eye, the man looked quickly down at his phone again. And then back at Khan. This happened three more times in rapid succession, and each time he stared at Khan, the man's face grew more hostile.

Khan ignored him. He made his way through the market. Despite his many years in this country, the sheer abundance of items in American grocery stores always amazed him. Whenever he passed overflowing displays of fruits and vegetables, he remembered the want of his childhood, and he counted himself lucky that he'd found his way here. And this was just a small neighborhood market compared to others in the city.

In aisle four, he passed a young mother with a baby boy in her cart. She smiled at him; he smiled at her. Khan made a silly face at the baby and wiggled a finger to say hello. The child kicked his legs happily.

"How old is your son?" he asked the woman.

"Five months," she replied.

"He's a beautiful boy. What's his name?"

"Thomas."

"That's a good name," Khan said.

"Oh, thank you."

Mothers liked it when you complimented their children.

He continued to the far end of the aisle. The market's baking supplies included hundreds of products. All kinds of flour and sugar. Chocolate chips. Molasses. He hunted until he found coconut on the lowest shelf, and he squatted to examine the brands and compare the prices. He had no idea what Ahdia usually bought, and he hoped he wasn't making a mistake by picking the cheapest package to save a few pennies.

As he got up with a plastic bag of shredded coconut in his hand, he glanced at the other end of the aisle. The man in the leather jacket was standing there. He had been in the checkout line; now he was back in aisle four.

The woman with her baby was gone.

When Khan looked his way, the man shifted his gaze, as if to examine cake mixes on the shelf. Khan had a chance to study him more closely. He was short and heavy, with a thinning crown of curly brown hair. He needed a shave. His hands were large. He wore a Timberwolves T-shirt under his jacket and loose-fitting gray sweatpants. When the man saw Khan watching him, he shoved his hands into the pockets of his jacket and strolled away.

Strange.

The whole thing gave Khan an odd feeling.

He took his coconut and marched back up the aisle, but he didn't spot the man in the leather jacket hovering nearby. In fact, he didn't see anyone at all. As he passed each aisle, he noticed that they were empty. No one was at the deli or meat counters. He checked his watch to make sure that he hadn't stayed past the store's closing time, but he was certain the market typically stayed open for at least another hour.

When he returned to the checkout area, he noticed that every aisle was now closed except one, and the only employee in sight was the manager with the tie he'd approached when he first arrived at the store. The man's Minnesota smile was still fixed in place, but Khan noticed that he was sweating, even in the cool air-conditioning of the market.

"Hello!" the manager greeted him with an unusually loud voice. "So, did you find the coconut you were looking for?"

Khan nodded. "Yes."

"That's good. Is that all you need? Is there anything else?"

"No, that's all. Where is everybody?"

The man shrugged. "It's like this every night. Crowds go up and down."

"Oh."

Khan took out his wallet and peeled off a five-dollar bill. The manager had the coconut in his hand, but he hadn't scanned the price yet.

"So what are you baking?" the man asked.

"My wife is making a dessert to bring to the office tomorrow."

"That's nice. Me, I love coconut dishes. Have you ever tried magic bars? Chocolate chips, butterscotch, sweetened condensed milk, and coconut on a graham-cracker crust. They're so good. My wife makes them for the kids, but to tell you the truth, I eat more of them than they do."

Khan checked his watch. "I'll have to try them."

"You won't be sorry." The man twisted his body and looked outside at the rain. "Whoo, it's still coming down out there."

"Yes."

"Summer in Minnesota, huh?"

Khan's brow wrinkled with mild confusion and annoyance. "Yes. How much for the coconut?"

"Oh, well, let me run it through." He scanned the plastic bag and announced the price and then said again, "Anything else?"

"No."

"Any coupons?"

"No." Khan handed him the five-dollar bill.

The manager opened the cash register and counted out Khan's change, but he stopped to open a new roll of nickels, even though it looked as if he had plenty of nickels in the drawer. He counted out the change slowly.

"There you go," he said.

"Thank you."

"Do you want a bag for that?"

Khan shook his head. "That's not necessary."

"Come back and see us again."

"Yes, I will," Khan said.

He headed for the automatic doors of the grocery store. The doors slid open, and Khan walked outside into the rain, but he stopped when he found the fat man in the leather jacket blocking his way. The man still had his hands in his jacket pockets.

"Excuse me," Khan said, but when he tried to change direction, the man stepped in front of him.

"Excuse me," Khan said again.

The man didn't move. "Is that your cab over there?"

"It is, but I'm sorry, I'm not taking fares right now."

Khan looked past the man into the store parking lot. Half the cars had vanished. Among those that remained, he spotted people inside, peering at the two of them through the windows. He could see others on the street corner, backing away. The mother he'd seen in the baking aisle was running across the street against the light with her baby clutched in her arms.

The rain poured down.

"Excuse me, I have to leave," Khan said.

"No, I don't think so," the man replied.

"What?"

"You're staying right here."

Khan began to push past him, but the man grabbed his wrist.

"Let me go!" Khan called. "Get your hands off me!"

The man dug a phone out of his pocket. "I've got a question for you, buddy. Is this you?"

"What?"

He held the phone in front of Khan's face. "I said, is this you? Because it sure looks like you."

Khan squinted at the phone, but he couldn't make out any details on the screen. "I have no idea what you're showing me, but please get out of my way."

"Until the police get here, you're not going anywhere," the man said.

"Police? What are you talking about? I'm going home now."

Khan shook off the man's grip and marched toward his cab, but before he got there, a heavy impact in the small of his back knocked him off his feet. The coconut bag flew from his hand. He hit the wet pavement, and the air burst from his lungs, leaving him gasping for breath. The fat man landed on top of him, pinning him to the ground.

Struggling, Khan elbowed the man above him and managed to squirm free, but the man hammered a fleshy fist down into Khan's chin. Khan's cheekbone struck the pavement, and the impact rattled around his head. He crawled away, but the man jumped on him again, and they grappled like wrestlers through the puddles of the parking lot.

He heard people nearby.

Someone shouted, "That's him! That's the guy!"

The two of them fought their way back to their feet beside Khan's cab. Another thick fist landed in Khan's face; his head snapped back. He lost his balance and grabbed for the man's jacket to steady himself, and something spilled from the man's pocket with a metallic clatter. He saw what it was, and he heard screams.

"A gun!"

"He's got a gun!"

It's not mine! Khan wanted to shout.

The man punched him hard in the chest, and Khan staggered back, colliding with the door of his cab. He saw the man squatting to retrieve the gun, and Khan took a step and shoved the man with all his strength. The stranger fell flush on his back, where his skull cracked against the asphalt. Khan kicked the gun under his cab, and then he ripped open the door and turned on the engine. Around him, people yelled and pointed and shouted for help.

The cab jerked forward. All he could think of was to get away. To go home. To see Ahdia. To see Pak. To find out why this nightmare was happening and put a stop to it. But he was trapped. Above the thunder of the rain, he heard a siren, and a police vehicle screamed from the north, cutting off the road that led home. He couldn't go that way. Instead, Khan turned left, away from his house, away from his wife and child. He glued his eyes to the mirror and watched the police car swerve into the parking lot of the grocery store behind him.

Then he sped around the curve, and he couldn't see anything more.

He drove, but he didn't know where to go.

19

Gayle Durkin spent an awkward hour with her parents at the home near Amity Park where she'd grown up. Some families grew closer after tragedy; some built walls. She loved her parents, but after her brother's death in Paris, she didn't know what to say to them. Being in the old house, which they'd kept as a shrine to Ron, made it worse. As soon as she got there, she wanted to leave.

She kept seeing things the way they used to be. She remembered the Christmas tree in the corner of the living room, where she and Ron had opened their gifts. The backyard swing set was still in the yard, where she'd pushed him as a toddler. Her matchbox bedroom was where she'd pounded on the wall to complain about Ron's bad guitar-playing. Right now, the volume of her memories was even louder than that awful guitar.

The report about Khan Rashid gave her a reason to escape. She kissed her parents and said she'd see them soon, which was a lie. When she headed out on the lonely stretch of Jean Duluth Road, she found herself torn between emptiness and anger. The Islamist terrorists had taken away more than her brother. They'd moved into her family home like monsters hiding in the coat closet.

Pulses of rain surged across the highway. It was nearly dark. She didn't see another vehicle ahead or behind. Birches and fir trees lined both sides of the road, with only an occasional house carved out of the woods. She drove fast; she always drove fast. Her tires skidded where the water pooled. She wanted to get back to work, because work was the only thing that made sense.

She remembered Khan Rashid's face, which bore all the tells of a liar. The nervousness. The fear. She wasn't surprised to learn that he'd been spotted in Canal Park moments before the explosion, even though he'd claimed he wasn't there. He was a typical terrorist coward, planting the bomb and running away. At least the bomber who killed Ron in Paris had done the world by a favor by blowing himself up, too.

Gayle had barely driven a mile when the report reached her that Rashid had been spotted at the Woodland Market. Adrenaline made her fists tighten on the wheel. She knew exactly where that was; her parents shopped there. Just ahead of her, Jean Duluth Road became Snively Road, and if she turned right at Woodland Avenue, she'd reach the grocery store in five minutes. Police were incoming. She accelerated to join them. She wanted to be there when they took Rashid down.

When she crossed over Amity Creek, where she'd hiked a hundred times as a teenager, she heard the next update. Witnesses at the scene had reported seeing a gun during a violent altercation at the market.

"Rashid should be considered armed and dangerous. Use extreme caution."

Gayle went faster, which wasn't safe in the rain, but she didn't care. She sped around a broad curve, and she was almost back in the heart of the city. Her sixth sense tingled. Every investigator knew that feeling, when something was about to happen. She was in the right place at the right time.

Headlights loomed ahead of her, and she *knew*. The car flashed by her in an instant, but she caught the streak of yellow in the rainy glow of her headlights. It was a yellow cab. It was Rashid. She shoved her brakes hard and spun the wheel, but she was going too fast. Her car did a 360 once, then twice, and she finally slid to a stop on the shoulder, pointed north.

She grabbed her radio and reported Rashid's position.

Then she chased the taillights of the cab.

* * *

Khan's first thought was to seek protection at the Muslim center near UMD, where he knew many of the students and faculty from the local mosque. Someone would know what was going on. Someone could help him convince the police that he'd done nothing wrong. However, when he stopped at the red light on Woodland at the intersection of Snively Road, he saw the whirling glow of police lights heading directly toward him. His cab was impossible to miss.

He ignored the red light and made a sharp left, heading along a high ridge. If he went far enough on the country highway, he knew a back road that would cut through the woods and take him to the city just north of his house. He could get home to Ahdia and Pak.

And then what? He didn't know.

Khan found a news station on the radio, and he caught the announcer in mid-sentence: "*. . . still don't know whether the man in the photograph that has gone viral really has any connection to the bombing. We've had no confirmation from the FBI that this man is a person of interest, but that hasn't stopped activists like Dawn Basch from declaring that the bomber has been found.*"

His heart sank.

He knew what had happened: He was the man. He was the suspect. Khan thought about the fat man in the parking lot at the store, shoving a photograph on a phone screen in his face: "*Is this you? Because it sure looks like you.*"

Oh, Ahdia, Ahdia, what have I done? They're going to kill me. When they find me, I'm dead.

He sped through the rain. Gauzy lights shined from houses on his left and in the valley to his right. People were home with their families, living quiet lives, which was all he'd ever wanted for himself. He tried to think about what to do. Where to go. Confusion and panic filled his mind.

For nearly a mile, he had the road to himself, but then another car passed him like a rocket flying in the opposite direction. Through the thunder of the rain, Khan heard the squeal of brakes. In his mirror, he saw headlights going around and around as the other car spun. He didn't need to ask what would happen next; the car came after him. Word had spread.

Look for the yellow cab.

Look for the bomber.

Khan made an immediate left turn from the highway. He found himself on a suburban street, and he drove fast with one eye on the mirror. Trees and lawns whipped by on both sides. He didn't see the other vehicle behind him yet. He drove four blocks, squinting to see past the end of his headlights, and he almost piled into a tree ahead of him as the road split. He jerked the wheel right. The asphalt vanished and became a dirt road. The ruts and mud made the vehicle vibrate like a roller-coaster.

He kept looking behind him. One block. Two blocks. Three blocks, deeper into the woods.

No lights.

Ahead of him, the road ended in a T. He was going too fast to stop. His tires clawed at the wet dirt, and the cab shimmied, riding up a short slope and crashing into a metal fence, which caved beneath it. He jerked into reverse and hit the accelerator, but the cab rocked and refused to move. The mesh of the fence trapped the car like a net.

Khan tried to open the door and couldn't; it was blocked shut. He rolled down the window and slithered through the small opening. Where he landed, sharp prongs from the broken fence tore his skin and drew blood. He had no idea where he was. The dirt road continued westward but dead-ended in the other direction. Behind him, on the other side of the fence, was a long stretch of darkness. Low-hanging fir branches blew in his face, and the storm pelted him.

Half a mile away, down the original stretch of the dirt road, he saw headlights getting larger and closer. The roar of an engine rose above the rain.

The car was coming for him. He was trapped.

Khan stood by his cab, paralyzed. He had to move. He clambered onto the hood of the cab and jumped over the fence into the weeds and flowers on the other side. Getting up, he ducked past the arms of the evergreens and started to run. Spongy wet grass sank under his feet. Rain blew into his face.

Lightning split the sky, turning night into day.

He was in a large cemetery, and he sprinted through rows of tombstones.

20

Officer Dennis Kenzie heard the radio update from the FBI agent who was on the trail of Khan Rashid.

"Suspect is on foot, heading west through Park Hill Cemetery. Requesting backup at this location."

Kenzie, who'd been heading toward the Woodland Market in response to multiple 911 calls, brought his cruiser to an immediate stop. He'd just passed the entrance road leading into Forest Hill Cemetery, which butted up against Park Hill on the west, making one of the largest graveyards in the city. He did a quick U-turn, turned off his siren and lights, and headed silently up the entrance road into Forest Hill.

If Rashid was heading west with Special Agent Durkin in pursuit, Kenzie was perfectly positioned to intercept Rashid by heading east.

He called in his plan and got out of his cruiser into the rain.

Kenzie was young and single, twenty-four years old, with the beefy build of a high school football player and a fuzz of Nordic blond hair on his square head. He'd joined the Duluth Police only six months earlier. He was a Bemidji boy, growing up in the shadow of the town's Paul Bunyan statue, and he'd gotten his criminal justice degree at Bemidji State. But his hometown wasn't hiring peace officers, and Duluth was.

Out of a hundred applicants, he was one of only four officers hired that winter.

In six months, he'd issued hundreds of citations for everything from speeding to indecent exposure. He'd intervened in domestic disturbances. He'd arrested a drug dealer outside the Seaway Hotel. He'd rescued an injured eagle on the Lester Park Golf Course and arranged its transport and rehabilitation through the local Wildwoods organization.

One thing he'd never done was draw his weapon.

Until now.

The grip of his gun was wet, and so was his hand, but he clutched the weapon tightly and kept it pointed at the ground.

"Assume that Rashid is armed and dangerous. Use extreme caution."

In a flash of lightning, Kenzie saw the cemetery spread out in front of him. Graves climbed the hillside in terraced rows among the evergreen trees. He jogged up a narrow asphalt path and made his way past crypts that surveyed the valley like a series of royal thrones. He kept wiping rain from his eyes with his free hand. With each lightning strike, he looked for the silhouette of Khan Rashid, but the gravestones, the evergreens, and the summer trees offered cover everywhere for someone who wanted to hide.

When he stopped to listen, he heard a drumbeat of thunder and the slap of the downpour through the trees. The volume of the storm drowned out everything else.

Kenzie was scared. People thought cops weren't bothered by fear, but that was crazy. If you were a human being running into danger, you got scared, and the only thing you could do was live with it and not let it stop you. He was still learning that trick. He could feel the speed of his heartbeat; he could feel a tremble in his muscles that he tried to quiet. He told himself: Don't stop. Stay focused.

He slowed to a walk in the northeastern corner of the cemetery. His tree-trunk body shuddered in the wind. Lightning was his only light. Otherwise, the night was black. He left the path and marched onto the sodden grass, past dozens of marble stones. His boots sank into the ground with each step. Low branches from the evergreens brushed his hair.

Blackness. Nothing but blackness.

Then lightning sizzled practically over his head, followed immediately by deafening thunder that shook the ground and made him twitch. He heard a crack, and close by, he smelled burnt wood. He was momentarily blinded, but in a split second, he saw the landscape of the cemetery spread out in front of him. He saw the chain-link fence that marked the eastern border of Forest Hill, and beyond it, the dirt road that split the graveyards in two.

The lightning vanished, the rain poured down his face, but he blinked and saw something else, too.

Not even thirty yards away, a man was running directly at him.

* * *

Behind him, Khan saw a flashlight sweeping back and forth across the cemetery. Whoever was chasing him was on foot now, pursuing him among the headstones. He ran, but between the lightning strikes, he found it almost impossible to dodge the nearly invisible tombstones in his way. His clothes were soaked. His ankle was twisted. He pushed water from his glasses with his thumbs, but the world was a blur.

He heard a shout, but in the storm, he couldn't make out the words.

Ahead of him, he stumbled up to a fence on the border of the graveyard. The mesh of the fence was low but slippery, and the top was unfinished, with sharp barbs twisted into forks. He tried to kick it down with his shoe, but the fence didn't yield. The stone support pillars were too small to give him any leverage, so he backed up and charged the fence and threw himself over. His feet slipped in the tall grass as he left the ground. The claws of the fence-top raked his arm and tore his shirt, and he fell, bleeding, into the weeds on the other side. He pushed himself up and staggered into the middle of a dirt road.

Run.

Khan limped along the road, but he hadn't gone twenty feet before he saw headlights beyond the curve and heard the whine of sirens. Turning back, he saw flashing red lights from the other end of the road, too. They were coming for him from both sides.

He thought about giving up. He stood, frozen, waiting for them to find him; then he panicked.

They'll shoot me.

If he stayed there, he was dead.

He ran for the fence on the opposite shoulder. He pushed himself up and over, and he picked himself off the ground and ran again, into the heart of another graveyard. He made it to the nearest headstone and stopped, catching his breath. The police were closing in. The flashlight behind him looked like the searchlight of a prison.

Khan sucked air into his chest and charged forward.

Lightning cracked, as bright as the sun. Thunder exploded like a bomb. He covered his face, but he didn't stop running.

In front of him, someone bellowed a warning.

"*Freeze!* Police! Khan Rashid, put your hands in the air!"

Startled, Khan put a foot wrong and spilled forward. His body sprawled into the mud, and he landed hard on his shoulder. His head struck the earth; his glasses flew from his face. He crawled, his body sheltered by the headstones. His hands pawed the earth, hunting for his glasses. Without them, he was blind.

He heard the police officer in front of him shout again.

"*On your feet right now!* Hands in the air!"

Khan's fingers brushed against stiff plastic stuck in the grass. His glasses. He grabbed them by the temple, where they dangled from his right hand. He pushed himself up from the ground, his feet slipping. He stood there, wet and cold, with nowhere to run. The night was black, and he couldn't see a thing.

Lightning.

Lightning erupted again, and he saw the blurry shape of a police officer not far away. By instinct, Khan went to put his glasses on. The frames glinted silver in the on-and-off illumination of lightning. His right hand moved higher.

And then he heard a shout. A female voice screamed from the fence behind him.

"*Gun! He has a gun!*"

Khan saw a pinpoint flame. The police officer in front of him fired.

* * *

Gayle Durkin leaped the first fence with the ease of a runner, and she was at the second fence leading into Forest Hill Cemetery when she heard the shout of a police officer, and she saw Khan spill to the ground. The police officer shouted again, and Durkin saw Khan scuttling in the grass like a crab.

Looking for something.

Something he grabbed. Something in his hand.

Everything happened at once. It was chaos. Police cars roared in from the left and right, sirens blaring, lights making a kaleidoscope on the dirt road. Lightning, like a comet, dazzled her. Thunder cracked like dynamite. She squinted through the pouring rain, seeing Khan standing up. A flash of silver glittered in his right hand. She saw his hand moving. Coming up. Pointing.

And then blackness again.

"*Gun!*" she screamed in warning. "*He has a gun!*"

Almost instantly, a shot cracked, its noise bouncing off the trees and headstones. Durkin dropped her flashlight and whipped her own gun into her hand and spun back to the fence. The aftereffects of lightning bloomed like orange neon in her eyes. Rain made a waterfall down her face.

"Light it up!" she shouted at the police as they got out of their cruisers. And then, to the darkness: "Rashid! Don't move! Drop the gun!"

Another shot rose above the storm.

Everyone ducked. Durkin took cover behind a tree, but in the next second, she twisted, squatted, and aimed through the fence. Swirling red light reached into the graveyard. The trees loomed like giants, and the headstones were squat soldiers. She saw Rashid, and she squeezed off a shot.

He began to fall.

Durkin fired again.

* * *

The first shot from the police officer missed but left Khan frozen in place.

He tried to move, but his muscles refused his brain's command. He heard the wail of police sirens and saw the carnival of red lights break up the darkness. And still he stood in the rain, his jaw slack, his arms and legs paralyzed, as the police officer in front of him fired again, his bullet missing wildly.

But Khan's luck was running out.

The next shot came from behind him. It was so close that he heard it buzz his head and whine in his ear like a mosquito. Finally, he threw himself to the ground, just as another shot hit the marble of a headstone and ricocheted into the night.

Khan slithered forward. He snaked past the line of graves, where the stones protected him. He shoved his glasses back onto his face, and the night took focus. He crawled faster, and he thought about shouting, "Don't shoot, stop shooting!" Instead, he kept his silence and pushed along the wet ground.

The cop in front of him had vanished.

He was just gone.

Behind him, Khan heard the noise of others leaping the fence, heading his way. He got to his feet, but he ran only two steps before he tripped and fell. When he looked sideways on the ground, he saw the face of a police officer staring at him, eyes wide, mouth open, mud on his cheek and chin.

A bullet hole bled in a single trickle down the middle of his forehead.

The cop was dead. Young, helpless, shot dead. Khan didn't understand. Who killed him? How did it happen?

It didn't matter. He couldn't stay here; he had only seconds to escape. The police lights sweeping the ground hadn't found him yet. His ankle and his injuries didn't slow him down. He picked himself up, and he ran through the cemetery the way a deer runs, panicked and fast, and the night swallowed him up.

21

Ahdia hummed as she tucked Pak into bed. The boy was asleep practically as soon as his head sank into the pillow. She envied that kind of innocent sleep. She was a worrier, letting everything keep her up in the middle of the night. Her job. Money. Her husband and the strangers in his cab. Her fears for her child and the kind of world he would inherit.

She turned off the light. She left a CD of songs by Pakistani singer Hadiqa Kiani playing softly, because Pak liked her music, and she hoped it gave him good dreams.

The grandfather clock in the living room ticked loudly, counting off seconds. The chimes rang every half hour overnight, reminding her of how long she lay awake. She wished Khan would sell it, but something about the dusty old clock appealed to him. Khan, like Pak, slept well, except when the occasional nightmare took him back to his childhood. On those nights, she would comfort him with her head on his chest, until the past gave up its grip on him.

She returned to the kitchen. She still had baking to do. It surprised her that Khan wasn't back with the coconut yet. The market wasn't far, and he'd left a long time ago, but she also knew that Khan had a soft heart. If someone spotted his cab and needed a ride, he'd be right there to take them home, even if it meant going halfway across the city in the rain and the darkness.

Then a sharp knock on their back door startled her. Khan never came in through the back; besides, he always had his keys. She pushed aside the flowered curtain on the window, and when she saw the man on their back porch, she opened the door immediately, letting him in along with an ocean of rain.

"Haq," she said. "What are you doing here? Why did you come to the back door?"

Ahdia knew Haq Al-Masri well. Every Muslim in Duluth did. He often gave the Friday sermon at the mosque, and he was an unofficial spokesman when Islam was in the news, as it too often was. He was a handsome man, like Khan, although Haq had more ego and liked to show off his professor's intellect. Even so, he'd been the first to welcome them when they moved to the city and to make sure they felt a part of the community.

"I parked on the dirt road on Hubbell and came through the trees," Haq told her.

"What on earth for?"

Haq didn't explain. "Is Khan here? Did he make it home?"

"No, he went to the market. I expect him any minute now." Then she saw the look on Haq's face. "What is it? What's wrong?"

"Have you seen the news?"

"No, why? Is it Malik?"

"Worse," Haq replied. "There's no time to explain. We need to get you away from here. Put some things in a small bag, and then we must take Pak and go."

"Go? What are you talking about? Haq, tell me what's going on."

He sighed in impatience. "Turn off your living room lights, and then look out the front window."

Ahdia hesitated, but she obeyed. She darkened the front room and peered carefully from one side of the curtains. At the curb, on both sides of the street, she saw police cars with their lights off. Under the streetlight, she saw a uniformed cop behind the wheel of one of the cars. He was studying her house and speaking into his radio.

"Police!" she said. "What do they want with us?"

"They want Khan," Haq replied.

Ahdia cupped her hands over her chin. "They found out he was at the marathon? They think he's the bomber!"

"Yes, some fool posted a picture of Khan in Canal Park before the explosion. He says he saw Khan carrying a backpack."

"Khan doesn't own a backpack!" Ahdia protested.

"It doesn't matter. It's too late. Dawn Basch spread the picture around the city. There was an incident at the market. Someone saw Khan and tried to stop him from leaving. They fought."

"They fought? Is Khan okay? Where is he?"

"I don't know. I haven't heard more since then. I came over here immediately."

Ahdia shook her head. "Haq, this is crazy. Khan is innocent."

"There are no innocent Muslims the day after a bomb goes off! You know that. Ahdia, people at the market claimed that Khan had a gun. Is that true?"

"Khan with a gun? Nonsense. Khan never held a gun in his whole life."

Haq shook his head. "Even so, the police are treating him as armed and dangerous."

"We have to find him!" Ahdia said.

"Right now, we have to get you and Pak away from here. Otherwise, the police will take you and interrogate you. And this house isn't safe. Basch is stoking the flames with her mob. We need to find somewhere for you and Pak to hide. Tomorrow we can find a lawyer, and we can try to clear Khan's name."

Ahdia stared at Haq through the shadows of the living room. She thought: This is how it happens. This is how the innocent become guilty. A stone rolls downhill, and soon it's going so fast, it cannot be stopped.

She glanced at the doorway to her son's bedroom and saw Pak sleepily wiping his eyes. "Mama, I heard voices."

"It's Uncle Haq," she told him. "He came for a visit."

Pak's face brightened as he saw Haq, who marched into the bedroom and scooped the boy into his arms. "Would you like to go on an adventure?" Haq asked. "Do you have the heart of a tiger in the jungle?"

Pak was immediately awake. "Yes!"

"Good. I knew I could count on your courage. The three of us will head into the woods, and you will be a brave hero like Amir Hamza!"

"Will Papa come, too?"

"Very soon. He will be with us very soon."

Ahdia stared at her son, who beamed in Haq's arms. She cast another glance toward the street, where the police waited.

"All right, Haq, whatever you say," she murmured wearily.

Haq gave her a reassuring smile. "It's the best thing. Now hurry. We should be gone in two minutes, no more. Take only a couple of things for you and the boy."

"My phone?"

"Take it with you, but turn it off."

"But what if Khan tries to call?" she asked.

"If your phone is on, they can track you. They'll find you wherever we go."

Ahdia squeezed her plump lips into a thin white line. The rose of her cheeks was gone. She grabbed her phone from the coffee table and turned it off.

She was ready to go in less than a minute. She always kept a travel bag ready on a shelf in their closet. Somehow, she'd known that a day might come when they would have to leave their lives behind that way. It was one of the things that kept her awake in the nights.

With a cloth bag over her shoulder, Ahdia turned off the last of the house lights, and then she, Pak, and Haq crept out the back door into the storm and made their way toward the safety of the trees.

* * *

Khan ran and ran.

He escaped from Forest Hill southward into the wooded streets and picked his way undetected through the backyards of houses. Behind him, he heard overlapping sirens, wailing and moaning as if they were calling out his name. He ran until the noise of the police cars faded behind the rain. He lost track of the streets and the direction he was going, but the downward slope of the hills told him he was headed toward the lake.

When he finally stopped to catch his breath, he found himself near a Christian church on the northeast end of Superior Street. It was built of red brick and had a sharp white steeple. He'd been here once before, during an interfaith dinner.

The sign that faced the street said: Give me your hand.

To Khan, in despair, that felt like an invitation. The church was dark, but he dragged himself up the driveway, staying close to the trees, and at the back of the church, Allah smiled on him. The rear door was unlocked.

He let himself inside into the darkness. He wouldn't stay long. He didn't know whether churches had alarms to warn of intruders. He took a chance by flicking a light switch, and when his eyes adjusted to the brightness, he found a church office with a phone on the oak desk.

Khan dialed his home number. It rang and rang with no answer. He hung up and dialed Ahdia's cell phone, but it went straight to her voice mail. Somehow, he realized, she knew what had happened to him, and she'd fled. That was good, but it left him alone, hunted, with nowhere to go.

He had another number in his head.

It was a number to use only in emergencies, but if this wasn't an emergency, nothing in the world was.

Khan dialed, and a familiar voice answered immediately. The voice of a friend who would drop everything to be there for him.

"Malik? It's me. I need help."

@mnwoodsygal tweeted:
SHOTS FIRED in Woodland area of Duluth. Heard the bombing suspect was spotted and is on the run.

@jeandulhut12 tweeted:
Wow! Sirens everywhere near UMD. I think every cop car in Duluth is here.

@jmbarker61 tweeted:
Got a sister in DPD. She says officer down. Asshole shot a cop. Hope they blow his brains out. :-(

@dawnbasch tweeted:
Duluth needs justice. The Muslim bomber is now a COP KILLER.
#marathon
#islamismurder
#noexceptions
2,261 people retweeted @dawnbasch

MONDAY

22

Stride found Dawn Basch in the lobby of the Radisson Hotel, where she sipped takeout coffee and took dainty bites from a blueberry scone. Her face was mostly hidden by large sunglasses. He noticed two private security guards stationed nearby, watching the hotel entrances.

The overnight storm had passed. Outside the hotel, Monday morning had dawned clear and sunny, and the high temperature was headed for the eighties. It looked like a beautiful day on the outside, but looks could be deceiving.

He took a seat next to her. "Good morning, Ms. Basch."

She folded up the copy of the Duluth *News Tribune* she was reading. He didn't think he'd ever seen anyone with longer fingernails.

"Hello, Lieutenant," she said. "My condolences on the loss of one of your officers. What a terrible tragedy."

Stride worked hard to keep his anger off his face. If there was one person he blamed for the events that had led to Dennis Kenzie's death, it was Dawn Basch. With nothing but a Twitter account, she'd provided the match and the fire that had consumed the young officer.

"Have you apprehended this man Rashid yet?" she asked.

"No."

"All these police everywhere, and one terrorist outsmarts them."

He took a deep breath but didn't take the bait. He didn't want an argument with Dawn Basch. He wanted to say what he needed to say and move on.

"Special Agent Maloney and I have a request," he told her.

"Oh?"

"We'd appreciate it if you would refrain from tweeting about the investigation while we have an active and dangerous situation in the city. We want people to remain calm and not put themselves in harm's way."

Basch pinched a chunk of scone between her fingers and popped it into her mouth. She brushed crumbs from her red skirt.

"More political correctness," she said. "Didn't the election teach you that people are sick of being told what they can and can't say because it might offend somebody? The president calls it the way he sees it on Twitter. So do I, and I don't intend to stop."

"I'm not trying to censor you, Ms. Basch," Stride continued. "I'm simply appealing to your good judgment. The city is on edge. We don't need to give a green light to vigilantes or inflame emotions any more than they already are. That's how people get hurt."

"What you call vigilantes I call engaged citizens. They found the bomber for you, didn't they? And then the police let him get away."

"We don't have any actual evidence yet that Khan Rashid was involved in the marathon bombing."

Basch removed her sunglasses. Her eyes were cold. "Other than a dead cop?"

Stride felt his fingers tighten like vises around the arms of the chair.

"The situation last night got out of control, Ms. Basch, and, speaking candidly, you played a role in making that happen. You practically invited your followers to attack Rashid."

"I did no such thing," she replied. "I'm not responsible for the way frustrated people behave, but I'm not going to blame them for wanting to do something. If radical Muslims start worrying about ordinary Americans fighting back, maybe they'll think twice and look for softer targets somewhere else. Or maybe they'll go home, where they belong."

Stride stood up.

"Mob revenge isn't justice," he reminded her. "You may be fond of saying 'no exceptions' about free speech, but inciting people to violence actually *is* an exception. Please be careful that you don't cross the line."

"Congratulations, Lieutenant," Basch replied acidly. "The terrorists blow things up and murder people, and you waste your time trying to stifle my Constitutional rights. Well, I won't be silenced by murderers, and I won't be silenced by local government officials, either. Remember, Washington is on my side now."

"Goodbye, Ms. Basch."

Stride walked away, but Basch stood up and called after him. "Lieutenant?"

He turned and waited for her as she walked up to him.

"Do you want to know what I believe?" she asked. "Do you want to know why I do what I do?"

He didn't answer, but she told him anyway.

"I believe this country is at war. We are in a war with Islam for the future of civilization, and either we win or we lose. There's no middle ground. No room for compromise. Believe me, there is no such thing as an innocent Muslim, because when they're forced to choose, they will choose their side over ours. Count on it. So we have our own choice to make. All of us. If we huddle in our homes like sheep, then we lose. The only ones who ever win a war are the wolves."

* * *

When Cat didn't return from her morning jog after two hours, Serena got into her Mustang and went to find her. She drove down the narrow strip of land called the Point, with the calm waters of the harbor on her right and the dunes of Lake Superior on her left. The road ended in a children's park, which was empty except for dozens of seagulls bathing in the puddles left behind by the night's storm.

She spotted Cat on a green bench by the bayside beach, her legs tucked beneath her. The teenager stared at the water, and strands of her long brown hair spilled across her face with the breeze.

Serena parked her Mustang and walked through the sand. She sat down next to Cat, but the girl didn't react. "Hey."

Cat said nothing.

She had a luminous face despite her sad eyes. It wasn't just the ordinary prettiness of youth; she was a beautiful girl on her way to becoming a beautiful woman. When she smiled, she lit up the whole house, but she didn't smile nearly enough. People had said the same thing about Serena at that age. You could walk away from your past, but it had a way of trailing behind you, like a shadow.

"I went to see Drew Olson yesterday," Serena told her. "I saw Michael, too."

Cat's eyes were fixed on the water. "I know. I saw you."

"You were there, too? Why didn't you come over?"

The girl shrugged. "I'm not ready."

"Drew said to make sure you know you're welcome."

"I know that."

Serena didn't push her. The more she pushed Cat about anything, the more the girl dug in her heels. That was another way in which they were alike. Cat had to make peace with giving up her child in her own way and in her own time.

"Was your tutoring session cancelled?" Serena asked.

"Yeah. Everything's cancelled. Everybody's staying home."

Cat was a year behind other high school students her age—she'd be a junior in the fall, rather than a senior—but she had a flair for math, and she was already a tutor for students older than she was. When she set her mind to anything, she was whip-smart about it. The trick was keeping her focused.

She'd had a successful year at school after giving birth to Michael. She aced every class. The one thing she hadn't done was make friends. She'd already seen more life and death than other kids her age, which made it hard to do normal things with normal girls. She'd had a boyfriend, Al, but she'd broken up with him at the start of the school year, because she said she couldn't handle classes and Al at the same time. Serena thought the real reason was that she was afraid of any relationship getting serious.

The strange thing was, she knew that Cat missed her old life. Living on the street was what she knew; it was what she was good at. Without it, she didn't know where she belonged.

"Listen, I need your help with something," Serena told her.

"With what?"

Serena handed her a mug shot of a bearded, middle-aged man. "Do you recognize him?"

"Sure, that's Eagle. Everybody knows Eagle."

"Tell me about him."

"He's like a lot of the older men on the street," Cat said. "He had a normal life until his drinking took over. Eventually, he drank his way out of his marriage, his house, his job. I liked him. He was smart, like me. He was always bugging me about school. Sometimes he would make up puzzles I had to solve, and he'd quiz me until I got it right. That was when he was sober, though, which wasn't too often."

"Have you seen him around the city recently?" Serena asked.

"No. Eagle's a hider."

"What's that mean?"

"If he doesn't want you to find him, you won't. A lot of the homeless hang out in the same places all the time. Once you know their spot, you can usually find them there. Not Eagle. He knows how to slip into places he's not supposed to be, and he's usually in a different place every night. He was the one who told me how easy it is to get inside the DECC after dark because there's almost always an open door."

"Does he steal to get money?" Serena asked.

Cat gave her a thin smile. "No, he's not one of those. Not like me. And he isn't much for handouts, either. Usually, he'll make a couple bucks mowing a lawn or shoveling somebody's driveway, and then he'll drink until the money is gone. Why are you asking about him, anyway?"

"Eagle was in the Duluth Outdoor Company shop last week," Serena told her. "He had some kind of episode, and they called 911, but he left before the police got there."

Cat frowned. "That's weird."

"Why do you say that?"

"Oh, it's just that Eagle doesn't like going near Canal Park. He hates tourists. It bugs him the way everybody looks down on him, you know?"

"Can you think of a reason he'd go to the shop, then?"

"I can't," Cat said. "Hey, you don't think Eagle had something to do with the bombing, do you? That's not his style. He's harmless."

"No, I don't think that," Serena said.

"Then why do you care?"

Serena kicked the sand at her feet and asked herself the same question. She had no reason to believe that Eagle's behavior at the shop was important, but for some reason, she couldn't let it go. When her instincts grabbed hold of something, she'd learned to listen.

"If I want to talk to Eagle, how do I find him?" Serena asked. "Given that you say he's pretty good at not being found."

Cat grinned. "You can't find him, but I can."

"How?"

"I can check in with some of my friends," Cat said.

Serena shook her head. "No."

"Hey, you can try to do it yourself, but they won't talk to you. Not a cop."

"I'm not letting you go back into that world," Serena told her.

"Well, then, come with me. We can do it together."

Serena studied the girl's face. She didn't like the idea of Cat having anything to do with people from her old life, but she also knew that asking for Cat's help was giving the girl something that mattered. Everybody needed a purpose in life.

"Okay," Serena said. "You win."

Cat looked pleased with herself. She knelt on the beach and let some sand slip through her fingers. A gentle wave lapped at her feet. She turned and looked back at Serena. "So what are you going to say to Eagle when we find him?"

"I want to know why he went to the shop that day," she replied. "Don't worry, I'm not trying to get him into trouble."

"What do you think he knows?" Cat asked.

"I have no idea. Probably nothing."

The girl squinted into the sunshine and shook her head. She knew Serena too well. "Come on, you must have a hunch. You always say your gut knows the truth before you do."

Serena bent over her and smiled. She pushed some of the loose strands of hair out of Cat's face. "Honestly? You're right. I don't know why, but my gut tells me that Eagle knows who the bomber is."

23

Maggie parked her Avalanche at the Cloquet airport, which was in the middle of flat fields west of town, surrounded by acres of woods. Among the handful of cars in the parking lot, she spotted an Escalade with the license plate MM.

Michael Malville.

She heard the whine of a small plane engine overhead. It dipped for a landing, its wings waggling in the breeze. The plane made a touchdown on the runway, but rather than slowing down, it accelerated into another takeoff and began a lazy arc into the sky. Someone was taking flight lessons.

Maggie's boyfriend, Troy, had his pilot's license, so she'd spent a lot of time in small airports over the past year. It said a lot for her faith in Troy that she would climb into a plane with him, because she was deathly afraid of flying. She still screamed at every updraft, and she refused to go up into anything but cloudless skies. Even so, she'd begun to appreciate the freedom that Troy felt in the air.

She found Michael Malville prepping a Cirrus SR22 for flight. It was a beautiful single-engine propeller plane, and it looked brand-new, with a dazzling midnight-blue coat of paint. Malville, like Troy, looked at home with his aircraft. He stopped what he was doing when he saw Maggie approaching him, and he folded his arms across his chest. His head was shaved bald and had a pink glow from too much time in the sun. He wore a red polo shirt, khaki shorts, and Ray-Ban's over his eyes.

"How did you find me?" Malville asked her.

"Your wife told me you were here."

He opened the cockpit door and reached in to grab a silver travel mug. He took a sip of coffee and wiped his mouth. "Well, what can I do for you?"

"For starters, you can tell me what the hell you were thinking last night when you posted that tweet," Maggie said, letting her anger show in her voice.

"I didn't break any laws," he retorted.

"I'm not talking about laws. I'm talking about common sense. You could have called me. You could have called the tip line. You could have called 911. Instead, you had to show off and try to look like a hero for your Twitter friends."

"That's not what I was doing."

"No? Whatever you think you were doing, you created a dangerous situation. A police officer died because of it."

Malville jabbed a finger at her. "Don't you dare put that on me."

"Why did you put that information out there, Mr. Malville? You're smarter than that."

He stripped off his sunglasses. "Why didn't I trust the police? Gosh, I don't know. It's almost as if there were something in my past that might make me believe they wouldn't listen to me when I told them the truth."

"I get it. You're still bitter about the Spitting Devil case."

"Damn right, I am," he snapped. "My faith in the government, and my faith in *you*, are right around zero. So don't lecture me, Sergeant. I got results. Things happened fast. If I'd called in a tip, how many days would it have been before anyone took it seriously or the information made its way through the FBI bureaucracy? In the meantime, this guy could have been on his way to another city with another bomb."

Maggie waited as the small plane she'd spotted earlier drifted down for another practice landing and takeoff. The noise made it impossible to talk. She didn't blame Malville for his anger at the police, even if there was nothing she or Stride would have done differently two years earlier. You asked questions and made choices based on the best information you had. Back then, the evidence had made Malville look like a serial killer.

"Tell me again what you saw," Maggie said once the plane was back in the air.

"I already told you on Saturday. A Muslim man with a backpack bumped into me when Evan and I were standing outside the Electric Fetus. He was heading toward Canal Park. That was a few minutes before the bombing. Ever since, I've been combing through the photos that people have posted online, to see if I could identify the guy. And I did. I found him steps away from the blast site, just seconds before it happened, with *no* backpack. Maybe that's not enough for you or the FBI, but it was enough for me."

"If you had come to us with that information, we would have taken immediate action," Maggie told him.

"Well, that's easy to say now. Look, I'm sorry about what happened to that police officer. I really am. If Rashid shot him, it just shows that I was right. Rashid is the guy. And he's dangerous as hell."

"Are you absolutely certain that Khan Rashid is the man who bumped into you on Superior Street?" Maggie asked.

"Yes."

"Because we've been going over photos, too, and we can't place him on Superior with a backpack."

"He was there," Malville insisted.

"How long were you studying online photos from the marathon before you found the one you tweeted?" she asked.

Malville hesitated. "Since I got home on Saturday."

"Did you sleep on Saturday night?"

"Not much," he admitted.

"I'm sorry, Mr. Malville, but the fact is, you were sleep-deprived, angry, and emotional, and you'd spent hours looking at thousands of faces, trying to find someone you admit you saw for no more than a split second a day earlier. Is it *possible* you made a mistake?"

"I know what I saw."

Maggie had seen that certainty in eyewitnesses many times before. They were absolutely convinced about what they remembered. They could picture a face in their mind. They could pick a suspect out of a lineup, and they could point him out in court.

And all too often, they'd been dead wrong.

"I'm not laying blame on you, Mr. Malville, but this is important."

"Why? Why do you think I'm wrong? Because you were hoping the bomber was a white Christian, like me? I'm sorry to disappoint you. Too bad it was yet another Islamic radical."

"I just want to know if you're really sure," Maggie said.

Malville slipped on his Ray-Ban's and went back to his plane. "I'm one hundred percent sure, Sergeant. Khan Rashid was the man I saw. Now how about you go find him before he kills anyone else."

* * *

Wade Ralston took tentative steps up and down the St. Luke's corridor. The surgical incision in his stomach made him grimace with pain, but the nurses all said he was doing better. He was wearing street clothes again. By tomorrow, he'd be home. He could go back to work and get on with his life.

In the hospital lounge, he saw Travis. The kid looked like death. Wade hobbled over to him and eased down onto the sofa. He took heavy breaths, waiting while the pain subsided. The room was warm, and he felt himself sweating. His jaw clenched, because seeing Travis made him angry. Angry about Joni. Angry about how things had worked out.

"Listen, man," Travis mumbled, as if he could read the bitterness on Wade's face. "I feel really bad."

"About what?"

"I should have saved her somehow. It doesn't seem fair. Me being here. Joni being gone."

"I'm not sure who told you life was fair," Wade said. "It's not."

"Yeah. I know."

"How's Shelly?" Wade asked.

"She's alive, for whatever that's worth."

"You tell her about Joni?"

Travis nodded without saying anything. His eyes welled with tears.

"How about her legs and all? She know?"

"Yeah. She was giving me the God crap. Jesus will take care of her. I don't know how she can say that. Me, I just want ten minutes with the guy who did this. Ten minutes to saw off *his* legs, you know? I want to *do* something."

Wade stared at Travis. Big, dumb Travis, strong as an ox, handsome as one of the Hemsworth brothers. The kid was right. He should be dead. Instead, here they both were, sitting side by side on a hospital sofa.

"You believe in God, Travis?" Wade asked.

"Nah."

"Maybe you should. Maybe Shelly's right."

Travis's face screwed up in confusion. "What are you talking about, Wade?"

"I'm saying, what are the odds that you survived the explosion? One in a million? That can't be an accident. Gotta be a reason you walked away."

"Yeah? Like what?"

"I don't know, but the way I see it, God saved you. You were in the path, man, and God saved you. Seems like He must have some kind of mission for you. Otherwise, you'd be on a slab, just like Joni."

Travis laced his big hands on top of his head. "Man, if that's true, He picked the wrong guy. I've never done anything that's worth shit in my life."

"Well, maybe now you've got another chance."

"A chance for what?" Travis asked.

Wade looked around at the hospital lounge to make sure they were alone. He lowered his voice. "Just what you said, man. A chance to *do* something."

24

Khan awoke in an empty house.

He lay on his back on a wood floor. When he pushed himself up on his elbows, his muscles ached. So did his face, where the man at the market had struck him. He had no idea how long he'd slept. All he remembered from his dreams was the police officer's face in the cemetery, haunting him like a dark angel.

The hole in his head.

The look in his dead eyes.

He was in an unfurnished living room, and he didn't immediately remember how he'd gotten there. Everything was unfamiliar. Hooks dangled from the walls where paintings had once been hung. Dust coated the floor, except for a slurry of dirty footprints. The thick curtains, which were closed, gave no hint of whether it was morning or night. He knew he'd missed prayers, but he didn't know how many.

Khan got up off the floor. Dried blood was streaked on his skin. He could feel the sting of cuts on his arms and legs. He walked to the curtains, but as he reached out to sweep them aside, he felt someone behind him. He spun, and Malik was there. His friend grabbed his wrist in a steel grip.

"Don't touch the curtains," Malik said.

"Why not?"

"Cops are all over the neighborhood. They're looking for you. We can't let anyone see that we're here."

Malik turned around and walked away, and Khan followed him into the kitchen. Like the rest of the house, it was empty. No table or chairs. No appliances on the counter. One cabinet door hung open, revealing a few crumbs of food and the white dust of flour. The refrigerator was unplugged. Malik picked up a plastic bottle of Lipton iced tea, unscrewed it, and drank. He held out the bottle to Khan.

"Want some?"

Khan began to say no, but he realized he was thirsty. He took the bottle and drank down the rest of the warm, sweet tea. When he was done, he wiped his mouth and said, "Where are we?"

"This house is on the end of Redwing Street across from the Ridgeview golf course."

"Who owns this place?"

Malik shrugged. "Now? Some bank. One of my friends in Minneapolis works in the foreclosure department. He gave me the keys. From the outside, it looks abandoned. Long grass. I have to come and go carefully to make sure the neighbors don't get curious."

Khan didn't ask questions about Malik's friends. He didn't want to know who they were.

"Does anyone else know I'm here?" Khan asked.

"Just me."

"I need to call Ahdia."

"No. I'm sorry, Khan. That's not possible for many reasons. I can't have you use my phone and risk people tracking it to us. And the fact is, Ahdia's phone is probably turned off, so that no one at the FBI can track *her*."

"Where is she?"

"Gone," Malik said. "She and Pak disappeared last night. It's all over the news. You are a wanted man, Khan, and so is your family."

"Where did she go?" Khan asked.

"I don't know. The good thing is, the police don't seem to know, either. Otherwise, you can bet they would have her in a holding cell somewhere, and your boy would be with Child Protective Services. I'm trying to find out through my channels where she went. She's probably still in the city and somewhere close by. If she escaped, it wasn't on her own. She had help."

Khan thought about it. "Haq."

"Yes, that's my guess," Malik replied.

"Call him."

"I can't do that. It wouldn't be safe for us to be in contact. And you know that Haq and I don't exactly see eye to eye. Don't worry, Khan. I'm sure Ahdia and Pak are safe. I'll talk to a friend, and a friend will talk to a friend, and somewhere in the chain, I'll find out where she is. Be patient."

Khan looked around the empty house, which felt like a prison. It had none of the smells, none of the comforts, of home. He wanted to smell sandalwood and jasmine. He wanted to kiss his wife and go out in the fresh air to drive his cab.

"Patient? How can I be patient? What's happening to me? Malik, what is going on?"

Malik didn't answer. He grabbed another bottle of tea from the floor and returned to the living room, where he sat cross-legged in the dust. Khan was too anxious to sit, so he paced back and forth from the curtains to the kitchen doorway. Then he knelt in front of his friend.

"Please, tell me what's going on."

"What's going on is exactly what I warned you about. Since Saturday, they've been looking for a Muslim face, and they finally found one. Yours."

"But how?" Khan asked.

Malik reached into his pocket for his phone and showed Khan a photo. Khan had seen it before. It was the same photo that the man at the market had shoved in his face. "*Is this you? Because it sure looks like you.*" And it was. The photo showed Khan rushing back to his cab from Canal Park on the day of the marathon. Seconds later, the bomb went off, and he'd reversed his steps to wade into the terrified crowd and help.

"This photo is all over Twitter," Malik told him. "Dawn Basch called you the bomber. Now everyone thinks it's true, and they're all looking for you."

"So I was there!" Khan protested. "What does that mean? And yes, I was a fool; I lied about it to the police. I was going to go there today and explain it to them."

Malik gave him a tight smile. "Explain what? That you were really looking for me? Thank you so much, Khan."

"I'm sorry, but if you did this terrible thing—"

"I didn't."

Khan's eyes narrowed. He tried to decide if Malik was telling the truth. "You weren't the bomber?"

"No."

"Malik, I was in your apartment. I found a marathon brochure. And a bit of copper wire, too."

"You call me for help, and I risk my life for you, and now you interrogate me?"

"I need to know what you did," Khan replied.

"You already know enough. I told you. It wasn't me. We talked about the marathon, but that wasn't the plan."

"Then what was?"

"Never mind. Everything has changed because of you."

"If you didn't do this, I can go to the police," Khan repeated. "I can explain what really happened. I can clear this all up."

"It's too late for that. The photo went viral because a man claims he saw you a few minutes before the bombing with a backpack. In this photo, you don't have one. Everyone leaped to the obvious conclusion. Your backpack wound up shredded all over the marathon course, along with the body parts of the people you maimed and killed."

Khan backed up in horror. He put trembling hands over his face. "That is insane! I don't even own a backpack!"

"Do you think they'll care about that? How do you prove a negative? Besides, you have other problems now. You killed a police officer in the cemetery. The cops are baying for your blood, my friend."

"I didn't kill him! I didn't have a gun!"

"Witnesses saw you with one," Malik told him.

"They're wrong! The man who accosted me at the market had a gun. That was his, not mine."

Malik got to his feet. He stood in front of Khan, and his face was filled with anger. "Don't you get it? The truth doesn't matter! No one cares about the truth! People said you had a gun, and now a cop is dead with a bullet in his head. As far as the world is concerned, *you did it.*"

Khan's eyes widened with disbelief. "I can't believe this. I don't even know how it happened. It wasn't me! I didn't shoot him!"

"Wake up, Khan. You are their bomber. You are their murderer. And once they find you and shoot you, you won't be able to say anything different."

"So what do I do?" Khan asked.

"For now, nothing. Read the Qur'an. I have my copy for you. Pray. Ask for guidance from Allah."

"I can't just sit here. Ahdia needs me. I need to go to her."

"I told you, I'm reaching out to friends. I'll find out where she's taken refuge. But you can't go *anywhere* during the daylight. Hopefully, I can exchange a message with Haq, and he can find a lawyer, and the lawyer can figure out a way to keep you safe. Until then, you have to sit tight, my friend. Stay away from the windows and doors. If someone knocks, don't answer. I'll be back as soon as I can."

"You're leaving?" Khan asked. "Where are you going?"

"I can't take the risk of turning on my phone while we're together. I don't know who's being watched and who's being tracked, and if they run a search, it will lead the FBI right to you. I parked a car on the other side of the golf course. I'm going to slip over there and stay on the move. Don't worry, I'll return when I'm sure it's safe."

Malik turned toward the back of the house, but Khan grabbed him and embraced him. "Thank you, my friend. Be careful."

"I will."

"I'm sorry that I doubted you," Khan said.

Malik gave him the strangest of looks and didn't reply. Then he disappeared into the shadows, and Khan heard the rear door open and close.

25

"I missed," Agent Durkin told Stride. "I missed *twice*."

He thought she wanted him to blame her. To yell. To swear. To tell her that he was going to ask Agent Maloney to call for her gun and her badge. Beating herself up wasn't enough. She wanted others to do it, too. Durkin was the kind of agent who had a hard time dealing with her own mistakes. He'd felt the same way for a long time.

"It happens, Durkin," Stride said.

"Not to me. I'm a great shot. I don't miss."

"The range isn't the same as real life—you know that. All the conditions were against you. It was dark. It was pouring. You had trees between you and Rashid. You'd been running flat-out across the cemetery."

"I'm not looking for excuses," she told him.

"Those aren't excuses. They're facts."

"I missed," she repeated, "and because of that, Rashid had a chance to shoot Officer Kenzie and get away."

"His death isn't your fault," Stride told her.

Durkin was silent. She sat at the end of a small conference table, and Stride sat across from her. For now, they were the only two people in the room. The air-conditioning hummed over their heads. The small meeting room had been loaded up with whiteboards and computers and equipped with videoconferencing. They'd been waiting for Agent Maloney to join them for half an hour.

"I know you don't like me," Durkin said, "so why are you trying to be nice to me?"

Stride shrugged. "I've been there. We all have things we'd like to take back. It would really be nice if we were superheroes like Mitch Rapp or Jack Reacher, but we're not."

"This was the first time I had to fire my gun at an active scene," Durkin told him. "It's not what I expected."

"No, it's not."

"Have you?" she asked.

"A few times."

"Killed anyone?"

"No."

"I always thought I'd be up to it," Durkin said. "You do what you have to do, right? Now I wonder if . . ." She stopped.

"What?" Stride asked. He could see a crack in her tough shell.

"I wonder if I missed because, deep down, I was afraid of killing someone."

"It's easy to second-guess what happens in a split second. Don't make it a judgment on what kind of agent you are."

"An agent has to be able to take a life when it's necessary," Durkin said.

"Right, but anyone who says it's easy . . . Well, I wouldn't want them on my team."

Durkin looked as if she wanted to thank him, but at that moment, the door opened, and Special Agent Maloney entered the conference room. He carried a foam cup of coffee, a crisp new legal pad, and two Uni-ball pens. Somewhere in the past day, he'd managed to get a haircut.

At her boss's entrance, Agent Durkin's face hardened like concrete, all emotion gone.

"I've already been on the phone today with the mayor, the governor, and the president," Maloney told them as he sat down. "I don't have any answers for them, and I don't like being in that situation. Let's review the status of the local police issues."

Maloney was all business. Stride liked that about him.

"Have there been any confirmed sightings of Khan Rashid since last night?" Maloney asked.

"We've been investigating dozens of calls to the tip line all day," Stride replied, "but so far, nothing has panned out. We've got an intense search going on inside the perimeter we established last night, but there's a lot of wooded areas and empty land up there. He could have slipped through our roadblocks, and if he did, he could be anywhere now. The good news is, his photo is all over the news and social media. It will be tough for him to move around without being spotted."

"What about his support network?"

"His wife is his only local adult relative. As far as we can tell, he doesn't have many close friends."

"Other than Malik Noon," Durkin interjected.

Stride nodded. "We're looking for him, too."

"Rashid's wife and kid didn't disappear on their own," Durkin added. "They had help. Somebody's hiding them. Maybe Rashid, too."

"Lieutenant?" Maloney asked. "Do you agree?"

"Yes, Ahdia Rashid didn't take her car when she left. I can't believe she got far on foot with a young boy without help. Particularly at night in the middle of a storm."

"Did anyone reach out to her before she disappeared?"

"There were no calls in or out of her land line or cell phone yesterday evening. Her cell stopped pinging right around the time of the manhunt for Khan. It hasn't been on the network since."

"They could have burners," Durkin said.

Stride frowned. "Maybe, but that assumes Ahdia was part of the conspiracy."

"Muslim wives aren't necessarily innocent little flowers," Durkin reminded him. "Remember San Bernardino? If they were in this together, they had to know that a moment like this was likely to come. Look at their house—right on the edge of a heavily wooded area. It's easy to escape to some prearranged meeting point."

"You could say that about half the homes in Duluth," Stride said. "So far, there's no evidence of radicalization with Ahdia Rashid. She works at Cirrus. We checked in there this morning. Her co-workers have nothing but good things to say about her. Same with her neighbors. They describe her as sunny, friendly, outgoing. No arguments, no religious disputes."

"That doesn't mean a thing," Durkin said.

Maloney nodded. "Unfortunately, Agent Durkin is right. Looks can be deceiving. What have we found out about Khan Rashid? Do we know anything more?"

"He's quiet," Stride said. "Neighbors say he keeps to himself. His behavior didn't raise any red flags with them."

"Religious?" Maloney asked.

"Very, but no indications of extremism. My source insists we're wrong about Khan."

Maloney absorbed this information without reacting. He sat up straight in the chair. He never leaned back. He never tapped a finger or a foot.

"The search of the Rashid house this morning revealed nothing of interest," Maloney told them. "We're still examining their computer for evidence of radical contacts, but there were no signs of explosives or bomb-making material anywhere on the property."

"Any weapons?" Stride asked.

"None."

Stride shook his head. "Khan didn't even have a concealed-carry permit. I have to say, this couple doesn't fit the typical terrorist profile."

"Perhaps, but that doesn't make them innocent," Maloney said. "Rashid was friends with the man your source identified. Malik Noon. If Noon was radicalized, he could have recruited Rashid and possibly his wife, too. It takes a while for people to spot a change in someone's behavior, especially if they're trying to hide it."

Stride knew that was true. He'd known plenty of killers who'd shown a benign face to the world. They had kids. They went to work. They smiled at their friends. And then, in their dark hearts, they planned and executed terrible deeds. He knew all that, but this crime still didn't make sense.

He thought about what Haq had told him on the phone. *"He's not your man, Jonathan."*

"You look troubled, Lieutenant," Maloney said.

"I am."

"Why is that?"

"Honestly?" Stride said. "It's the coconut."

Maloney's mustache wrinkled with puzzlement. "I'm sorry?"

"Rashid went to the market to get a bag of shredded coconut. We found it on the ground outside the store. I know it's just a little thread, but when you pull on those threads, things start to unravel. Why was Khan Rashid running out to get coconut on the day after he bombed the marathon? It doesn't make sense."

"Dzhokhar Tsarnaev hung out in the dorms after Boston like nothing had happened," Durkin said. "With all due respect, Stride, you're being naïve."

"Durkin," Maloney murmured, with an admonition in his tone.

"No, it's okay," Stride replied. "She may well be right. It looks like Rashid shot Officer Kenzie, and if that's true, he's obviously not the man he appeared to be on the outside. I just don't think we have the whole picture yet."

"Well, we need to examine every aspect of their lives to see where there may have been radical influences on the Rashids," Maloney said. "In the meantime, the priority is to find them. Lieutenant, talk to your source again. If someone in the Muslim community is helping them, we need to find out who."

"I will."

"What about the death of Officer Kenzie?" Maloney asked. "Has the autopsy been completed?"

Stride nodded. "Yes, the medical examiner recovered the bullet that killed him. Typically, we'd send it to the Bureau of Criminal Apprehension in Saint Paul for analysis, but your people wanted it done at the FBI lab."

"The bullet and the weapons from the scene are being hand-carried to Quantico by one of our agents," Durkin added. "It's top priority. We should have more information tomorrow."

Maloney nodded. "Good. Is there anything else?"

"I have a question about the marathon photos," Stride said. "One of my people talked to the witness who first brought Rashid to our attention. Michael Malville. He's convinced he saw Rashid with a backpack on Superior Street a few minutes before the bombing. I was wondering if we'd located any photo or video evidence to confirm it."

Maloney shook his head. "No."

"What about in Canal Park itself? Do we have any photos of Rashid arriving there with a backpack?"

Maloney and Durkin exchanged glances.

"The investigation in Canal Park has been troublesome," Maloney replied.

"How so?" Stride asked.

"I'm sure you know that the marathon maintains a high-definition camera on the roof of their building that captures images along the street. So we have excellent coverage of the entire area throughout the marathon. We've been through it numerous times from the beginning of the day through the bombing and the aftermath. That's in addition to materials provided by the public."

"And?"

"And nobody with the right type of backpack went inside the Duluth Outdoor Company shop. Not one. We didn't know what to make of it until Durkin pointed out something we hadn't immediately realized."

"The shop has a back door," Durkin interjected. "It was open throughout the morning for people coming in from the alley."

"There's no camera coverage back there," Stride said.

Maloney nodded. "Unfortunately, that's right. For the moment, our theory is that the bomber brought in the backpack from the alley and left it near the front door. Then he simply walked out into the crowd. It makes suspect identification extremely difficult, which is why the information from Mr. Malville is important. He says Rashid had a backpack."

"Except we have no photographs of Rashid to confirm it," Stride pointed out.

"That's true," Maloney said, "but we do have this."

He leafed through the pages of his legal pad and extracted a piece of shiny photo paper. He pushed it across the conference table to Stride.

Stride picked up the photo.

It showed Khan Rashid emerging from the doorway of the Duluth Outdoor Company shop on the morning of the marathon.

26

"Curt Dickes," Serena said to Cat in exasperation. "Do we really have to talk to Curt Dickes?"

Cat grinned. The open top of Serena's Mustang swirled her chestnut hair as they headed north on London Road past the Glensheen Historic Estate.

"Hey, I know you don't like Curt, but he knows the score with all the street people. If anyone has seen Eagle lately, it's Curt."

"I don't like him because he was the one who pimped you out and nearly got you killed," Serena said. "Remember?"

"Oh, yeah, but he's still a nice guy."

Serena shook her head. There was no talking to Cat about Curt Dickes. She kept going back to him like a beautiful bee buzzing around a mangy flower.

Curt wasn't really dangerous. He was mostly an irrepressible scam artist, and he'd been that way since he was fifteen years old. Every month, he wound up at police headquarters because of a different con game he was running on convention-goers at the DECC. Once it was "Canadian" Viagra made from ground-up Flintstone vitamins. Another time it was half-price tickets to a free folk concert at Amazing Grace. If he'd devoted half the energy toward honest work that he put toward his schemes, he probably would have wound up as a billionaire entrepreneur. However, Curt and honest work never found themselves in the same city at the same time.

"There!" Cat called. "There's the sign!"

Serena spotted a hand-painted sign on the highway shoulder near the scenic bypass toward Two Harbors. She couldn't help but remember that this was the marathon route, leading along the lakeshore between the two towns. On Saturday, she'd run past this very spot. She could still feel the drizzle on her face and hear the in-and-out of her breath and see the midnight blue of the lake sticking by her like a friend.

The sign on the highway said in stencil:

CRAFT BEER

And below it, scrawled in heavy marker:

*Yes, we are **OPEN!***

Serena turned onto the road that led toward Brighton Beach. She followed it until the trees opened up at the sun-swept lake, where waves bubbled against a tiny strip of rocky beach. From this angle, the city was invisible, making the lake look endless. She parked her Mustang between a Subaru Forester camper and a Prius. On the beach, two children splashed in the cold water, and a woman about her own age lounged on the rocks with a paperback book. Beyond the family, she could see two men farther along the beach, drinking from red Solo cups. They stood beside a kid in a yellow canvas chair that was planted a foot deep into the lake.

Curt Dickes.

"Hey, Curt!" Cat shouted. Serena didn't like the excitement she heard in the girl's voice.

The teenager ran for the beach, and Curt, recognizing her, nearly toppled backward in his chair as he scrambled to get up. Serena followed, with her badge clearly visible on her belt. As she neared the water, the two beer drinkers spotted the badge and did a quick-march back toward the Prius.

Curt splashed from the water and hugged Cat. He was surrounded by half a dozen coolers of various sizes and colors, and two giant bags of plastic cups dangled from the arms of his canvas chair.

"Serena!" Curt said to her with a big smile. "Or should I say Mrs. Stride? Congrats on the big wedding! Mazel tov!"

Serena tried not to laugh. The strange thing about Curt was that he always seemed genuinely happy to see the police, even when they were about to bust him.

He was twenty-six years old and built like a stalk of skinny aspara-gus. His black hair was greased back and hung down to his shoulders. His skin oozed musk cologne that somehow overpowered all the fresh smells of the lake. He wore baggy jean shorts and nothing else, other than a wolf tattoo on his forearm and piercings through both nipples.

"So what's with all the coolers, Curt?" Serena asked.

"Craft beer! I make it myself. Really good stuff, really strong."

"You make it yourself?" she said skeptically. "I never thought of you as a Dave Hoops kind of guy."

Curt began flipping up the lids of his coolers to reveal dozens of growlers. "Oh, yeah! I've got jalapeno IPA, Elton John Island Girl stout, piss-it-away lager, Mauer's Tripel Belgian ale, and a honey-wheat beer that I call Lesbian Honey because it tastes just like—well, never mind. You want to try something?"

"No, thanks," Serena said.

Cat held up a growler of Lesbian Honey. "I'll try it!"

"No, you won't," Serena told her. "I know it's a waste of time to ask, Curt, but do you have a license to sell alcoholic beverages? Because I'm pretty sure you don't."

"License? Come on, Serena. I'm a libertarian guy. Live and let live. Down with government bureaucracy."

"Yeah. I guess."

"How are sales going?" Cat asked.

Curt gave a thumbs-up. "Couldn't be better. Most of the liquor stores are still closed, so I'm here with all the provisions people need for a week at the cabin."

"Leave it to you to make money off this tragedy, Curt," Serena said.

His smiled vanished, and he looked genuinely hurt. "Now that's not fair. I want to see you catch this guy as much as anybody. I'm a Duluth boy, born and raised. Nobody messes with our marathon."

Serena sighed. She couldn't deny that Curt had an odd, incorrigible charm.

"Okay, I'm sorry to insult your reputation as an ambassador of the Zenith City, but the growler party's over. When we leave, you leave—got it? And you get a free pass today, but next time, the beer goes into the lake."

Curt frowned but didn't protest. "Yeah, yeah, okay. So what do you guys need, anyway?"

Cat leaned over to examine the piercings through Curt's nipples with an unhealthy curiosity. Curt showed a similar interest in the mocha-skinned cleavage visible through the top of Cat's marathon T-shirt.

"You seen Eagle lately?" Cat asked him.

"Eagle? No, not since last week."

"When exactly was that?" Serena asked. "Do you remember the day?"

"Wednesday, I think. I picked up a scone at the 3rd Street Bakery, and I spotted Eagle in an alley down the block."

Cat cocked her head. "Sober?"

"No, I almost called 911, because he was so out of it. Looked like he'd gone through a few liters of booze."

"Damn," Cat said.

"Any idea where we can find him now?" Serena asked.

Curt dragged an Island Girl growler from the ice. He poured a cup, took a drink, and wiped foam from his mouth. "Eagle? No, good luck with that. I hear he sneaks into the old Nopeming Sanatorium sometimes if he can hitch a ride up to Midway. Or he gets into the downtown basements where it's warm. Or he just finds a porch or an open window to do a sleepover at somebody's house, and he's gone before they wake up. Nobody finds Eagle unless he wants to be found."

"I told you," Cat said to Serena. She flicked one of the miniature silver barbells on Curt's chest. "So did it hurt a lot to have that done?"

Serena spoke up before Curt could answer. "I'm sure it hurt so much that no human being would *ever* want to do that to themselves."

Cat smirked. "I didn't say I wanted them. I was just curious."

"Yeah, let's keep it that way." Serena didn't want to think about the day when Jonny spotted Cat with new accessories under her shirt. "Curt, we really need to find Eagle. Help us out."

"Well, most people would buy a growler for a favor like that," Curt replied, winking.

"I'm not most people," Serena replied.

"Oh, fine, fine. For the wife of the Lieutenant, it's free. Look, I meant it when I said you're not going to find Eagle yourself, but I can put the word out. If anybody spots him, they call me, and I call Cat. Okay?"

"You call *me*," Serena told him. "This girl here, she's like plutonium. Very, very radioactive. Understood?"

"Yeah, message received loud and clear," he replied with a salute.

"Don't worry, Curt," Cat said, rolling her eyes. "Serena's just being Mom."

It was amazing how Cat could always find ways to throw Serena off-balance, in good ways and bad ways. This was a good way. Serena had never, ever heard Cat use the word Mom to describe her, and the way it had simply rolled off the girl's tongue hit Serena with an emotional punch she hadn't expected. She liked it.

"We need to go," she murmured with a catch in her voice.

"Growler for the road?" Curt asked, sitting back down in his canvas chair. "Bring one home for Stride?"

"Don't push it," she told him.

"Yeah, okay. What do you want with Eagle, anyway?"

"There was an incident at Duluth Outdoor Company last Tuesday," Serena said. "Eagle had some kind of breakdown. I want to find out more about it. Do you know anything?"

"Duluth Outdoor Company? You mean, where the bomb went off?"

Curt was many things, but he wasn't stupid.

"That's right," Serena said.

Curt rubbed his chin thoughtfully. He sipped his beer and dangled his other hand in the water.

"Why, does that mean something to you?" Serena asked.

"Well, I did notice something on Wednesday when I saw Eagle. I don't know if it's important or not."

"What?"

Curt pointed at his bare feet. "Eagle had new shoes. Nothing's ever new about Eagle, but instead of his usual ratty sneakers, he had brand-new, right-out-of-the-box hiking boots. And speaking as someone who spends a lot of time in Canal Park, I can guarantee you, they were from Duluth Outdoor Company."

27

The luxury SUV carrying Dawn Basch stopped in front of an old two-story house across from the UMD campus. The driver ran around to the rear of the vehicle to open the back door for her. Two security men climbed out of the backseat before her. She smoothed her red skirt and fluffed her curly hair.

"Now this is a gorgeous day, boys, isn't it?"

"Yes, ma'am," they replied in unison.

Dawn slid her large sunglasses off her face and secreted them in a case inside her shoulder purse. With a toothy smile, she marched in her high heels onto the sidewalk in front of the house and examined the exterior with her hands on her hips. It was a small house but well maintained. The siding was beige, and the roof was covered in red shingles. Leafy hedges obscured most of the downstairs windows. Two side-by-side windows on the second floor looked out on the street, and she could see several young men crowded at the glass, staring out at her.

"Is this the place?" she asked one of the guards.

The retired Marine with the red crew cut nodded. "Yes, it is."

"You're absolutely sure? There's no sign outside."

"This is it, ma'am. I confirmed it this morning."

"Excellent."

The front door of the house opened. A Somali man, no more than twenty years old, stepped out onto the porch. He wore a *kufi*, a paisley shirt, and jeans, with open sandals on his feet. His face was grim.

Dawn waved cheerily.

She took out a selfie stick from her purse and snapped her phone into the plastic frame. Ignoring the men at the upstairs windows and the man on the porch, she undid the joints of the metal stick and extended it to its full length. She unlocked the phone, switched to the front camera, and turned around so that her back was to the house. She extended the selfie stick in front of her and squeezed the button to snap a photo.

When she was done, Dawn checked her phone. Her smile was wide in the photograph—she always had a good smile—but her eyes were half-closed, and the house was partly cut off below the roof by the angle of the photo. She extended the selfie stick to try again.

"Hey!" a voice called.

Dawn turned around. The Somali man came down off the porch and marched down the house's front walk toward her. Her security guards edged closer, ready to step between them.

"Hey, what do you think you're doing?" the man called to her.

"I'm exercising my free-speech rights, young man."

He pointed at the camera. "You can't take pictures here."

"Oh, but I can," she replied with a sunny smile. "Maybe in your country, you could stop me, but this is the United States of America, and I will take pictures of whatever I want, and there is nothing you or your terrorist friends can do about it."

The man shouted over his shoulder. "Call Haq!"

Dawn returned her attention to her selfie stick. She propped it higher, but with the camera five feet away from her face, she couldn't see well enough to figure out whether she was using a better angle. "Mark, I'm totally blind here," she told the red-haired guard. "Can you see if this looks right?"

He ducked behind her shoulder. "You're only getting the second floor."

"How about now?" she said, nudging the stick downward.

"Better."

Dawn squeezed the button again, but her hand jiggled as she tried to keep the stick steady, and the photo was blurry. She shook her head. "No, that's no good. I'm so bad at this."

"Hey!" she heard again.

Three more young men joined the Somali youth on the front lawn of the small house. Two looked Arabic. One looked Southeast Asian. The taller Arabic man, who had thick dark hair, a large nose, and black-as-coal eyebrows, folded his arms across his chest.

"You're Dawn Basch, aren't you?" he asked.

"Yes, I am."

"You're a racist, you know that? You call all Muslims terrorists."

"You're right, that's what I do, and I'm proud of it."

"What gives you the right?" he demanded.

"It's a little document called the Constitution, sir. If I want to get on my knees and draw a chalk painting of Muhammad taking a dump on the sidewalk right here, well, I can do that, too. I don't care if it offends you."

"You are a disgusting human being."

"No, the Muslims who blow up bombs and throw people off buildings and cut off heads are disgusting human beings," Dawn replied.

The Somali youth took an angry step toward her, and one of her guards swiftly intervened and pulled aside the flap of his jacket to reveal a handgun in a holster. The Somali man stopped and backed up.

"This is our property! Get off our property!"

"No, actually, the sidewalk is not your property; it's public property. Now, if you'll excuse me, I need to figure out this silly selfie stick."

"Would you like me to just take the picture for you, ma'am?" the redheaded guard asked.

Dawn laughed. "Well, Mark, that is why I keep you around. You're so much smarter than me. Here I am wasting my time with this thing, and there you are to save me all the trouble."

She turned her back on the men on the lawn and disconnected her selfie stick. As she slid the device back into her purse, she spotted another man running toward them at a sprinter's pace from the UMD campus. She knew him, and he knew her. They'd tangled repeatedly ever since Dawn arrived in Duluth.

"Mr. Al-Masri," Dawn said as the man skidded to a stop on the lawn of the house, prompting her guards to tense like dogs with their hackles raised. "Are you here to harass me again? It's nice to know that the Council on American-Islamic Relations has its priorities in order after yet another Muslim bombing."

"Ms. Basch," Haq replied. "What are you doing here?"

"Right now, I'm trying and failing to take a decent picture, but I think Mark should be able to handle it for me."

She handed her phone to the guard, who lined her up in the frame.

"Make sure you can see the whole house in the background," Dawn told him. "The whole house. We don't want to miss anything."

"Why are you taking a picture of this house?" Haq asked her. "This is the Muslim Student Center building."

Dawn smiled. *Click.*

"Oh, take a few more, won't you, Mark? I want to make sure we have a good one, and you know me, I always wind up with a funny expression."

"Ms. Basch?" Haq asked. "What do you think you're doing?"

"Hang on, Mr. Al-Masri."

The guard took several more pictures. *Click. Click. Click.* He handed the phone back to Dawn, who scrolled through them.

"Wonderful! These are much better. Thank you, Mark. You're a lifesaver. We can move on to the next spot now."

"Ms. Basch, would you mind telling me *why* you're taking these pictures?" Haq asked again.

"I'm taking my Twitter followers on a little photo tour of Duluth," she said.

"What kind of tour?"

"Oh, I'm just showing them places I think they should know about."

Haq's face turned dark. "And why would your followers want to know the location of the Muslim Student Center building?"

"It's a cute little house. I like it. Everyone who comes to Duluth takes pictures of the lift bridge or the Enger Tower or Split Rock Lighthouse. I'm more interested in urban minutiae. It's a hobby of mine."

"I know exactly what you're doing. You're encouraging vigilantes to harass the Muslim community in this city. You're putting innocent people at risk by deliberately inciting violence."

Dawn laughed. "A Muslim complaining about inciting violence? I'm sorry, Mr. Al-Masri. That's rich. You're a funny man."

She opened up her phone and fiddled with the screen. She selected the best photo from the pictures that Mark had taken, and then she found the Twitter app and typed a quick message. She flicked her thumb on the blue button.

"There, all done. Tweet-tweet. Sorry to interrupt our conversation, Mr. Al-Masri, but I have more places that I need to go."

"What did you post?" Haq asked.

"You can look it up yourself. You follow me, don't you? I'm sure you do. Always know your enemy, right?"

"We don't have to be enemies, Ms. Basch," Haq said.

"You're wrong about that," Dawn replied. She gestured at the guards. "Come on, boys. We don't have all day."

"Where are you going next?" Haq asked.

"There's a little bakery I want to check out. I think the name of it is Angels of London. Because it's on London Road—that's pretty cute, don't you think? Do you know it?"

Haq stared at her with a fierce expression. "Angels of London is a Muslim-owned bakery."

"Is it?" Dawn replied. "What a coincidence. Well, I'm sure they'll like the publicity. Maybe I can drum up some new customers for them."

* * *

@dawnbasch tweeted a photo:
Greetings from #radicalduluth.
#islamismurder
#noexceptions

* * *

Travis Baker let himself into the garage at Wade's farmhouse on Five Corners Road. The house and land doubled as the headquarters for Ralston Extermination. A big sign near the dirt road advertised THE BUG ZAPPERS. For Travis and Shelly, this was their home away from home. She did the accounting and scheduling out of an office in Wade's basement. Travis and Wade were in and out of the garage for supplies during the workdays. Joni was the eye candy of the business. Wade liked showing her off. She appeared in all Wade's newspaper ads, with her blond hair and her tight body suits. She was like a tattooed supermodel waging war against cockroaches.

And now Joni was gone. Dead.

And Shelly had lost her legs.

Travis couldn't believe it. Saturday morning his life had been perfect, and with one big bang, it all went away. He didn't know what would happen next. It would be weeks before Shelly could work again. Or months. Or maybe not ever. Travis didn't even know how long he'd have a job himself. Maybe Wade would open the business again, or maybe he'd kiss off the Duluth winters and move to Key West. That was where he always said he wanted to be. It's not like anybody wanted to squirm through a tunnel, laying down traps and poison. The only reason you did it was for the money.

Travis popped open the rear doors of the van. He needed to load up. Tomorrow was Tuesday, and Wade figured the city would be open for business again, regardless of whether they'd caught the Muslim bomber. Time to make the rounds on their accounts. Zap more bugs. Haul out the gray bodies of the rats. This was what he did every day, but suddenly it felt hollow and empty to be there alone. His chest felt heavy. He left the garage and watched the breeze blow in ripples across the huge lawn. He couldn't see another house beyond the fields, just trees. Wade liked his privacy.

Travis walked to the main house. The door was unlocked. Nobody locked their doors up here. Inside, he went to the kitchen, where Wade kept a special refrigerator just for beer. He popped a can of Bent Paddle and sat down at the table. The house was dead quiet, but he could hear voices in his head, like echoes. He could smell Joni's perfume, which reminded him of a fresh apple blossom. He sat there drinking, and tears ran down his face. Big fat tears like he hadn't cried since his parents died.

He finished his beer and crushed the can in his fist. He imagined having his hands around somebody's throat.

Travis went back to the garage and the van. He started loading up poison again. Was that all there was? Life goes on? Joni gets killed, Shelly can't walk, and he was just supposed to go back to work like nothing was different? That wasn't right. He couldn't sit on his ass and pretend that everything was fine.

You were in the path, man, and God saved you.

Wade nailed it when he said that. Travis was alive, when he should have been dead. He'd stood in front of a bomb, and the bomb had passed him by. That had to be a sign. God didn't save his sorry life so he could do nothing.

Seems like He must have some kind of mission for you.

A chance to do *something.*

Travis stood alone in the garage and realized the answer was staring him in the face. Right there on the metal shelves was a row of plastic gasoline cans that Wade kept for the machines around the farm. He went over, picked one up, and unscrewed the cap, letting out the sickly aroma of gasoline into the musty garage. Some splashed on his sleeve. He put the fabric to his nose and inhaled. The smell made him dizzy, because it was so strong.

He knew what he was supposed to do. He knew why he was alive.

Just like that, Travis had a plan.

28

When Malik still hadn't returned by dusk, Khan began to wonder if something had gone wrong. He was hungry, lonely, and scared. The house was dark behind the closed curtains, and he wandered from empty room to empty room amid the shadows. He thought about walking into the street with his hands up and letting the police take him away. Or he thought about finding a phone and calling the media to say: "I didn't shoot that cop. It wasn't me."

Malik was right. No one would believe him.

More than anything, he missed Ahdia and Pak. He wanted to know where they were, and he wanted to be with them. He could picture his wife's face and hear her voice, and he could feel Pak's small arms hanging on when he carried him. He hoped Allah would bring them all together again soon. He had no idea of the time and when he should perform *salat*, but he prayed throughout the day, anyway. It was the only thing that gave him comfort. His relationship to God was the only piece of the world that made sense.

Saturday morning his life had been perfect, and then, with one big bang, it all went away. He didn't know what would happen next.

His stomach growled, but there was no food in the kitchen. The toilet, which had no water, smelled of waste. Every remnant of human life in the house had been stripped away. No furnishings. No clothes. Just the dust and debris of what had once been a place where a family lived. He didn't even see where Malik slept, which was strange.

Everything about Malik felt strange.

Why had he taken refuge here, instead of his apartment? What was he doing in this place?

His friend was hiding something, and Khan wanted to know what it was.

He began opening doors, because he was sure the answer was there somewhere. One door, which he'd assumed was a closet, was actually the entrance to the basement. Wooden stairs led down into darkness. He flipped the light switch, but there was no electricity. He returned to the living room to retrieve a small flashlight that Malik had left behind, and with that light guiding him, he took the stairs to the underground level.

The air was cool and damp. He reached the bottom of the steps, where the foundation was made of concrete. His light lit up only a small portion of the space in front of him. The basement was unfinished. Pink insulation filled the seams where the beams of the house were joined to the walls. On the floor, scattered like confetti, he saw mouse droppings. Water and venting pipes made a maze above his head.

He saw a sleeping bag and pillow. This was where Malik spent his nights. He also saw a rickety wooden table and an open bag of vanilla sandwich cookies and a jar of chunky peanut butter. He scooped out peanut butter with his finger, and he wolfed down the rest of the cookies in the bag. His mouth felt sticky and sweet.

Khan shot his light around the walls. He saw barred windows and grew nervous when the light passed over the dirty glass. Anyone outside could see it. Malik had rigged heavy drapery that could block the windows at night, but he hadn't lowered them yet.

It was time to go back upstairs.

As his flashlight beam swept across the floor, he spotted a worktable and a chair in the middle of the basement. He felt a wave of horror when he realized what he was seeing. The concrete around the table shined with bits of wire. The table itself was a mess of tools, nails, black powder, plastic jugs, and electronic circuits. Beside the table, hanging by shoulder straps on the back of the chair, was a black vinyl vest, in which multiple pockets had been sewn. The pockets were filled with sealed jugs that had been carefully wired together.

Khan wanted to scream.

He knew Malik's secret now, and it was worse than he'd imagined. It was a suicide vest. It was a human bomb, with only one purpose. To kill the person wearing it and everyone around him.

He swung around sharply, and as he did, his flashlight beam lit up a face, and he jumped. Malik stood directly behind him. His friend's face was bone white in the light, like a corpse. His eyes were dark and devoid of emotion.

"You shouldn't be down here, Khan," Malik told him. "I was outside. I saw the light. Others can, too."

"Who cares about that?" Khan asked.

He shoved angrily past his friend, their shoulders colliding. Khan made his way by feel, bumping into the wall with his hands until he found the wooden stairs. He took them two at a time, back into the deep shadows of the house, and he heard Malik running behind him.

"Khan!"

Malik caught up with him in the hallway and grabbed his shoulder. Khan spun around and pushed Malik hard. His friend lost his balance. Khan marched for the rear door of the house, and Malik charged after him. They wrestled in the hallway, but Malik was strong and soon pinned Khan's shoulders to the wall. His friend's breath was hot on his face, although he could barely see him.

"What do you think you're doing?" Malik demanded.

"Leaving."

"Are you crazy?"

"I don't even know who you are anymore," Khan said.

"I'm a fighter for Islam," his friend replied.

"Don't disgrace my religion with that garbage. You are a fighter for *nothing*. I don't want to have anything to do with you."

Malik breathed heavily, and then he let Khan go. "Fine. Get out of here."

Khan wanted to run out the door, but he didn't. He stood in silence. He tasted peanut butter on his tongue, making it feel thick. His veins coursed with sugar and adrenaline.

"Did you lie to me?" he asked finally. "The marathon bomb—was it you?"

"No."

"Do you know who did it?"

"No, I don't."

"So who are you planning to kill, Malik? Other than yourself."

Malik didn't reply for a long time. Then he said, "You wouldn't understand."

"You're right. I don't understand at all. It's against *everything* I have ever believed. And from you? A man I call a brother? No, I will never understand."

"I'm part of something larger than myself for the first time ever," Malik said. "If I lose my life to fight back for Allah, then I've done something glorious."

"Fight back against whom?" Khan asked.

"Dawn Basch."

Khan pounded the floor. "So you murder this insufferable woman. And you kill yourself at the same time. Maybe others, too. Then what? What does it accomplish? Where does it end? All you do is bring down more violence on our heads. You give her exactly what she wants—proof that every Muslim is no better than a murderer."

"Maybe that's what we need to be!" Malik replied. "She's right about one thing. This is a war, and I'm proud to be a soldier."

"I won't listen to this," Khan told him. "Good-bye, Malik. I'm going to the police right now. I'm sending them here for you. If you want to escape, you'd better do it now. That's all I can offer you."

Khan headed for the door, but Malik called after him.

"What about Ahdia?" he said. "What about your son?"

Khan stopped. "What about them?"

Malik walked to Khan in the darkness and clapped a firm hand on his shoulder. "I know where they're hiding. I came back here so I could take you to them."

29

Serena found Special Agent Durkin on the pedestrian bridge between the DECC and Canal Park. The FBI agent had a sandwich in her hand, but rather than eating it, she tossed bits of bread into the water, where ducks fought for the prize. It was dark, but streetlights gave the area a yellow glow. The giant ore boat *Charles Frederick* floated in the channel.

"Agent Maloney said I'd find you here," Serena said.

"Yeah, I just needed ten minutes to clear my head." Durkin turned around and leaned against the railing. The lift bridge shimmered in silver a hundred yards away. "You're Stride's wife, right?"

"I am."

Durkin took a quick, obvious glance at her from head to toe. Serena waited for the usual snarky comment about her looks. Even at forty years old, she maintained her showgirl face and body, and most cops assumed that she'd gotten where she was because of her sex appeal. However, Durkin surprised her.

"Sergeant Bei tells me you're smart. Smarter than Stride. Even smarter than her, too."

Serena laughed. "Maggie said that? Really?"

"Yeah. She said it made the size of your boobs doubly annoying."

"Now, that sounds like Maggie," Serena said.

"I know she's not one of my fans," Durkin added.

"Oh, I don't know about that."

"Please. Even my own people have started calling me the Gherkin."

Serena suppressed a smile. "Well, Maggie can be a little sharp-edged. She and I have had our ups and downs over the years, too. The fact is, you're a Fed, and you stole our investigation. It really doesn't matter that you grew up in Duluth. She's going to resent you."

"I don't mind sharp-edged. I'm sharp-edged myself. And I really don't care whether people like me."

"Still, this has to be a tough case for you," Serena said.

"Because of my brother?"

Serena nodded.

"Believe me, the best thing I can do for Ron is catch Khan Rashid. The only thing I regret is not drilling a bullet through Rashid's head before he shot Officer Kenzie. If I face the same opportunity again, I won't miss."

"Well, let's hope we can bring him in without more violence," Serena said.

Durkin didn't rush to agree with her. It made Serena wonder whether, in her heart of hearts, Durkin really wanted to arrest Rashid or whether she'd prefer to face him down again, gun to gun. To make up for her mistake. To make up for Ron.

"So what's on your mind?" Durkin asked.

"Stride tells me you have a photo of Khan Rashid coming out of the Duluth Outdoor Company shop during the marathon."

"That's right."

"But no actual link to the bomb yet?"

"No, if the bomb was his handiwork, he didn't do the assembly at his house. We're checking GPS records in his cab to see where he's been in the last few weeks. Hopefully, that will lead us to his hiding place."

"Okay."

Durkin read the hesitation in her voice. "You and Stride don't sound convinced that we have our man, but the circumstantial evidence is piling up fast."

"Yes, it looks that way."

"But?"

"No buts," Serena said. "I'm just trying to rule a couple of other things out."

"I know you've been looking into this incident with the homeless guy at the shop," Durkin said.

"Yes, I'm trying to find the guy and talk to him."

"It's pretty thin," Durkin said.

"Normally, I'd agree with you, but there's something about it I don't like."

The FBI agent threw the rest of her sandwich into the water, which caused a frantic cackling of ducks as they fought for what was left. "All right. Tell me about it."

"The day after the incident at the shop, somebody spotted the homeless guy, Gary Eagleton—Eagle—drunk out of his mind and wearing a brand-new pair of boots from the Duluth Outdoor Company."

"What's your take on that?" Durkin asked.

"Eagle had money to buy booze. Where did he get it? If he'd stolen the boots, the store personnel would have spotted it, and they didn't. So somebody *gave* him the boots after the incident. That tells me there's a third party in the mix that we haven't identified yet. I'd like to know who it was."

Durkin thought about it. "I don't see much of a mystery here. Eagle teams up with somebody to rob the store. He goes up into the loft and fakes a breakdown, and while the staff is distracted, his partner walks out with a bunch of merchandise. Eagle gets his share, fences some of it for drinking money, and keeps the boots for himself."

"Yes, I thought the same thing," Serena said. "Except the word on the street is that Eagle avoids Canal Park, doesn't steal, and keeps to himself. None of that fits with him being part of a burglary scheme."

"An alkie who needs a fix will do just about anything to get his hands on booze," Durkin pointed out.

Serena knew that was true. She'd fought her own battle with vodka long ago and lost. In her twenties, in Las Vegas, drinking had almost killed her. Since then, she'd spent seventeen years on the wagon. The closest she'd come to a drink was the day two years ago when she'd found out about Jonny and Maggie's affair.

"Maybe so, but I'd still like to know exactly what happened," Serena said. "I'm canvassing local fences to see if anybody moved merchandise from the shop last week. I'd also like to talk to Eagle about who got him to go into that store."

Durkin shrugged. "Do what you need to do, but it still sounds to me like you're chasing zebras."

Serena smiled. A "zebra" was a wild or overly complicated explanation for a simple crime. Some cops, when they heard hoofbeats, looked for zebras instead of horses. "It wouldn't be the first time," she admitted.

"Since you're looking into the shop, I have another question for you," Durkin went on. "How well do you know Drew and Krista Olson?"

"Pretty well. They adopted Cat's baby." She could hear an undercurrent of suspicion in Durkin's voice. "Why? What is this about?"

"I did some research on the businesses affected by the blast," Durkin replied. "The Olsons are having a difficult stretch. The shop fell behind on a lot of its bills this spring."

"It's retail," Serena said, "and we didn't have much of a spring. The weather kept a lot of tourists away."

"Yes, but I found something strange. The Olsons purchased a terrorism rider on their commercial insurance policy last year. If this incident is certified as a terrorist attack, they're fully covered."

Serena shrugged. "So they were smart."

"Maybe, but you have to wonder why a struggling business in a small city like Duluth would pay extra for that kind of protection," Durkin went on. "It's almost like they knew something was going to happen."

* * *

"When did you hear the shot?" Stride asked.

He examined the broken window and turned around to find the matching hole in the bedroom ceiling where the bullet was lodged. The sharp angle suggested that the shooter had been across the street from the Muslim Student Center house.

Haq Al-Masri checked his watch. "An hour ago. Just after dark. We heard glass breaking and then the noise of a car speeding away. By the time I got outside, the car was gone. I think it headed west, but that's all I can tell you."

"No one was hurt?" Stride asked.

"Fortunately, we were all downstairs when it happened. If someone had been in this bedroom, they could have been killed."

"I'm sorry. I'm glad your students are all okay."

"They're not okay, Jonathan. They're scared and angry. Dawn Basch tweeted a photo of this house, and we immediately became a target for her followers."

"I'll try to position a squad car on the street outside the house for a few hours," Stride said. "That should dissuade anyone else who gets ideas about targeting the place. The challenge is, we're spread thin because of the manhunt."

"Yes, there are always resources to hunt Muslims," Haq replied acidly, "but when vigilantes shoot at *us*, the police are nowhere to be found."

Stride's eyes were dark in the bedroom. "I lost a man last night. Try to remember that."

"I do. And I'm sorry."

"Let's go downstairs," Stride suggested.

He took the narrow staircase to the main floor of the student house, with Haq close behind him. A cluster of young men sat in a circle on the living room floor, far from the windows. The room was lit only by candles, which left their faces in shadow. He could see suspicion and mistrust when they looked at him, as if he was an enemy. He went through the screen door onto the porch and then onto the grass near College Street. Haq followed.

"Can you arrest Basch?" Haq asked.

"She hasn't committed a crime," Stride replied.

"No crime? She's out there encouraging vigilantes to act against Muslims. She knows exactly what she's doing. And the result is a bullet through our window."

"Haq, I wish there was more I could do, but she hasn't even come close to crossing a legal line. It's hard enough getting a stalker who sends actual threats of violence behind bars. Basch calling Muslims radicals in her tweets is protected speech. I can't stop her."

"And you wonder why we get frustrated," Haq said. "Where are *our* Constitutional protections?"

"We'll do everything we can, but you should tell your community to be cautious. The city is hot. Everyone's on edge. People lost friends and family, and they're angry."

"We want justice as much as you do, but shooting at our windows isn't justice. Hounding Khan Rashid isn't justice. This is a lynching of an innocent man and of an entire people."

"Do you still think Khan is innocent?" Stride asked. "He shot a police officer."

"I'm sorry, no, I don't believe that. There's some other explanation. Khan doesn't even own a gun."

"Witnesses saw him with one," Stride said.

"Then the witnesses are wrong."

Stride sighed and shoved his hands into his pockets. "Where is he, Haq? Where's Khan hiding?"

"I don't know. That's the truth."

"Would you tell me if you knew?" Stride asked.

"Honestly? I'm not sure. It's not you that I don't trust, Jonathan. It's all the others. I'm afraid of what they'll do to him."

"Then help me arrange a peaceful surrender," Stride said.

Haq hesitated. "I'm trying do that."

"So you do know where he is."

"No, but I've reached out to a lawyer, and we're trying to work out a plan and find a way to get a message to Khan. There has to be a way to do this without bloodshed and to make sure his rights are protected."

"That's what I want, too," Stride said.

"Forgive me for saying that that doesn't count for much right now," Haq replied.

"What about Ahdia Rashid? And her son? Where are they?"

"Safe," Haq said.

"If you know their location, you should tell me. Wherever they are, they'll be safer in protective custody."

"Right now, I think it's better to keep them hidden. They know nothing about any of this, Jonathan. All they want is to get their lives back. Ahdia is no radical, and neither is Khan. They are decent, hard-working, religious Americans."

"What about Malik Noon?" Stride asked.

"Khan is not Malik."

"Do you know where Malik is?"

"No."

"Would Khan turn to him for help?"

"Maybe. If he's desperate, he might turn to a friend."

"Don't you see how this looks, Haq?" Stride asked. "Malik is a radical, but Khan isn't, except now they may be together. I can't take claims of innocence at face value, not with a dead cop in that cemetery. The FBI already thinks I'm naïve to give Khan the slightest benefit of the doubt."

Haq grabbed Stride's arm. "I know you're making a leap of faith to trust me. I promise you, if I find Malik, I will tell you. And I'm doing everything in my power to arrange for Khan to turn himself in peacefully. When he does, and you talk to him, you'll see that I'm right. I don't know what happened in that cemetery, but it's not what you think."

"I have to go," Stride said. "I'll get an officer to park in front of the house. Until then, stay away from the windows."

"It's not just this place," Haq replied. "Basch has been going all over the city with her 'radicalduluth' hashtag. She posted a picture in front of our mosque. She posted at a Muslim-owned bakery. She posted in front of a house owned by an Indian doctor. Is there really *nothing* you can do to stop this?"

"I wish there was," Stride said, "but she's within her rights."

Haq exhaled in disgust. "People in our community are on guard, but we can't be everywhere all night, Jonathan. And yes, I know, you're spread thin."

"Get me a list of the places she's tagged," Stride told him. "I'll do what I can."

Haq slid his phone from his back pocket. Immediately, he went to Twitter and ran a hashtag search and scrolled through a series of posts from Basch and her followers. "Look, she's already posted three more photos in the past hour. And do you see what people are saying in their comments? These are *threats*. What more does it take to show incitement?"

"Get me the list," Stride said again. "I'll make sure we do drive-bys at all the locations throughout the night."

Haq didn't answer. He stared at the screen on his phone. His face bloomed with fear.

"What is it?" Stride asked him.

"She just posted another photo," Haq murmured.

"Where?"

"A gallery in Woodland. The owner is a Muslim artist. She's a friend of mine. Jonathan, we have to get over there right now."

"Why?" Stride asked.

Then he read Haq's face, and he knew the answer already. "That's where you're hiding Ahdia and her son."

30

Ahdia huddled with Pak in a corner of the gallery attic, near the two small windows that looked out on Woodland Avenue. Stifling air gathered in the tiny loft, making them both sweat. The artist, Goleen, did much of her work up here, so the room had a faint chemical smell of paint and turpentine. Her huge, twisted bronzes of Arabic letters, mounted on pedestals, were lined up like a parade against one wall. In the gloomy darkness, the sculptures looked like monsters, and Pak was afraid of them.

When cars passed outside, their headlights lit up a spiderweb on the dusty old windows, which were painted shut and divided into chambers like prison bars. Ahdia could see a large black spider gliding along the web's sticky surface, laying a trap for the moths and gnats that sought out the light. It made her shiver. Pak was afraid of monsters, but Ahdia was afraid of spiders.

"Where is Papa?" Pak asked in a loud voice.

Ahdia's eyes shot to the staircase that led to the main floor of the gallery, which was housed in a brick building no larger than an old one-room schoolhouse. She was sure they were alone. Goleen had gone home hours ago. Even so, Haq had said to take no chances of being found out.

She put a finger gently on her son's lips and smiled at him. "Softly now. We must be very quiet."

"I miss Papa," Pak whispered.

"I know. So do I. He will be with us very soon."

"Will you sing me a song?" the boy asked.

"Oh, Pak, I don't know—"

"Please," he urged her. "The song about the crow, okay?"

Ahdia could never say no to him. She rustled his hair and put her lips near his ear and breathed the song to him, barely aloud, in Urdu. It was a fable about a clever, thirsty crow who found water in the base of an urn and added stones until the water rose high enough for him to dip in his beak. She could remember her mother singing the same song to her in a warm, noisy bedroom in Karachi; it was one of her earliest memories.

When she was done, Pak made her sing it again. The music relaxed both of them.

Holding her son always made her feel blessed. He was her everything. She knew physical love for Khan, but the love of a husband and wife made her feel selfish, because it was about her own happiness. Her love for Pak was something that tiptoed into the deepest parts of her soul, and it was not about happiness; it was about fierce, selfless devotion.

"Mama, I'm thirsty," Pak murmured.

"Like the crow?" she replied, smiling.

"Yes."

"Shall I look for pebbles to make the water rise?"

Pak giggled.

"Okay, stay here, and I'll see if there is any water downstairs," she told him quietly.

"What about the monsters?" he asked, pointing at the sculptures.

"Don't worry about them. The crow will keep you safe."

Ahdia crossed the attic floor, which was messy with old drop cloths that bore the remnants of Goleen's work. She found the wooden stairs in the pitch-blackness, and she took them one at a time, blindly, wincing at the loud creak of every loose floorboard. She reached the gallery, where the air was cooler. Tall, rectangular windows broke up the walls on three sides, letting in light from the street. She saw more sculptures, like those in the attic. Wall hangings as intricate as a kaleidoscope. Hand-painted pottery. Jewelry made from colored beach stones. She wished she had a talent like Goleen, to create something beautiful out of nothing, but her own mind worked like a mathematician's, full of numbers and computer formulas.

At the back of the gallery was a small office, with a desk, a bathroom, and a half-size refrigerator. Goleen had told her she was welcome to anything in it. Ahdia found two small bottles of water. She drank one herself, realizing she was thirsty from the dry, dusty space and the salty sandwiches Haq had smuggled to them earlier in the day. She clutched the other bottle in her hand as she returned to the gallery.

Through the tall windows, Ahdia saw the twin eyes of headlights, and she felt exposed. A large vehicle pulled into the dirt driveway beside the building, and she heard the crunch of its tires on loose rock. She threw herself to the floor and held her breath. The gallery itself was elevated six feet above street level, so she was higher than the truck that had passed below her. Its lights disappeared into a parking lot in back that was sheltered by trees and led to a small side street near the fringe of Hartley Park. She no longer heard its engine.

Maybe it was gone.

Ahdia flew across the gallery. She took quick steps back up to the attic, not caring about the shrieking of the wood under her feet. With almost no light to guide her, she collided with one of Goleen's heavy sculptures and caught it just as it fell to the floor. She rested it at her feet, and then she made her way to the far corner where Pak was waiting for her. She sat down and gathered him up in her arms.

"Mama, I'm still thirsty," he said loudly.

"Shhh. Okay."

She unscrewed the cap on the bottle and handed it to him. As he drank, the plastic crinkled as the air was sucked away. She tensed, wanting him to finish quickly. When he was done and wiped his mouth, he exhaled with a sigh of satisfaction that seemed to shake the building.

Ahdia took the bottle away. "Be very, very quiet now."

He opened his mouth to speak, but she shook her head, and he could see in her stern eyes that she was serious. Pak buried his face in her chest. They held on to each other, dead still. The only movement in the room was the black spider, scuttling about the strands of its web, its legs flicking like knitting needles. She had a feeling that the spider was a sign of bad things to come.

Below her, muffled, she heard the shattering of glass.

Moments later, the wooden floor of the gallery groaned. Someone was downstairs.

* * *

Travis had parked the van where it couldn't be seen from the street.

He checked the photo on Twitter, because he didn't want to make a mistake. When he compared the brick building in front of him to the picture that Dawn Basch had posted, he could see that he was in the right place.

His original plan had been to burn Khan Rashid's house to the ground. He'd filled up half a dozen gasoline tanks from Wade's garage by stopping at four different gas stations around the city. He'd headed for the dead-end street where Rashid lived, but when he got there, he found the house watched by two police cruisers. Rather than let himself and his truck be seen, he'd backed away into the side street, made a U-turn, and headed to Woodland Avenue.

He needed a different target. A new focus for his rage and revenge, something that would send a message. He'd found it online. Dawn Basch had tweeted a series of photos with the hashtag 'radicalduluth,' and one of the photos showed a Muslim-owned gallery barely two miles away.

Good.

He'd start there.

Travis made sure he was alone as he got out of the van. The night air was damp. He heard frogs in the woods like a deafening chorus. The back door of the brick gallery was immediately in front of him. He had to decide. Stay or go. Fight or run. It had sounded so easy when he was standing in Wade's garage, but now he was actually here.

You cross a line, and you can't go back.

Travis climbed steps to the back door of the gallery. He tried the knob; it was locked. He peered through the window, but it was dark inside, and he couldn't see anything. He checked his surroundings again and then peeled off his shirt and wrapped it around his fist and forearm. With one swift punch, he broke through the glass beside the door.

He reached through the window frame, undid the dead bolt, and let himself inside.

The floor shifted under his heavy feet as he followed the corridor. He listened, but no one moved. No one shouted. No one came running. The gallery was empty. He studied the odd artwork, which looked foreign, as if this were some desert kingdom, not Duluth, not America. Looking at it reminded him of why he was there. His fists clenched. He'd been angry in his life, but he'd never felt soul-sucking hatred before, thinking about what these people had done to Joni and Shelly.

Travis returned to the van and popped the back doors. He reached in and grabbed three of the red gasoline tanks and carried them into the gallery. He put one tank down and brought the other two to the front door that faced Woodland Avenue. There was no traffic outside; the night was quiet. He unscrewed the caps and walked back and forth between the walls, pouring down trails of gasoline. He coated everything. The floor. The art. The window ledges. Gasoline splashed onto his skin and clothes. Soon the shut-in space had a choking smell of gas that rose into his head and made him dizzy. His eyes teared.

When he emptied those two tanks, he retrieved the other and continued his work. He moved fast, and he moved silently, with no sound except his labored breathing.

Then he stopped.

Above him, he heard a sharp crack in the ceiling, as if someone had taken a step. He looked up, and he waited. The sound didn't recur. He went to the wooden staircase and peered up into the dark shadows.

He saw no one, and when he listened again, he heard nothing but the distant song of the frogs outside.

His mind was playing tricks on him. He was alone.

Travis saw a car pass on Woodland Avenue, and it reminded him how exposed he was. He poured gasoline on the steps, and it dripped onto his shoes. By now, the third tank was nearly empty, too. He backed toward the rear door, making a ribbon of gasoline that stretched along the hallway, down the outside steps, and through the dirt, grass, and leaves. Near the van, he stopped. He screwed the cap onto the tank, put it in the back, and shut the door. He was having trouble catching his breath, partly because of the fumes, partly because of his fear.

He could still drive away. He didn't have to light the match.

But he owed it to Joni, to Shelly, to Wade, and to God to do what he'd come here for.

Travis went back to the van and started the engine. Once the fire started, all he had to do was speed forward onto the side street and disappear. From his pocket, he slid out a silver Zippo lighter. It had been a birthday gift from Joni. His skin smelled of gasoline, and his shoes were soaked in it, and he didn't want to set himself on fire. He opened the driver's door, with the engine still running, and climbed out. The wind was at his back, blowing toward the gallery. That was good. He reached inside and grabbed an empty Budweiser can that had been clanging around the van for weeks. He rolled up a take-out menu from a local Chinese restaurant and shoved it into the hole of the can, leaving six inches of paper sticking out at the top.

Travis popped the top of the lighter. All he needed to do was spin the wheel. He wondered what kind of fire he would get and how fast the flames would spread.

You cross a line.

You can't go back.

The lighter spat up a tiny flame. With his arm extended, he held the flame to the take-out menu and let it curl into fire and ash. Like a softball pitcher, he made an underhanded toss, hurling the burning can toward the ribbon of gasoline.

It fell short. And then it rolled.

Fire touched gas, and the trail burst into a wall of flame that roared like a racecar across the parking lot, up the stairs, and into the gallery.

Travis waited.

Tick-tock, tick-tock.

The building exploded.

31

Khan and Malik waited until dark before they slipped out of the house. Malik went first. He crouched and dashed across the lawn into the empty street. With his body barely lit by the gleam of stars, he beckoned for Khan to follow. Side by side, they pushed through dandelion weeds and a fringe of dense trees onto the rolling fairway of the Ridgeview Country Club. The grass was lush like a fur rug under their feet. Individual pines dotted the slope. A breath of wind whispered in the branches.

"Stay close to the trees, and stay quiet," Malik whispered. "There could be patrols out here."

Malik led the way. They were both dressed in dark clothes. With the woods beside them, they were invisible. The golf course dipped and rose as they headed south. He saw the silhouette of the clubhouse and its flags on the hill above them, and then they dropped into a valley, following a cart path that took them past manicured greens and sand traps.

All Khan could think about with each footfall in the wet grass was Ahdia and Pak. His wife and son were not even two miles away—less than an hour's walk through the golf course and the trails of Hartley Park. Then they would all be together again. In each other's arms.

Crying. Smiling. The past day of loneliness in the house on Redwing Street had been the longest of his life, but it would be over soon. Every nightmare ended at dawn.

He tried *not* to think about Malik and his suicide vest and his awful plan. It was impossible to reconcile the image of his best friend with that of a man who would do something like that. For now, Malik was leading him to his family, and that was all that mattered. Khan didn't know what to do next, but soon he would be with Ahdia again, and she would make all the choices seem easy. His heart felt so full, he found it hard to breathe.

If he listened, he thought he could hear Ahdia, her voice like a musical instrument. "*Come to me.*"

And Pak, too. "*Papa, where are you? It is time to pray.*"

I am here, my boy. I am on my way.

In front of him, Malik held up a hand. "Stop."

"What is it?" Khan asked.

"Someone is out there," Malik murmured. "Take cover."

Together, they ducked into a stand of trees and squatted behind the thickest trunk. Khan squinted into the darkness. Malik was right. A dark shape moved on the fairway under the stars, no more than fifty yards away. It wasn't human. It was a doe, putting its head down to feed on the grass.

"It's just a deer," Khan said. He was impatient.

He began to stand up, but Malik stopped him. "Wait."

Much closer, almost close enough to reach out and touch, Khan heard a stealthy rustle in the brush, accompanied by a low, violent growl. The sound made him freeze. He could see an animal now, breaking cover. It was a wolf, its body low to the ground, slinking from the rough to the fairway. Heading for the doe.

"Another," Malik whispered, pointing.

Khan followed Malik's hand and saw the silhouette of a second wolf, approaching at an angle. The two hunted together.

"We should do something," Khan said.

"Do what? It's nature. Either the deer lives or the deer dies."

"We can shout."

"And bring the wolves to us? Or the police? Come on, quickly, let's go. Silent running."

Khan eyed the wolves, but they were focused on the deer, not on the scent of men. He followed Malik, and soon the animals became part of the night, indistinguishable behind them. He tried not to listen for the sound of the hunt and the capture. It might be nature, but he couldn't abide the death of innocents. He hoped the doe was able to escape.

Moments later, they reached the end of the golf course and crossed a gurgling creek onto the wooded land of the Hartley Nature Center. The forest was dense. A soggy trail barely a foot wide wound into the trees. With a flashlight Malik illuminated the standing water of a swamp.

Khan was lost, but Malik walked with confidence. Mosquitoes feasted on their skin, and gnats flew up into the moist part of Khan's nose. The swampland got deeper, and a floating boardwalk carried them to the next trail, making their boots sound like the clip-clop of horses on the planks. Where two trails intersected, Malik stopped to get his bearings, but then he led them onto a new trail with his light. The park felt claustrophobic at night, with the trees crowding around them and grabbing at their arms like the street urchins in Lahore. Khan couldn't see anything except the flashlight beam on the ground.

Malik stopped again, but this time, there was no cross-trail. He swung his flashlight as if looking for something, and finally, his light stopped on a white handkerchief tied to a tree branch that dangled over the path. His friend looked back with a dark smile.

"The going gets tough from here."

"It wasn't tough before?" Khan asked.

Malik pushed directly into the thick trees. Their boots splashed into several inches of water. Sharp branches clawed their faces. The bugs were even more voracious here. The two of them fought their way forward through a cage made of tree branches, and what was probably no more than a tenth of a mile felt longer and harder than everything they'd hiked before. They made noise. Too much noise. But it couldn't be helped.

Finally, with a jolt, they burst out of the woods onto a paved residential street. It was the intersection of Harvard Avenue and Oxford Street. Malik gave him a thumbs-up and pointed down Oxford, which was lined with trees and telephone wires.

"We're only three blocks from Woodland Avenue. The gallery's there."

Khan found it almost impossible not to run, knowing that Ahdia and Pak were so close. Even so, they went more slowly, because the risk was greatest here. Houses and driveways appeared among the trees. Some had lights on inside. After one more block, the trees gave way to an open neighborhood where houses were packed closely together. He saw a school building on a slope to their right. Streetlights lit them up. He was conscious that they were two Muslim men, wanted by the police.

"It's not far now," Malik said.

Khan felt his adrenaline surge. He was so close. Where he was now, the world was chaos and violence and confusion, but two blocks away, in the loft of a tiny gallery, was happiness. He could feel the pieces of his life come together again. He walked faster and faster, because he needed to escape the guns and the bugs and the wolves.

And yet he felt something else, too.

A dark cloud. A sense of unimaginable dread.

Something was wrong. He had no idea how he knew, but something was very wrong. He felt it. The closer he got to Woodland Avenue, the more he could hardly contain himself from sprinting. It was as if angels were falling from the sky and beating their wings in despair. As if disaster were on the wind. They passed house after house and finally crested the shallow hill, and when he saw the stop sign below him, he said, "Malik, run."

"What? Why?"

"Don't you smell it?"

Malik lifted his nose to the air, and his face fell, and without a word, they both ran. Khan had never run faster. No sprinter would have passed him. But none of it mattered; none of it chased away Iblis. Shaitaan. Satan. The explosion rocked the ground. It lifted him off his feet; it threw him down. He was dazed and terrified. He got up and ran again, and already he could feel the heat. When he turned into the cracked asphalt drive that led to the rear of the gallery, he had to dive away to avoid a van that nearly ran him over. He didn't see what it looked like. He didn't see who drove it. It was there and gone, and all that was left was the hell in front of him.

Fire roared like a beast from every window. Smoke clouded the air, poisonous and black. Glass covered the ground like diamonds.

Khan screamed from the bottom of his soul.

"Ahdia! Pak!"

He ran for the gallery. Malik tried to grab him and hold him, but he shook himself free and ran. Nothing would stop him. He would walk through fire. He would breathe smoke. He would suffer any pain to reach them and free them and save them. His family.

His wife. His child.

But the fire was stronger. Satan was stronger. He charged in, and the flames drove him back. Again and again. The ground was on fire. The trees were on fire. The conflagration sucked away his breath. He fought to the front of the building, hoping to see an open window, hoping to find his wife and son safely on the street, hoping to see them ready to jump into his arms.

No.

Every window was smoke.

Every window was fire.

"Khan!" Malik shouted.

Tears poured down Khan's face. Tears filled his soul. He wailed like a baby.

"Khan!" Malik called again, trying to shout down the roar of the fire.

Sirens screamed, drawing close, but not soon enough, not fast enough. They were too late.

"Khan, we have to go, there's nothing you can do."

Khan tried to call their names again, but his mouth and tongue were black and dry and unable to form a word. The tears dried on his face, like burns. He felt Malik pulling him, yanking him back toward the park. He squeezed both hands against his skull, as if he could crush the bone and pull out his brain and destroy life and memory and breath and consciousness. He wanted to curl up and die. He wanted to run into the fire and let it consume him. If he could, he would have become nothing but black ash floating in the air.

"Khan," Malik said again.

He could barely walk, so Malik dragged him like a child. Even when they were blocks away, he could still hear the guttural throb of the fire. The boastful, evil, murderous fire. It followed him back into the woods, and he knew it would never be gone from his memory.

32

The fire was out, but the smell of smoke clung to Stride, a stench that couldn't be washed off. Black soot streaked his skin. He leaned against the door of his Expedition and felt every one of his fifty years. Around him, Woodland Avenue was closed and taped off in both directions. Media crowded the perimeter, looking for answers. Special Agent Maloney had already spoken to them; so had the mayor and the police chief. They'd said what they had to say—words of outrage and comfort, appeals for calm, promises of justice. Stride knew that words didn't change a thing.

Haq Al-Masri stood next to him. His body had the tight coil of a rattlesnake. His gaze never left the scorched remains of the gallery.

"This is what happens," Haq said, hissing out the words. "Politicians prattle about free speech, and in the real world, people die. Every one of us in our community knew this was coming. Every one of us knew something like this would happen sooner or later. You can't have this kind of vicious hatred spread around without someone paying the price."

Stride had nothing to say.

"I want that woman arrested for murder!" Haq went on. "She killed them. If she put a gun to their heads, she couldn't have been more responsible. You know that's true."

Stride put a hand on the man's shoulder. He didn't want an argument about justice, especially when he knew there was no likelihood of Dawn Basch ever being prosecuted for murder. "Haq, I feel the pain of this every bit as much as you do. I'm devastated."

Haq was in no mood to listen. "Basch already spoke to the press. Did you hear her? Expressing sadness at the loss of life? That lying hypocrite. She got exactly what she wanted. And her followers! Have you seen the things they've been posting? Calling Ahdia a terrorist. Saying she got what she deserved. Saying the death of *a child* takes a future terrorist from the world. It is unbelievable. You wonder where violence comes from? You wonder where radicals come from?"

"I don't defend extremists of any kind," Stride said.

"I know you believe that, Jonathan, but you're the one protecting Dawn Basch. You have to live with that, and I don't know how you can."

Stride wanted to fire back, but he didn't. He was angry, but he held himself in check, because blind anger was the root of everything that had gone wrong. He wanted to tell Haq that if he'd trusted Stride, there would have been no loss of life. If he'd brought Ahdia to him, instead of hiding her away, she and her child would still be alive. It didn't matter. He found it hard to blame Haq for his choice, because trust was in short supply.

"Where is Khan?" Stride asked.

"I have no idea."

"Haq, I want him *safe*. If he reaches out to you, you need to tell me. No one else. Just me. I'll make sure nothing happens to him."

Haq shook his head. "No. I'm sorry, Jonathan, no. We are done. We are over. No more information. No more secrets. I will not betray my community. You stay in your world, and we stay in ours."

"That's not how it works," Stride said.

"It is now."

Haq stalked away toward the crowd of reporters. Seeing him come, they shouted questions and lit him up with klieg lights. Stride could hear Haq begin to unleash his bitterness in front of the press, and he walked away, rather than hear the next volley of hatred. Tit for tat. It never ended.

Maggie waited for him in the middle of the street. "You okay?"

Stride wanted to say no. No, he was not okay. He'd lived too long and worked too hard to accept the notion that his city was going backward.

"I was thinking about something Scott Lyons told me when he was the chief," he replied. "He said he became a cop to save the world, and it took him a long time to realize that the world had no interest in being saved."

Maggie blew the bangs out of her face, which was dirty with ash, like his. "We're just Dutch boys, boss. Fingers in the dike."

Stride knew she was right. It was late, and there was nothing more he could do there. He wanted to go home; he wanted to watch Cat sleep; he wanted to get into bed with Serena and talk to her, because he knew he'd never sleep himself. This was a night that made him glad he was married.

"Remember I told you about that case twenty years ago when I was filling in as interim chief in that small town for the summer?" Stride asked.

"The missing boy? Joshua?"

"That's the one. He was out walking with his brother on a dirt road. Brother hears a car while he's in the woods, and when he comes back, Joshua's gone. I figured it was all a misunderstanding and Joshua would be back home by nightfall. I mean, a stranger kidnapping in the middle of nowhere? What were the odds of that? But Joshua never came home. I spent the whole summer looking for him, and I swore I wouldn't leave that town until we solved the case. But summer ended, and we didn't find him. Twenty years later, his parents still don't know what happened to their boy. I didn't deliver. I didn't do what I'd promised to do."

Maggie was quiet. Then she said, "What's your point, boss?"

"The day I left that town at the end of the summer was the only time in my life I thought about quitting the job," Stride said. "Until now."

"It's a bad day. There are always bad days."

"Yeah. I know."

"Go home, boss."

Stride nodded wearily. He headed for his Expedition, but then he backtracked. "I want you all over this one, Mags," he told her. "Find out who did this."

TUESDAY

33

Cat knew that Curt Dickes would call her, not Serena, when he found out where Eagle was hiding. And he did.

She spent the morning spying on Drew Olson and her baby from the parking lot behind the elementary school basketball court. She watched them through binoculars as she sat on the hood of her beat-up Civic. Even from far away, Cat could see a lot of herself in her son. There was something about his smile that made her think she was looking in a mirror. His eyes were her eyes. Even the shape of his ears, with the sharp little edges like wing tips, reminded her of photos she'd seen of herself as a baby.

Yes, Michael was her son. He had a stable home, which was more than she could have given him herself. He had a father and mother. He had everything he needed in life. It should have made her proud, but it made her feel lonely.

She put down the binoculars. She didn't want to watch anymore.

It was summer, and summer made her restless. When she was in school, she had things to do. She was good at her classes, and Serena watched her like a hawk to make sure she got her homework done. Now she had nothing constructive to do until September. Serena kept lining up tutoring sessions and volunteer work for her, but some days

Cat had an itch to do bad things. An itch to steal or drink or smoke or run away to the Graffiti Graveyard. That was who she really was. There was no point in trying to change.

"Cat?"

Her head flew up. Drew Olson, holding Michael, stood on the edge of the school basketball court, no more than twenty yards away. He'd spotted her from the backyard of his house.

"Oh, damn," she murmured, sliding off the hood and throwing open the driver's door.

"Cat, wait!" he called.

Cat didn't listen. She sped off in the opposite direction, casting a glance in the rearview mirror to see father and son behind her. Drew waved at her to come back, and part of her wanted to turn the car around, but she kept driving. The house disappeared in her mirror. She couldn't see them anymore, and she was glad they couldn't see her. Her face felt hot from embarrassment.

As she turned on Grand Avenue, her phone began to ring. She wondered if it was Drew calling her, but when she answered it, she heard the all-too-familiar voice of Curt Dickes.

"Hey, babycakes!"

Cat pulled to the curb. She knew she should hang up. Tell Curt to call Serena and put down the phone. But talking to Curt made her feel as if she was back in her old world, and that was where she felt comfortable. Besides, she liked Curt. He always had crazy ideas, but he was funny and knew how to make her laugh.

"Hey," she said to him.

"You guys still looking for Eagle?" he asked.

"Yes. Did you hear something? Do you know where he is?"

"Maybe." His voice teased her.

"Come on, what does that mean?"

"I mean, maybe I can help you, and maybe you can help me."

Cat squirmed in her seat. "Help you how? What are you talking about?"

"Well, here's the thing. Everybody's bored. The whole city is shut down because of the bombing. One of my customers called—guy over on Congdon Park Drive—and he's trying to set up a party for tonight. High-class, lots of champagne, the works. He said he'd pay two hundred bucks to every pretty girl who shows."

"Yeah, and what do you get?"

"A tiny finder's fee. The big money goes to the girls."

"No, thanks."

"It's a party! That's all!"

"That's all? They're not expecting any action?"

"Fun, friendly, cute, nothing else. I swear on my five sisters. Somebody gets fresh, you can slap 'em."

Cat chewed a fingernail and debated with herself. She'd been down this road with Curt before. She'd been at one of his parties on the *Charles Frederick* and knew what the men expected. It was more than fun and friendly. Even so, two hundred bucks was a lot of money. And she had an itch.

"I don't know."

"Come on, Cat, it's summer in the city!"

"I'll think about it. Where's Eagle?"

"You'll think about it? Kitty Cat, we're talking hot tubs and a DJ and probably lobster and shit. I'll pick you up at ten o'clock, okay? Sneak out your window, meet me at Lafayette Park."

Cat hated herself for being weak, but she hadn't snuck a drink in weeks. And she liked lobster. And it was cool having men hang on her, which they always did. And Curt was right; it was summertime.

"I want the cash in advance," she said.

"It's in your purse before we walk in the door."

"You make it clear, I'm dressing up the party, and that's *all*. I'm not screwing anybody, Curt, you hear me? I don't do that anymore. Any guy sticks a hand up my dress, and my knee is in his balls."

"Understood. You're the best."

"Where's Eagle?"

"I don't know," he said.

"Aw, Curt, you're messing with me," Cat snapped.

"I don't know where he is, but I know where he *was*. As of last Friday. Guy saw him hiking along the railroad tracks near Becks Road."

"Last Friday?" Cat complained. "That was four days ago. He could be anywhere by now. That doesn't tell me anything."

"It's more than you had before," Curt pointed out.

"Forget the party."

"Oh, don't be like that. You've got the whole day to check out the tracks, and then you can have fun and make some money tonight."

Cat sighed. "Where exactly did this guy see Eagle?"

"Maybe half a mile from I-35. He was heading north."

She thought about the location. One advantage of her time on the street was that she knew areas around Duluth that most people didn't. The parks. The railroad tracks. The abandoned buildings. If she knew them, Eagle knew them, too. And one of the creepiest places in the area was within spitting distance of Becks Road and I-35.

"That's near the old Nopeming Sanatorium," Cat said. "Didn't you say that Eagle likes to hang out there sometimes?"

"I did."

"So maybe he was heading there."

"Maybe so, Kitty Cat. Be careful if you sneak into the ruins, though. They say the place is haunted from all the TB patients who died there. Don't let the ghosts get you."

* * *

"So Cat was here?" Serena asked Drew Olson.

"Yes. She was watching us from the school. I tried to get her to come over, but as soon as she realized I'd seen her, she took off."

Serena studied the empty basketball court on the other side of the alley. "It's not the first time. She told me she was here on Sunday, too. She keeps coming back, so maybe that's a good thing."

"Well, I hope I didn't scare her off," Drew said.

"Not likely. Cat's tough. It's not about being afraid with her."

Drew bounced Michael in his arms. Serena found it hard to take her eyes off the baby whenever she was near him. This time, though, she didn't make any effort to hold him.

"So what's up?" Drew asked. "Is there more news? That was a terrible thing last night about the fire in Woodland. Even if that man

Rashid is guilty, it's horrific to lose a mother and child like that. Krista was in tears over it."

"Yes, it's awful." Serena hesitated. "Listen, Drew, I need to ask you something."

"Sure."

"Why did you and Krista take out a terrorism rider on your commercial policy last year?"

Drew's eyes widened. His face clouded over. He put Michael into a stroller on the back lawn, and then he folded his arms tightly together. "Do you honestly think—"

"I don't think anything, Drew. I have to ask. It raised a red flag with the FBI. Your business was having trouble, but even so, you bought extra insurance to cover an event that most people would consider pretty unlikely around here."

"And yet look where we are," Drew said.

"Yes. That's what makes the FBI curious."

Drew's face had an angry cast, but then the anger faded. He sighed. "Look, I know you're just doing your job. I guess I'm not surprised that someone would ask the question. The fact is, the rider wasn't particularly expensive for us. Apparently, the insurers didn't think a terrorism event here was very likely, either."

"Then why do it?" she asked.

"Isn't it obvious? We did it because of Boston. Our shop is at the finish line of a major marathon, Serena. After Boston, we realized that if something terrible did come to Duluth, it might well happen at our front door. I'm not going to apologize for taking precautions. Everybody did. There are a lot more police at the marathon now for the very same reason."

"You're right," Serena said.

Drew put a hand on her shoulder. "Please tell the FBI that Krista and I had absolutely nothing to do with what happened."

"I will."

He retrieved Michael from the stroller, as if the boy could soothe him. He didn't say anything else. Serena understood. Trust was a casualty of every crime, but Duluth was still a small town, which made it worse. It was hard to think that a friend believed you were capable of something evil.

"I have to go, Drew," she said. "Take care of yourself."

She wondered if she'd crossed a line with him and whether she would ever be invited back. Drew must have realized what she was thinking. "You're always welcome here, Serena. And Cat, too, of course."

"Thanks."

As she walked away, Drew called, "Did you find that man you were looking for? The homeless man who was in our shop?"

Serena turned and shook her head. "No, we're still looking."

"And do you think he's important?" Drew asked. "Do you think he knows something about the bombing?"

"Yes," she replied. "I do."

34

Maggie took intermittent bites of a Quarter Pounder as she scrolled through Twitter on the MacBook balanced on her lap. Beside her, Max Guppo feasted on a Coney Island chili cheese dog. She had a rule about not staying in enclosed spaces with Guppo, and she opened all the windows in her Avalanche as a precaution. The barrel-shaped sergeant had a way of poisoning anyplace he inhabited for more than ten minutes with near-lethal quantities of gas.

"Who the hell are these people?" she complained with her mouth full. "I've never seen so many whack-jobs making threats. It would take us a year to run these all down."

"Yeah, Twitter is like walking into a crowded stadium where everyone is screaming obscenities at each other," Guppo replied. "They're big talkers, but the ones to really worry about are the people who don't say anything."

"So you're saying we're chasing our tails here?"

"Pretty much."

Maggie scowled. She knew he was right. Whoever firebombed the gallery on Woodland Avenue had obviously seen the Twitter post from Dawn Basch, but that was a universe of thousands of people, and most of them were hidden behind anonymous accounts. She'd hoped for a clue among the users who'd reacted to the post, but instead, the sheer volume of haters overwhelmed her. It wasn't going to help them find a suspect.

"Uh-oh," Guppo said, lifting up in the passenger seat. "Sorry. Incoming."

"You mean outgoing," Maggie said, opening her door quickly. She jumped down and exited the truck before the memory of the chili cheese dog could waft her way.

She stood in the street and studied the burnt shell of the gallery. A light drizzle fell, tamping down the ash into wet tar. Police and firefighters combed through the wreckage. She had officers going up and down the surrounding streets to interview neighbors. So far, no one had seen anything that would point them toward a suspect.

"What do you think about timing?" Guppo asked, joining her on the street as he fanned his backside with a clipboard. "I figure this guy probably didn't spend more than ninety seconds on site."

"Yeah, it didn't take him long," Maggie agreed.

Ninety seconds sounded right. One and a half minutes. That was how long it had taken to incinerate a mother and son. She understood how Stride felt. There were moments as a cop that made you want to throw it all away.

Maggie thought about the facts they'd already gathered. The fire investigation team had traced the ignition point to the rear of the building. There were ruts in the dirt but not enough to give them tire tracks. The bomber had broken inside, dumped gasoline, set it ablaze, and sped off. If there was forensic evidence in the building, the fire had destroyed most of it.

"What about security cameras up and down Woodland?" she asked.

Guppo shook his head. "Nothing. No help there."

"Sometimes I think it would be easier to work in a city where Big Brother is always watching."

"No, thanks," Guppo said. "I'm staying here."

Maggie crossed to the gallery, where the smell of smoke remained strong. She'd talked to the owner, a woman named Goleen, who'd been numbed by the death and destruction. Goleen had shown her pictures of her art, none of which had survived the fire. Maggie recognized the woman's talent, but the geometric designs and Arabic sculptures reminded her that many Muslims lived in a world apart, with a culture she simply didn't understand. Some walls were hard to climb.

"Mind if I ask you something, Max? Just between you and me?"

"Sure."

"Do you think Dawn Basch is right? Is there some kind of problem with Islam that causes violence?"

Guppo scratched his comb-over. "Wow. I don't know. When it happens over and over, you can't help but think that, right? How could anyone do some of those crazy things without a hole in their heart? The thing is, we live next door to a Somali family who are the sweetest people you're ever going to meet. There's nothing wrong with *their* religion. I think about them whenever I get angry about terrorism."

"Sometimes I feel like the Muslim world has a few centuries of catching up to do when it comes to civilization," Maggie said.

"Yeah, well, so does the guy who did this. Look, I blame the leaders, not the followers. You've got wannabe Hitlers overseas who spread poison and a cult of deluded young people who swallow it."

"I suppose you're right. I know being prejudiced about it just makes it worse. Be honest—do some of the cops around here still have a problem with me being Chinese?"

"If they do, they're smart enough not to say it to me," Guppo replied.

Maggie smiled. No matter how much of the dark side Guppo saw of the world, he retained a sunny outlook on life. He had a wife. He had his daughters. He had a house and a pontoon boat. As far as Guppo was concerned, he couldn't be more blessed. Maggie wished she could segment her life into good and bad the way he did, but, like Stride, she sometimes carried the dark side home with her.

"So we have no witnesses, no cameras, and no evidence," she said.

"Right."

"And the suspect pool is everyone on Twitter."

"Right."

Maggie clucked her tongue in frustration. There had to be a way to narrow it down. Somewhere, somehow, this guy had left them a clue. Standing on the sidewalk, she caught a whiff of gasoline rising from the ashes, and that gave her an idea. "Hey, how much gas did the fire guys think the perp used?"

"Hard to be exact, but several gallons," Guppo said. "Maybe ten or more."

"Most people don't have that much gas hanging around their garage," she said.

"Probably not. What are you thinking?"

"I'm thinking the gallery bombing feels spontaneous, right? Nobody decided to do this days or weeks ago. They came up with the plan after the marathon and probably after Khan Rashid hit the news and Basch tweeted her Muslim-owned hit list."

"Agreed," Guppo said.

"Okay, so odds are this guy bought a lot of gasoline recently."

Guppo saw immediately what she had in mind. "If he was at a gas station, he was on camera. I'll get some uniforms to start gathering up video feeds from every station within five miles of here. We can start working our way backward in the hours before the fire."

"Exactly," Maggie said. "If we're lucky, we'll spot somebody filling up a bunch of gas cans."

* * *

Cat stared through the woods at the ruined Nopeming Sanatorium. The day was quiet around her except for a chorus of birdsong. Rain spat in her face from gray clouds.

She'd been here many times. Never legally. One of Curt's crazy parties had been held here in the dead of a winter night, until the police broke it up. Street people and urban explorers found abandoned buildings irresistible, and Nopeming was notorious. A reality television show about ghost investigators had featured the site on one of their episodes, and ever since, the owners had struggled to keep out trespassers who wanted to sneak inside to prove their courage.

A homeless Ojibwe man had told Cat that Nopeming meant "out in the woods." The facility dated back to the early part of the last century, when it had served as a place for tuberculosis patients to live and die. Years later, it became a nursing home, and then it fell into disrepair, too expensive to tear down, too expensive to rebuild. The owners had dreams of turning it into a charter school, but for now, it was the haunted house of the Northland, hidden behind a fenced road and locked gate.

Cat didn't want to get caught. She'd parked on the frontage road and hiked up the long driveway and then ducked into the woods when the building came into view. She saw no sign of the caretaker today. If a truck was parked outside, you knew to stay away. From the outside, the four-story yellow brick building looked like a sprawling old hotel, and it was only when you looked closely that you could see the broken windows and torn curtains flapping in the breeze.

Cat ran across the wet lawn. She knew how to get in. Several of the upper-floor windows were open to equalize the indoor and out-door temperatures and prevent mold. She found a birch tree leaning toward the building and scrambled up the trunk into the thick of the branches. One branch, just sturdy enough to support her weight, faced an open window, and she scooted along it until the branch bent down and ushered her onto the sill. She slipped nimbly inside one of the old sanatorium bedrooms.

Plaster dust littered the floor, and electrical wires hung from miss-ing ceiling tiles. Remnants of a tattered sheer, flimsy curtain danced in the wind, sagging on a broken rod. Rainwater puddled under her feet. It was a small, warm room, and it creeped her out to think of the many people who had occupied the beds here, dying slowly and horribly.

She made her way to a corridor that stretched the length of the building. Up and down the walls, paint peeled, looking like the white wings of hundreds of gulls. The hallway was a mix of sun and shadow, filled with a minefield of debris. The wooden banisters were covered in dust. It felt humid.

Cat listened but heard no signs of life.

She peered into each empty room as she walked, passing through open fire doors from one end of the building to the other. No one was inside. When she found a stairwell, she climbed to the next floor, crunching dried paint shards with each step.

Upstairs, she called softly, "Eagle?"

And then again: "Eagle? It's Cat."

No one answered, but she squelched a scream as something moved in the ceiling immediately above her. She looked up into a hole where several ceiling tiles were missing, and the bandit face of a raccoon stared back at her. It was huge, hunched up on its back legs, and not scared of her at all. Cat backed away from the animal, turned, and ran. The floor was wet, and she slipped and fell, and a cloud of dust blew into her eyes. Her jeans tore, and something sharp scraped her knee. Getting up, limping, she blinked and wiped her face with one arm. When she could see again, she found herself staring into one of the bedrooms.

There was Eagle.

He lay on top of a purple sleeping bag, facing away from her, with his head on a pillow. His body was stretched out; his feet wore no shoes, just socks that were worn through at the heels. Two empty plastic vodka bottles were tipped on the floor near him, along with an empty bag of Jack Link's beef jerky and an open can of tortilla soup.

"Eagle," Cat called. "Hey, it's Cat. I need to talk to you."

She took a step closer. That was when she noticed the smell. She also noticed that the wall near Eagle's face dripped with a burst of something that looked like pus and snot.

"Eagle?"

She squatted next to him and tugged on his shoulder. His body drooped onto his back.

Cat couldn't stop the scream this time.

Eagle had no face. Someone had shot it away.

35

"Settle down, buddy," Wade Ralston told Travis. "You need to be cool."

The two men stood on the sprawling lawn outside Wade's farmhouse on Five Corners Road. It was raining hard, but Wade wasn't about to let Travis track evidence into his house. The kid reeked of gasoline that had soaked into his clothes, and his skin was almost black.

The hospital had discharged Wade an hour earlier, and he'd ordered an Uber ride to get home when he couldn't reach Travis. When he'd spotted the Bug Zappers van parked askew outside his garage, he'd told the driver to drop him off on the deserted farm road rather than approach the house. He'd waited until the Uber car was gone and then hiked past the huge evergreens and found Travis asleep in the front seat of the van. When Wade yanked open the door and smelled the interior, he knew exactly what the kid had done. And the idiot had done it in the company van! Sometimes Travis was nothing but a swearing, drinking, cheating waste of a sperm cell.

"Be cool?" Travis exclaimed. "Are you kidding? How am I supposed to do that?"

"I'm saying, you're in big trouble, so you better not panic."

Travis eyed the dirt road for the twentieth time to make sure they were alone. "Man, you have to believe me, I didn't know anybody was there! Far as I could tell, the place was empty! How was I to know those people were upstairs?"

"You think that's going to matter to the cops?" Wade asked.

"I know! Shit, I can't believe this. I *killed* those people, man. I burned them up. They're going to put me away."

That was true.

Wade knew Travis was looking at twenty-five years behind bars, maybe more. They might even hang a terrorism charge around his neck and call it murder one and put him away for life. Wade couldn't imagine what that would be like. He'd rather die than spend year after year staring at the walls of a small cell.

"Did anybody see you?" Wade asked.

"I don't know. I don't think so."

"What the hell were you thinking, huh? Are you out of your mind?"

"I was just so pissed," Travis told him. "I mean, seeing Shelly like that, and thinking about Joni. I wanted to *do* something. Just like you told me. God saved me so I could hit them back."

"Don't be saying I put this idea in your head, Travis," Wade snapped. "This was all you."

"Yeah, but you told me—" Travis stopped talking and shook his head. "No, I get it, man. This is on me. I'm not bringing you down with me. The thing is, what the hell do I do now?"

Wade thought about it. He'd expected Travis to do something stupid, but he'd never thought that the kid would do something *so* stupid. Regardless, he didn't want any fingers pointing his way. Travis had probably gotten lucky, because if anybody had spotted The Bug Zappers on a truck speeding from the firebombing, the cops would already be knocking on his door. But they were alone, and there were no sirens. Not yet. They had a little time.

"What do I do, Wade?" Travis asked again.

"First thing you do is air out the truck. Thing smells like a Texaco station. Open the doors and windows and spray the whole thing down with Lysol. Wash the exterior, too. What did you do with the gas tanks?"

"They're still in back. I was gonna put 'em back in the garage."

"You used my tanks?" Wade asked. "Shit, Travis, are you kidding me?"

"I'm sorry, man. I saw the tanks, and I thought, yeah, that's it. That's what I'm supposed to do. Burn down a Muslim building. Eye for an eye."

"The tanks were empty. Where'd you fill them up?"

"I stopped at a bunch of different places. I figured, if I did it all in one place, somebody might notice, you know?"

"No kidding."

Wade thought about any evidence that might trace this whole thing back to Travis and from Travis to himself. He wasn't sure if the cops could match gasoline from the fire to gasoline that was left in the tanks, but he wasn't taking any chances. His own fingerprints were on those tanks. And the Feds loved a conspiracy.

"Take the cans into the woods and bury them. Then dump leaves, branches, and pine needles over the whole area. Got it? I better not be able to go back there and figure out where you did it."

"Yeah. Yeah, will do, man. Then what?"

"Then strip naked behind the house and hose yourself down. Wash everything— your hair, your eyebrows, your nose, your fingernails, your toenails, everything."

"What about my clothes?" Travis asked.

"Burn them. You got any spare clothes at my house?"

"Uh, yeah, I think so. Joni did some laundry for me after I got caught in the last storm."

"Okay, I'll get it," Wade told him, frowning. "Don't you set foot in my house, you got that?"

Travis nodded. "Yeah. Yeah, I got it. Thanks, man."

"Don't go anywhere near Shelly's place tonight," he told Travis. "Hide the van somewhere, and stay under the radar. If the cops come after you, you're a sitting duck staying at her apartment, and I don't want you anywhere near me."

"Yeah, no problem," Travis replied. "Do you think they'll figure out it was me?"

Of course, they will, you dumb shit.

"I have no idea," Wade said. "If they do, we never talked about any of this, right?"

"Right."

"Okay, get the shovel, and get moving."

Travis stood frozen on the ground. He blinked back tears. "I didn't mean for this to happen, Wade. Really. No way I wanted to kill anybody. Especially not a kid."

"It's too late to cry about it," Wade said.

"Shelly's going to be so mad."

Wade jabbed a finger in the kid's face. "Do *not* tell Shelly."

"She'll know," Travis said. "She always knows when I've done something wrong."

"Then don't go see her until you can keep it together."

"No, I gotta see her. I told her I'd be back at the hospital tonight. I don't want her all alone."

"I'll go," Wade said. "You lay low until we figure out if the cops are on to you."

Travis shook his head. "I'm telling you, Shelly will figure out the truth. She always does. And her and her God stuff, she'll say I'm going to hell."

Wade reached out to grab a fistful of Travis's shirt, but he pulled his hand back. He smothered the rage he felt. He wanted to take the shovel from the garage, swing it into the kid's brain, and bury him in the forest with the gas cans. He never wanted to see Travis's face again. He wished he'd never met him. He wished Shelly had never brought her brother to work at Ralston Extermination and that Joni hadn't twisted his arm to hire the kid.

"Maybe you *are* going to hell," Wade told him. "I don't know how those things work, Travis. Fact is, you crossed a line. You're a murderer. All you can do is get used to the idea, because there's no going back."

* * *

Michael Malville sat on his front porch in Cloquet with a copy of the photograph of Khan Rashid in his hand. He'd studied it a thousand times, until he could see it even when he closed his eyes. The man's face. His expression. His torso, twisted as he looked back over his shoulder, waiting for the bomb to explode. The anticipation. The nervousness. The guilt.

It was the same face that he'd seen on Superior Street. The same face, filled with hatred. It was him.

Michael swallowed down his regrets about what he'd done. Khan Rashid was guilty. He was the bomber. And yet Michael's whole world was filled with doubt now. Ever since the news about the gallery fire and the death of the Rashids, he'd done nothing but replay the last few days in his head. He wondered, if he could go back in time, whether he would still push the button and tweet the photo of Khan Rashid, knowing what would happen next. Knowing that two people would die.

Beside him, Alison was quiet. She'd been quiet all day. Through the open windows, he could hear Evan playing inside, waging an imaginary battle against imaginary monsters. In front of them, gentle rain soaked the lawn and played music on the metal gutters.

"Are you going to tell me what's wrong?" he asked, although he already knew.

Alison had one foot tucked beneath her on the Adirondack chair and one on the porch. Her blond hair was unwashed. "It's nothing."

"Come on, we're past those games," Michael said.

"Well, then, I don't want to get you angry. Not today."

He was self-aware enough to know that her worries were well founded. He got angry easily and too often. "I'll try not to—that's all I can say."

"Okay. I'm upset. I keep thinking about that woman and her child dying the way they did. It's horrible."

"And you think it's my fault?" Michael asked, unable to keep the bitterness out of his voice.

"I didn't say that. If you're going to get like this, then I don't want to talk about it."

"You're right. I'm sorry."

"It must have been so terrifying and painful. And for a mother—to know that her child was going to perish in her arms . . ."

"Try not to dwell on it," he told her.

"I know, but I can't think of anything else." She reached out and took his hand. "I do *not* blame you, Michael."

"Thank you."

"But I do blame Dawn Basch," Alison went on. "I told you from the day she arrived in town. that woman made me uncomfortable, and this is why. She had no reason to tweet out those photos except to incite people."

Michael didn't reply for a long time. "It's still free speech. It's not against the law."

"Maybe, but we both know it's wrong."

"She couldn't have known what would happen," he said.

"Yes, she could. You're not naïve."

"Come on, Alison."

"I'm serious. Innocent people died because of what she did. She knew something like that could happen."

"We don't know for certain that the wife was innocent," Michael said. "I'm not excusing what happened, but I'm just saying, she could have been a co-conspirator."

"And the child?"

Michael hesitated. "That was a terrible thing, of course."

"I have a request." Alison's voice was soft but firm.

"Okay."

"I don't want you to have anything more to do with Basch or her No Exceptions crowd. No rallies. No books. Throw away the buttons and the hats. I don't want them in our house. I don't want Evan hearing about any of this."

He was about to protest, but he had to make a choice, and he chose his wife. "Okay, if that's what you want. I'll give it up."

She closed her eyes in relief. "Thank God."

"I don't support what she did, you know. She went too far."

"Yes, she did."

Michael stared at the photo in his hand again. "Are you being honest with me? Or do you think I'm partly to blame?"

"What do you think?" Alison asked.

"I think I pushed a stone downhill, and I had no idea how far it would go."

His wife got up and knelt beside him and reached out to stroke his face. "You feel guilty, don't you?"

"A little."

"Well, unlike Dawn Basch, you couldn't have predicted any of this," Alison said. "I know you, Michael. Sometimes you rush in where angels fear to tread, but it's never with malice. You're a good man, and you have a good heart."

"But you wish I'd never gotten involved," Michael replied.

"You're right. I wish you'd been able to let it go, even though I knew you couldn't. I worry about the heartache this will cause you for the rest of your life. I hate that."

"Yes, but I know what I saw. I had to say something."

Alison kissed him before he could dive into his pool of self-justification. "I know what you think you saw, but it's easy to convince yourself of things that aren't true. I've been there, remember? Two years ago, I thought my husband, the love of my life, was capable of being a killer. I couldn't have been more completely, horribly, terribly wrong. I still live with that guilt. That's what scares me, Michael. What if you're wrong, too? What if you simply made a mistake?"

36

"A single gunshot wound to the back of the head," Stride said, staring down at the body of Eagle amid the debris of the Nopeming Sanatorium. Hot, damp air blew through the open window.

Serena stood in the bedroom doorway. "Based on the amount of alcohol he'd consumed in here, Eagle was probably passed out cold. It wouldn't have been hard to sneak up on him. Guy comes in, takes the shot, and makes his escape."

"Did anyone hear anything?" Stride asked.

"Not that we know of. There's a caretaker apartment on the other side of the complex, but apparently it's been empty for weeks. Otherwise, we're in the middle of nowhere, so if you're going to shoot someone, this is a good place to do it."

Stride joined her in the hallway, which was a wreck of standing water, fallen ceiling tiles, and broken glass. He saw hundreds of tiny yellow paint pellets, remnants of mock battles played inside the ruins by war gamers. Among the debris was the head of a chicken, too, and the horned skull of a ram, surrounded by candle wax. Even Satanists found their way to Nopeming.

"Good luck with the forensics in this place," he murmured.

"Yeah."

"Assuming nobody else heard the shot, what do we know about time of death?"

"The M.E. thinks somewhere from two to four days ago. The autopsy may tell us more, but the heat and humidity won't make it easy to narrow down. It could have been before the marathon, could have been after. According to Cat, Curt Dickes said that someone spotted Eagle on the railroad tracks near Becks Road on Friday. He was heading in this direction."

Stride studied the corridor

"You said Eagle was hard to find," Stride said, "so how did the perp locate him out here?"

"It could have been an arranged meeting. Or our guy could have slipped a GPS tracker onto Eagle to follow him. Based on the way this played out, I think the murder was premeditated. This guy came out here specifically to kill him. The guy took Eagle's boots, too. Eagle wasn't wearing any shoes. That's important."

"Why? What do you mean?"

"Curt saw Eagle wearing brand-new boots from the Duluth Outdoor Company. That was last Wednesday, the day after the incident at the shop. The boots aren't here, which means the killer took them with him."

"So maybe the killer wanted the shoes for himself," Stride said. "It wouldn't be the first time a homeless guy killed another one over something like that."

"Okay, yeah. You're right, that's possible. Or maybe the killer didn't want us to make a connection to the store, because that would have given us a connection to the marathon bombing."

"You're convinced Eagle's murder is related to the bombing?"

"I am. The timing is too coincidental to think anything else. Eagle was inside the Duluth Outdoor Company shop creating a scene just days before the bomb went off at the marathon. Then Eagle turns up with a bullet in his head. Whoever did this was tying up loose ends."

Stride nodded. This time, the coincidences went too far. He thought Serena was right.

"Where's Cat?" he asked.

"Outside. She's pretty shaken up."

The two of them made their way to the ground floor of the complex. Outside, spitting rain tapped on the green grass. The yellow brick building loomed above them. Stride could see Cat standing against a tree fifty yards away. Her arms were folded, and she stared at the sky.

"So what was Eagle really doing at the shop last week?" Stride asked Serena.

"I have a theory," she said, "but you and the FBI aren't going to like it."

"What is it?"

"Durkin thinks Eagle was at the store to cause a diversion. Throw a fit, and distract the staff. She thought it was part of a burglary scheme, and, yeah, okay, she might be right. But I just don't believe anybody killed Eagle over a pair of boots."

"Then why the diversion?" Stride asked.

"That's when the guy planted the bomb," Serena said.

Stride stared at her. "You think the bomb was sitting on the floor of the store for days, and no one noticed it?"

"Not on the floor," Serena said. "He could have slipped it into the front display window. It could have been sitting there with a dozen other backpacks, and no one would have paid any attention to it. But to do that, he needed a few seconds with the staff distracted. Eagle gave him those few seconds."

Stride shook his head. "You're convinced of this?"

"I may be crazy, Jonny, but I think we've all been on the wrong track from the beginning. The bomb was already in the store long before the marathon."

"That's a big risk for this guy to take," Stride said. "The thing could have gone off at any time."

"Yes, but he also didn't have to get the bomb into the store on marathon day, when we have Canal Park flooded with security. All he had to do was set it off remotely. For all we know, the bomber wasn't even *at* the marathon. He could have dialed a phone number to trigger it."

"If you're right, the suspect pool just got a lot bigger," Stride said.

"It also means we don't have any real reason to suspect Khan Rashid of anything," Serena added.

"Except Dennis Kenzie's murder."

"I know. I'm not necessarily saying he's innocent. But whether Rashid had a backpack or not doesn't mean a thing if the bomb was in the store before the marathon even started."

Stride tried to rewire his thinking. He'd spent three days looking at the bombing one way, and suddenly, he had to go back and start over. If Serena was right, the whole investigation needed to start over. They'd been looking for a needle in the wrong haystack.

"How do we find Eagle's partner?" he asked her. "Eagle was part of the homeless population, but there's no way someone from that community had the resources or know-how to build this bomb. So how did the bomber even cross paths with Eagle?"

"I don't know," Serena admitted. "Cat says Eagle hung out all over town, so they could have bumped into each other anywhere. However, if my theory is right, they were both in Canal Park a week ago. Eagle went into the Duluth Outdoor Company shop on Tuesday evening, and so did the bomber. Our guy was *there*. And the marathon people keep a high-def camera on the roof of their building that takes pictures up and down the street. Maybe they caught him on the camera feed that evening."

"Okay, except that camera's visible from the street. Everybody knows it's there. Why wouldn't he use the back entrance to the shop? Why take the risk of coming in on the Canal Park side? There are no cameras in the alley."

Serena nodded. "True, but I'm betting he used the front door, anyway."

"Why?"

"If I'm carrying a fifty-pound bomb on my shoulder, I don't want to walk all the way across the store with it and hang out where the staff can see me. I want to stand outside the shop until Eagle does his thing. Then I slip in, plant it, and slip out. Twenty or thirty seconds max."

Stride put himself in the mind of the bomber.

The less time inside the store, the better.

"Okay, go check it out," he told Serena. "I'll talk to Durkin, and you talk to the marathon people. Let's see who showed up on their camera on Tuesday night."

* * *

As she headed back to her Mustang, Serena stopped to check on Cat. The girl leaned against a tree and chewed her fingernails, and her face was streaked with tears. Serena didn't say anything. She simply walked up to Cat and put her arms around her and held her tightly.

"You okay?" she asked.

"I feel like that kid in *The Sixth Sense*," Cat murmured.

"What do you mean?"

"Everywhere I go, I see dead people."

Serena smiled. If Cat could joke about it, even a little, that was a good thing. "Yeah, I get it. You've seen more than your share."

"I don't know how you and Stride deal with it, you know?"

"It doesn't get easier, the more you see it," Serena told her.

"Do you have any idea who killed Eagle?"

"Not yet."

"He was a good guy," Cat said. "He had problems, but he was okay."

"I know." Serena hesitated, and then she went on, "I wish you'd called me rather than going in there yourself. This isn't a safe place. It's private property, too, and you shouldn't be trespassing."

"I've been here before."

"Maybe so, but we're in the middle of a dangerous situation. I don't want you getting hurt."

Serena didn't want to chide her, but she worried that the girl's impulsive behavior would catch up with her sooner or later.

"I also want to know why Curt called you, not me," Serena added.

The girl's eyes shifted to her feet. "You know Curt."

"Yes, I do. That's what worries me. What did he want from you?"

"What do you mean?"

"I mean, what did Curt want you to do for him in exchange for information about Eagle?"

Cat shrugged. "Nothing."

Serena took the girl's chin and lifted it up until their eyes met. "Hey. This is me. Don't lie."

"He wants me to go to a party tonight with some rich guys over on Congdon," Cat said. "It's a lot of money."

"Curt's *paying* you to show up at a party?" Serena asked.

"Not to do anything. Not for sex or crap like that. Just to look pretty and hang out."

A private party. For money. Cat talked about it like it was no big deal. Serena took a deep breath and tried not to scream at her. She realized that this was a Mom thing, and she still wasn't used to being a Mom. She could tell the girl not to go and hope she obeyed, but Cat typically didn't follow orders. If you told her what to do, she did the opposite.

Serena decided to try something different. Mom to daughter.

She would trust her.

"Okay, you can go or not go," Serena said. "This is your call."

The girl stared at her. It was the last thing she'd expected Serena to say. "What? What do you mean?"

"You decide for yourself."

"Come on, I know you don't want me to go," Cat said.

"What I want isn't the issue. You're seventeen years old. You're smart as hell. You know what's right, and you know what's wrong, so don't pretend you need me or Stride to tell you what to do. We're done with that. It's up to you, Cat."

Serena kissed the girl's head, and then she walked away without another word.

She hoped that she hadn't made an awful mistake.

37

Khan beat his fists on the wooden floor and cried, but nothing brought his family back.

For hours, he wailed to Allah, looking for answers where there were none. Malik kept trying to quiet him, because he was afraid the neighbors would hear. Khan didn't care. He thought: Let the police come. Let them draw their guns and kill me. His life was as good as over. He thought about strapping on the awful vest that Malik had built. End everything in a brilliant flash of light, rather than face the long, empty years of loneliness ahead of him. Even so, he couldn't do it. He sat in a corner of the deserted house, surrounded by dust and darkness, with no idea how to go on.

Khan was devastated, but Malik was angry.

"Now do you understand?" his friend demanded of him, his face reddening with outrage. "Now do you see what I've been saying for months? This country *hates* us. It would murder us simply for who we are. All your talk of peace—what did it get you? You thought you could hide in your little town, your little neighborhood, your little house, but you can't."

Khan had nothing to say, but this time, he knew Malik was right. There was no place to hide. He'd run from Pakistan. He'd run from

Chicago. He'd asked nothing from life except to live in tranquility with his wife, his son, and his God. But no. You can't run forever. Sooner or later, the monster always finds you.

"Don't you see the truth now?" Malik went on. "*Muslim* is tattooed on your forehead, Khan. It's all they see. You can never be a part of them; you can only be a part of *us*."

Khan stared at his friend from red-rimmed eyes. "Who is us?"

"Those who would fight and die for Allah," Malik said.

Khan shook his head wearily. "What does violence do? Violence solves nothing."

"So what, you're afraid of them calling you a terrorist? They'll do that, anyway. Meanwhile, the real terrorists are right here. The terrorists are the ones who murdered Ahdia and Pak last night."

"Don't even speak their names," Khan told him.

Malik took a slow breath. He slid down the wall and sat next to Khan. "I know. I'm so sorry for your loss. This tragedy is beyond anything a man should have to bear."

"The wound will never close," Khan replied. "Never. I keep thinking about what they went through. I can feel the fire on my own skin. I choke on the black smoke. I should have been able to save them, Malik. I should have sacrificed myself, and instead, I was a coward."

"Nonsense."

"I wasn't strong enough," Khan murmured, mostly to himself. "The fire drove me back. I should have been stronger."

"Even if you'd made it inside, all three of you would be dead. There was no way out."

"Then I wish we'd all died together."

Malik grabbed Khan's hand. "I know you have to grieve, but you also have to think about what comes next. You don't have the luxury of mourning them in peace. You don't have time."

"I don't care what comes next."

"So instead, you walk outside and let the police fill you with bullets? That may sound preferable right now, but is that what Ahdia would want? For you to give up?"

Khan felt the tears again. He stared at the ceiling in resignation. "What do you want from me, Malik?"

"I want you to get *angry*. Underneath your grief, anger boils. This was your wife! Your son! These people took them away from you. Murdered them. If you give up, they win."

"Nothing boils inside me," Khan said. "I can't feel anger. I can't feel anything. Don't you see that? I'm dead inside. I'm going to walk out that door with my hands up. If they shoot me, so be it."

Malik squeezed Khan's hand until his fingers hurt. "No. I won't let you do that. I'm going to get you out of here."

"How? There's a police car not even fifty yards away. Two police officers watching the street."

"We wait until dark, like last night," Malik said.

"There are still streetlights. We're not invisible."

"I'll draw the police away somehow. Once they leave, you'll be able to escape."

"And then what? Where do I go? You said it yourself. There's nowhere to hide. Sooner or later, they'll find me."

Malik pushed himself off the floor. They were in the living room, hidden in shadows. Outside, just beyond the window glass, Khan could hear the trill of a cardinal. The red birds with their tufted hats had been Ahdia's favorites. She'd put up a feeder and bought food to attract them, but it seemed as if cardinals couldn't be tempted by easy offerings. They kept their distance, even when their song was in the trees; they showed up only on rare occasions to grace the humans with their presence. It made every sighting special.

He wondered if Ahdia had sent the cardinal to him now and what message she wanted him to hear.

What would you tell me to do, my love?

"I'll set up an underground railroad for you," Malik said.

"What do you mean?"

"I'll make contact with my friends in Minneapolis. They'll arrange a meeting point and a safe house. From there, someone will drive you out of state. You can take refuge in another city. Chicago. New York.

Los Angeles. If necessary, if it comes to that, they can find a way to smuggle you out of the country."

"My home is here," Khan said.

"Your home *was* here. You have no home now—don't you realize that?"

Khan took a deep breath. Malik made it sound so easy to pick up and go. He found it hard to imagine a world outside Duluth, where he'd always assumed he would spend the rest of his life. But Malik was right. His home wasn't this city. His home had been his wife and child, and now his home was gone. It didn't matter where he went. He had nothing to leave behind.

"Assuming I left," Khan said, "how would that even happen? How would we get from here to Minneapolis? As soon as we tried to run, we'd be spotted."

"We'll stick to back roads. We avoid the freeways."

"You don't think they've thought of that? There will be roadblocks. They'll have the entire city in a box. As long as the search goes on, we're marked men."

Malik nodded thoughtfully. He looked like an engineer contemplating a design flaw that seemed impossible to solve. "True. You're right."

"So what do we do?"

His friend shook his head. "I'll worry about that part of the plan later. First things first. I need to make sure the car I was using is still safe. It's not registered to me, but any car that's been parked in the same place for a while may have attracted the attention of the police. If they found it and they're watching it, then I need to find something different."

"How will you get to the car without being seen?"

"Carefully," Malik said, smiling. "Don't worry, I can slither on my belly when I need to. Once I reach the car, assuming it's safe, I can map out our route and arrange a welcome from my friends in Minneapolis."

"And what do I do in the meantime? Sit here alone?"

Malik squatted in front of him. "For now, yes. Get some sleep if you can."

"I'm not sure I'll ever sleep again."

"Well, try to rest, anyway. It's going to be a long night. And listen to me, Khan. Whatever happens, don't be foolish. These people would put a bullet between your eyes on sight. To them, you're a cop killer. Do you understand?"

"I don't understand anything," Khan replied. "Nothing makes sense."

"Well, I can't leave unless you give me your word that you will stay put. Do *not* walk out that door. You may think you're alone, but I'm here to help you, and others will do the same."

Khan glanced around the shut-up house, which already felt like a prison. Two days here had been an eternity. A life sentence. Inside or out, he was an innocent man in jail.

"And what do I do if you don't return?" he asked.

"I will."

Khan put both hands on Malik's face. "Not if you're dead, my friend."

"Okay, if the night passes and I don't come back, assume I'm dead or arrested. There's a backup plan—a plumber named Abdul who lives in Chester Park. Call him and tell him you have a flood in your basement and give him this address. Tell him there is so much water, you thought you heard Noah pleading with his son not to stay with the Unbelievers."

Khan's eyes narrowed. "What?"

"It's a code. Abdul will understand. He'll know it's an emergency. He'll find a way to get you out."

"Malik, this is crazy," Khan said.

"The world is crazy. I'll leave you an extra phone, but don't use it unless you need to reach Abdul. That should be your one and only call. And assume that somewhere a federal agent will be listening. Act natural, and don't use your name or mine. It's just a call about a leaky basement. Understand?"

Khan felt overwhelmed. "Yes."

"One more thing," Malik said. He got up and retrieved a small shoulder satchel from the other side of the room. He dug inside and found a silver flip phone, which he tossed to Khan. Then he brought out something else and cupped it in his hand. It was a gun. A pistol with a black barrel and wooden handle.

Khan shook his head. "No."

"I have a gun," Malik said. "You need one, too."

"I've never fired a gun in my life. I don't even know how."

"I'll show you."

"*No*. No gun. If I have a gun, then I become exactly what they say I am—don't you see that?"

Malik acted as if Khan hadn't said a word. He picked up the gun and demonstrated how to prep it, taking the magazine in and out, cycling the slide, and loading a cartridge. How to aim. How to fire. Then he reversed the process, emptying the weapon. He did it twice and made sure Khan was watching the whole time.

"See? That's all you do."

"Under no circumstances will I ever fire a gun," Khan said. "Take it with you."

Malik ignored him. Khan's protests meant nothing. He put the gun on the floor next to Khan and yanked the satchel over his shoulder. "Hopefully, you won't need it, but I'm leaving it here for you, anyway. Do you understand the plan?"

Khan nodded without replying.

"Good," Malik said. "I'll be back as soon as I can, and I'll have a way out of Duluth for you. Trust me, my friend."

Malik left, but Khan barely heard him go.

All he could do was stare at the gun on the floor.

38

Maggie blew the black bangs out of her eyes.

"Minnesota is just not a donut state," she said to Guppo, pressing pause on the video feed. "What's that about, anyway?"

"What are you talking about?" Guppo replied. "I love donuts. I can plow through a dozen chocolate cake donuts in a sitting."

The two of them sat on opposite sides of a conference table in front of computer monitors. They'd already spent hours reviewing footage of people buying gas in Duluth in a five-mile radius around the site of the gallery firebombing. Watching identical clips of cars and trucks coming and going from the pumps had made them punchy.

"Yeah, okay, but where do you *buy* your donuts?" Maggie asked.

"I don't know. Super One sometimes. Holiday or SA, if I'm filling up."

"See, that's my point. Grocery stores and gas stations do not sell donuts. Donut shops sell donuts. Go anywhere else in the country, and there are actual donut shops that sell actual donuts. Duluth is a donut wasteland. The whole state is a donut wasteland."

Guppo, who resembled an enormous filled donut himself, leaned back in the chair, which groaned precariously under his weight. "Yeah, I still miss House of Donuts. Those were the days."

"You and Stride and House of Donuts," Maggie said with a sigh. "How many decades ago was that? Anyway, at least Dunkin' finally came back to town. That's progress. And don't get me started on the lack of pancake houses, either. When Troy and I went to Chicago in the spring, we passed pancake houses every other block. Up here? Nothing. I mean, I love Duluth Grill, but I also want a place that sells Swedish pancakes and silver dollar pancakes and Dutch apple pancakes and blueberry pancakes and buckwheat pancakes. And I want them to have a logo of a pancake with a happy face on it. That's a pancake house."

"You sound crabby," Guppo said.

"I'm sick of watching people buy gas."

"Well, here's another guy filling up a portable gas tank," Guppo told her. "Monday afternoon, 3:45 p.m. at the Spur on Central Entrance."

"Just one tank?"

"Yeah."

"What does he look like?"

"I think he's about eighty," Guppo said. "He's wearing a short-sleeve plaid shirt, shorts, and sneakers with black socks."

"I'm going to take a gamble that our firebug is not a great-grandfather, but print it out, tag the feed, and add it to the stack."

"Done."

Maggie rolled the feed on her laptop again, reviewing footage from a Holiday station on Arrowhead Road. Each store had multiple cameras; each camera had multiple hours of video, starting from Monday morning. It was a long job. They'd found dozens of people filling up portable tanks, and they'd kept records on each purchase, but so far, they hadn't identified anyone whose behavior looked suspicious.

Eventually, she knew they would have to run down each buyer individually, in order to cross them off the suspect list. She also knew that she and Max might be heading down a dead-end road. Someone planning a firebombing might have been smart enough to use gas stations outside the city, where there was less likelihood of being spotted. Or maybe they had gallons of gas already stored in their garage for lawn mowers and snowblowers. Even so, for now, this was their best chance at finding a lead. If the bomber was angry enough and emotional enough to lash out violently on the spur of the moment, then maybe he wasn't overly careful about covering his tracks.

Another half hour passed as they studied the videos in silence. The only noise was a low belch from Guppo and the occasional hum of the printer when they found a clip of someone filling a portable tank. When Maggie did long video review sessions alone, she usually played Aerosmith, which kept her adrenaline pumping late into the night. But Guppo, like Stride and Serena, was a country music fan, and Maggie categorically refused to listen to country. The only compromise that worked between them was no music at all.

"So what's up with you and Troy?" Guppo asked as he dipped a rippled potato chip into a tub of Dean's onion dip. "Are you guys serious?"

"Did Stride ask you to grill me about that? Or Serena?"

"Both."

Maggie chuckled. "Troy and I are taking it one day at a time."

"Hey, if you're eating donuts and pancakes together, that sounds pretty serious, for you," Guppo said.

"Yeah, but the man refuses to try a McRib sandwich. I don't know what the deal is with that. He may have some kind of serious character flaw."

"Hey, Maggie?" Guppo said.

"I'm not saying I didn't think the whole pickle-and-onion thing on the ribs was weird," she went on as if Guppo hadn't said a word, "but you have to have faith in Mickey D's. It works."

"Hey, Maggie?" Guppo said again.

She noticed the change in his voice. "What's up?"

"Check this out."

Maggie got up from her chair and went around to Guppo's side of the table. He froze the video on the monitor and rolled the footage back. She found herself staring at an open rear door of a white van. A tall man had his back to the camera as he filled a red plastic gas tank on the pavement. He wore sweats, a red T-shirt, and a baseball cap planted backward on his head.

"What am I looking at?" Maggie asked.

Guppo paused the camera feed as the man replaced the pump. He tried to zoom in on the image, but the resolution was blurred.

"Look inside the back of the van," Guppo said. "I know it's not very clear, but does that look like the edge of another gas can behind the van door?"

Maggie squinted. "Hard to say."

Guppo rolled the feed a few more clicks. "How about now?"

"Maybe."

"The shape looks right," he said. "I think it's another gas can."

Maggie watched the man slide the full tank into the back of the van and slam the door. "Is that the only can he fills?"

"Yes."

"Can you see his face?" she asked.

"Just a quick profile. The rest of the van gets blocked by an SUV as he's driving away. I'll run the plate and see what we get."

"What's the time stamp on the footage?"

"7:03 p.m."

"Is this still the Spur on Central Entrance?"

Guppo nodded.

"Well, if he's our guy, it looks like he's only filling one tank at a time to avoid suspicion," Maggie said. "So maybe he went straight from there to a different station to fill another tank. Or maybe he was coming to the Spur from somewhere else. Let's take the two closest gas stations nearby and see if we spot him again."

Maggie found the flash drives they'd collected from a SuperAmerica station on Miller Hill. She booted up the video for the evening feed and scrolled forward until the time stamp showed 6:30 p.m. She ran the video in quick mode, hunting for a white van. When the time stamp rolled to 7:10 p.m., she said, "Bingo. I got him."

Guppo squeezed out of the chair and lumbered closer. His breath smelled of onion dip as he leaned behind her. "That's him, all right, and he's filling another red gas can. Think this is our guy?"

Maggie studied the face of the man filling the tank. Unlike in the other feed, she could see him clearly. He had long brown hair and a piercing in his lower lip. He was tall, good-looking in a bad-boy way, and built like an ox, with tattoos covering both arms.

She could see the logo on the truck, too.

The Bug Zappers.

"Yeah, I think that's our guy," Maggie said, "and I know who he is."

* * *

"Serena thinks the bomb was in place *four days* before the marathon?" Durkin asked.

"That's her theory," Stride said.

The two of them stood outside the ruins of the Duluth Outdoor Company shop in Canal Park. The store was taped off, and the broken windows had been sealed with plywood. The rest of the street was open again, but tourists had been slow to return. Everyone knew the bomber was still on the loose. No one felt comfortable on the city streets.

Durkin studied the large gaps in the brick wall where the store windows had been. "No way. Someone would have spotted it."

"Not necessarily. I called Drew Olson, who owns the store. He told me that the display windows only get overhauled every few weeks. Backpacks in the window are typically stuffed with paper to make them look full. So another backpack in the window—with a bomb—wouldn't stand out."

"You really believe this idea?" Durkin asked.

"I didn't until we found Eagle's body, but now I think Serena may be on to something. She's with the marathon people now, trying to isolate street-level photos from Tuesday evening, to see if we can spot Eagle and his partner."

Durkin didn't hide the skepticism on her face. She shoved her hands into her pockets and wandered across the street, and Stride stayed with her. They crossed between two of the hotels and headed to the boardwalk that fronted the lake. Durkin sat on a bench, and Stride sat beside her. They heard the horn of the lift bridge and saw a giant red freighter taking aim at the narrow ship canal to make its way into the harbor.

"I miss it here," Durkin said. "Although I think I mostly miss being a kid up here."

"It's a great place to grow up," Stride said.

"You never wanted to leave?"

"No. Whenever I've left, it hasn't worked out well, so I always came back. Besides, Duluth grounds me. I have a place to call home. I know I'm lucky."

"You are lucky," Durkin said. "You have a beautiful wife, too."

"Thanks."

"Living together and working together must be hard, though. Are you married to each other or to the job?"

"To each other, but some days it doesn't feel that way. We didn't even get to take a real honeymoon. Not yet, anyway. Maybe we can get away this winter."

"My job is my life, too," Durkin agreed, "so I get it. It is what it is."

She said it matter-of-factly, not as if she was complaining, but there was a loneliness about Agent Durkin, beyond the intensity she showed the world. He also knew that the FBI culture wasn't easy for female agents.

"I was sorry to hear about Ahdia Rashid and her son," Durkin said. "I hate to see the violence spreading. Things are getting out of hand."

Stride nodded. "That's the way some people want it."

"Dawn Basch?" Durkin asked.

"Right."

"Yeah, she's not helping. Look, Stride, I may come across as a hard-ass, but I hope you know I don't support vigilantes."

"I never said you did," he told her.

"That doesn't mean I'm not angry, because I am."

"We're all angry, Durkin."

The FBI agent hesitated. "To be totally honest, I've always had a certain amount of sympathy for what Basch says. And not just because of Ron."

"She knows what buttons to push," Stride acknowledged. "That's what makes her so dangerous. If there wasn't a kernel of truth in what she's saying, no one would listen to her. Even so, don't believe the hype. Dawn Basch isn't a martyr. She's a narcissist who loves attention, and she's making a volatile situation worse. I'm afraid that unless we solve this case soon, Basch is going to get exactly what she wants."

"Which is?"

"War," Stride said.

39

Serena climbed the stairs to the Duluth Marathon headquarters in Canal Park. Inside, she found a somber mood among the handful of staff who managed the race operations. The days following the marathon would normally be a time for celebration, but the tragedy had cast a pall over this year's event. Even so, in typical Duluth fashion, the group had already set their sights on the future. On a chalkboard in the crowded main office, someone had scrawled in huge letters:

WE WILL BE BACK
BIGGER and BETTER!

Serena didn't doubt it for a minute. Nothing kept Duluth or Duluthians down. If they could survive the winters, they could survive anything. That was one of the things she loved about the character of her adopted hometown.

Most of the police knew the staff at the marathon, because they worked closely together on the race every year. There were no tears among any of them, just fierce determination, and that was true of the marathon runners, too. The race director, Lorena Baylor, told her that inquiries about entering next year's race were already up 30 percent.

In the conference room at the back, Serena found the man she was looking for: Troy Grange. Maggie's boyfriend.

Troy's full-time day job was as the senior health and safety manager for the Duluth port, but he'd coordinated safety issues for the marathon as a volunteer for years. Like Stride, he was a Duluth lifer, one of those solid, decent men who made the city work. Troy got up to shake her hand, and Serena, in her heels, towered over him. He had a shiny bald skull, cheekbones like pink golf balls, and a deceptively heavy physique. He was as round as Max Guppo, but Troy was a muscleman who could bench-press three hundred and fifty pounds without breaking a sweat.

"Detective Stride," he greeted her formally, even though they were friends. He added with a smile, "I like calling you Stride, you know. It fits you."

"I like hearing it," Serena replied. "You know, Maggie nearly choked when I told her I was changing my name, but I never had much of an attachment to Dial. It came with a lot of baggage."

"I understand. Have a seat. Do you want some coffee?"

"I'd love some."

Troy poured her a cup from a silver Thermos on the shelf near the window. She could see the back-alley parking lot behind the marathon building. The coffee was lukewarm and not very good, but she drank it, anyway.

"Speaking of Maggie, there's a little less bark in her snark these days," Serena said. "Do we have you to thank for that?"

Troy laughed. He had a big Santa Claus laugh. "Well, I try to keep her smiling, but she does like to blow off steam. When she's mad at me, wow. She can be like a ninja with that tongue of hers."

"I've had the pleasure," Serena said, grinning.

"You should see her with my girls, though. She's amazing. You wouldn't believe it."

"You know, I actually would," Serena said.

Troy leaned across the conference table with his big hands folded together. His brow knitted into wrinkles. "So, what's the latest? How can I help?"

Serena gave Troy the background about Eagle's murder and explained her theory about the placement of the bomb. When he heard it, Troy rocked back in his chair and stroked his multiple chins.

"You think the bomb was there before the race began?" he murmured. "Intriguing idea. That would explain a lot of things. I was honestly puzzled by how this guy could have gotten a bomb past the dogs."

"Me, too."

"So I assume you want to check our photo records from Tuesday night?" Troy asked. "To see if you can identify the guy that Eagle was working with?"

Serena smiled. Troy was smart. "Exactly. If we can spot Eagle, I'm betting our bomber isn't far behind. Even if he wore some kind of disguise, it would be helpful to get eyes on this guy."

"When exactly did this happen?"

"According to the 911 call, the incident happened at 8:35 p.m. last Tuesday. That's less than half an hour before the store closed. Some of the staff had already clocked out, which I assume wasn't an accident. This guy must have checked out the store multiple times to pick the optimum time to make the drop."

Troy pushed himself out of the chair. He was nimble despite his heft. "Okay, let's check our feed. We archive the photo records on a computer in the main office. The FBI already has copies of everything from Friday and Saturday, of course."

"The camera itself is mounted on the roof, right?" Serena asked.

"Right."

Troy shouldered through the office, and Serena followed. He had an open-toed, muscle-bound walk, and his footsteps were heavy. He found an empty cubicle near the office door and squeezed himself onto the three-legged stool in front of the computer. His thick fingers manipulated the keyboard like a pro.

"This is from thirty seconds ago," he said, pulling up a photo aimed toward the boardwalk beyond the Inn on Lake Superior. "The camera shoots every few seconds, shifts angles, and shoots again. We get 180-degree coverage along Canal Park Drive. It's always on."

"How's the resolution?" Serena asked.

Troy zoomed using the computer mouse. He enlarged the photo, focusing on a Chevy pickup in the hotel parking lot across the street, until the license plate of the truck was crisp and clear.

"Pretty darn good," he said, smiling.

Serena felt a rush of adrenaline. She wanted to see the bomber's face. "Let's go back to last Tuesday."

"Sure."

Troy called up files in a subdirectory, and he scrolled down, hunting for the photo archives from Tuesday evening. As he did, Serena saw his face take on a darker cast. He reviewed the list three times, and then he opened up the directory of deleted files. When he didn't find anything, he pushed away from the desk and bumped his right fist against his chin.

"What's up?" Serena asked.

"The files from Tuesday night are missing," Troy told her.

"Missing? Were they erased?"

"It doesn't look that way. They just don't exist. We have photos up to Tuesday afternoon, and then nothing again until Thursday morning."

"How does something like that happen?" she asked.

"That's what we're going to find out." Troy called out in a booming voice. "Hey, Decker? You here? Where are you?"

A young man who couldn't be more than twenty years old popped his head around the side of the cubicle. He had bushy blond hair and an equally bushy beard. "What's up, Troy?"

"Serena, Arlin Decker. He's our PR and marketing intern. Arlin, Serena's with the DPD."

"Nice to meet you," Decker said. He wore a marathon T-shirt and jean shorts, and he leaned against the cubicle wall. "What do you need, Troy?"

"The photo files from Tuesday are missing," Troy said.

Decker's face fell. "Oh, yeah. Shit, sorry, I kept meaning to tell you about that. We got it fixed before race day, so I figured, no big deal."

"Got what fixed?"

"The camera feed went down last Tuesday, but nobody even noticed it until Thursday, when we started testing everything. You know what it's like in those last few days before the race. Everybody's crazed. As soon as we realized the camera was down, we got the video people in to check it out and get it up and running again."

"What was the problem?" Serena asked.

"The cable was unplugged. Stupid, huh? Thing just came loose from the computer here, and somebody must have stepped on it, because the prongs were bent. Had to have the company bring a new one. The camera was working fine, but we lost all the data."

Serena looked at Troy, who waved Decker away. When they were alone, she murmured, "Somebody sabotaged that cable."

"Looks that way," Troy agreed.

"Is there a way of pulling together a list of people who were in the office on Tuesday afternoon? I need to track them all down."

Troy groaned. "Four days before the race? We had people in and out of here all day long."

"Like who?"

"Oh, man. The chaos is pretty much twenty-four hours a day at that point. You want a few examples just off the top of my head? We had meetings with the advance teams for the bands who were performing on Friday and Saturday nights. We had a VIP tasting for the spaghetti dinner, and believe me, nobody misses that. We finalized arrangements for transport and housing of the elite runners and several of the specialty runner groups from various charities and religious organizations. We had reps from the health care group sponsoring the fitness expo having a meltdown about the map for the booths, because two participants dropped out at the last minute. We had a mouse in Lorena's office, so she was going nuts about that. We had the bus company CEO warning us about a possible drivers' strike, which never materialized. Do you want me to go on? Because that's just scraping the surface, Serena."

"No, I get it. It was a zoo."

"Always is," Troy said.

"I'm sorry, but I still need the list," she told him. "Make it as complete as possible. Have every person on staff write down all the people that they can remember being in the office on Tuesday. I want copies

of everyone's calendar for that day, too, as well as incoming and outgoing e-mails and phone records. I need to go through all of it. Someone
pulled the plug on that camera. Someone was here, inside the marathon office. Either it was the bomber himself, or it was somebody who
got paid to do the job."

Troy saluted. "Okay. I'm here to help. I'll get it all to you this
evening."

"Thanks."

"Mind if I walk you out?" Troy added, and Serena knew from the
look on his face that Troy had something else to tell her that he didn't
want to say in front of the others in the office.

They descended the stairs to the outer door that led to Canal Park
Drive. Beside them was a storage area where the race staff kept everything from bottled water to T-shirts to boxes of lanyards. It was dark,
with the light off, but Troy unlocked the door and beckoned Serena
inside. He closed the door, and they were alone in the warm space.

"Did you want to tell me something?" Serena asked.

Troy's face was unhappy. "Look, you know me. I don't have a prejudiced bone in my body."

"I know that."

"The thing is, I was thinking about the groups that were in here
on Tuesday."

"Okay," Serena said.

Troy hesitated. He shook his head, as if he was angry with himself.

"Tell me what's on your mind," she urged him.

"Well, part of our marketing effort is diversity, okay? This year,
members of the local mosque reached out to us to expand the repre-
sentation of Muslims running in the race. It was very successful. We
had almost forty new Muslim participants, and we worked with local
sponsors to make sure they had housing and that we were attuned to
any special religious or dietary concerns."

"And on Tuesday?" Serena asked.

"We met with several members of the mosque for a final check-in
about the needs of the Muslim runners," Troy replied. "They were all
in the marathon office upstairs."

40

Maggie found Shelly Baker in her hospital bed. Wade Ralston sat in a chair beside her. Talking to witnesses never bothered Maggie, but this time, she had to gin up the courage to go inside. She knew that Shelly had suffered grievous injuries in the marathon bombing, and she was reluctant to add to her burden by telling her that her brother, Travis, was now a suspect in a double homicide.

In the doorway, she cleared her throat, and the two people looked up. For Maggie, that first split second with someone always told the tale. Shelly's expression was blank, but Wade Ralston's eyes darted back and forth with beady, nervous alarm. That was as good as a confession.

He knew exactly why Maggie was there.

"Mr. Ralston, I'm glad to see you up and about," she said. "Ms. Baker, my name is Maggie Bei. I'm a Sergeant with the Duluth Police. I'm sorry to bother you during your recovery."

The woman in bed looked drained of energy. "What do you want?"

"I'm trying to find your brother, Travis. Do you have any idea where he is?"

"Travis? At my place, probably. I have a Central Hillside apartment, and he usually stays with me. He doesn't have a place of his own."

"No, he's not there. I already checked. When did you last see him?"

"Yesterday afternoon," Shelly replied. "What is this about, Sergeant? Why are you looking for Travis?"

"I just need to ask him a few questions. Can you think of anywhere else your brother might be?"

"At Wade's house, I guess," Shelly said, turning to Ralston with a curious expression. "Have you talked to Travis today, Wade?"

Ralston's face was suddenly as empty as a fresh sheet of paper. "Nope."

"Travis works for your company, doesn't he, Mr. Ralston?" Maggie asked.

"That's right."

"Does he ever drive your white van?"

"Yes, he does. It's got a big logo for The Bug Zappers on the side. Termites, cockroaches, ants, rodents, wasps, Asian beetles. If you have any critter issues, we're the ones to call. You can count on us to kill 'em all." He said it with a grim smile, as if he was reciting the copy from a television ad.

"When did you last see Travis?" Maggie asked him.

"Same as Shelly. Yesterday afternoon, here in the hospital."

"Have you talked to him today?"

She could read Ralston's eyes and the twitch in his mouth, and she knew he was about to lie.

"I haven't, no."

"You're sure about that?"

"Positive," Ralston said.

"Would he be driving your company van?"

"Probably. I like him to ride around in the van. It's good advertising."

"Was he working on any jobs for you today?" Maggie asked.

"No, not unless somebody called with an emergency. This was my first day out of the hospital. I cancelled all of our jobs. I'm sure we'll be back at work tomorrow, though, crawling into the basements downtown. It's a glamorous job, but somebody has to do it." His mouth bent into a sarcastic grin.

"I wonder if you'd mind calling Travis for me," Maggie said. "Maybe he'll answer the phone for you."

"Sure, if you'd like."

He dug into his pocket for a phone, and he turned on the power. He dialed a number but then immediately ended the call.

"It went straight to voice mail," he said. "Sorry. Do you want me to call back and leave a message?"

"No, that's fine. Where is your business located, Mr. Ralston?"

"I run it out of my house on Five Corners Road. Shelly is our accountant and scheduler. Travis and I do the dirty work."

"Have you been home today?"

"Yes. Got out this morning, went straight home. I took a nap. I was pretty worn out. I've been through a lot."

"Yes, I'm very sorry for your loss. Did you see Travis while you were there? Did he come to the house?"

"I already said no," Ralston replied. "Unless he stopped by while I was asleep."

"Tell me something. I'm afraid I don't know much about the extermination business. Do you require supplies of gasoline in your line of work?"

Ralston's face was frozen. "Gasoline? No, we don't kill bugs with gasoline."

"These seem like very odd questions," Shelly Baker interrupted. "Do you suspect Travis of doing something wrong, Sergeant?"

"Well, as I said, we'd just like to talk to him," Maggie replied. "Can you think of anywhere else that he might go, other than to your apartment or to Mr. Ralston's house?"

"He has a lot of friends," Shelly replied.

"Mostly women friends," Ralston added. "You've never met a bigger horndog than Travis. Kid loves to drink and party, and his body is nothing but muscles and tats. Girls go for that sort of thing, I guess. It's not his brains they're after, that's for sure."

Shelly shot Ralston an impenetrable look, and Ralston smiled back at her with no warmth at all.

"Does he have a specific girlfriend he might stay with?" Maggie asked.

"No, he'll go home with whoever happens to be at Curly's on any given night," Ralston replied.

"Ms. Baker, when you talked to your brother yesterday, did he mention any plans he had?"

"What do you mean?"

"Did he tell you what he was going to do last night?" Maggie asked.

"No."

"Was he angry about what happened to you?"

"Yes, he was very upset. Wouldn't you be?"

"Of course. Mr. Ralston, what about you? Did Travis talk about any plans with you?"

"Travis isn't much for plans," Ralston replied. "He's a spur of the moment guy. He does whatever pops into his head. Was he angry? Yeah, he was angry. We're all angry. We're all pretty frustrated, too, because you people don't seem any closer to catching the bomber."

"As soon as we know anything, we'll be communicating with all the victims and their families," Maggie said. "In the meantime, if you do see Travis, or if he contacts either one of you, please ask him to get in touch with the police immediately."

"We'll do that," Ralston replied.

Maggie turned and left the hospital room before they could ask her anything else. Being there made her claustrophobic. She walked to the end of the hallway, where the windows of a patient lounge looked out on the lake. It was almost dark. She checked her phone to read an update from Guppo, but the white van hadn't been spotted yet.

Travis Baker was out there somewhere, probably holed up for the night.

She knew he was guilty of killing Ahdia and Pak Rashid and burning down the art gallery. And so did Wade Ralston.

* * *

Silence hung like a suffocating pillow over the hospital room. Wade didn't say a word, but he felt Shelly watching him and waiting for him to look back at her. He got up and stretched. The surgical incision still hurt. He turned on the television without the sound. He stood watching it, his back to the hospital bed.

"Wade?" Shelly called to him. "What was that all about?"

"Hell if I know," he murmured.

"I think you do know. I could see it in your face. What's going on?"

Wade scowled and turned around. "Nothing."

"Where's Travis?"

"I have no idea."

He'd told the kid to lay low, which had turned out to be good advice. He wasn't surprised that the cops had zeroed in on Travis already. The kid always left a trail a mile wide whenever he did something stupid.

"Why are they looking for Travis?" Shelly asked.

Wade returned to the chair and sat down next to her. "Don't worry about it. It's probably nothing."

"He's my brother. Of course, I'm worried. You know what he's like. Travis doesn't think before he does things."

Wade fired back at her. He didn't care what he said anymore. "Maybe if you held him accountable for his stupid shit once in a while, instead of making excuses and telling him that God loves him no matter what he does, he wouldn't be in such a mess."

He could see her heart rate escalate on the monitor.

"Wade, please tell me what's going on," she said.

He said nothing.

Shelly began to protest, but then her eyes widened as she stared at the television screen. He glanced over his shoulder and saw video footage on CNN of the burnt-out Woodland gallery behind him. He swore under his breath. He didn't need to connect the dots for her. She could do that all by herself.

"Gasoline," Shelly murmured. "That policewoman asked about gasoline."

"Yeah, she did."

"They think Travis did this!" she went on. "Wade, did he? Did Travis burn down that building and kill those people?"

"We shouldn't be talking about it, Shelly."

"Oh, my God. Oh, Travis, what did you do? Wade, did you put this awful idea into his head? Was it you? He wouldn't come up with a plan like this on his own. He does whatever you tell him."

Wade hissed at her to be quiet as her voice rose. He got up and quickly closed the door to the hospital room. "Shut the hell up, Shelly.

I had nothing to do with this, do you hear me? Nothing. This is all your baby brother's fault. He got himself into this shit on his own, and now it's too late."

Tears crept down Shelly's pale face. "He only did this to avenge what happened to me and Joni. You know that. If they catch him, he'll go to prison for the rest of his life. Is that what you want?"

Wade couldn't keep the harshness out of his voice. "No, that's not what I want. I never said I wanted him in prison."

"The terrorists are the real criminals. Not Travis. They did this to me. They killed your wife."

"That doesn't change anything," Wade said. "The police don't care."

Shelly closed her eyes, and he heard her murmuring a prayer, calling on Jesus as if he were in the next room and could stop by to work out a plan. Religious people were so naïve. They didn't live in the real world.

"Praying won't help him," Wade told her. "You're kidding yourself. Even God can't help Travis now. It's too late for that."

Shelly opened her eyes again. "Then *you* have to help him, Wade."

41

Malik arrived back at the house after dark. He slipped silently through the rear door and then fell back against it, breathing heavily. He looked hopped up and jittery, and his face was bleeding.

"What happened?" Khan asked, pointing at the blood. "You're hurt."

His friend wiped his cheek with a sleeve. "It's nothing. I made my way through the woods to avoid being seen. Thorns scratched me."

Malik went into the living room and paced nervously. He couldn't seem to stay still. His muscles twitched, and he rubbed his hands together. He kept going to the curtains and looking outside, despite his own warnings that it wasn't safe to do so.

"Are you all right?" Khan asked.

"Don't worry about me."

Khan let his friend bounce from wall to wall like a pinball until he couldn't stand it anymore, and then he blocked him with his hands firmly on his shoulders. "You're hyperventilating. Stop and relax."

Malik closed his eyes. His chest swelled with a deep breath. "Yes, you're right."

"Something's wrong," Khan said. "What is it?"

"Nothing is wrong. I'm fine. I know what to do. I have a plan."

"Well, good. What's happening outside? Can we escape?"

Malik laughed, which sounded strange and inappropriate, like a joke told in a cemetery. "Oh, no. Escape is impossible right now."

"The police?"

"They're everywhere. Squad cars are going up and down the streets. I don't know if the mayor declared a curfew after dark or whether people are simply scared, but the entire neighborhood seems to be sheltered in place. I was lucky to get back here unseen. One of the police cars used a spotlight on the woods, and I ducked down just before it lit me up."

"And yet you have a plan," Khan said dubiously.

"Yes, trust me. The good news is that the car appears to be safe. It's not being watched." Malik dug in his pocket and found a set of keys, which he shoved into Khan's hand.

"Why are you giving me these?" Khan asked.

Malik ignored him and paced again. "It will be best for you to leave around midnight, I think. It should be safe then, but you'll know if it is. You'll be able to tell. The car is a burgundy Taurus parked in the woods at the dead end of Gordon Street on the other side of the golf course. You can't see it unless you hike into the trees. There's a house near there, but the owners appear to be gone, so no one should see you."

"I don't understand," Khan said.

"Then listen! Pay attention! It's important. There's a GPS navigator in the glove compartment of the car. Stay off the freeway. My advice is that you go west to the town of McGregor and then head south on Highway 65. They won't be watching out there. Start making your way to Minneapolis. You don't need to go all the way. If you want to rest for a couple of hours in one of the parks, that should be okay. Tomorrow will be a long day."

Khan stared into his friend's dark eyes. "What about you?"

Malik shook his head. "This is your journey, Khan. I can't go with you."

"You're sending me alone?"

"It's the only way. Be alert, because we don't have much time. Even outside Duluth, you're still recognizable. Your photo has been everywhere. I found an old baseball cap for you. Keep it on. If you find a convenience store where it looks safe, buy a razor, shaving cream, and some other sundries so it doesn't look suspicious, and shave off your beard. Get sunglasses, too, for the morning."

"Where do I go?"

"Drive to West River Parkway in Minneapolis. Go to a place called Mill Ruins Park near the Mississippi. Park there by ten in the morning, and wait. A man will approach you. Go with him, and leave the Taurus and the keys behind. Someone else will take care of the car. After that, you're in their hands. That's the start of your new life, Khan."

Khan laced his hands on top of his head. He could feel the sweat of his own anxiety gathering on his skin. "I don't know if I can do this."

"Yes, you can."

"Not without you," Khan said.

"It has to be this way."

Khan walked to the front window and nudged the curtains aside an inch. He could see that Malik was right. The swirling lights of a police cruiser lit up the night where it was parked at the end of the street, near the golf course. Another police car swept past the house, even as he watched. They were in a box. He aligned the curtains again and shook his head.

"I'll never make it," Khan said. "They'll grab me as soon as I leave."

"Let me worry about that. I told you, I have a plan."

"What is it?"

Malik didn't answer. He crossed the room and embraced Khan tightly. He put both hands on Khan's cheeks. "I know you never wanted to be in this position. Right now, the pain seems like it will never end, but someday it will get better."

"Unlikely."

"Think of the winds that scatter," Malik told him, quoting the Qur'an. "They lift and bear away heavy weights."

"I'd like to feel those winds. Right now, the burden feels impossible to carry. I'm lost."

"Well, you'll have time to find yourself, after tomorrow. Don't for-get what I told you. Wait until midnight. By then it should be safe to go to the car and make your escape."

"Why?" Khan asked. "How can it be safe?"

"Because by then they will no longer be looking for you," Malik said with a mysterious, serene smile. "At least not for a day or more. It will give you time."

"How is that possible?"

"I told you, trust me. And remember to take the gun with you."

Khan scowled. The last thing he wanted was to hold a gun in his hand. He couldn't imagine it. He could never point it at another human being. The thought of it was immoral.

"No gun," he insisted.

Malik sighed long and hard, as if Khan, who was years older, was as foolish as a little child. "Fine, give it back to me, then. I just hope you never need it."

The gun was exactly where Malik had left it hours earlier, on the floor near a corner of the dusty room. Khan walked toward it, and Malik followed as closely as a shadow. Khan bent down to retrieve the weapon, although he was reluctant even to take it in his hand. The gun was an ugly thing. Behind him, he could hear the quick, nervous rush of Malik's breathing and the rustle of his clothes.

"I'm very sorry, my friend," Malik murmured in his ear.

Over his head, Khan felt rather than heard a rush of air.

Then something hard crashed down onto the bone of his skull, which erupted like a bomb of pain and light. His jaw clamped shut; he bit his tongue. His scalp burned. The room spun before his eyes. It was over in an instant. He didn't feel himself falling into an abyss. He was already unconscious by the time his body collapsed to the floor.

42

Gayle Durkin tried to read Special Agent Maloney's face as he sat down behind the desk. That was what she did; she read faces. She knew when people were hiding things. She knew when they were lying. Her insights typically gave her an advantage when she was face-to-face with someone. Most people couldn't keep secrets from her, but Maloney was one of the few who could. The things that were so expressive in others—eyes, mouth, the tilt of one's head, the positioning of hands—gave her no clues with him.

He'd asked for a private meeting. Just the two of them. Drop whatever she was doing, and come back to the DECC. She had no idea what to expect, and that made her nervous.

"Thank you for joining me, Agent Durkin," Maloney told her in the same emotionless voice he always used. The desk in front of him was empty except for a slim file folder.

"Of course, sir."

"Can you review for me the events on Sunday night that led up to the death of Officer Kenzie?" Maloney asked.

Gayle was confused. "Yes, sir. I did write up a full report about that yesterday."

"I know. I've read it." Maloney folded his hands together and waited. He didn't say anything more.

She found herself stuttering, which was unlike her. "Okay. Well, I passed Rashid's vehicle as I was responding to the reports from the Woodland Market. I reversed course and gave chase. I followed him to a road bordering the Park Hill Cemetery, where I found his taxi crashed. At that point, I pursued him on foot through the cemetery. I reached the road that divides Park Hill and Forest Hill, and at that point, I spotted Rashid on the other side of the fence. Backup was arriving from both directions, and I heard the voice of Officer Kenzie shouting at Rashid to stop."

"Where was Officer Kenzie in relation to you?" Maloney asked.

"Based on the direction of his voice, I believe he was about thirty yards directly in front of me. That was also where his body was found."

"And Rashid?"

"Rashid was at a forty-five-degree angle to me, about twenty-five yards inside the fence."

"What happened next?" Maloney asked.

Gayle looked for any clues at all in Maloney's face and voice as to what this interrogation was about. She found none. Even so, with each question, her anxiety soared.

"Well, there was a flash of lightning, and I saw a gun in Rashid's hand, so I shouted a warning."

"Are you sure about the gun?"

"Am I—well, it was dark and raining, and it happened fast, but, yes, I'm sure. And Officer Kenzie is dead, so obviously—"

Maloney interrupted her. "How many shots did you fire?"

"Two."

"Did any of the backup units fire?"

"No, sir."

"What about Officer Kenzie? How many shots did he fire?"

"I'm not sure. There were at least two shots from the other side of the fence before I fired, but I don't know which shots came from Officer Kenzie and which came from Rashid."

"Thank you, Agent Durkin." Maloney opened the file folder in front of him. "I'm afraid I have upsetting news for you."

Gayle could almost hear the roar of the blood pumping in her head. "What's that, sir?"

"This is the ballistics report from Quantico," Maloney told her, gesturing at the file. "They were able to match the bullet taken from Officer Kenzie's body to the gun that fired it."

"How is that possible? We didn't recover Rashid's gun at the scene."

"I'm sorry, Agent Durkin. The bullet that killed Officer Kenzie didn't come from Rashid's gun. It came from your gun."

Gayle blinked. "What? That's not possible."

"I'm afraid there's no question about it. At my request, they ran the test again to be one hundred percent certain."

She bolted from her chair but had to grab the desk to keep from falling. She felt as if a tornado were swirling in front of her face, threatening to suck her in. "Sir, I fired at *Rashid*. He was at an angle to me. Officer Kenzie was nowhere near my line of fire. I couldn't possibly have hit him."

"I understand. Based on stone residue found on the bullet, the ballistics team believe the bullet likely ricocheted off a headstone in the cemetery and struck Officer Kenzie."

"Oh, my God."

"It was a freak accident," Maloney told her. "It wasn't your fault."

Gayle tried to find words, but she didn't have any. She could feel the rain on her skin again. She remembered the heaviness of the gun in her hand. The lightning blinded her. She heard her own voice, shouting. She felt the recoil as she fired.

Her gun.

She'd killed a police officer.

"What—what happens next, sir?" she asked.

"There will be a full investigation, which should be completed within two weeks. Given your report and the ballistics findings, I don't believe any blame will attach to you."

"Thank you, sir," Gayle replied, trying to keep her voice steady.

"Typically, we encourage agents involved in shootings to take five days of administrative leave. If you wish to do so, you should, and we'll make mental health support services available to you."

"Am I required to take leave, sir?" she asked. "Because with the bomber still out there, I'd rather stay."

"No, it's optional at the agency, and if you'd prefer to continue working, I'd prefer that for now, too, because I need you on this investigation. But if there's any hint of this situation affecting your performance, I'll pull you from active duty immediately. Is that understood?"

"Yes, sir."

"That'll be all, Durkin."

"Thank you, sir."

Gayle turned around and left the office. She put one foot in front of the other, not wanting Maloney to see any hesitation in her walk. She squared her shoulders, keeping her expression blank for any of the other agents who might be looking her way. Outside, she made her way to the restroom at the far end of the hallway, and she made sure she was alone before she locked herself in a stall.

Then she sank to her knees and threw up.

She closed her eyes and made sure she was done, and she stood up unsteadily and left the stall. At the sink, she rinsed her mouth and washed her face. Her skin was pale, but it was always pale. Another agent entered the bathroom. They didn't know each other. Gayle nodded at her, and the other woman nodded back but didn't take any special interest in her. That was good.

She left the DECC and stepped outside into the darkness of the Duluth night. She crossed the street, where a strip of sidewalk and grass bordered the calm water of the harbor. Her eyes squeezed shut. Her breathing came faster. A ferocious headache pushed against her forehead. She wanted to scream, and she wanted to find a wall and beat it with her fists.

Gayle heard footsteps. Someone was following her. Quickly, she wiped her eyes, which had leaked tears. She pasted a calm expression onto her face and turned around. Stride stood facing her, only six feet away.

"You heard?" she asked.

"Yes, Pat told me."

"Are you here to blame me?"

"I'm here to make sure you're okay."

Gayle didn't answer. She spun back to the harbor, because she felt her face grow hot, and she knew she was going to cry again. She couldn't let him see that. She couldn't risk being taken off the case. Her tears were silent, but he came up behind her and put a hand on her shoulder.

"This wasn't your fault, Durkin," Stride said. "A ricochet? That's a one-in-a-million bad break."

She still said nothing, because she knew her voice would be a mess.

"I don't blame you," Stride went on. "No one on my team is going to blame you. And Officer Kenzie's family will understand when we tell them. It's a tragedy, but you didn't make this happen."

Gayle stared up at the stars in the night sky. Finally, she turned around, and her glassy, tear-streaked stare met his eyes, which were watching her closely. "Come on, Stride. Maloney already asked me. You can ask me, too. I know what you want."

"Okay," he said quietly. "Are you still absolutely certain that Rashid had a gun?"

She saw it again.

The flash of silver in Rashid's hand.

"Stride, I've been replaying that moment over and over in my head. Everything happened so fast. Rain was pouring down. The lightning came and went like a flashbulb. I'm telling you, I *saw a gun*. I saw Rashid raising his arm, pointing toward Officer Kenzie. If you asked me to swear on a stack of Bibles, I'd do it. Except I've talked to enough eyewitnesses to know they make mistakes about this shit all the time."

"Yes, they do," Stride said.

"So am I sure? No. Not anymore. And, yeah, I know, it's a big deal, because without Rashid killing Kenzie, we don't have any evidence of him being guilty of anything. Maybe he was just in the wrong place at the wrong time. For the life of me, I don't know. If he's innocent, he's already paid a horrible price for my mistake."

She stared at Stride, as if he could give her answers, even though she knew he couldn't. She felt as if she could unburden herself to him, as foolish as it was. He owed her nothing. His team didn't like her. If he wanted to get her kicked off the investigation, he probably could. Even so, he had a way of commanding trust, and she typically didn't trust anyone.

"I understand there's a box on the FBI job application about being perfect," Stride said. "Did you forget to check that?"

Gayle gave him a broken laugh. "I guess so."

"Look, if I see what I think is a gun, I call it out," Stride told her. "The alternative gets people killed. And, yeah, sometimes human beings make mistakes, and the results can be tragic. But if my best judgment tells me it's a gun, I still call it out. If I'd been standing in your shoes, I would have done exactly the same thing."

"Thanks."

Stride's phone rang. He backed up and took the call, and he didn't say much as he listened. Gayle replayed the moment in the cemetery in her head. She knew she wouldn't do anything else for a long time. She'd see it in her waking hours, and she'd see it in her dreams.

He hung up the phone and gestured to her. "Come on, Durkin, let's go."

"What's up?" she asked.

"Someone just called 911," Stride said. "Rashid was spotted in the Woodland neighborhood on Kolstad Avenue. We're surrounding the area."

43

Malik moved like a ghost through the backyards. In the darkness, he was mostly invisible. He wore a loose-fitting XXL black sweatshirt with the hood pulled over his head, dark jeans, and black sneakers. Despite the night, he used sunglasses. He didn't want anyone to see his face too clearly. If the police or the neighbors spotted him, they'd realize that the man on the run was not Khan Rashid. And then the plan would fail.

He stayed hidden, except when he crossed from one street to the next like a cat. The lots here were flat and big, dotted by tall trees. No one had fences. Without a light, he had to move slowly, ducking past detached garages and swing sets and pushing through wooded lots that were dense with weeds. Every now and then, a chained dog barked and growled, but no one came outside to investigate. Near one house, he had to wait for a man to finish a cigarette and return inside from the redwood deck before he could slip across the yard.

When Malik was ten blocks away, more than a mile from the house where Khan was hiding, he made the call. He had a pay-as-you-go phone, and he found a quiet place to dial 911. He was nervous, but nervousness was fine. Anyone making this call would be close to panic, and it was okay for the police to hear it in his voice.

"I was just driving home from the Woodland neighborhood, and I saw a man run across the street right in front of my car. He looked right at me, and I recognized him. It was that man the police have been trying to find. The bomber? The man named Rashid? I was headed east on Mankato Street toward Woodland Avenue, and this man was running south on Kolstad Avenue toward Hartley Park. He was wearing a black hoodie and jeans."

Malik hung up and started moving again.

He kept an ear to the wind, expecting sirens, and he wasn't disappointed. Barely a minute passed before he heard them. They were distant, but they grew louder, and they came from every direction, like insects to the light. They'd all be here soon. The police. FBI. SWAT. Helicopters overhead. They'd bring their assault rifles and their robots. They'd abandon their other positions and leave Khan a path to escape across the golf course and drive south out of the city.

Malik kept off the street, but he stayed parallel to Kolstad Avenue, heading south on a dense trail through the woods. He'd hiked here many times, so he knew the area well. Where the path ended near Wabasha Street, he found himself between two little white houses. A streetlight made it impossible to stay in the dark. He jogged to the corner, catching his breath and leaning against a fat elm tree where the shadows protected him. The streets were still empty, but the police were close. Silhouettes appeared in the house windows as the sirens became screams and neighbors realized that something strange was happening just outside their doors.

Everyone would know soon.

The bomber was here.

Malik broke cover and crossed the street. His timing was bad. Headlights flooded to life not half a block away, from a police car coasting silently down the street. It accelerated with a screech as the driver spotted him, and a bullhorn crackled through the air.

"Freeze! Stay where you are!"

Malik ran down the middle of Ewing Avenue. As he did, he drew his pistol from inside his belt. Behind him, tires squealed as the squad car jerked around the street corner. He stopped, cocked the weapon, and turned around and fired toward the windshield of the police car. Once, twice, three times. Brakes jerked the car to a stop. Glass shattered. He saw the driver's door fly open, and Malik spun away and ran again.

Bullets followed him.

The police officer fired again and again. The game was on. *Here I am. Chase me.*

He cut from the street into the nearest yard, where the frame of the house blocked him from the cop. He wasn't concerned about noise now. He ducked between a red pickup truck and an open garage and fought his way through a swath of lilac bushes. He heard boots behind him, but there were no more gunshots. He jumped a low chain-link fence and zigzagged from house to house, hugging the walls. When he stopped and listened, he heard sirens everywhere, almost on top of him. He sucked in a breath and charged down a narrow driveway that broke out onto Anoka Street.

Another squad car was there, its lights off. Another police officer was there, covered behind the open door of the cruiser.

"Stop! Hands in the air!"

Malik fired. A bullet hit the cruiser door. Another sailed high. The cop ducked down but then spun from the car and fired back multiple times. Dirt and gravel spit from the ground around Malik, and he leaped toward the cover of the nearest tree, but he was too late. A bullet hit his leg, shattering bone, and his weight carried him down. He rolled over onto his back, the gun still in his hand.

The cop stood up.

Mistake.

They both aimed. They both fired again, over and over, a hail of bullets. Bark from the tree exploded. Dust made a cloud. The cop shouldn't have missed, but somehow, he did. Malik, dizzied by pain, took a wild shot that never should have hit a thing, but somehow, his bullet drilled through the cop's throat, sending up a spray of blood. The cop's gun fell; his hands flew to his throat. Malik pushed himself to his feet immediately. His right leg dragged like dead weight. The street was dark, and the cop couldn't see his face, so he didn't waste time firing again. He needed to get away, so he crossed in front of the squad car and lost himself in the maze of trees and yards.

He limped as fast as he could. More cops would be converging on the area in seconds. Blood trailed behind him, running in a warm stream down his skin and leaving a path for anyone to follow. He passed a back porch and found someone's T-shirt draped over the wooden railing. He grabbed it and tied it around his leg, soaking up the blood, and then he pushed his way into the trees to cover his trail.

He kept going. The lights of the police cars were bright enough and close enough to light up the sky above the trees like fireworks. He heard their radios and the bark of voices nearby. Cops were in the woods. Dogs bayed. Close by, windows and doors slammed shut. As word spread, the neighborhood locked down. He was lost and dizzy. His leg was numb, and blood overtook the tourniquet. Pain throbbed with his heartbeat, like a hot poker pressed over and over to the hole in his skin.

He knew he couldn't go much farther.

He staggered across another street, but he didn't know which one. An open stretch of grass lay in front of him, between a stand of trees and a two-story beige house with a screened porch in the rear. Behind the house, he spotted a windowless aluminum storage shed with a red door.

Malik crossed the grass. He couldn't support his weight anymore. When he slipped to his knees, he crawled. There were lights on in the house, but no one came to the windows, and no one looked outside. He dragged himself past a fenced garden filled with tomato vines and stopped at the door of the storage shed. It slid upward on tracks, and he threw up the door and rolled inside. With a bang, the door slammed closed behind him. The interior smelled of soil and fertilizer. In the blackness, he couldn't see anything, but he heard the buzz of bees as he disturbed a hive nestled in the beams overhead.

Your Lord told the bees, build homes in the hills and trees and in the structures made by men.

Malik sank backward, his body wedged against the metal door. He listened to the angry bees, and he waited for the end.

* * *

The neighbors on Northfield Street had given Ethan only one rule for house-sitting: Don't let the cat out.

They were spending two weeks on an ecotourism vacation somewhere in the mountains of Costa Rica. For Ethan, who was sixteen years old and lived a block away, this was the best summer adventure ever. His neighbors, the Carlsons, had stocked the fridge with Mountain Dew and homemade cookie dough and frozen Heggies Pizza. He could play Minecraft all night long. He could binge-watch *Game of Thrones* on their sixty-inch television and replay the nude scenes as many times as he wanted.

It was an easy gig. Water the plants. Scoop the litter box. Mow the lawn. And above all, above all, don't let the cat out.

Now he was screwed.

The sirens had brought Ethan to the front window, where it looked like a Jason Bourne movie outside. Police cars roared up and down the street. Floodlights scanned the woods and the yards. His mother had called to tell him: Stay inside the house, and make sure everything's locked. He'd followed instructions, but when he spotted three police officers in military gear walking side by side down the street with rifles in their hands, he couldn't stop himself. He cracked the front door and called out: "Hey, guys, what's going on?"

One of the cops shouted, "Get back in the house, lock the door, and don't come out!"

Ethan did, but he was too late. The door was only open a few inches, but a few inches were plenty for Fuzzball. Like a streak of orange lightning, the cat was out the door and gone.

"Crap!"

He bolted down the steps into the driveway to chase the cat. The cop saw him and had a fit.

"Son, I said, get inside the house *right now!*"

He started to explain about the missing cat, but when a cop with a rifle marched up the driveway toward him, he turned around and ran back inside and locked the door. That was half an hour ago. He was still inside, the cops were still outside, and so was Fuzzball. He didn't dare open the front door again.

Ethan went downstairs to the finished basement. He let himself out through the patio doors onto the screened porch that bordered the garden, the storage shed, and the woods behind the house. The evening was warm and dank. A mosquito whined in his ear, and he slapped it away. He went to the screen door that led outside and peered into the darkness.

"Fuzzball!" he hissed. "Fuzzball, come!"

But Fuzzball was a cat, and he didn't come when he was called.

Ethan went back inside and retrieved a flashlight and brought it to the screen door and shined a light into the yard. He checked the garden. No cat. He cast a beam up and down the grass. No cat.

"Fuzzball!"

Ethan unhooked the lock on the screen door and stepped outside. He wasn't visible from the street here, so he figured the cops wouldn't see him. He left the porch light off to keep the mosquitoes away, but they dove for him, anyway, as if he'd bathed in sugar water. He walked to the wire fence around the garden and cast the light along the rows of tomatoes. Despite the fence, rabbits still got inside sometimes, and he wondered if the smell of rabbit had encouraged the cat to go streaking out of the house.

But Fuzzball wasn't in the garden.

He lit up the crabapple tree and the spireas growing along the foundation of the house. No cat. Then he walked deeper into the yard, past the garden, toward the old metal storage shed, swinging his flashlight beam along the grass; it was short, because he'd mowed it that afternoon.

There was Fuzzball, outside the shed, lapping up water that had pooled near the door.

"Hey, buddy, there you are," Ethan said quietly, not wanting the cat to scamper for the woods. If the cat did that, he'd never see him again. "You know, if you were thirsty, we've got water inside."

He approached with slow, careful steps, but Fuzzball paid no attention. The cat let Ethan come right up next to him, and Ethan bent over and scooped the cat up by its stomach.

"Gotcha!" he said with a sigh of relief. Fuzzball fussed, but Ethan held him tightly.

The cat's paws were wet. Soaking wet. Ethan turned the flashlight around to light up his white T-shirt, and he was puzzled to see red paw prints smudged all over his chest. He lit up Fuzzball's paws. They were red, too. The underside of the cat's fur was all red. So were Ethan's hands.

He swung the cone of light back to the ground. He could see a puddle leeching from under the door of the metal shed, but it wasn't water. The liquid was dark red, like wine. He sniffed his fingers, and he knew what it was.

It was blood.

Ethan stared at the storage shed and saw that there was blood everywhere. On the ground. On the grass. On the door. It was a lake of blood, growing larger. From inside the shed, someone groaned, and the frame of the door rattled.

With Fuzzball still in his arms, Ethan spun around, shouted, and ran for the street.

44

"Khan Rashid! Open the door, and keep your hands in the air!"

The voice of the FBI negotiator boomed through the speaker in the DECC conference room that served as the command center. There was no answer from the metal shed on Northfield Street. There had been no answer for an hour.

As the FBI, police, and SWAT teams communicated back and forth between the Woodland neighborhood and the DECC, Stride found himself scribbling on the legal pad in front of him.

He wrote: *Rashid shot a cop.*

Then he changed it.

Rashid shot a cop?

Special Agent Durkin, who was seated next to him, glanced at the pad and whispered into his ear. "What's up? What are you thinking?"

Stride was thinking that none of this made sense.

"I don't know. I was shocked when the report came in that we had an officer down. I know Rashid was on the run, but I didn't think he'd turn violent. I really didn't think we had the right man."

"Khan Rashid! You're bleeding. You need medical attention. Open the door, and keep your hands away from your body."

Again there was no answer.

"Do we have any options for getting the door of the shed open?" Agent Maloney asked the tactical commander on the scene.

"We sent in the robot, but we couldn't unjam the door," the commander replied. "Either the suspect locked it from inside, or he's got it blocked. It means we're blind for now. All we can do is listen."

"What are we hearing?" Maloney asked.

"The suspect doesn't seem to be moving. We think he's on the ground. We can hear the occasional moan, but that could be a fake to mislead us about his condition. However, he's lost a lot of blood, and there's still blood coming from under the door. Sooner or later, he'll be critical, if he isn't already."

Maloney turned to the people in the command center. "Thoughts?"

"If he dies, we lose the chance to question him and find out if he was part of a larger network," Durkin said. "We should go in."

"Yes, I'd like him alive, if possible," Maloney agreed. He turned to Stride. "What about the officers who had eyes on him? What can they tell us about the magnitude of the threat?"

"He fired at them," Stride replied, "so we know he has at least one gun. Beyond that, it was too dark to assess if he had other weapons or additional ammunition."

"Have we found any unclaimed vehicles in the neighborhood? Do we know if he came by car or by foot?"

"Nothing on that yet," Stride said.

Maloney tapped the eraser of a pencil rhythmically on the conference room table. The point of the pencil was perfectly sharp. The agent's face was a mask as he wrestled with the decision. What to do next. To go in or to wait.

Stride had been in Maloney's shoes more than once. There were no easy answers when a suspect was injured and trapped. You could storm the hideout and risk the lives of your officers. You could wait and risk walking away without the truth. He knew what he would do if the decision were his alone. He'd wait. He'd let Rashid die, if it came to that, rather than put more men in jeopardy. He hoped that Maloney, who was a cautious man, would do the same.

And yet something still bothered him.

He had a hard time reconciling the Khan Rashid he'd met on the stairs of the house near UMD with the man who could put a bullet into a police officer's throat. He was certain then that they'd made a mistake about Rashid, but here they were, anyway. A cop was in the hospital; Khan Rashid was bleeding to death in a shed. He'd been wrong about suspects plenty of times in his life, but he was honestly surprised to be wrong about Rashid.

Agent Maloney spoke into the microphone. "Commander, tell him again to toss out his gun."

There was a pause from the scene in Woodland, and then a voice blared through the loudspeaker.

"Rashid! Slide open the door, and toss out your gun. We're trying to save your life."

Silence took over the communications channel. Stride heard nothing from the radio feed. He wanted to hear the metal shed door slide upward on its tracks, but he didn't. The robot outside the shed broadcast a faint noise that sounded like Rashid's ragged breathing.

"Any movement on site?" Maloney asked.

"Negative."

Then everyone in the room flinched in surprise. Gunshots burst over the speaker, one after another in rapid succession, muffled shots from the interior of the shed. It was Rashid, shooting, and the sudden noise triggered a response from the tactical team, whose jittery fingers were already on their weapons. Outside the shed, someone fired, and then someone else fired, and the entire scene erupted in gunfire banging into the metal walls. Fifteen seconds of chaos filled the room before the commander regained control and silenced the weapons.

"What the hell was that?" Maloney demanded.

"The suspect opened fire, sir."

"Is anyone hurt?"

"No, sir."

Maloney placed his hands flat on the table. "I guess we have Rashid's answer."

The room was silent, but then Agent Durkin said, "Not necessarily, sir."

"What do you mean?"

"I mean, the gunfire on its own doesn't make any sense. Rashid can't see anything from inside the shed. Maybe he was *emptying* his weapon. We asked him to open the door and toss his gun out. If he's not physically strong enough to do that, he might have been trying to prove to us that he's no longer a threat. He fired until he ran out of ammunition."

Maloney frowned. "Stride?"

"Or he may be trying to lure us in."

Maloney opened his mouth to reply, but a voice over the microphone interrupted him. It came from the transmitter mounted on the robot at the scene, and it was almost impossible to interpret.

"Commander, what was that? Was that Rashid?"

"I think so, sir." And then, louder, over the bullhorn: "*Rashid, repeat your last communication.*"

They all heard it this time.

"*I surrender.*"

* * *

Khan awoke on the floor in the house at the end of Redwing Road. The pain made him feel as if his skull had been split in two. When he touched the back of his head, the slightest graze of his fingers set off lightning bolts. He pushed himself to his knees, feeling dizzy. When he stood, he fell against a wall, barely able to keep himself upright.

He was alone.

"Malik?" he called, but he knew his friend was gone. The gun that Malik had left for him was still on the floor at his feet. Next to it was a folded sheet of white paper. Khan squatted, feeling the whole world spin, and he retrieved it. He tried to read the note, but the darkness was too black, so he carried it to the front window, where the glow of a nearby streetlight reached inside.

I'm sorry, my friend. This was the only way to set you free. Leave the way I told you, and don't look back.

Khan wondered what time it was. Was it midnight yet? Malik had said he'd know when it was safe, but he had no idea what that meant.

And then he realized, looking outside to the street, that something was different.

The police were gone.

There were no flashing lights. No parked squad cars. No uniformed officers going house to house. He was alone. Somehow, Malik had drawn them all away, just as he'd promised.

Wherever the police were, the emptiness in the neighborhood wouldn't last. The window of escape would only be open for a brief time. Khan realized that Malik was right. It was time to go. He'd thought it would be difficult—impossible—to leave his life in Duluth behind, but now that he was at that moment, he realized he had nothing else to do but walk away. His wife was gone. His son was gone. The only thing he had left were memories, and he could bring those with him.

Standing there in the house, Khan felt something ugly inside his chest. He realized he was bringing something else with him, too.

Hatred.

Anger.

He didn't like those feelings. They were foreign to him. He wished he could drive them away, but they clung to him like ticks that had dug their way into his skin and were feeding on his blood.

Khan walked over to the gun on the floor, picked it up, and shoved it into his belt. He had nothing else to take with him. His head throbbed. It was hard to walk. But he couldn't wait any longer.

He opened the front door. He expected lights and rifles and angry shouts, but instead, the darkness welcomed him. Crickets sang, and frogs croaked out a chorus in the swampy woods. The trees fronting the golf course were on his left. All he had to do was cut across the hilly fairway under the protection of the night and find the burgundy Ford Taurus that Malik had left for him. Get into the car. Drive. Escape. Leave his life behind.

Start over.

He tried to go, but he hesitated on the threshold. He couldn't stop thinking about Malik. Where was he? What had he done?

What was his plan?

By then it should be safe.

Why?

Because they will no longer be looking for you.

Khan's headache made it hard to think. To understand. To puzzle out the answer to the riddle. It made no sense for Malik simply to draw the police away. Once they captured him, it would be clear that it was Malik in their hands, not Khan. The search would begin again. He wouldn't be safe, not here, not on the road, not in Minneapolis. There was nowhere to run.

A day or more. It will give you time.

A day for what?

Think, Khan.

And then he knew. Horror crept into his body, starting in the soles of his feet, wriggling up his back. It was hard to breathe. He spun around, too fast, and he lost his balance. He went back inside the house, leaving the door open, and braced himself against a wall. The darkness and dizziness followed him. He could barely see. Like a blind man, he stumbled forward, and he realized that, along with the shuddering pain in his head, tears had begun to fall from his eyes, as heavy as rain. He felt for the door to the basement; he knew it was there. He ripped it open. The stairs felt impossible, as if he had to lower himself into a cave. He only made it two-thirds of the way before he fell, crashing down, feeling his shoulder hammer the concrete floor.

When he got up, he squinted. Faint light glowed through the window wells. He let his eyes absorb it, and he let the room slowly stop spinning in his brain. He inched across the floor, kicking debris. He wanted to shout. He wanted to scream. The curtain of tears turned the basement into a gauzy dream.

Khan knew what he would find down there.

Nothing.

The wooden chair was empty. The suicide vest that Malik had assembled was gone.

* * *

I surrender.

Malik knew that was what they wanted from him.

Give up the fight. Offer no sacrifice at the end. He could never do that. He was going to die, and when he did, he wouldn't die alone. He'd take as many of the Unbelievers with him as he could in a single moment of bright light. It was a glorious thing, to walk with head held high into the Hereafter.

And the others?

Taste the penalty of the blazing fire.

It would be days before they could run their tests on blood and tissue and realize that they had all been fooled. By the time they knew who had died here tonight, Khan would be hidden in another life.

Malik lay on his back. He stared upward, seeing nothing. His heart pumped; his blood spilled to the floor, leaving him light-headed to the point of euphoria. He felt keenly aware of everything around him. In the fierce buzz above his face, he could distinguish the flutter of wings of each individual bee. He could identify each leg of each beetle that traversed his skin. Somewhere nearby, he smelled roses and honey, rising like sweetness above the manure in the shed.

His breathing came with difficulty now. When he tried to move his legs, he found that they didn't obey his brain anymore. Instead of pain, he felt numbness. He didn't have much time. It didn't matter; he had no fear and no regrets. The flat, plastic trigger was already in his hand, and all he needed was the barest touch of a finger to fulfill his goal. One spark, sent along the wires, exploding flesh and bone into a billion fragments. Online, his brothers had assured him that he wouldn't feel a thing. One moment, he would be here in the dirt and darkness, and a millisecond later, he would be walking in the Gardens of Paradise.

"*Rashid, we are coming to get you now.*"

Yes, yes, come, he whispered soundlessly to himself. Bring as many as you can. Meanwhile, hopefully, Khan was already gone, on his way to freedom.

"*When we open the door, do not move. If you move, you'll be shot.*"

And by then, we will all be gone.

Malik waited. He wished he could pray aloud, but he knew his prayers would be a warning. His lips moved, but his voice was silent.

Instead, the verses ran through his head. He could hear them as clearly as if his brothers were there with him, reciting them in unison.

By the Glorious Morning Light,
And by the Night when it is still
Your Guardian Lord has not forsaken you, nor is He displeased
And verily the Hereafter will be better for you than the present
And soon will your Guardian Lord give you what shall please you.

Outside, the boots of the police splashed and thundered. He didn't know how many there were. They crept toward him inch by inch, and they shouted at him, and their armor and guns clattered as they came closer.

So close.

So very, very close.

* * *

"They're moving in," Special Agent Maloney said.

Three different oversize monitors in the conference room tracked the progress of the SWAT team. Stride could see the Woodland yard lit up like daylight by the hot klieg lights on the street. A camera atop the black tactical van broadcast the panorama of the scene. Uniformed men converged on the metal shed from three sides. One camera, mounted on the helmet of the lead officer, shuddered as he moved, giving them a real-time perspective on the assault.

Stride could see them getting closer. The command center was as silent as a church. Beside him, he realized that Agent Durkin was holding her breath.

At that moment, he felt his phone vibrating in his pocket. He wanted to ignore it, but when he slipped it into his hand, he saw that the 911 call center was trying to reach him. He got out of his chair and found the remotest corner of the room, where he answered the phone and murmured, "Stride."

He recognized the voice of the 911 supervisor for St. Louis County.

"Lieutenant, I'm sorry to bother you, sir, but we've got a caller who insisted on being forwarded to you. He claims it's an emergency, and he says he won't talk to anyone else."

"What's his name?"

"He won't give us a name, but he says he's a friend of Khan Rashid. That's the only reason I thought I should check with you."

Stride's eyes were glued to the monitor.

"Put him through," he said.

"Yes, sir."

He heard a clicking on the line and then the sound of someone breathing rapidly and frantically.

"This is Stride," he whispered.

The phone line was silent except for the breathing.

On the monitors, he saw the SWAT team within ten yards of the shed. Among them were men he'd known for years. He trusted them and their training. Move in, throw open the door, immobilize the suspect.

"Who is this?" Stride continued. "What do you want?"

Finally, the man spoke. "It's a trap."

"What?"

"It's a trap. He's wired. Keep your men away!"

Stride threw his phone to the floor and shouted, "*Pull them back! Pull them back! Pull them back!*"

But he was too late.

The monitors went white with light, blinding them. An instant later, the noise of the explosion erupted through the speakers. Chaos and screams followed. When the scene revealed itself again, they could see only smoke, but as the smoke drifted, they could see the bodies of good men on the ground.

45

Serena studied the closed door to Cat's bedroom from where she sat. She hadn't knocked. She hadn't gone inside or listened at the door. It was nearly midnight, and she wanted more than anything to know whether the girl was still there. Either Cat was asleep in bed, or she'd slipped out her window to go to Curt's party.

If Serena got up and opened the door, it was like admitting that she would never really trust Cat to do the right thing.

She was sitting at the dining room table of their cottage, papers spread around her. Phone records. Calendar printouts. E-mails. She'd been there for hours, working her way through the chain of events the previous Tuesday at the marathon headquarters. Somewhere in all the people coming and going from the building was the person who had disconnected the street camera. Hours later, someone had placed the bomb inside the Duluth Outdoor Company shop.

For all the research she'd done, for all the phone calls she'd made, she had to admit to herself that she was nowhere close to finding a lead. Nothing leaped out at her. The sheer volume of visitors inside the marathon headquarters that day made it almost impossible to identify a likely suspect. All she could do was go down the list name by name and number by number.

Her phone, which was sitting on the table, buzzed. She picked it up and saw that Jonny was calling.

Her husband.

A smile crept onto her face, but when she answered and heard him tell her what was going on, her smile vanished. She closed her eyes. A quiet moan of anguish escaped from her throat.

"How many?" she asked.

"Two dead, eight injured," he said.

"Do you need me there?"

"No. I'll be home when I can."

She could hear the sheer exhaustion in his voice, and she wished she could help him and hold him. It wasn't just the days without sleep. It was the weight of violence. It was the hopelessness of one man pushing against a glacier.

"I love you," she murmured.

"I love you, too."

Then she was alone in the silence of the cottage again. She couldn't work anymore. She got up from the dining room table and went into the great room, where she sat in the red leather chair by the fireplace and stared into space. The lights were low. The room was warm. Part of her wanted to sleep, but she couldn't. Part of her wanted to drink, but she couldn't do that, either. Part of her wanted to believe in God, but judging by all the evidence around her, God had left the building.

She'd run out of anger. She was numb, and that was the scariest thing of all.

People never changed.

Then the door to Cat's corner bedroom opened. Cat, the most beautiful teenager Serena had ever seen, padded in her bare feet into the great space. Her chestnut hair was mussed, and her face was full of sleep, with no makeup, not that she needed any. She wore her usual roomy pink nightshirt. It had a stenciled slogan on the front: PRIS-ONER OF LOVE.

"Hey," Cat said. "You still up?"

"Yeah."

Serena couldn't stop herself. She began to sob. She'd never been the kind of person to cry, but she cried, anyway. Cat, her face alarmed, ran across the room and slid to the carpet in front of her.

"Serena, what's wrong?"

Serena shook her head. She could have said that everything was wrong. There was absolutely nothing right with the world. And yet that wasn't the truth. She didn't know how to explain that she wasn't crying because she was sad. She was happy. It made no sense at all, but in the midst of everything, at that moment, she was happy. Cat was still there. She hadn't gone out.

"Do you know what I'd like right now?" Serena asked.

"If I had to guess, chocolate," Cat said.

"That's exactly right."

Cat grinned and got to her feet. She disappeared toward the kitchen, but a moment later, when Serena looked up, Cat stood in the dining room doorway. She leaned her head against the frame. Her face was serious.

"You thought I was going to go to Curt's party, didn't you?" she asked.

Serena smiled. Cat was always a step ahead of her. It was scary sometimes.

"Honestly? I had no idea what you were going to do."

"Honestly," Cat said, "I didn't know myself."

"So why didn't you? Because you thought I didn't want you to go?"

"No." The girl smirked. "You know that wouldn't have stopped me."

"Then why?"

Cat shrugged. "Because I'm someone else now. I decided I like this person better."

She turned around with a swish of her brown hair and headed for the kitchen, where they kept the chocolate. Serena could hear the girl singing softly to herself, but she didn't recognize the song.

WEDNESDAY

46

Khan woke up at dawn in the parking lot of Grand Casino Mille Lacs.

Following Malik's instructions, he'd headed west out of Duluth in the darkness and made his way via back roads to the town of McGregor. His plan had been to turn south there, but when he spotted a Highway Patrol vehicle near the intersection, he'd gone straight for another fifteen miles to Highway 169. Then he drove as far south as the town of Onamia on the shore of Lake Mille Lacs.

Despite the late hour, dozens of cars had dotted the casino parking lot. He'd decided there was safety in numbers. He found an empty spot between an SUV and a vintage Cadillac, and he closed his eyes. The uncomfortable space made it hard to sleep, and when he did drift off for short stretches, he dreamed of Malik. It was a pleasant dream, about the old days, but when he woke up in the morning, he remembered that his friend was dead. Even from a mile away, he'd heard the explosion and felt the ground vibrate under his feet. He knew that Malik was gone.

There was nothing else to do but run.

Now it was a new day. Sunrise hadn't come yet; it was time for *fajr*. If he went inside the casino to pray, he would attract unwanted attention, so he started up the Taurus and backtracked half a mile north to a wayside rest by the lake. It was deserted. He parked and found a grassy spot near the pier, and he performed his morning ritual the way he had every day of his life since puberty. Normally, it brought him peace, but not today. He'd never felt lonelier or farther from Allah. Even the refuge of prayer had been stripped from him by the horrors of the past three days.

The morning was still young. He needed to be in Minneapolis by ten o'clock, and the city was only two hours to the south. Staying here, by the water, was the safest thing to do, so he rolled down the window and waited. The time passed slowly, as if every second were a kind of torture. He wondered if anyone was looking for him yet. He didn't know how long it would be before the world realized he was still alive. It didn't matter. As far as Khan was concerned, he was already dead.

By seven in the morning, he decided it was time to leave.

He had one stop to make, so he drove back to the casino and parked near the entrance. He was conscious of the numerous cameras and security personnel, so he kept a baseball cap planted low on his head and his face down and his hands in his pockets as he went inside. No one paid attention to him. He threaded his way through the slot machines, dismayed to see so many old people frittering away their retirement money in a kind of bored trance. His throat tightened as he passed through clouds of cigarette smoke.

He found a shop where he bought a razor and shaving cream and several other items, and he took the bag with him to the restroom and locked himself inside a handicapped stall that included its own mirror and sink. He ran hot water and inhaled the steam.

Khan stared at his reflection. He'd had a beard since he was sixteen years old. Ahdia had always loved his beard and how neatly he kept it trimmed. Pak had asked him how old he would have to be to grow his own beard. Khan fought back tears, bathed his face in shaving cream, and slowly used the razor to cut away his beard until his chin was smooth. He only nicked himself once. He washed his face and then used a pair of scissors to shorten his hair and give himself a higher forehead. When he was done, he didn't even recognize himself in the mirror.

He was a stranger. A new man for a new life.

Leaving the bathroom, Khan realized he was hungry, and he didn't know when he was likely to eat again. With his disguise in place, he felt more comfortable being around other people. The casino's breakfast buffet was open, so he got a table and overloaded a plate with eggs, spicy potatoes, and cut fruit. However, when the food was actually in front of him, he found that his appetite was a mirage. He ate a few bites without enthusiasm and then put down his fork. He drank half a glass of orange juice, but the acid unsettled his stomach.

There was a television in the restaurant. He couldn't tear his eyes away from the morning news. He was the star of the show, and he was dead. His awful driver's license photo was on the screen, and when he saw it, he looked down, certain that everyone in the restaurant was staring at him. But no one was. They didn't recognize him. When he looked again, he saw the scorched aftermath of the events in Woodland. Burnt grass. Broken windows. Twisted metal debris. He saw the photographs of the police officers that Malik had murdered.

His heart was sick.

Two tables away, he heard an elderly man mutter, "It's always Muslims."

Khan wanted to scream. He wished he could go to the man and shout, "Yes, Malik did a terrible thing, and I hate him for it! Yes, he disgraced the religion that I cherish! *But what about my wife and child?* Who mourns for them? Who gets justice for them? I did nothing to anyone, and now my whole life, everything I love, has been stolen from me. Who will give it back? Who even cares?"

He sat in the chair, staring at his cold food, and said nothing. The old man got up and left. No doubt he was going back to his lucky slot machine. Khan wondered if the man had a wife who was still alive. He tried to swallow his own bitterness. Sooner or later, we all end up alone.

The face of a friend filled the television screen. It was Haq Al-Masri, doing a live interview. Haq had the thankless job of mourning the loss of innocent lives while separating Islam from the violence done by Malik in its name. No one listened or cared. Khan thought about the last time he'd talked to Haq, when they'd shared their concerns about Malik. They'd laid out a plan: Separate him from his friends in Minneapolis; keep him away from the online recruiters; try to cure the disease in his heart. Khan knew what people would say: You should have turned him over to the authorities. But it wasn't that easy. Malik was a friend; he was practically family. And it was impossible to know what was mere talk and what was a real plan that would leave police officers dead on the burnt grass.

He heard the reporter ask Haq, "Did you know Khan Rashid?"

On television, Haq's face was full of sadness. "Yes, I did. The man I knew could never have perpetrated this atrocity. Not Khan. If it really was him, then it was the act of someone who'd lost everything. If you push an innocent man past the breaking point, sometimes he breaks."

Khan couldn't listen anymore. He was done with this life. He paid his check and stood up to leave—to drive south, to meet up with Malik's friends in Mill Ruins Park and be smuggled somewhere new—but then everything changed for him. He turned his back on the television, but as he did, he heard a new voice. A voice he recognized. A voice that was like the roaring of a train in his head.

He swung around and walked to the television and stared up at the face on the screen.

Dawn Basch.

In that one moment, all his anger and hurt suddenly had a focus. Dawn Basch came to Duluth, Dawn Basch sowed hatred, Dawn Basch spread poison, and now that poison had cost him *everything*. Without her, Malik would be alive. Without her, the police officers in Woodland and in the Forest Hill Cemetery would be alive. Without her, Ahdia and Pak would be alive, and Khan's life would still be what it was before. Innocent. Perfect.

She was the cause.

She'd made it all happen.

She was Satan.

Khan felt a murderous passion in his heart like no emotion he'd ever experienced. The transformation rolled over him like a tidal wave. The old Khan was gone; the man in the mirror was someone new. He had died, but now he was reborn with a purpose. Every man needed a purpose.

Ahdia and Pak are dead. Who mourns for them? Who gets justice for them?

I do.

He stalked from the restaurant. His breath was loud in his ears, blocking out every other sound. He was conscious of the weight of the gun that was still secured under his belt. It didn't seem strange or fearful now to hold a gun. To point a gun. To pull the trigger and wreak havoc.

Khan got into the Taurus. He made the engine roar like a snorting bull.

To the south was Minneapolis, freedom, and a new life.

To the north was Duluth and Dawn Basch.

Khan turned north and sped away.

47

On Wednesday morning, they found the Bug Zappers van.

Maggie bumped her Avalanche over the curb as she parked outside a boarded-up storefront on First Street. She climbed out and dropped down to the grease-stained, cobblestoned pavement. The still, sticky air gave her face a sheen of sweat. She crossed to the four-story U.S. Bank parking ramp that took up most of the opposite block. She trotted up the steps to the roof, where she found Max Guppo waiting next to the van. One of their uniformed officers had identified the vehicle an hour earlier.

"Morning, Max," Maggie murmured, stripping off her sunglasses. She matched the license plate on the panel van to the photo from the SuperAmerica gas station and confirmed that this was the same van Travis Baker had used to fill up multiple gasoline cans.

"Morning," Guppo replied, chewing on a peach scone that left crumbs in his mustache.

They were both grim. It had been a bad night and a bad stretch of days. Maggie put her hands on her hips and squinted at Lake Superior through the haze. Her lips bent into a frown.

"Do we know how long the van has been here?" she asked.

"I reviewed the ramp cameras with the security staff. The van entered the lot yesterday evening at about eight o'clock."

"Was Travis Baker driving?"

"Yeah. Kid looked scared to death."

"Anybody else in the vehicle?"

"No, he was alone. Two minutes after he pulled into the ramp, the cameras caught him on the sidewalk outside. He headed south on First Street on foot. I added what he was wearing to the BOLO."

Maggie did a circuit around the van. "The truck's clean. Not a speck of dirt on it. Travis was trying to cover his tracks."

"Yeah, but check out the paint near the rear tire on the driver's side," Guppo told her.

She squatted and examined the chassis between the left rear tire and the tailpipe. She saw what Guppo had seen. An inch of white paint was bubbled and blackened, as if scorched by fire.

"He set off the blaze a little too close to the van," Maggie concluded. "Flames licked the paint."

"Looks like it."

"Kid's lucky he didn't blow himself up."

Maggie walked to the rear of the van. She cocked her head and assessed the vehicle. Something didn't look right. "Does this thing look lopsided to you?"

Guppo came and stood next to her. "Little bit, yeah."

"The right rear tire is low," Maggie said.

She grabbed a flashlight from her pocket and bent down and aimed the beam deep into the jagged treads of the tire. She whistled and moved to each of the other tires and did the same thing. Everywhere she looked, she saw the shiny glint of something like diamonds.

"What is it?" Guppo asked.

"Glass. There are fragments of glass stuck in the treads on all the tires. One of them must have gone deep enough to produce a slow leak. The gallery blew, the windows shattered, and Travis drove through a field of broken glass as he was getting away. He brought all the evidence with him."

"It's nice when criminals are stupid," Guppo said.

Maggie gestured at the locked rear doors of the van. "Let's take a look inside and see what else he left for us."

"Sure."

The round detective finished his scone with a large bite and waddled to the back of his tan 1998 Oldsmobile and popped the trunk. He took out a thin aluminum stick with a hooked end and gracefully slid it into the window well on the van's driver's door. In a few seconds, he undid the lock. With a gloved hand, he opened the door and pushed a button inside to unlock the remaining doors of the vehicle.

Maggie swung open the rear panels. The interior of the van was lined with metal shelves, and she saw a supply of animal cages, rubber gloves, ventilator masks, and plastic canisters labelled as poison. She also saw a large, clear plastic bag on the nearest shelf, and when she squinted, she realized that the bag was stuffed with the corpses of at least thirty rats. Where an orange bucket had tipped, she saw hundreds of dead cockroaches spilling across the rubber-matted floor.

"Holy crap, it's like a Stephen King novel in here," she said.

Guppo's mustache wrinkled with distaste as he assessed the van. "But no gasoline cans," he said.

"No, he must have jettisoned them. Hang on, though."

Maggie bent forward until her nose was almost touching the floor of the van. She avoided the bodies of the bugs. The strong odor from the mat made her jerk backward, and she saw drips of dark liquid staining the floor.

"He spilled," she told Guppo. "The tanks leaked when he was taking them in and out. The floor reeks of gasoline."

"So we've got him," Guppo said.

Maggie nodded. "Yeah, we've got him. Now we just need to find him."

* * *

Travis froze as he was about to push open the glass door that led to the roof of the parking ramp. Not far away, the rear panels of his van were open. He recognized the Chinese police officer from the hospital, and his whole body convulsed with fear. They'd found him. They knew what he'd done.

The cop's head swiveled in his direction, and Travis stumbled out of sight before she could spot him. With heavy, lumbering footsteps, he ran down the stairwell. He stopped before he reached the street, at the entrance to the second-floor skywalk over Lake Avenue. On the street, any cop in a squad car could come around the corner and pick him out. In the skywalks, he could blend into the workday crowd.

Travis shoved his hands into his pockets and wandered across Lake Avenue in the glass tunnel. He tried to hide the anxiety that swirled in his brain.

The skywalks connected buildings throughout miles of downtown, which meant that Duluthians could avoid the subzero temperatures in January and get around the city without ever going outside. The corridors were long and dark, with a shut-in smell. Popcorn littered the carpet. Air-conditioning hummed. As Travis hurried from building to building, other pedestrians passed him, but no one looked at him twice. He glanced over his shoulder, in case the cops from the parking ramp were following him, but for now, he'd eluded them. Even so, the police were everywhere. When he crossed over Second Avenue, he spotted two squad cars roaring through the intersection, and he turned around to make sure his face wasn't visible through the glass.

Travis knew they were looking for him.

He ducked into a café in the Holiday Center and bought a cup of black coffee. He nervously eyed the businesspeople moving back and forth around him. He took a seat near the tall windows looking out on the street, away from the skywalk traffic, and dug his phone out of his pocket. He wondered if the police were already monitoring it, but he turned it on, anyway, and dialed Wade's number. The phone rang and rang, until he got Wade's voice mail.

"Wade," he murmured. "Hey, man, it's me. Call me."

Travis sipped his coffee. The caffeine added to his jittery nerves. As he sat there, the reality of his situation sank into his brain. When the police found him, they'd arrest him. They'd put him on trial, and the jurors would stare into his face with their hard eyes and say, "Guilty." Travis Baker, murderer. They'd put him in a cell, and that was it. End of story.

The thought of being stuck in prison for the rest of his life overwhelmed him. He squeezed his coffee cup so hard that he crushed it, and coffee squirted up like a fountain over his clothes and the table. It burned his hand. Now everyone was looking at him. One of the café employees came running over with a towel. She looked straight at his face. She'd remember him. When she saw his photo on the news, she'd say, *That's him. That's the guy who spilled his coffee.*

"Are you okay, sir?"

"I'm fine, I'm fine."

"Let me get you a refill."

"No, it's okay, never mind."

Travis got up, toppling his chair. He dried his hand on his T-shirt. He shoved his way through the tables and back to the skywalk without looking behind him. He felt a flush on his face.

He couldn't stay there.

Travis hurried through the food court and was about to cross over Superior Street when he spotted a security guard heading toward him. He reversed direction and exited the building into an alley behind the hotel. He waited outside, making sure that the guard wasn't following him, and then he jogged across Third Avenue. Already, he felt unsafe. The intense sunlight was making him sweat. Cars were parked up and down the block. When he took a quick glance down the hill, he saw the perfect place to lie low.

Half a block away, on the sidewalk, was a small iron railing bolted to a building wall, with a gate that gave access to a set of dirty concrete steps leading into the subbasement of the building. He and Wade probably spent more time underneath that building than anyone else in the city. They'd waste hours there, alone, playing music and cards, without a soul disturbing them, other than the occasional rat.

Travis hurried down the street. No one looked his way. He swung open the gate and hugged the brick foundation wall to the bottom of the steps. The stairwell was barely wide enough to let him through. Where the steps ended, he found a locked metal door. Moisture leached from underneath. Garbage had been tossed from the sidewalk overhead, and Travis kicked it aside with his boot. He yanked keys from his pocket, and then he took out his phone, too. He backed up out of view from anyone on the sidewalk above him and dialed Wade's number again.

This time, Wade answered on the first ring.

"What do you want, Travis? Why are you calling me?"

"I got trouble, man. I need help. The police are on to me. They know I did it."

He heard a loud sigh from Wade. "Yeah, that cop came by the hospital and talked to me and Shelly. She was asking lots of questions about you. Do they have any proof?"

"They found the van. I tried to clean it, like you said, but they'll figure it out. They know it's me, man."

Wade was quiet for a long time. "What do you want from me, Travis?"

"I need help. I need to get out of town."

"You're going to run?"

"What choice do I have, man? They catch me, they put me away—you know that. I need a car and some money. Soon as I'm settled, I'll pay you back."

Wade laughed. "Sure. That'll happen."

"I mean it. And, hey, Wade, I probably need a gun, too. You got one I can take with me?"

"I'm always carrying, Travis, you know that. Where are you planning on going, anyway?"

"I don't know. Somewhere south."

"Where are you now?"

"I'm heading into the subbasement at the building on Third. You know, the one where we hang out sometimes? I figure it's safe there for a while."

"Yeah, I know the one," Wade said. "Okay, hang tight, Travis. Get out of sight, and stay out of sight. I'll be there in half an hour."

48

Stride found Michael and Alison Malville waiting for him in the interview room at police headquarters.

He remembered both of them from the investigation two years
earlier. Since then, Alison had ditched her long red hair for a short,
blond, soccer-mom style, and she was dressed down in a way she
never would have been when she lived in her McMansion in Duluth.
Michael hadn't changed as much as his wife. He still looked tense and
angry. He was a poster child for the fact that having all the money in
the world didn't make you happy.

Stride sat down across from them. He noticed that Alison reached
out and took her husband's hand. It was good to see them still together.
Back then, he hadn't been certain that their marriage would survive.

"Hello, Mr. and Mrs. Malville," Stride said. "What can I do for
you?"

Alison looked at her husband, but Michael stared down at the table.
His face and his bald head were beet red. "We're very sorry about the
deaths of your police officers," she said.

"Thank you."

"Can you tell us if Khan Rashid was the man who blew himself up
last night?" Alison asked.

Stride didn't answer immediately. He tried to anticipate where this conversation was going, but all he saw was a cauldron of emotion bubbling under Michael Malville's skin, even when the man didn't say a word.

"The FBI will be conducting DNA tests to be sure," Stride replied. "Until then, we're not confirming the identification."

Michael spoke for the first time. "Do you know if Rashid was guilty? Was he the one who bombed the marathon?"

"We're not sure yet. Why do you want to know?"

Alison looked at Michael, and Michael looked at Alison. They waited for each other. Finally, Alison said under her breath, "It doesn't change anything, Michael. Even if Rashid really is guilty, they need to know the truth."

Michael scowled. He didn't want to talk. It was obvious that Alison had dragged him here without his consent.

"My husband has something to tell you," Alison announced, not giving him a choice.

"And what's that, Mr. Malville?" Stride asked.

Michael stared back without blinking, as if he didn't want to give Stride the satisfaction of not looking into his eyes. "I made a mistake," he announced.

"A mistake?"

"When I saw the photograph of Khan Rashid in Canal Park, I was certain that he was the man who bumped into me on Superior Street. The man with the backpack. You have to understand, Lieutenant, I was sure he was the guy. I didn't have the slightest doubt."

"Now you're not sure?" Stride asked.

"Now I realize I was wrong. It wasn't him."

Stride wasn't surprised at all. Eyewitnesses got it wrong all the time. Even so, he had to bury his anger at the man in front of him, because this eyewitness mistake had rippled into a violent disaster. Dennis Kenzie was dead. Ahdia Rashid was dead. Pak Rashid was dead. So were two more police officers, along with a man they assumed was Khan Rashid.

All those deaths had begun with Michael Malville's tweet.

And Michael Malville was wrong.

"Didn't you tell Sergeant Bei that you were one hundred percent certain that the man you saw with the backpack was Khan Rashid?" Stride asked.

"Yes, I did, but—"

"And now you're one hundred percent certain that it was *not* him," Stride said.

"That's right."

Stride allowed a long stretch of silence to linger in the room. "Okay. Well, thank you for coming in, Mr. Malville. I'll have an officer show you both out."

Michael leaned across the table. "That's it? Don't you want to know who I really saw?"

"No."

"Why the hell not?" he demanded. Alison frowned and shot him a look that said: *Calm down.*

Stride ran both hands back through his wavy hair. His face was stone. "Mr. Malville, right now, your memories of what you saw or didn't see have no credibility with me. We're done listening to you, and my advice is that you keep any information you think you have off social media, too."

He stood up to leave, but Alison interrupted him. Beside her, Michael stewed with resentment.

"Lieutenant, wait," she said. "We are both very sorry. I know that doesn't change a thing, but it's true. Michael won't give you any excuses, but I can tell you he simply made an honest mistake. He didn't post that photograph with malice toward anyone."

"You're right, Mrs. Malville. That doesn't change a thing."

"At least *look*," Michael interjected. He pushed a white piece of paper across the desk. "I'm not going to pretend I didn't screw up. I was wrong about Rashid, and I have to live with that. The reason I made a mistake is that I never saw the *real* man in any of the photographs online. If I had, I would have identified him immediately. I didn't see him until today, and as soon as I did, I recognized him."

Stride moved the piece of paper closer with one of his fingers. "Where did you see him?"

"On television. He was being interviewed. I did a quick screen capture from the CNN website and printed it. This is the guy, Lieutenant. He had a backpack, and he bumped into me on Superior Street. I know what I said before, but this time, I'm right."

Stride took the page into his hands and turned it over. The photo taken from the video feed was blurry, but he knew the face.

It was Haq Al-Masri.

* * *

Stride found Serena waiting for him in his office. She handed him a can of Coke. "You don't like the Malvilles very much, do you?" she asked.

He sat down next to her and took a swig of pop from the can. "Not really. In fairness, they have plenty of reasons not to like me, either. The Spitting Devil case almost broke up their marriage."

He was conscious of the silence from Serena, and he knew what it was about. She hadn't been a part of that investigation, and that was because it had happened during the winter months two years earlier when she and Stride were split up. Those were the short-lived days when he and Maggie had been sleeping together, before they both realized they'd made a terrible mistake. The case wasn't a bad memory just for the Malvilles. It was his own dark time, too.

"Anyway," he murmured. The past was the past, and he couldn't change it.

He put the photograph of Haq Al-Masri on the desk between them.

"Do you think Malville is right this time?" Serena asked. "Was Haq at the marathon?"

"I don't have much confidence in anything Malville says at this point. His memories are too colored by everything that's happened. I do believe that he was wrong about Khan Rashid. Malville and Dawn Basch destroyed that man's life, and he didn't do a damn thing."

"What about last night in Woodland?" Serena asked.

"That's a good question. Durkin thinks Khan was pushed so far that he finally pushed back. The working theory among the FBI is that Malik Noon gave Rashid a suicide vest."

"You don't think so?"

"No."

"What's another explanation?"

"That it wasn't Rashid who died last night," Stride said. "The voice on the phone call sounded familiar to me. I think it was *Rashid* calling to warn me. Plus, the original 911 call that identified Rashid in the Woodland neighborhood came from a burner phone. It was untraceable. Somebody wanted us to walk into that situation thinking Khan Rashid was the man in the shed."

"Why?" Serena asked.

"If we were convinced Khan was dead, we'd stop looking for him. He'd be able to escape."

"Have you told Maloney or Durkin about your suspicions?"

"I haven't. I don't have any proof; it's just a hunch. We'll wait to see what the DNA results tell us." He hesitated, and then he added, "If Rashid is alive, I'm not sure it's a bad thing if he gets away. He's a victim, along with all the others."

Serena leaned back in the chair. She had a strange look on her face. "Every now and then, Jonny, you surprise me."

"What, you think I'm getting soft?"

"Maybe a little."

He smiled. "Sometimes you have to know who to arrest and who to let run."

"What about Haq? Are you going to talk to him?"

"Because of what Michael Malville said? No. I know Haq. He's not the marathon bomber."

Serena frowned. "It's not that I don't trust your instincts, Jonny . . ."

"But?"

"But I really think you should talk to Haq."

His brow furrowed. "Because he bumped into Malville at the marathon? Because he had a backpack with him? You're the one who's been telling me the bomb was probably in place for days before the race."

"Yes, but there's something else," Serena said.

"What?"

"I'm still working my way through the parade of people who were in the marathon offices on that Tuesday," she told him. "The list includes representatives from the local mosque who were making arrangements for a special group of Muslim runners. Haq was one of them, Jonny. He was at the marathon office on the day the street camera was disabled."

49

Haq ran hard. His anger propelled him. He went out the back of his house to avoid reporters who might be waiting for him, and he made his way to College Street, where he headed west along the border of the university. He got into a rhythm. The air was heavy, and his body poured sweat, but when exhaustion tempted him to slow down, he ran faster.

He followed College Street to the end and turned south. His route was downhill, with the wind at his back, and he raced along a mostly wooded route until he reached Skyline Parkway. There he turned back uphill, on a scenic drive high above the lake, where the steepness made each step a battle. He barely noticed the view. He was too consumed with his own thoughts.

Skyline Parkway twisted and climbed until he reached the bridge over the waterfall at Chester Creek. He'd met Stride in the park there on Saturday night. Four days seemed like a lifetime ago, when the violence and bitterness in the city was just beginning.

He climbed one last hill, and he was back on the wide lawns near the Aftenro Home, a senior center only a block from the UMD campus. He bent over, his hands on his thighs, and let his breathing come back to normal. He unhooked a water bottle from his belt and squirted warm water into his mouth. It was cooler in the shade of the firs, and he slid down the trunk of a nearby tree and sat with his eyes closed. He undid the laces of his sneakers. He may have slept for a while.

"*Salaam Alaikum*, Haq."

His eyes shot open as heard the quiet voice above him. He squinted into the shadows and saw a man standing among the evergreen branches. He didn't recognize him at first, but when he did, he scrambled to his feet.

"*Khan!*"

They embraced, but it was a sad embrace. As they stood with linked arms, Haq could see that Khan was a different man. It wasn't just that he'd changed his physical appearance. There had always been an inner peace to Khan, but that was gone. Hardness had taken its place.

"They said you were dead," Haq told him, "but I didn't believe it."

"I'm not dead, but I don't know if I'm alive, either. My heart still beats—that's all I can say."

Haq glanced around the sprawling lawn to be sure they were alone. "Was it Malik?"

Khan nodded. "I tried to stop him, but I was too late."

"Malik was beyond rescue," Haq said. "Don't blame yourself."

"Do the police think I'm dead?"

"For the moment, yes, but it won't take them long to figure out the truth. You realize it's not safe for you to be here. You could be recognized. Whether you wanted him to do it or not, Malik gave you a head start to escape the city. My advice is that you take it."

"Guilty men run," Khan said.

"So do smart ones."

Their heads both turned as a car engine rumbled from the nearest driveway. Instinctively, Haq backed into the shadows, and so did Khan. Beyond a green hedgerow, an SUV backed out of the driveway and headed down a spur toward Skyline Parkway. There was no way the driver could have seen them, but they waited until the car was gone before they spoke again.

"We're as bad as everyone else," Haq said with an ironic smile.

"What do you mean?"

"How do you define a conspiracy? Two Muslims talking."

"That's not funny," Khan said, frowning.

"No, it's not, because the rest of the world thinks it's true."

Khan was silent. Then he said, "Malik claimed that he wasn't responsible for the marathon bombing."

"Do you believe him?"

"He swore to me."

"I'm not sure the word of a suicide bomber means very much, Khan," Haq replied. "Did Malik know who really was responsible?"

"He said no, but he might have been protecting his friends in Minneapolis. Why, do you know who did it?"

"You're assuming it was one of us, too."

"I guess I am," Khan admitted.

Haq bent down and retied his shoelaces. He was tired. He wanted to go back to his house and put on Egyptian music and purge his soul of anger. Every time it built up, he needed a release. He put a hand firmly on Khan's shoulder. "Listen, my friend, I need to ask your forgiveness."

"For what?"

"I tried to save Ahdia and Pak. I was the one who went to your house and told Ahdia she needed to leave. I hid them at Goleen's gallery because I thought they would be safe there. Instead, they died. It's my fault."

"It's not."

"I shouldn't have interfered," Haq said.

"You had their best interests at heart. You couldn't have predicted what would happen. Besides, we both know who was really responsible for their murders, don't we?"

Haq's eyes narrowed. He didn't like what he heard in Khan's voice. "What do you mean?"

"I mean, *Iblis* walks among us. The Devil is right here in Duluth. You know who I'm talking about."

Haq did. He knew exactly who Khan meant.

"And as the Qur'an says, do you intend to fight the friends of Satan?" he asked.

"Yes, I do."

Haq shook his head. "No, Khan. You should leave. Go. Start a new life. Forget all the tragedies here."

"I can't do that."

"Why not? Why make this your fight?"

"Because Allah put me in this whirlwind for a reason," Khan replied. "The last four days led me to this place."

Khan lifted up his shirt, and Haq saw the gun concealed in the loop of his friend's belt. Haq wanted to scream. It never stopped. Hatred led to violence. Violence led to hatred. If only there were a way to stop this sickening ride long enough for everyone to get off.

"I can't help you," Haq said. "I *won't* help you. Not with something like that."

"I just want information. That's all. If you really think you need my forgiveness about Ahdia and Pak, then that's the price of it. This is my journey, not yours."

Haq felt a weariness that never went away. "All right. What do you want to know?"

"I have only one question," Khan said. "Where is Dawn Basch right now?"

* * *

Wade descended into the bowels of the Third Avenue building.

He knew every inch of the tunnels that wound like a maze under the streets. Ordinary people took the skywalks. He preferred the subbasements. The dripping water, the smell, the hum of machinery, the rough brick walls—they were all old friends to him. The calendar on the nearest wall was his own. The supplies on the shelves and the traps on the floor were his. Aside from Travis, almost no one else came down here; he could spend hours all by himself. He joked that it was like his Florida office, right down to the humidity and the giant roaches.

He used a flashlight in the corridor, rather than turn on an overhead fluorescent light. Mortar chips and plaster dust littered the damp floor. The ceiling, which was a web of pipes and wires, was low. If it was eighty degrees outside, the temperature was nearly one hundred

down here, and the air didn't move at all. He was sweating, but he
didn't mind the heat.

Key West. That was where he needed to go. Uproot, leave the winters behind, and get drunk and stay drunk in Margaritaville. He'd
always said he'd head for the steamy South someday. This was finally
the time.

He reached another dark tunnel. He dodged around steel support
columns and plastic-covered pallets. The bricks here were covered in
green mold. He turned a corner and found a flickering light illumi-
nating one of the underground rooms. Plywood walls made storage
enclosures for the building's tenants, but most of the doors were open,
with boxes stacked as high as the overhead pipes and filing cabinets
stuffed with paperwork from decades-old contracts. He figured all the
secrets of Duluth were buried down here somewhere.

Not far away, he heard music. Something loud and modern. That
was Travis. Stupid kid didn't know to keep quiet anywhere. He found
Travis at an old desk, next to a boom box playing a raspy track of
Van Halen. Wade had spent hours working at that desk, listening to
cassette tapes from the 1980s. His supplies were stored in paint cans
on top of the dusty filing cabinets. The fluorescent light flickered; it
was near the end of its life. Travis's face went in and out of darkness.

"Thanks for coming, man," Travis said.

Wade shrugged. "Yeah, whatever."

"Did you tell Shelly what's going on?"

"No. The fewer people who know, the better."

"Right, you're right."

"Where are you planning to go, Travis?" Wade asked.

"I don't know. Arkansas, maybe. I was in Little Rock once. I can
get settled under a new name, and maybe Shelly can come down and
join me. She's going to need help."

"Yeah, she is."

"You'll tell her, right? I'll send for her when I can?"

"Sure, I will."

Wade knew it was all a pipe dream. Travis didn't have the smarts to
run or to hide out or to live under a false name without giving himself

away. He'd last a month. Maybe two. And then somebody would figure out who he was, and the police would come and drag his sorry ass back to Minnesota.

He stared at Travis's face. Sweat poured down from the kid's hairline like a waterfall. Oh, yeah, he'd last a long time in Arkansas.

"We had fun, huh?" Travis asked.

Wade laughed. He saw a dead rat under the desk. Half a dozen cockroaches were stuck in a glue trap. "Yeah, killing shit is a blast, Travis."

"You think I should leave now or wait until dark?"

"Whole damn city is looking for you. Wait until dark."

"I hate to ask, man, but I need cash. A few hundred."

"I've got money for you," Wade told him, "but if it ever comes up, I didn't help you at all, right? You didn't get nothing from me."

"Right, yeah, I got it. What about a car?"

"I know a guy in Mora. I'll call him. A couple hundred will get you a beater, no questions asked. You can drive it until you're out of state and then ditch it for something else."

"You're the best, man. I don't know what I'd do without you."

"Yeah. Sure. I'll go up to the street and make the call. There's no signal down here. Plus, I want to make sure there aren't any cops casting eyes on the tunnels. With any luck, we'll have a car for you by dark."

Wade turned on his heels, but Travis called after him.

"Hey, Wade?"

"Yeah?"

"I'm sorry, man. I just wanted you to know that."

Wade folded his arms across his scrawny chest and stared at the good-looking young kid. "Yeah? What do you have to be sorry about, Travis? Tell me."

"You know. Everything. I mean, things didn't work out the way I figured they would."

"How did you think they were going to work out?" Wade asked.

"Not like this, that's for sure."

"Well, sit tight and don't worry," Wade said. "I'll take care of it. Believe me, there's not a problem I can't fix."

Wade wasn't lying.

Travis had a problem, and he knew exactly how to fix it.

He retraced his steps through the tunnels and let himself out through the metal door to the steps below Third Avenue. He grabbed his phone from his pocket and dialed the number from the card in his pocket. He figured she'd answer right away, and she did.

"Sergeant Bei, it's Wade Ralston," he told her. "I need to talk to you about Travis Baker. Can you meet me right away?"

50

Stride knocked on Haq's door. Haq answered immediately, but he didn't look happy when he recognized Stride on the porch. Four days had aged Haq. His worry lines were deep, and his face was flushed. He checked the street, and then he waved Stride inside without a greeting.

Haq led them into the house's front room. Heavy curtains kept the room dark. One wall was lined with bookshelves, and the books were mostly leather-bound, Arabic volumes. A brick fireplace took up the opposite wall. Haq sat down in an overstuffed easy chair and gestured for Stride to take the yellow sofa.

"What do you want, Jonathan?" he said finally. "I thought I made it clear we had no more business together."

"You did."

"So I guess this will be a short conversation."

"Maybe so," Stride said. "I wanted to share some news with you."

Haq said nothing. His eyebrows arched impatiently.

"The original identification of Khan Rashid was incorrect," Stride told him. "The man who said Khan bumped into him on Superior Street now admits that he was mistaken."

"Of course, he was. I told you from the beginning that Khan wasn't involved. You should have listened to me."

"That's true, but you weren't being completely honest, were you? You left out the most important part."

Haq's face darkened. "What do you mean?"

"You knew that Rashid didn't bump into Michael Malville on Superior Street. You knew for a fact that the identification was wrong, because the man on Superior Street with the backpack was *you*."

Haq was silent, and Stride could see the man weighing what to say. Wondering whether Stride had any real proof. Debating whether to deny it or whether to acknowledge what they both knew. Finally, an arrogant smile crept onto Haq's face.

"Okay, yes, I heard this rich white suburbanite talking about No Exceptions. Explaining to his boy about Americans being entitled to say whatever they want. Typical simpleminded nonsense, dressing up racism in the gown of Lady Liberty. I admit, it made me mad, so I 'accidentally' bumped into him. Hard."

"You should have told me," Stride said. "If you'd admitted it, we could have released a definitive statement that the identification on Twitter was an error. That Khan Rashid was not a suspect. Things might have turned out differently."

"Are you saying this is my fault?" Haq asked.

"No, I'm not saying that, but it makes me wonder. Why didn't you tell me it was you?"

Haq rubbed a hand thoughtfully along his beard. Their eyes met across the dark room. The realization of what Stride was saying dawned on him slowly. "You consider me a suspect in the bombing. *Me*."

"You lied," Stride said.

"I said nothing that was untrue."

"Let's not parse words. It was a lie of omission, Haq. It raises questions about what you were hiding."

Haq stood up, clenching and unclenching his fists. "So I should have served myself up as a suspect? When I knew I did nothing wrong? Look at what happened to Khan! You're saying I should have volunteered for the same treatment? The same vigilantes out for my blood? I bumped into a man on the street, Jonathan. That's all. Nothing more.

I was doing exactly what Khan was doing that day. Looking for Malik. Trying to keep the marathon safe."

"Malville said your backpack felt heavy," Stride pointed out.

"Because I'm a professor, and I had *books* in it, as I typically do."

"Where is the backpack?" Stride asked. "Do you still have it?"

Haq laughed bitterly and shook his head. "You want me to show it to you? Is that what it's come to between us? You actually need physical proof that I am not a terrorist?"

Stride said nothing. He waited.

Haq stared at him in disbelief and then left the room with quick, impatient steps. Seconds later, he returned, carrying a bulging navy-blue backpack that he threw at Stride's feet. The zipper was half open. Coffee-stained textbooks pushed from inside. "There. Are you satisfied?"

"I'm sorry, Haq. I had to ask. I also need to know more about a meeting you had at the marathon building last Tuesday."

"What about it?"

"What was the meeting?" Stride asked. "Who was involved?"

"A half dozen of us from the mosque met with marathon officials about the Muslim runners we'd recruited for the race. Why is that important?"

"Someone disconnected the cable for the marathon's street camera that day," Stride said. "It happened inside the marathon office."

"And you think it was one of us." Haq made it sound like a statement more than a question.

"Is that possible?"

"No."

"You sound pretty sure," Stride said.

"I am sure. We walked in as a group, we met in a conference room, and we left as a group. I think I would remember someone crawling around on the floor unhooking cables. Now, is that all? Because I'd like you to leave my house, Jonathan."

"I have one more question," Stride said, making no move to get up.

"What?"

"Is Khan Rashid really dead?"

Stride could see a crack in Haq's composure. "You're the one with the forensic experts. Talk to them, not me. What makes you think Khan might be alive, anyway?"

"You," Stride replied.

"Me? I said nothing."

"When you first called me about Khan, you said he was a good man. I believe in your judgment about people. If that's who Khan is, then I can't see him luring police officers to their deaths with a suicide vest."

Haq's chest swelled as he took a deep breath. "Well, even good men have their limits."

"Enough to commit murder?" Stride asked.

"Maybe."

Stride stood up and went to Haq. They were eye to eye. "Tell me the truth. Was it Malik Noon in the shed?"

He saw a battle going on in Haq's face. His friend had begun to see him as an enemy, and you didn't extend a hand of support to your enemies. Even so, they had a history together.

Without a word, Haq slowly nodded.

"Khan's alive?" Stride asked.

Another silent nod.

"Is he on the run? Where is he? I want to protect him."

Haq's mouth made a grim line. "He was on the run, but he came back. He came to see me."

"Why? What did he want?"

"I told you, Jonathan. Even good men have their limits."

Stride heard alarm bells in the man's tone. "Haq, what is Khan doing?"

"He wants revenge. I tried to dissuade him. He wouldn't listen."

"Revenge against whom?" Stride asked, but he already knew the answer. "Dawn Basch? He's after Dawn Basch?"

"He has a gun," Haq told him. "He's going to kill her."

Stride clapped a hand on Haq's shoulder. "Thank you, my friend."

He headed for the front door, his phone in his hand, but Haq called after him. "Jonathan."

Stride stopped. "What is it?"

Haq came to the doorway.

"I want you to remember something. This wasn't easy for me, not after everything that's happened. But you told me you believe in my judgment, and I believe in yours. So please do the right thing. Keep Khan safe."

Stride nodded. "I'll do my best. You need to remember something, too."

"What's that?"

"Building trust between us isn't a sprint," Stride said. "It's a marathon."

* * *

Khan sweated in the shut-up space of the Taurus. He had a sinking feeling in the pit of his stomach, because he didn't know whether he had the courage for what came next. He was terrified and filled with doubt. When he stared at the gun on the passenger seat, he struggled with whether he could actually take it in his hand again.

He was parked in a small lot near the loading dock of the Radisson Hotel. The hotel's cylindrical tower rose above him. He'd backed into a parking space in the shadow of a concrete retaining wall. Near the loading dock, he saw green trash bins and empty laundry carts. The noise of the physical plant made a roar through vents in a brick wall. Every few minutes, an employee came through a gray metal door to take a cigarette break, and he caught the aroma of smoke.

Whenever he saw someone, he hunched low behind the wheel. Everyone in Duluth knew his face, and despite the changes in his appearance, he was afraid of being recognized. He kept an ear on the street, expecting to hear sirens coming for him. He checked the clock on the dashboard and saw that the man who was supposed to meet him was late. Maybe he wasn't going to come at all. Khan couldn't blame him if he didn't want to get involved.

Five more hot, interminable minutes passed.

Near the loading dock, the metal door opened again. Another hotel employee came out, looking nervous. He was tall, his skin very dark, his wiry hair buzzed short. He wore black slacks and a crisp white dress shirt, and he carried a plastic laundry bag. His glance shot around the parking lot and then landed on the burgundy Taurus.

Khan turned his lights on and off. He put the gun on the driver's seat between his legs. The man hurried toward him, his head bobbing left and right to be sure no one was watching. Khan could feel the man's impatience, as if his mission couldn't be over fast enough.

The man climbed into the passenger seat. His eyes examined Khan, trying to match the face to the photo he'd seen everywhere.

"You know who I am?" Khan asked.

The man nodded. He didn't offer his name, and Khan didn't ask.

Khan had used his burner phone to call the emergency number Malik had given him. He'd reached the plumber named Abdul and used the code phrase about Noah and the Unbelievers to let the man know he needed help. Abdul had called back almost immediately, on a phone he said was secure, and Khan told him what he wanted.

Someone who could get him inside the Radisson Hotel.

The man in the car handed him the laundry bag. "Put on this uniform. It should fit. If you come out of this alive, you stole it, yes? You didn't get it from me. You never met me. Are we clear?"

"Yes," Khan replied.

"I have a family," the man said.

"I understand. I'll keep you out of it. Is the woman in the hotel?"

"She just arrived at Astor's. That's the revolving restaurant on the top floor. She's in a booth by the window, but you'll have to walk around the circle to find her. Take the service elevator. Go through the kitchen. Act like you belong there, and no one will challenge you. Do what you have to do, and get out."

"What about security?"

"Her guards aren't with her. She must think she is safe with you dead."

"Okay. Good."

"Regardless of whether you succeed, you know you are likely to die," the man told him. "Sooner or later, the police will kill you. Are you prepared for that?"

"If I die, I'll get to see my wife and child again," Khan replied. "It's a blessing."

"*Allah u akbar.*"

The man checked the parking lot and then climbed out of the car and hurried back inside the hotel. They'd been together for less than a minute. Khan was alone with his gun, his waiter's uniform, and his plan. He bent forward across the steering wheel and stared up at the floor-to-ceiling windows of the restaurant on the top floor of the hotel.

Dawn Basch was up there.

Their destinies were about to collide.

51

"Shelly Baker?" Serena asked.

The woman in the hospital bed turned her face from the window. She was heavyset with curly brown hair that lay on the pillow like a deflated balloon. Without makeup, she looked older than her age, which Serena guessed was mid-thirties. Her nose was flat and wide, and her eyes were rimmed in red.

"What do you want?" Shelly asked.

"My name is Serena Stride. I'm with the Duluth Police."

"I already talked to that other cop, the Chinese woman," Shelly replied in a voice that made it clear she didn't want to be bothered.

"Yes, I know. I'm sorry. This won't take long."

For an entire day Serena had been working her way through the list of marathon contacts from Tuesday morning. Shelly Baker was just one name among dozens of phone calls, but she was also a victim of the bombing, and that was enough of a connection for Serena to investigate. Not that she suspected Shelly of being involved. She wanted to ask the woman a few questions, cross Shelly off the list, and move on.

"Is this about my brother?" Shelly asked. She half lifted her torso off the mattress, causing a shock of pain that made her face twitch. "Did something happen to Travis?"

"No, Sergeant Bei is still trying to find him," Serena told her.

"You have to understand, Travis does stupid things sometimes, but it's not because he's a bad person. Think about what he went through in the past few days. His sister's a cripple, and Joni's dead. Travis thought he should be dead, too. He felt guilty that God spared him and not us. He can't even look at me."

Serena sat down in the chair next to the bed. "I'm very sorry for what happened to you, Ms. Baker."

"Don't be sorry for me. There's no point in second-guessing God's plan. I put my faith in Jesus. I always have."

Serena didn't say anything. She'd given up on God years earlier, as a child, at the hands of her mother's drug dealer. It was hard to trust in God after something like that. If Shelly Baker could still believe that Jesus was looking out for her, after everything that had happened, then Serena admired her faith.

"You know what Travis did, don't you?" Serena asked. "You know he set fire to that gallery. A mother and child died."

Shelly blinked over and over. Her big lips pressed into a thin, unhappy line. "Is that why you're here? So I can help you put my little brother in jail? I'm sorry, I won't do that. I won't say a word."

"No, that's not why I'm here," Serena told her.

"If Travis did anything, then it was an *accident*. I mean, I'm heart-sick about that poor woman and her son, but I'm sure nobody *meant* to hurt them. Not like me. Not like Joni. Whoever put that bomb at the marathon knew that people were going to die. It was deliberate. It was murder. The three of us happened to be the ones standing there. We were in the path."

"Yes, it was a terrible thing," Serena said.

Shelly closed her eyes and said nothing. Her blood pressure was climbing.

"I apologize for upsetting you," Serena went on. "The reason I'm here has nothing to do with Travis. I just need to check something with you, and then I'll be on my way, and you can rest."

"What is it?" Shelly asked.

"I'm going through a list of calls made by marathon staff on the Tuesday before the race. It's just routine. That Tuesday morning, someone at the marathon called your cell phone number. Do you remember what the call was about?"

Shelly's eyes opened. Her face was confused. "What? Why does that matter?"

"As I say, it's routine follow-up. Do you remember the call?"

"Tuesday?" Shelly asked.

"Yes."

"Okay, sure. MIH."

"What's that?"

"MIH. That's what we call it. Mouse in the house. Lorena from the marathon called to say they had a mouse infestation in the office. They'd spotted three or four of them already. She wanted someone out there to take care of it right away. That's what we do. I'm the office manager for Ralston Extermination."

"Do you know why Lorena called you specifically?"

"Yes, the marathon has been a client of ours for years. They store a lot of perishables as they get close to race day, and they can't afford to have bugs or mice or anything like that getting into their supplies."

"Was there anything unusual about the call?"

"No. I mean, Lorena was a little annoyed with us, because she said they pay us to prevent that sort of thing. Anyway, it was four days before the race. She was stressed, so I just apologized and said we'd deal with it immediately. That's what we did."

Serena nodded. "Okay, thank you for clearing that up, Shelly."

"Sure."

Serena stood up. She was done; she had the answers she needed. It was time to walk away. And yet she found herself still standing there in the hospital room. She hadn't moved; she was frozen. Something about the conversation felt wrong to her. It was the kind of wrong that set off alarms in her brain. Right now, her mind was screaming so fast and loud that she could hardly separate out all her thoughts.

She heard Shelly's voice in her head again.

Whoever put that bomb at the marathon knew that people were going to die. It was deliberate. It was murder.

The three of us happened to be the ones standing there. We were in the path.

Serena sat down by the bed again. She felt the pounding of her heartbeat. It was hard to get out the words. "I'm sorry, Shelly. I have just a couple more questions for you. Who exactly is Joni?"

Shelly looked at her in confusion. "What?"

"You mentioned Joni. She was one of the people killed in the bombing, wasn't she? Did you know her?"

"Yeah, of course. Joni was Wade's wife."

"Wade?"

"Wade Ralston. He owns the business. Travis and I work for him."

"And where was Joni at the time the bomb went off?"

"She was standing right next to me," Shelly said. "Travis, me, and Joni were all together."

Serena tried to collect her thoughts and take them one at a time. "I'm sorry to go over this again, but you said Lorena was annoyed when she called you about the mice. Why was that?"

"Because they have a contract with us to prevent things like that. We keep bait stations down. Poison. It doesn't keep them out, but if they get inside, they don't last long."

"Except four days before the race, they found themselves with mice, and they had to call you," Serena said.

"Yes, that's right."

"This is a weird time of year for mice to get inside, isn't it?" Serena asked. "Don't they usually try to get in when it's cold out?"

"It happens, but you're right, it's not very common."

"Who handled the call?"

"What?"

"Who went to the marathon office to deal with the mice?"

"Wade," Shelly said.

"Wade is Joni's husband?"

"Yes, that's what I told you."

"Where was Wade during the marathon?" Serena asked.

"What do you mean? He was in it. He ran it."

"Wade *ran* the marathon? Do you know where he was when the bomb went off?"

"Like, twenty feet away? He was across the street from us. He got some shrapnel in him from the explosion."

Serena stood up again. She turned her back on Shelly and went to the window. Thoughts bounced around her head like atoms colliding. She tried to isolate each fact, because, individually, the facts didn't mean a thing. But when she put them together . . .

The marathon camera went down on Tuesday. Wade Ralston was in the marathon office on Tuesday. Coincidence.

Wade's wife was one of the victims of the bombing. Coincidence.

Wade was twenty feet away when the bomb went off. Coincidence.

Put them all together.

Not a coincidence.

Serena spun around again. "Why were you guys standing there? Why were you, Joni, and Travis outside the Duluth Outdoor Company in that particular spot?"

"We wanted to see Wade finish," Shelly said.

"Did he know you'd be there?"

"Of course. He told us where to stand. He said he wanted us there to see him cross the finish line."

Serena dug her phone out of her pocket and scrolled to her photos. She found the picture she was looking for. "This is going to be a strange question," she told Shelly, "but do you know this man?"

She could read the confusion on Shelly's face. Confusion hadn't become suspicion yet. Shelly studied the photo on Serena's phone, and when she spoke, all the pieces began falling into place.

"Sure, that's Eagle. What about him?"

"*How do you know Eagle?*" Serena practically shouted.

Shelly looked scared now. Confused and scared. "He's just a homeless guy. Wade and Travis deal with them all the time. They handle extermination work under the downtown buildings. In the subbasements. It's warm there, so homeless people break in during the winter, and Wade and Travis are the ones who have to roust them out."

"So Wade knew Eagle?" Serena asked.

"Of course. Wade found him hiding in the tunnels all the time. What is this about, anyway?"

Serena didn't answer. She was already running for the door.

She realized that if the bomb was in place on Tuesday in the Duluth Outdoor Company shop, then anyone could have triggered it.

Anyone at all.

Even a runner.

52

Maggie followed Wade Ralston down the steps of the Third Avenue building to the metal door that led underground. "You did the right thing by calling me, Mr. Ralston," she said.

"I just don't want Travis getting hurt," he replied. "He's met you. He'll listen to you."

Ralston opened the door and let her brush by him as she crossed the threshold and took the next set of steps into the subbasement. As she did, her phone buzzed, and when she grabbed it from her back pocket, she saw that Serena was calling. She answered the phone, but she was too late. She'd lost signal deep under the building.

"Where is he?" Maggie asked.

"He's waiting for me in one of the inner rooms. I told him I was arranging for a car so he could get out of town."

Maggie lit a flashlight. Pipes ran along the ceiling just over their heads. The brick walls felt like the inside of a crypt. She saw glue traps on the wet concrete floor, with dozens of dead cockroaches stuck in the adhesive. They were just bugs, and she was the first to admit that spiders never made it out of her condo alive, but she wasn't crazy about what exterminators did. Seeing it up close made it feel like mass murder.

"You spend a lot of time down here?" she asked.

"This is my life." Ralston had a smile on his face, which made him look like a grinning skeleton in the flashlight beam. "People don't like thinking about how meat gets into those grocery store packages. They don't like knowing how we keep critters out of their nice warm buildings, either. Kill them all, but don't tell us how you do it."

"I suppose that's true," Maggie replied, feeling a twinge of discomfort.

Ralston didn't move. "So that Muslim guy Rashid blew himself up, huh? I'm not shedding any tears over him. Guess it saves us taxpayers the cost of a trial. Sorry about your cops, though."

Maggie said nothing.

"I should tell you," Ralston went on, "I'm not defending what Travis did, but I know where he was coming from. People are angry about these Islamic terrorists, and they want to hit them back, you know? Especially when all they get from Washington is politically correct bullshit."

"Let's just get this done, okay, Mr. Ralston?"

"Yeah, okay. Come on."

He led the way through the heat and darkness. Being down here, among the rough brick walls, was like going back in time. At street level, the world had changed, but down here, the decades peeled away. Men who were long dead had layered this mortar and brick in a deep hole in the earth.

Ahead of them, she saw light and heard static-filled rock music. They continued into a basement room lit by a flickering fluorescent tube and lined with metal shelves, bankers boxes, and filing cabinets. Rock dust littered the floor, making it slippery. The air baked. She was conscious of her gun in the holster, and she was ready to slip it into her hand if necessary.

"Hey, Travis, you here?" Ralston called.

"Yeah, glad you're back, man. What took you so long?"

Maggie let Ralston walk ahead of her. From behind a wall of boxes stacked as high as the ceiling pipes, she saw Travis Baker bound into view. He wore a tank top that showed off his sweaty muscles and tattoos. His long, greasy brown hair hung loose.

Travis spotted Maggie, and his face screwed up in fury.

"What the hell, man," he barked at Ralston. "What the hell. You called the cops on me?"

"I'm trying to keep you alive, kid."

Travis twitched; he was ready to run. Maggie wondered if he'd taken any drugs while he was down here, because he looked wired. His eyes shot past Maggie to the dark tunnel behind her that led back to the world. Maggie stood between him and freedom, and they both knew it.

"Mr. Baker, turn around, get on your knees, and put your hands on your head," she ordered him.

Travis didn't move. He focused his anger on Ralston. "I thought we were friends, man."

Ralston leaned casually against the open top drawer of one of the filing cabinets pushed against the wall. Old, yellow-streaked paint cans were perched atop the cabinet. The two men were ten feet apart, and Maggie worried that Travis might charge the smaller man. She could see Ralston keeping a wary eye on Travis for the same reason.

"You thought wrong," Ralston said. "You're my employee, Travis. You work for me. That's our relationship, kid. Maybe if you'd remembered that along the way, things would be different."

Travis pointed a finger at Ralston and then shouted at Maggie. "The whole thing was *his* idea! He said God saved me for a reason. God wanted me to do it!"

"Yeah, like me and God are so tight," Ralston replied, chuckling.

"Mr. Baker, get on your knees," Maggie repeated. "*Right now.*"

Behind his bluster, Travis was used to taking orders. He did what he was told. He slid to his knees on the dirty floor. He put his hands over his head. Maggie came around behind him, her cuffs in her grip. She grabbed one of Travis's wrists, yanked it behind his back, and snapped the cuff tightly around it. She did the same with his other wrist.

"On your feet," she said.

Awkwardly, Travis stood up. She kept her fist around the belt on his jeans. The heat in the tight space felt like the blast of a furnace. She could see Ralston, who hadn't moved from where he stood beside one of the filing cabinets. There was something odd about him. He watched her and Travis with a strange, self-satisfied look. The dying fluorescent light made his face flicker in and out of darkness.

Travis's hair spilled across his face. "Is this about Joni, Wade? You knew, didn't you?"

Ralston didn't say a word, but Maggie saw the man's expression mutate into a hatred that he made no effort to hide.

"Let's go, Travis," Maggie said, but pushing on the kid from behind was like shoving the trunk of a tree. He didn't move.

"Say it, Wade!" Travis demanded. His voice grew louder as he threw his words into Ralston's face. "You knew I was screwing Joni, didn't you?"

Maggie felt the danger in the room. The silence between the two men crackled with electricity. When Ralston finally spoke, his voice was low and venomous, like poisonous sulfur boiling out of a hot spring.

"*You're fucking right I knew.*"

Travis bellowed like a warrior and attacked. He ripped himself from Maggie's grasp and lurched across the dark space toward Ralston. He was fast. Ralston didn't have time to react, and neither did Maggie. Travis crossed the room in two steps and hurled the weight of his body against the smaller man, knocking him away from the filing cabinet and upending him onto his back. The filing cabinet crashed down, spewing drawers and papers. Paint cans spilled onto the floor and bounced, and their lids popped open and rolled away.

Travis planted his weight on one foot and launched a vicious kick toward Ralston's head. Seeing the blow coming, Ralston rolled clear, and Travis, off-balance, skidded backward. He lost his footing, banged his skull against the stone wall, and swayed like a drunk. Blood leaked from his mouth where he'd bitten his tongue.

"Knock it off!" Maggie shouted at both of them. She yanked Travis's tank top with two hands and pushed him face-first to the wall. "Don't make this any harder on yourself, Travis."

She spun him around and pushed him forward.

"Both of you, let's go!"

Ralston was on his feet again, watching her closely. His hands were in his pockets. Between Maggie and Ralston was the fallen filing cabinet. Two of its drawers had slid out, leaving the frame looking like an open mouth. The concrete floor was littered with debris from inside the old paint cans. The light flickered on and off over her head, as if they were in a disco.

It took a moment, with the light blinking, for her brain to register what her eyes were seeing.

The stone floor was strewn with ball bearings and nails. Round silver balls, no bigger than marbles. Sharp, one-inch nails.

Shrapnel.

Fine powder spilled from inside one of the paint cans. The black dust looked like coffee. It wasn't.

One of the cabinet drawers had overturned, spreading its contents at her feet. She saw coils of copper wire. Sticks of fireworks and rockets. Circuit boards. Half a dozen rubber athletic fitness trackers, cut open to reveal electronic components. Everything the homegrown terrorist needed to build a bomb and construct a remote-control trigger was on the floor in front of her.

It was only a second before the reality of this place caught up with her. Automatically, her hand dove for her holster, but she was too late. Looking up, she saw Wade Ralston pointing a gun at her head.

* * *

Dawn Basch sipped ice water as she stared out at the Duluth panorama through the restaurant's tall windows. The motion of the revolving floor was almost imperceptible, but even so, she felt the slightest nausea. Right now, the window faced northeast, where the land hugged the giant lake on its way into the arrowhead that ended at the Canadian border.

Her menu sat in front of her, unopened, as she composed her latest tweet. She always considered it a challenge, fitting pearls of wisdom into 140 characters. It was like changing the world one little sound bite at a time.

Her long fingernails made it difficult to type on the phone's keyboard.

@dawnbasch tweeted:
Another Muslim suicide bomber. As expected.
When will we face the truth about the Religion of Peace?
#islamismurder
#noexceptions

Dawn put her phone faceup on the table. A few seconds later, it began to vibrate again and again. Retweets. A tiny smile played across her bright red lips. Word was already spreading. More deaths meant more anger, but anger was essential if anything was going to change.

She mourned the deaths of the innocent. The spectators at the marathon. The police. However, sacrifice made people understand the stakes. Injustice led people to take up arms.

"What can I get you, ma'am?"

Dawn looked up into the smiling face of the waitress standing beside the booth. She was young, in her early twenties, probably a college student at UMD. Pretty girl. Dark skin, dark eyes, thick eyebrows. Her black hair made a V on her forehead. She wore the restaurant's uniform, but she also had a scarf wrapped around her head and pulled back around her neck.

Dawn smiled back. "I'm sorry?"

"I said, what can I get you, ma'am?" the waitress repeated.

Dawn looked down at the phone on her table. She was getting a phone call, and she saw on the screen that the caller was Lieutenant Stride. Another policeman, blind to the threat in front of his eyes. Another government stooge who invariably chose peace over freedom. She had no interest in talking to him.

With the tap of a finger, she declined the call. The phone kept vibrating. More retweets. More patriots.

"What can you get me?" she said to the Muslim girl. "Well, first of all, dear, you can get me a different waitress."

53

Maggie stared into Wade Ralston's eyes, and she knew the truth. This was never about terrorism. This was murder, evil and simple.

She put her hands up slowly. As she did, she measured the distance between herself and Ralston, gauging the likelihood of his getting off a good shot or of her being able to take him down before he fired. The fluorescent light gave her a flicker of darkness every second, but it wasn't much.

Next to her, Travis's face was blank. He still didn't get it. "What are you doing, man? What's with the gun? What's this about?"

"I think this is about Wade killing his wife and her lover," Maggie said, never taking her eyes off Ralston. "He tried to blow you and Joni up, Travis. Is that right, Wade? Was that the plan?"

Ralston blinked through his sweat. "Yeah. That was the plan."

Travis looked back and forth between them. "*What?* What are you talking about? What is she saying, Wade?"

"She's saying I was the one who blew up the marathon, you moron," Ralston told him.

Blink on. Blink off. Light. Dark. In the next flash of shadow from the flickering fluorescent light over her head, Maggie took a quick step forward.

Travis shook his head in disbelief. "No way. No way, man. You killed Joni? How could you do that, you son of a bitch? And Shelly? She'll never walk again. All because of *you?*"

"Maybe you should have thought of that when you were sticking your dick between my wife's legs," Ralston fired back. "The two of you, acting like I didn't know. Throwing it in my face. Did you really think there wasn't going to be some kind of payback?"

"You wanted me dead, too," Travis murmured, his eyes wide.

"Damn right I wanted you dead. The bomb was supposed to blow both of you to ribbons. The two of you gone, and me on my way to Key West with half a million dollars in insurance. I couldn't believe it when I woke up, and there you were, barely a scratch on you. Like I said, you're a lucky man, Travis, but your luck is about to run out for good."

Darkness.

Another step forward.

"You built the bomb here?" Maggie asked, stalling for time, trying to get close enough to jump across the space and grab the gun.

Ralston grinned. He was proud of himself. "Yeah. If some teenager in Boston could build a bomb, I figured, how hard could it be? And nobody would ever be looking for a runner, right? All I had to do was rewire my athletic tracker to send the signal. Soon as I got close, soon as I saw Joni and Travis, I pressed the button. I wanted to see their faces right before the end. *Boom.*"

"You're sick, man!" Travis shouted. "You're a sick, sick bastard!"

"You think you're so innocent, Travis? You burned up that building. You killed those people."

"You said I had to do something!"

Ralston laughed. "Yeah, I knew if I pushed you, you'd do something stupid. Stupid is your middle name, Travis. I figured, having you rot in prison for the rest of your life, squeezing your ass cheeks shut, that might be okay. But no, it's not enough. I missed you once with the bomb. I'm not going to miss again."

Flicker, flicker, flicker. Maggie inched forward.

"What about Eagle?" she asked. "Why was he involved?"

"You know about him?" Ralston's eyebrows nudged upward in surprise. "One crazy homeless guy gets popped, I didn't think anyone would make the connection."

"You sent him into the shop and paid him to distract the staff. That's when you planted the bomb."

Ralston cocked his head. "Yeah, I knew I could set the bomb off in the middle of the race, but obviously, I couldn't plant it. It had to be ready to go before the marathon ever started. And I didn't want Eagle around to talk about what he did. Even a shit-faced drunk like him might have put two and two together after the bomb went off."

"And the marathon camera?" Maggie asked.

The light went off. It stayed off a fraction of a second longer this time. She assessed the distance. Assessed how far she could jump.

Ralston shrugged. "The marathon people like to show off their camera. I've known about it for years, ever since we started zapping their bugs. I figured I'd wear a disguise on Tuesday to plant the bomb, but I didn't want anybody getting curious and taking a close look at the pictures. The safest thing was to make sure the camera went down. So I stopped by the marathon offices on Monday evening and left a little present behind. Mice. I knew they'd be calling the next day, soon as one of the little guys took a run across somebody's desk. And they did. So I crawled around the office on Tuesday afternoon, and it was easy enough to disable the cable to the camera."

Maggie shook her head. "And you didn't care about murdering total strangers when the bomb went off?"

"Collateral damage," Ralston replied, "but necessary. If you take out a big insurance policy on your cheating wife, and she and her lover boy are the only ones who die, the cops and the insurance company take a long, hard look at you. But a terrorist attack? They just cut you a check."

He chuckled to himself, as if he couldn't stop admiring his perfect plan.

"So what are you gonna do now, Wade?" Travis bellowed. "You gonna shoot me? Is that how this works?"

"No, the sergeant here is going to shoot you. But too bad for her, you've got enough left before you kick it to land a shot between her eyes. Of course, no one will know that she actually took the bullet in her brain first."

Maggie knew time was running out.

Ralston squinted at her, and his gun arm tensed. The barrel was aimed at her head. He wouldn't miss.

Light on. Light off.

Maggie ducked and jumped. The gun exploded over her head, deafening in the enclosed space. She could feel the burning passage of the bullet grazing her hair. She hit Ralston low, ramming his thighs, bringing both of them down. Another bullet fired, this one wild, and it banged against a metal pipe, throwing off fragments that shattered the single lightbulb and bathed the subbasement in total darkness.

She heard Ralston getting up. She crawled away, just in time, as he fired blindly. And then another shot. And another. And another, raking the underground. Nearby, she heard a puff of breath from Travis, like a whimper of surprise. He collapsed, like dead weight falling, and never made another sound. Maggie crawled faster. Nails on the floor cut her hands. Dirt and dust filled her face. She bumped against something heavy and metal and realized it was one of the old filing cabinets. She squeezed herself behind it, her back against the stone wall, and she pulled her own gun out of her holster.

The world was black.

She heard footsteps. Boots crunching on rock.

Ralston was coming for her.

* * *

Khan was sure that everyone was looking at him as he got off the service elevator and marched through the JJ Astor kitchen. The cooks. The dishwashers. The waiters. Someone on the hotel staff would realize he was a stranger, and they would shout at him and block his path. They'd stare into his eyes and recognize him and tackle him to the ground.

Instead, in the tumult of lunch service, no one paid attention to him. People shouted orders. Meat sizzled on the flat-top grill. Dishes clattered.

He crossed the kitchen and pushed through the swinging door into a curving hallway that led past the guest elevator, the hostess desk, and the bar. The tables of the restaurant were in front of him, winding in a circle around the building, overlooking Duluth, the lake, and the northern wilderness. His eyes hunted for Dawn Basch, but he didn't see her in the outer ring of booths that was visible from where he was.

Behind him, a waiter flew through the swinging door, nearly colliding into his back with a full tray of food. The man whispered in annoyance, "Out of the way, you fool! Don't stand there!"

Khan mumbled an apology and let him pass. He spotted a pitcher of water on a tray near him and grabbed it. He walked slowly around the circle, studying each person at each table, searching for Basch. He pasted a smile onto his face. He tried to swallow down his terror, and he was sure that the smell of his sweat trailed after him. Some people asked for water. His hand shook as he filled their glasses.

Where was she?

"Are you all right, young man?" an elderly woman asked. She was at a table with a teenage girl, and they were both eating shrimp salads. The older woman had a sweet, puzzled smile.

Khan blinked. "I'm sorry?"

"Well, you've been standing there for a minute, not moving. I wanted to make sure that nothing was wrong."

"Oh. Oh, no. Sorry. Do you want some water, ma'am?"

The woman pointed at her glass, which was full to the rim, and the tablecloth underneath it was wet. "You already filled it."

"Yes, I'm very sorry."

The teenager at the table watched him as if he were under a microscope. She had her phone in her hand. Her eyes darted from the screen to his face and then back to the screen. Khan felt his legs begin to cave beneath him. He took a step, tripped, and took another step. He waited for the shout from the girl behind him. *That's the man! That's the terrorist! Get him!*

She didn't say anything. Maybe he was safe.

Khan walked a little farther, and then he took a risk and glanced over his shoulder. The girl was still staring at him. Her eyes glittered.

As he watched, she leaned forward and whispered something to the old woman across from her, and she turned around, too, her face pale. They were both staring at him now.

He went faster, although his legs barely supported him. He studied each table. Dawn Basch wasn't there. Maybe she'd left. Beneath his feet, the slight motion unsettled his stomach. The chatter in the restaurant sounded like a thousand annoying birds in his ears. He couldn't stop blinking. The gun behind his belt ground like a screw into his spine.

"Hey, how about some water?"

Khan looked down. A man in a suit held up his empty glass and stared at him impatiently.

"Yes. Sorry."

He tried to fill the glass, but his hand shook violently. Water went everywhere. The man cursed at him, and Khan apologized, but his eyes were drawn back to the table behind him. The older woman and the teenage girl were talking to a manager now and pointing around the circle. Pointing at him.

Khan left the pitcher of water on the table. The man protested loudly, but Khan walked away, fast. He felt eyes following him. When he took a look back, he saw the manager, a large man with a white shirt and a tie, heading his way. Their eyes met, and the man called out across the restaurant.

"Excuse me!"

Khan turned away. He was halfway around the circle now. The manager's voice grew louder behind him.

"Excuse me! You!"

Khan put his head down and charged forward. They would all know who he was soon. They'd be coming for him. He passed more tables and booths. More diners. More strangers. He saw the city spread out beyond the windows.

And there she was.

Dawn Basch.

Her head was down as she ate her lunch. Her fingers, tipped with long red fingernails, tapped the screen of her phone. He knew what she was doing. Spreading hate. Spreading poison. Getting people killed.

She didn't look up as he drew closer. He was nothing to her. He didn't matter at all.

All he had to do was pull his gun and fire. Find the courage. Avenge the murders of his wife and child. After that, nothing else mattered. What happened to him didn't matter. Let the police kill him, too, and he would be free.

Khan reached behind his belt. His fingers closed around the butt of the gun.

Then he heard a woman's voice.

He'd heard that same voice once before, in the cemetery, in the midst of the darkness, rain, and bullets.

"*Rashid!*"

* * *

"I'm in the restaurant," Gayle Durkin told Stride through the Bluetooth transmitter in her ear. "Where are you?"

Stride replied into her phone, "I'm in the elevator now. I'm thirty seconds away. Any sign of Basch or Rashid?"

"Not yet."

"I haven't been able to reach Basch. She doesn't know about the threat."

"Understood."

Gayle began a slow rotation around the restaurant. Her hand was in the purse that was slung around her shoulder, and inside the purse, she had a firm grip on a Glock. She smiled at each table. No one was familiar. No one was a threat.

A waitress passed her, heading in the opposite direction, toward the kitchen. Gayle stopped her with a gentle hand on her shoulder. She grabbed her phone and opened up a driver's license photo of Rashid. "Have you seen this man anywhere in the hotel today?"

The waitress, a pretty Muslim girl, shook her head. "No, sorry."

"What about Dawn Basch?"

The girl rolled her eyes, and her mouth pinched into a frown. "Oh yes, she's here. Keep going—she's at a booth on the other side."

"Thank you."

Gayle studied the tables beyond the curve. She couldn't see Basch yet. She kept walking. The tower had a faint sway. Out the window, she saw the city where she and Ron had grown up. They'd eaten here once, years earlier. The four of them, Mom, Dad, Gayle, Ron. It was their first experience at a revolving restaurant. Ron, who was probably no more than ten, got sick. She couldn't even remember why they were there or what they were celebrating. Mom's birthday, probably. That was in January, and she could still remember the snow flying past the high windows like a flight of angels.

Now she was back.

She couldn't help picturing Paris in her mind. Another restaurant. Another terrorist. Each step reminded her of the tables in the outdoor café. She thought about Ron's text. His photo. The Eiffel Tower behind him. Two tables away was a twenty-one-year-old Syrian who was ready to die and take Gayle's brother with him in the explosion.

Not again. *Not again.*

Gayle's grip tightened on the gun.

This time, she wouldn't miss. There would be no bad shot in the rain and darkness. No ricochet.

She continued around the circle. Something was already happening; she heard voices, someone shouting. She started to run. Ahead of her, she saw a dark-haired woman in a booth, and even seeing the back of her head, she knew it was Dawn Basch. A clean-shaven waiter stood near her table. Behind him, also running, she watched a manager hurrying through the aisle, calling out. "Excuse me! You!"

She took a second look at the waiter. She'd expected a beard, but when her brain took it away, she recognized him.

"*Rashid!*"

The waiter stared at her. Their eyes met. He had his hand behind his back, and when she saw it again, he was clenching a pistol, his finger on the trigger. He slid into the booth across from Dawn Basch and pointed the barrel into her face.

54

One of the downtown patrol officers spotted Maggie's truck on Superior Street near the Holiday Inn. The yellow Avalanche, pockmarked with dents and scratches, was impossible to miss. Serena parked around the corner from the vehicle on Third Avenue, and she dialed Maggie's cell phone again as she got out. The call went to voice mail, as it had done for the last half hour. Maggie was off the grid.

She noticed a navy-blue Cadillac in the spot next to Maggie's truck. It caught her attention because of the plastic toy hanging from the rearview mirror; it was an oversize mosquito. With a quick call, she checked the license plate and confirmed the owner of the Cadillac.

Wade Ralston.

Serena didn't know where to start searching. The street. The hotel. The skywalks overhead. Then, standing on the corner, she saw the iron railing around the steps that led into the subbasement of the Third Avenue building. She thought about what Shelly had said.

Wade and Travis are in the downtown basements all the time.

It was a great place to hide. Or a great place for an ambush.

She called in her position and then jogged across the street. When she peered down the steps to the landing below her, she saw the metal door ajar. She ran to the bottom, and as she did, she unhooked the holster of her gun.

Beyond the door, more steps led into darkness. She followed her flashlight beam into a narrow tunnel with brick walls. She was tall enough that her head nearly grazed the utility pipes mounted above her. She listened, but she heard only the buzz of machinery. At the end of the tunnel, the corridor turned at a sharp angle. She saw what appeared to be storage rooms, many of them open, stuffed with file cabinets and old office equipment. She checked each cubbyhole as she inched forward. Ahead of her, the tunnel widened, like the entrance to a cave.

Serena called out, "Maggie?"

Instantly, from somewhere inside the next room, Maggie shouted, "Serena, turn off the light! Ralston has a gun!"

Serena spun into the shelter of a storage room, and as she did, a gunshot banged off the walls inches from where she'd stood. She switched off her flashlight, leaving the basement dark. She drew out her gun from the holster. When she checked her phone to call for backup, she had no signal.

She listened again. No one was moving.

She squatted, staying low, and inched beside the stone wall into the hot, larger room. She tried to keep her footsteps silent, but debris crunched under her feet in the quiet space. She couldn't see anything. The interior was darker than a cloudy night.

Her foot bumped against something metal. She bent down and ran her free hand along the smooth surface of a toppled filing cabinet. Reaching out, she found a drawer that had come loose, and the floor was littered with paper. She nudged around the obstacles, but she made noise, and another wild gunshot made her dive to the floor. Rock and glass scraped her hands. She heard someone moving, but she didn't dare fire back, not knowing where Maggie was.

Serena crawled now, using only one hand to prop herself up and the other to keep her gun pointed ahead of her. Her fingers landed in something sticky and damp. When she extended her arm, she felt warm skin. It was a man's arm, but whoever was lying on the floor wasn't moving. She followed the arm to the man's wrist and found no pulse. He was dead.

She climbed over the body. When she stopped and listened again, she thought she heard the faint noise of someone hiding close by. She took a risk and whispered, barely louder than a breath.

"Maggie?"

Someone grabbed her wrist. Serena tried not to scream. She felt herself pulled sideways and then yanked down. Someone's mouth was at her ear.

"It's me," Maggie said.

Serena found Maggie's ear and whispered back. "There's a dead body a few feet away."

"It's Travis Baker. One of Wade's bullets hit him. Wade blew up the marathon."

Their voices were too loud.

Another bullet pinged off the filing cabinet near their heads.

"His gun has to be almost empty," Maggie murmured.

"Okay, hang on."

Serena felt around the floor until she found something hard and round, like a marble. She heaved it toward the opposite side of the basement, where it landed with a sharp knock on the wall. The noise drew Ralston's fire. He shot twice toward the wall, and the bullets ricocheted off stone and metal.

And then they heard it. *Click*.

"You're out, Wade," Maggie called immediately. "Give it up."

They switched on their flashlights and scoured the basement. There were hiding places everywhere, behind the debris and among the tunnels and storage closets. Their weak beams barely cut through the shadows. They each had their guns in their hands, and with silent signals, they split up, taking opposite routes through the space. Serena veered back toward the tunnel that led to the outside steps, to make sure Ralston wasn't able to slip out behind them.

"Hands up, Ralston, and come out where we can see you," Serena called.

Ralston didn't answer. Slowly, they cleared the interior of the basement from front to back. Twenty feet away, Serena saw Maggie's flashlight beam swishing across the floor.

And then she heard something.

Something sizzling.

"Maggie, what the hell's that? It's coming from near you. *Get down!*"

The warning came too late. A fireworks rocket exploded, as loud as a bomb, and a shell designed to burst in the sky instead hit the low ceiling and went off in a rainbow shower of color and flame. Serena saw the concussive wave knock Maggie off her feet, and her flashlight rolled away. Before it went dark, she spotted Wade Ralston jumping forward, a shovel in his hands, hoisting it high and arcing it toward Maggie on the stone floor.

"Maggie! Roll!"

Serena heard the shovel bang hard against the floor, but she heard a screech of pain, too. He'd hit Maggie. She charged toward Ralston, but he was already directly in front of her, swinging the shovel like a baseball player toward her head. She ducked and fired. The bullet missed, but the shovel smashed the flashlight out of her hand, leaving them blind again. The burnt smell of the rocket was in her nose. She heard a rush of air as he hoisted the shovel again, and she threw herself down hard and fired toward the ceiling. In the muzzle flash, she had a glimpse of Ralston with both hands over his head as he swung the shovel toward her like an ax.

She fired again.

Ralston screamed. The bullet hit his leg. The shovel kept coming, but it didn't clear the ceiling. Instead, it slammed into one of the building water pipes and knocked it free. A fountain sprayed into Serena's face. She fired again, up, aiming where Ralston had been, but he was already gone. Water flooded around her. It pooled on the floor, hissing as it surged from the open pipe.

She heard footsteps dragging on the floor. Heading away, heading toward the outside.

"Maggie!" Serena called, her ears still ringing from the fireworks shell.

"I'm here," Maggie shouted back from six feet away.

Serena followed the muffled sound of the voice and found Maggie on her back on the basement floor. They were both drenched by the broken pipe. Smoke clouded around them and made them choke.

"Are you hurt?" Serena asked.

"He grazed my shoulder. Feels like an elephant stepped on it. Come on, we have to go."

Serena helped Maggie to her feet and let her lean against her. They couldn't see, and both of them coughed and gagged. Their shoes splashed in the standing water. Serena grabbed her phone from her pocket, and it gave them a faint glow. They navigated around debris back to the main tunnel, and ahead of them, they saw a crack of light at the stairs that led up to Third Avenue.

"Run," Maggie told her. "Go."

Serena left her behind and charged for the stairs. She took them two at a time, first the subbasement steps, and then the stairs up to the metal railing at the street. Her eyes squinted into the sunlight. She ran to the corner of Superior Street, and a blood trail on the asphalt led the way. She'd hit him, badly, but he'd already escaped. The Cadillac that had been parked next to Maggie's Avalanche was gone. She looked up and down both streets but didn't see the car speeding away.

Ralston was on the run, and he had a head start.

When she got back to the basement stairs, Maggie was already at the top, grimacing and holding her shoulder as she leaned against the building wall. Their faces were streaked with dirt and ash, and their hair was matted to their skin. Their clothes were completely soaked.

"Call Maloney," Maggie said. "We need to get choppers up and road-blocks back in place. This son of a bitch is not getting away from us."

55

Khan saw the face of Dawn Basch at the end of his gun. All he had to do was pull the trigger, and she would be dead. And then the FBI agent would pull the trigger on her own gun, and he would be dead, too, and the nightmare would be over. It was easy. It was the only thing to do.

"Hello, Mr. Rashid," Basch said to him, in a falsely pleasant voice that made him think: *Yes, she is the Devil.*

She didn't blink. She didn't tremble. He didn't know if he'd expected her to be afraid, but she wasn't. He realized she was just like the martyrs who had stolen his own religion. She was ready to die for her cause.

"Go ahead, pull the trigger," she urged him. "Aren't you a little bit curious what happens next? Is there really a heaven? Is there really a hell? Pull the trigger, and in a millisecond, we'll both find out the answer to the mystery."

Khan tried to keep his hand steady. He wanted to speak, to say something, but his throat was as dry as dust.

"Put the gun down!" the FBI agent shouted at him.

His eyes flicked to the woman by the booth, with the big black gun pointed at his head. Would she fire first? In that instant, would he have time to shoot Basch, or would he be gone?

Did any of it matter?

"Because of you, my wife and child are dead," Khan murmured to Dawn Basch.

"I didn't start this, Mr. Rashid. Once violence begins, it's impossible for anyone to control it. It spreads, it mutates, it evolves. The ripple effects can't be predicted. It has a life of its own, gobbling up friends and enemies."

Khan felt tiredness in his arm as he held the gun. The tiredness was in his whole body. "My wife was a good woman. A computer scientist. A hard worker. A mother. An American. My son was innocent. He played soccer. He liked pizza. They were no one's enemies."

"Maybe not now, but sooner or later, Mr. Rashid, we will all have to choose. No one is neutral in this war. Think about it. Here you are, with a gun pointed at my head. You made your choice. You're a terrorist."

"I am *not*."

"No? And yet here we both are, willing to sacrifice ourselves for what we believe in. Go ahead, kill me. I don't care. Show the world who you really are."

"I'm what you made me," Khan told her.

The FBI agent shouted again. "Khan, put the gun down! I'm not going to tell you again. Put it down, and put your hands in the air."

Khan knew he had to keep his arm motionless. If he so much as flinched, he was dead. He wondered if he had the time to pull the trigger, before the agent saw his finger pulling backward and fired herself.

He stared at Dawn Basch, whose expression was cool. Seeing her, staring into the emptiness behind her eyes, he didn't want to be like her. He was a man of peace. Killing anyone was against everything he believed. And yet, if he walked away, she would go unpunished. She would never pay a price for what she did to Ahdia and Pak. Her flames would spread far and wide on a trail of gasoline. She had to be stopped.

He couldn't put the gun down.

He couldn't betray them.

His eyes shifted to the FBI agent, and his whole soul was sad. "I'm sorry," he said. "This woman is poison. The only good thing to come out of all of this would be to put an end to her. If you have to kill me, then go ahead. I'm ready to die, but she dies first."

* * *

The adrenaline in Gayle's veins flowed like a river flooding its banks.

Her arms were rock-steady. Her right hand cradled the Glock, and her left hand cradled her wrist. No mistakes. She had Khan's forehead on the other end of her barrel, lined up in her sights. He was no more than six feet away, with his own gun inches from Dawn Basch. Gayle's concentration was centered on his trigger finger. The slightest twitch, and she would blow him away.

"Lower the gun, put it on the table, and put your hands in the air," she told Rashid. "Right now."

"I can't."

"Look at me, Rashid. Tell me the truth. Do you really want to kill this woman? Is that what you want to do? Is that who you are?"

He stared back at her, as if he wanted to answer. Their eyes met. His mouth opened and closed without saying a word, but she didn't need words to understand him. This was her job; she read people. She knew what was in their heads. She was the Lie Detector. It should be easy for her to know if he was serious. She should have been able to see the truth in his face, in his body, in his voice. Either he was capable of murder, or he wasn't. Either he was going to pull the trigger, or he wasn't.

But her gift failed her. She had no idea. She couldn't read him; he was a closed book. She felt blind. She knew her head should be clear right now, but it wasn't. She should be alone in the moment, but she wasn't. Her past was with her, sitting in the booth next to Rashid.

Officer Kenzie was there.

Ron was there.

Both of them, dead.

A terrible realization overwhelmed her. She wanted to pull the trigger. If Khan gave her the slightest excuse, she would do it. She would fire, the bullet would blast through his brain, and she would have the tiniest amount of vengeance. It didn't matter who Khan was or what he'd done or hadn't done. He was the symbol. He was every deluded fool who'd walked into a café and thought that killing innocent people was a ticket to paradise.

Her jaw hardened.

Her fingers tightened around the gun. She could do it right now. She'd waited long enough. He wasn't going to give up. He wasn't going to put the gun down. If she waited, if he fired first, then she'd failed. No one would blame her or judge her for taking the shot.

No one would know what it was really all about.

The truth screamed at her, like a monster baying for blood. She hated this man. She hated him; she wanted him dead. She wanted all of them dead. Every single one of them who had killed her brother, who'd killed hundreds, thousands, who cut off people's heads, who threw people off buildings, who sent children to die.

She *hated* them.

And even if she couldn't kill all of them herself, she could start here, with this one man. Pull the trigger. He dies. It wasn't much, but it was something. Ron would never forgive her if she did nothing at all. If she let him go unavenged. If he was in Paris in a million pieces of dust, and she simply accepted it without striking back.

Right?

This is what Ron would want her to do.

"Durkin."

She heard the voice beside her, calm and quiet. Her eyes didn't leave Khan Rashid, but she knew who it was.

Stride.

"*Durkin*. Put your gun down. I've got this."

* * *

Stride ran through the now-empty restaurant with his gun in his hand. His officers had cleared out the guests and staked out positions on both sides of the semicircle where the confrontation was taking place. He saw the three of them, in and near the window-side booth. Dawn Basch, Khan Rashid, and Gayle Durkin.

As he got close to them, he slowed to a walk. One step at a time. He could feel the electricity in the air. One wrong word, one wrong motion, and they would all burn. His focus was on Khan Rashid, with his arm outstretched, pushing a gun into the face of Dawn Basch. He could see that Rashid was torn and exhausted. He didn't know whether Rashid would really pull the trigger, because the man clearly didn't know himself.

Then Stride looked at Gayle Durkin and realized he had a more immediate problem.

Durkin's face was a stony mask of loathing. She didn't see Rashid at the end of her gun. She saw something else, and whatever it was, she was going to kill it. Her arm was as rigid as a steel pipe. Her fingers were tight enough to crush the butt of her Glock. Stride read her face and knew that she was a millisecond away from pulling the trigger.

"Durkin."

He extended his gun at Rashid and edged close to the FBI agent, feeling the aura of violence from her body like a black cloud.

"*Durkin*. Put your gun down. I've got this."

"No." Her voice was robotic.

"I have Rashid. Stand down. Lower your weapon."

"He's going to fire."

"*No one* is going to fire," Stride said.

"He's a terrorist."

"This man? He's a taxi driver. He didn't blow up the marathon. He didn't blow up our officers. He's a man whose wife and child were murdered, and he's out of his mind with grief."

He wanted Durkin to hear him, but he wanted Rashid to hear him, too.

"He's not going to put the gun down, Stride. I tried that. He's going to shoot her."

"Rashid isn't going to shoot anyone." *Do you hear me, Khan?*

"You don't know that. Let me do my job."

"*Gayle*. Listen to me. Officer Kenzie's death was an accident. You'll learn to live with it. But if you pull the trigger now, that's it. You're done. There's no going back. And if Ron were here right now, he'd be saying the same thing. You know that."

Stride's eyes were focused on Rashid, but he could sense Durkin turning her head toward him. He'd broken through. Ron had broken through.

"Come on, Gayle," he went on. "Help me. Talk to him."

Her Glock, which was at the corner of his vision, sank toward the floor. Durkin holstered her weapon.

"He's right, Rashid," Durkin said. Her voice took on a quiet urgency as she pleaded, one human being to another. "He's right. This isn't the answer. Don't listen to Basch. You're not a terrorist. Put down the gun."

Stride saw tears in Rashid's eyes.

"I can't," the man said.

"Think about what you told her about Ahdia," Durkin went on. She squatted beside the table. "Your wife was a good woman. A good mother. An American. She would tell you to put the gun down. This isn't you. This isn't who you are."

"Khan, the man who murdered your family is dead," Stride told him. "My team found him. You don't have to get justice. You *have* justice."

Hesitation flickered on Rashid's face. "Is that really true?"

"It is. I got the call coming over here. His name was Travis Baker. He set the fire. And he's dead. We know who killed the people at the marathon, too. He's on the run, but we're going to get him. It's over, Khan. It's a tragedy, but you don't have to make it any worse."

"This woman . . ." Rashid murmured.

"This woman wants you to kill her, but if you do that, you become exactly what she says you are. And I know you. Haq told me about you. Right from the beginning, he said you could *never* turn to violence. Never. That's why you called me about Malik, isn't it? You didn't want him to hurt anyone. You knew that was wrong."

Khan blinked. His body began to shake. "But Ahdia is dead. Pak is dead."

Stride kept his gun trained at Rashid's head, but he lowered his voice, and he tried to catch the man's eye. To make him turn his head.

"I know. They're gone. So is this agent's brother. So are good people at the marathon and good police officers who were friends of mine. We've lost too many people already. It's time to stop. It stops right now with you, Khan. Put the gun on the table. Please."

Time seemed to stand still.

The silence was complete.

He could feel the movement of the rotating floor under his feet, slowly going in circles.

He didn't know what Khan would do, but he was ready either way.

Tears fell down the man's cheeks. His body convulsed in sobs. He lay the gun on the table and pushed it with a fingertip toward Gayle Durkin, who scooped it up and secured it. Rashid put his hands up. Stride took out his cuffs and helped Rashid out of the booth and cuffed the man's hands behind his back. Rashid continued to cry, as if there would never be an end to his tears.

Before Stride could lead him away, Rashid leaned over and spoke to Dawn Basch, whose face was as pale and motionless as a museum statue.

"There is a hell," he told her quietly. "It exists, and I'm sorry for you, because someday, you will see it."

56

Wade Ralston heard the throb of the helicopter.

He squinted through the windshield of the Cadillac and saw it floating over the evergreen trees not even a half mile ahead of him. It was an FBI helicopter, black, with its logo painted in huge white letters on the side. They'd found him. It hadn't taken long. The chopper was low enough that they could broadcast a message that blasted through the windows of the car.

"Pull over and stop."

Like hell. That wasn't going to happen. Wade accelerated, taking the engine of the Cadillac up to seventy miles an hour. He was on the old scenic highway, the marathon route, two miles south of Two Harbors, heading toward the Boundary Waters wilderness. Railroad tracks paralleled the road, both of them arrow straight. Lake Superior was just beyond the trees, but he couldn't see it.

He had survival gear in the trunk. He always did. His plan had been to take refuge in the wilderness and hike his way into Canada. The trouble was, he wasn't going to survive. He knew that. His leg continued to bleed where the cop had shot him. Blood pooled and soaked into the front seat and dribbled down to the floor. The blood was turning dark, and that was a bad sign. It didn't hurt or burn anymore. He didn't feel anything.

His breathing had become heavier, as if he were dragging air into his lungs. His vision was blurry. Even so, he drove faster, reaching eighty miles an hour, as if he could run from the police and run from death at the same time.

"You don't have much time left, Wade."

He glanced over at the passenger seat and saw a ghost. Travis sat there. Travis, who was already dead under the Third Avenue building, with a bullet hole in his skull.

"Go away," Wade murmured. The blood loss was playing tricks on his mind. "Go away. You're not real."

He looked again, and Travis was gone. The seat was empty.

He swooped past the FBI helicopter hovering above the highway, but it rose up and kept pace with him effortlessly. There was nowhere to go. He looked in the rearview mirror, and he could see the lights of police cars behind him. As fast as he went, they went faster. They were closing in on him. In less than a minute, they'd roar around the Cadillac and run him off the road.

They could probably save him if they caught him now. Tie off the leg. Put him in an ambulance. And for what? So they could put him on trial and convict him and send him to rot in a hole for the rest of his life? So some gangbanger could pay off a guard and shove a knife into his gut during the one hour per day the prisoners were allowed outside?

That was no life. That was torture.

He went ninety miles an hour, but the police still kept getting closer.

"You know I never loved you, right?"

Wade looked at the passenger seat, and there was Joni. Another ghost. Joni, in a tank top and shorts, with the amazing body and the tattoos and the piercings and the supersized breasts that no one but him was supposed to touch. Joni, who'd been humiliating him ever since they got married.

"I hung around for the money," Joni said. "I mean, you figured that out, huh?"

"Yeah," Wade said. "I figured that out."

Then she was gone, too. He was alone.

"*Pull over and stop*," the FBI said again.

He looked northward on the highway. Coming toward him on the opposite side of the road was a semitruck, one of the big rigs, thundering toward the city. It was going fast, and so was Wade. They'd pass each other in seconds. He would feel the vibration in its wake, nearly blowing him off the road.

Wade tapped his brakes.

Behind him, the police slowed, too. They saw his brakes and figured he was pulling off the highway. Instead, Wade undid his seat belt. The truck stormed closer, loud enough that its thunder reached him. He had to time it just right. He had to be in the other lane at the perfect moment. He didn't want the truck to brake; he wanted the impact at full speed. He'd fire as fast as a bullet, as fast as a rocket, and be gone.

Travis was back in the passenger seat next to him. The kid sang a chorus of "Rocket Man" and began to laugh. Wade laughed, too. Rocket man—that was funny. The two of them laughed and laughed.

The helicopter was right there ahead of him, like a crow in the sky. The police were right behind him. They thought they had him. They thought he had nowhere to go. The truck barreled down the opposite lane, and the driver was probably wondering what the hell was going on.

They were so close. They were about to pass, car and truck.

Right.

Now.

Wade flicked the wheel of the Cadillac and lurched into the other lane. The truck was on top of him, horn blaring.

Travis stopped laughing.

EPILOGUE

Khan answered the door at his Woodland home. He had a wedding picture of himself and Ahdia in his hand as he did.

He hadn't done much else in recent days, other than look at family pictures and talk to his lawyers about a plea deal that would keep him free despite his pointing a gun into the face of Dawn Basch. Around him, the house was still a mess from the search the FBI had made. He hadn't had the energy to clean up. He'd slept on the sofa, rather than going into their bedroom. Eventually, he would have to decide about Duluth and this house. Stay or go. But Haq had told him not to rush anything, and Haq was right.

He opened the door, but he didn't recognize the man on the porch. He appeared to be in his forties, with a muscular build and shaved head. At first, Khan assumed the man was a reporter, but he wore a suit and tie, which ruled out most of the journalists he'd met lately. Beyond him, on the street near the woods, Khan saw a pretty blond woman waiting in the man's car. There was a little boy in the backseat.

"Mr. Rashid?" the man said.

"Yes."

"My name is Michael Malville."

Khan shook his head in confusion. "I'm sorry, I don't know who you are. Are you a reporter? Or a lawyer? Because I already have plenty of both."

"No."

Oddly, the man on the porch began to cry. It was strange, seeing a strong man break down so completely in front of him. He realized that the man was staring at the photograph that Khan carried in his hand.

Malville wiped his face and tried to form words. "I'm—I'm the man who destroyed your life."

"What?" Khan asked.

"I made a mistake. I thought—I was sure—that you bumped into me on Superior Street during the marathon. I was tired, I was angry, and I was just wrong. And I—I told the world about it. And now you've lost your wife and son, and you've been through so much pain, and it's all my fault. So I needed to come here, to see you face-to-face. I need to apologize. To tell you I am so, so sorry. If I had ever dreamed—"

Khan held up a hand to stop him. His face clouded over. He tried to find something to say, but he had nothing. No words. He had to brace himself against the doorframe to stop himself from falling.

"It was you?" Khan said finally.

"Yes."

He thought about the night in the Woodland grocery store, the night when it had all begun. Someone had thrust a phone in his face. *Is this you? Because it sure looks like you.* One photograph had turned his life upside down. One photograph had destroyed his family. One photograph, sent around the world by the man standing in front of him.

"You can do whatever you want," Malville went on. "Scream at me. Hit me. Sue me."

"I want nothing from you, Mr. Malville," Khan told him brusquely.

He closed the door; he didn't slam it. Malville waited on the porch, but then, a few seconds later, he walked away with his head down. Khan turned around and leaned against the glass, and soon he was crying, too. Crying for everything that was lost. Crying for his empty house. He wished he could blame Michael Malville. He wanted to feel hatred for this man, but he realized he didn't. He couldn't. Hatred was what had killed Ahdia and Pak. Hatred didn't solve anything. He had already made a vow to himself never to hate again.

Khan opened the door quickly. "Wait," he called.

Malville was halfway down the walk. He stopped as he heard Khan's voice. Khan joined him in the warm summer afternoon and saw the man's face twisted in tears and pain, like his own.

"Why did you come here, Mr. Malville?" Khan asked.

"To tell you I'm sorry."

"Do you want me to forgive you? Is that what you expect?"

Malville struggled with his words. "I don't expect anything. Believe me, I'm not asking for anything from you. I just felt I needed to tell you in person that I was the one who wronged you and that I'm sorry."

Khan took a long, deep breath. He gestured at the car in the street. "Is that your wife?"

"Yes. Alison."

"And your son?"

"Evan."

"How old is he?"

"Twelve," Malville said.

"A handful?"

That brought a smile. "Oh, yes."

"I imagine they are your life," Khan said.

"They are. And not long ago, I came very close to losing them. So for me to be responsible for what happened to you is more than I can bear—"

Khan stopped him again. "You've apologized, Mr. Malville. You don't need to do so again. I was wrong, though. I do want something from you."

"What is it? Anything."

"I'd like to tell you about Ahdia and Pak," Khan said. "I'd like you to know who they were. All of you. Your wife and son, too. Would you do that for me?"

Malville drew himself up to his full height. He was a big man, and he had his voice back. "It would be an honor. Thank you."

Khan waved at the people in the car to join them. He saw them both getting out. Alison Malville was smiling, her pretty eyes rimmed in red. Evan's eyes were drawn to the soccer ball in the front yard. Children were all the same.

"Have you ever been to a Muslim home, Mr. Malville?" he asked.

"No," the man replied. "We haven't."

"Then come inside," Khan said.

* * *

"How's the truck driver?" Cat whispered into Stride's ear. The noise of the crowd in the brewery almost drowned out her question.

"Don't worry, he's out of the hospital and doing fine," Stride told her.

"Wow, that's great."

"Yes, it is."

Stride hoisted a glass of Derailed Ale in his hand and stood up at the table, where he was surrounded by Serena, Cat, Maggie, Troy Grange, and Gayle Durkin. He used a loud voice to make sure they could all hear him. "Let it be known, to all of you who think I am incapable of change, that we are here at Thirsty Pagan in Superior and *not* at Sammy's. I did not protest. I did not complain. I am willing to acknowledge that there are other pizzas in the world."

Durkin giggled. They were on their third pitcher of beer and most of the way through their second deep-dish pizza. "Yes, but that's only because he had Sammy's delivered to the DECC every single day we were there."

"I didn't hear complaints," Stride said.

"No, no, no complaints."

They all laughed. It felt good to laugh. One week after the marathon tragedies, the city was slowly making its way back to normal. It was a new weekend, a new summer festival, a new crowd of tourists. Dawn Basch was gone; she'd cancelled her free-speech symposium after hundreds of Duluthians sent back their tickets. The FBI was out of the DECC, and Gayle Durkin was spending the weekend with her parents and then returning home to the Twin Cities. The evening at Thirsty Pagan Brewing was her going-away party.

"You guys are great," Durkin told them. "Really. Duluth is lucky to have you."

"You're not so bad, either, Gherkin," Maggie replied, laughing so hard that she snorted and nearly slipped off her chair. She'd been anesthetizing her shoulder with beer, which seemed to help.

"You realize that's going to be my nickname for the rest of my career, don't you?" Durkin asked.

"You're welcome," Maggie replied. "I'm very proud."

"Anyway, it means a lot to me to have a night like this after a long week, but I need to go home now," Durkin continued. "I just wanted to say thanks and tell you how much everyone at the FBI appreciates all your help. Especially me."

"Well, don't be a stranger," Stride said. "Once a Duluthian, always a Duluthian, Gayle."

"I'll remember that." Durkin's eyes met Stride's, and a silent message passed them. "Really, thanks," she said. "For everything."

Stride lifted his glass in a toast.

"We'd better go, too," Maggie announced, swallowing the last of her ale and dragging Troy out of his chair. "We've got an early day tomorrow. Troy and I are helping Shelly Baker get home from the hospital. She's got a lot of physical therapy ahead of her, but her attitude is pretty good. We're working with the city to locate a ground-level, handicapped-accessible apartment for her, but for now, we'll make sure she's okay."

"Do you need more hands on deck?" Stride asked.

"At some point, yeah, but we'll be okay tomorrow."

"If you need us, call," Serena said.

There were hugs and goodbyes, and then Durkin, Maggie, and Troy were gone, and the three of them had the table to themselves. Cat eyed the beer, and Stride eyed her back with a look that said *No*. Serena took another bite of pizza. On the small stage in the crowded room, a folk guitarist began to play, and a college girl with purple hair crooned a mellow cover of an Alison Krauss song. The conversation died as the people began to listen. Soon the only sound was the girl's voice and the clink of glasses being filled at the bar.

"I'm going to go, too," Cat murmured. "Assuming the two of you can be trusted alone."

"Where are you off to?" Stride asked the girl. "Got a date?"

"No, I called Drew and Krista Olson to see if I could come over," Cat replied, hooding her eyes so she didn't have to look at them. "You know, to see how Michael was doing. And whether I could help at all."

Stride and Serena both smiled.

"I think they'll like that," Serena told her. "So will Michael."

"Yeah. That's what Drew said."

"Do you want us to go with you?" Stride asked.

"No, that's okay. I can do it myself."

As she left, Cat looked like seventeen going on thirty. Full of mistakes but full of promise. Stride's gaze followed the girl until she was gone, and so did Serena's. That was how it was when you were parents.

Serena pulled her chair close to him and sank back into his shoulder. He wrapped an arm around her and held her hand. The singer on stage was good. It was just her and the guitar and the Alison Krauss song, "When You Say Nothing at All," one of Stride's favorites. He felt the easy buzz of the ale in his head, and he loved the smell of Serena's hair near his face.

Darkness was everywhere but not here. Not tonight. The darkness would still be there in the morning, and so would the grief, but he didn't have to go looking for it.

"So, are you going to the run the marathon next year?" he whispered into her ear.

"You bet I am. *Everyone* is going to run next year."

"Biggest and best ever," Stride said.

"Exactly."

"You know, we haven't spent much time together lately," he pointed out.

"You're right. We haven't."

"Sorry. We'll change that."

"Don't worry, it's not about measuring time, Jonny," Serena replied. "It's about this moment right now. That's all that matters."

She was right. This moment was perfect, regardless of what had come before and what would come tomorrow. He wouldn't change a thing. The evening. The music. The food and drink. The people in his life. The good and the bad, exactly the way they were supposed to be. He drank his ale, held his wife, listened to the song, and said nothing at all.

FROM THE AUTHOR

Thanks for reading the new Jonathan Stride novel. If you like this novel, check out all my other books, too.

You can "like" my official fan page on Facebook at www.facebook .com/ bfreemanfans or follow me on Twitter, Pinterest, or Instagram using the handle bfreemanbooks. For a look at the fun side of the author's life, you can also "like" my wife, Marcia's, Facebook page at www.facebook.com/theauthorswife.

Write to me with your feedback at brian@bfreemanbooks.com. I love to get e-mail from readers around the world, and, yes, I reply personally. Visit my website at www.bfreemanbooks.com to join my mailing list and find out more about me and all my books.

Finally, if you enjoy my books, please post your reviews online at such sites as Goodreads, Amazon, BN, and other sites for book lovers—and spread the word to your reader friends. Thanks!

ACKNOWLEDGMENTS

In April 2013, the world witnessed the horror of the bombing at the Boston Marathon. That tragic moment and its aftermath had a special meaning for people in Duluth, because the annual marathon there is one of the great traditions of the city. As a result, this was an extremely difficult and personal book to write, because of the intensity of the emotions involved, both on the page and in real life. I'm grateful for the help of the many people who offered their counsel and insight.

Former Duluth Police Chief Scott Lyons was extremely helpful in discussing police strategy in major crises and working relationships with the FBI. Darlene Marshall of the Duluth Greater Downtown Council and Chuck Frederick of the Duluth *News Tribune* helped arrange a tour of the downtown subbasements (and were brave enough to accompany me and Marcia down there). Kevin Schnorr from Oneida Commercial Real Estate made a great tour guide.

I had the honor of discussing Muslim life, culture, and religion with members of the Islamic Society of Woodbury and the East Metro and the privilege of attending their Friday prayer service. They were extremely gracious and generous in talking about daily Muslim life and about the struggles of extremism. If I have made mistakes in this book in relation to Islamic culture, they are entirely my own.

I am always grateful to my team in the publishing world, including my agent, Deborah Schneider, and my editor at Quercus, Nathaniel Marunas, and to the many booksellers and librarians who make sure that readers discover my books. My advance readers on **MARATHON** included Ann Sullivan and my wife, Marcia. They make every novel better with their detailed analyses and insights.

Of course, Marcia makes *everything* in my life better, just based on who she is. I'm thankful for her every single day.

ABOUT THE TYPE

Typeset in Adobe Garamond at 11.5/15 pt.

Adobe Garamond is named for the famed sixteenth-century French printer Claude Garamond. Robert Slimbach created this serif face for Adobe based on Garamond's designs, as well as the designs of Garamond's assistant, Robert Granjon.

Typeset by Scribe Inc., Philadelphia, Pennsylvania.